Novah Burns

Robert Reynolds

DEDICATION

This book is dedicated to the stubbornly persistent inner voice which for years has insisted that I write a book. I finally listened, and this is the result. We'll see if the voice is appeased.

CONTENTS

ACKNOWLEDGMENTS

Thank you Andrew, Brad, Cort, and Kim for your great feedback and help during the creation of this book. Thank you Lisa for creating such a great cover.

i

CHAPTER ONE

D'kob awoke with a mercilessly persistent buzzing between his temples, as if he'd stuck his head into a container of G'narian mosquitos. Such was a common side-effect of absorbing a plasma-bolt shot to the back of the skull. The outcome could have been worse – the stunning plasma-bolt could have been a kinetic-bolt, which would have burrowed deep and fatally into his skull instead of merely bouncing off of it. He knew why he'd been spared. He'd stolen the *R'ptyr*, the crowning achievement of Khamek technology, and only he knew where it was hidden. S'heil wouldn't force him into misadventure until the secret hiding location and the access codes were extracted.

The mammoth vessel floated right where the Lord Commander had told him it would be, tucked behind the largest of N'ala 5's moons in the middle of the Khamek fleet, a giant amongst a swarm of much smaller, protective attendants. The *R'ptyr* had survived the journey from the V'jima Prime Shipyards completely unscathed after being properly launched with greater fanfare than any other vessel in Khamek history. This ship was the primary Khamek piece of the plan for the Humans, but the Humans weren't ready yet.

D'kob had stowed away on the final maintenance shuttle, remaining behind after the maintenance crew had completed their ship shutdown procedures and hastily departed, wanting nothing to do with the oversized, cavernous ship. Khamek felt uneasy on the *R'ptyr*, and

D'kob was no exception. The ship was in a dormant state, cool and dark, and each footfall of his white synthetic boots echoed hauntingly into nothingness. The spaces on the ship consumed him. Curiously tall ceilings and long, wide corridors projected his insignificance at every turn. Everything was too big, designed for taller beings with larger needs and purposes alien to Khamek thinking.

D'kob found the main security terminal just aft of the bridge and reprogrammed the security settings to deny entrance to anyone but him. He then descended down a hollow-ringing ladder to the deck below where the less-than-formidable missile launch tubes sat cold and unfired. From his pack he withdrew a four-folded electro-magnetic pulse bomb. He unfolded it slowly, and after a quartet of soft clicks, he held in his hand an intricate metallic device no larger than his head. He pressed the arming sequence code into the small display on the bomb, placed it into the launch tube, and finally pulled a single, short lever to activate the manual launch override. By the time he crawled back up the ladder to the bridge the surrounding Khamek ships were dark and helpless, floating harmlessly around the *R'ptyr*. Engaging the engines and the cloaking device, D'kob piloted the *R'ptyr* through the drifting cluster of ships. The *R'ptyr* – invisible and un-trackable – was long gone before the fleet recovered.

Hiding the *R'ptyr*, in spite of its size, wasn't difficult either. D'kob stashed it on N'ala 3 at the coordinates he was instructed to then fled the scene as fast as his shivering, scrawny legs could carry him. Those same scrawny legs had kept him ahead of his angry and persistent pursuers for nearly nineteen-hundred years since. His orders were simple: don't get caught, and wait for further orders. He had become quite adept at the first part, but impatient with the second. Nineteen hundred years, even for a Khamek, is a long time. Over the centuries his body had slowly ceded its resilience, its firmness turning soft. Sinew and muscle did not respond as they once did in this, his third body. He desperately wanted his clone and to move his consciousness into the new, fresher version of himself. Guaranteed for fifteen hundred years of normal wear and tear, the 2317 years of spectacularly abnormal wear and tear on his current body was – though remarkable – untenable for continued escape. Sure enough, even though he willed his body to leap the six foot high fence behind a non-descript bar in Indonesia, it only managed five. The subsequent fall provided his pursuers just enough time to get a clean shot.

S'heil wanted him close by so had converted an unused crew-quarters room on his flagship into a makeshift prison cell. The cell door slid shut and the stifling blackness was pierced only by a small shaft of light beaming through the cell door's window. He could feel the omnipresent rumble of the *L'ghorsk* through his thin boots.

Patience, D'kob told himself. The Lord Commander, who seemed to know everything that happened everywhere, had predicted that D'kob would eventually be captured. It was inevitable. The Lord Commander also said that D'kob's confinement wouldn't last long. He remembered the Lord Commander's soothing words, telling him it would only be three hours before the means of his escape would be revealed, that he would indeed escape, and then rendezvous with a Human whom he was to take to the *R'ptyr*.

D'kob sat patiently on the bed, eyes closed, waiting for the time to pass. His dark meditation was eventually interrupted by the bright translucency of his eyelids indicating a visitor, a visitor who re-enabled the lighting of the room.

By the time his eyes adjusted to the sudden increase in brightness, however, his mysterious visitor was gone. The light thankfully remained, along with a small metal tray upon which rested a small metal cup which contained his meal – a pair of familiar, standard-issue nutrition capsules.

Finding the paper-thin circuit re-router and the thumbnail-sized disc taped to the bottom of the tray surprised him. Written on the re-router in Khamek type barely large enough to read were his instructions detailing how to get off the ship, and what to do afterwards. D'kob sat on the bunk and thought. *Hmm… the R'ptyr is now needed. Yet which Khamek provided the re-router? How could such a secret delivery have been accomplished? Which Khamek on this ship would help D'kob?* He decided the questions could wait. Every fiber of his being screamed "trap," yet fiber-screaming is a distant third to desperation and duty.

He had to get out of the cell and off of the ship.

Beads of nervous perspiration formed on his wide, white brow. It was time to go. The instructions were simple – go left out the door, cross three hallway junctions, make a right, and then through the bay doors on the left.

He hoped his mysterious co-conspirator wasn't just setting him up. S'heil was cruel and deceptive, and sometimes liked to toy with his prey before shooting them in the face.

D'kob had his orders though. His role was pivotal. He knew he mattered, and the sooner he was done with this mission, the sooner he could go home and get his clone. He knew why he was living all of these centuries on the run – to buy time. Time for the humans and time for the Lord Commander, time which his current body was running out of. Now he was faced with either escaping or walking into a trap. Either way, he thought, the odds of transference in the near future were against him with his clone so far away. When this body was done, he was done. D'kob inhaled deeply to force his growing anger back into the pit of internal frustration from which it would snarl from time to time.

He sat on the sterile bunk and crossed his right leg over his left thigh and – just for a moment – admired the low, red pulse of the organic tracking band that circumnavigated his ankle. The red pulse throbbed in time with D'kob's heartbeat as if it was a part of him. Any disruption in the *whump-ka-thump, whump-ka-thump* rhythm would set off an alarm. *Trap or not, the time has come.* Warming the band with his hands and humming a low, melodic tune, he focused his thoughts on the beating tissue surrounding his ankle. At every third beat, he hummed just a little louder and ever-so-slightly stretched the band. Even as he worked to incrementally enlarge the band enough to slip over his foot, he sought to make it a part of him. In his mind, the notes he hummed stitched the organic fabric of the band to his essence, and the essence bled back into the band. By the time he had finally rolled it beyond his toes, the band and he were one – separate but together – at least for a short while. He gently set the band on the bed and watched it silently throb for a few seconds. D'kob was torn, satisfied at having managed to succeed, yet regretful, as if abandoning a beloved pet. *The band is simply an organic construct, no part of D'kob*, he told himself, refocusing on his mission.

He went to the door. He expected to be ambushed the second he swiped the circuit re-router along the inset locking mechanism, but to his surprise and relief the door simply and quietly slid into its pocket. He paused for a moment, but there was nothing to do but proceed. Either the cameras were disabled or they weren't. He'd know shortly.

Three hallways. Turn right. Doors on left. Be quick.

He didn't dare look any direction but straight ahead. After twenty-six seconds he entered the doors of docking bay one which housed six shiny, triangular scout ships. He quickly moved to the ship at the back end of the bay. The hard part was over. Now came the *harder* part. Any sign of electronic operations, either in the launch bay or the scout ship, would sound the alarm. He couldn't use the electronic launching system. He'd have to manually crank the launch doors open and hope that the static force field was in place. He doubted that the magnetic downforce arms had enough kinetic potential to get a scout craft pushed out, but it was too late to worry about that. D'kob grabbed the manual cranking mechanism in his hands and paused. Either he'd see the familiar blue shimmer of the shield, or he'd see nothing, except for perhaps his skull being strained through the slightly-opened seal as he was sucked out into the vacuum of space. He took a deep breath and began cranking open the massive metal doors. He could see the shimmer of the shield, and sighed in relief. The shield would part at a sub-molecular level as the scout ship dropped through it. He climbed up onto the ship, and placing his hand on the clear dome in the center caused it to dissolve into the frame. He slid inside and the dome re-congealed above him as he buckled in. He wouldn't start the ship engines. It had to be a freefall escape. D'kob calculated his odds of survival, frowning at the final percentage that failed to reach into double-digits.

He lightly pressed his short forefinger against the manual release trigger and the downforce arms shoved his craft with surprising effectiveness down through the force field. As he watched for signs above that his escape had been noticed, nothing happened. No alarms. No attack squadron. Only the slowly shrinking visage of the massive frigate slipping out of sight as the nose of his ship angled down into the bright blue and swirling white atmosphere below of N'ala 3, or as the Humans called it, Earth.

The planet slowly spun below him but D'kob had no time to admire it. He had quickly reached terminal velocity, and maintaining the angle of descent using only manual resistive controls was already taxing his strength and coordination. His hands and forearms quivered and strained with fatigue, struggling to keep the craft on the proper trajectory. The margin of error was small. The correct angle of descent was critical – three degrees too deep or too shallow would cause vaporization. Not the instant kind – the merciless kind that boiled off your skin and made you wish you were dead for twelve seconds before you actually died.

The silence of space grew into a crackling roar as his craft rocketed through the atmosphere. The noise hurt his ears. His sweaty hands strained at the controls, and that ancient tickle in his gut known as panic began to quickly gnaw at him. D'kob released the breath he had been holding and drew in a fresh one. Somewhere in that breath he found the strength to ignore the vibrating pain in his arms, the stinging sweat pouring down into his eyes, and the drum of fear pounding in his heart.

D'kob's ship was a brighter than normal meteor as it passed beyond the penumbra of dawn into N'ala 3's dark side. He instinctively looked at the control panel for an altitude reading, but it was dark. He'd have to engage the parachutes soon – but not too soon. He was doing all he could to keep his angle right, so had little choice of landing spots. Ahead on the horizon, boiling and rising towards his position at great speed, was a dark and unfriendly weather system.

He pulled the parachute release lever and three parachutes, spaced symmetrically at the three points of his ship, tore violently out of the hull and snapped open, straining the thin connecting cables. The instant resistance jostled him violently, as did what he saw through blurry eyes out of the canopy. *Too fast*, he thought. The storm ahead grew ever closer. *Too much lightning.*

His craft disappeared into the black, lightning-filled cauldron of thunder and rain. One of the parachutes then broke free causing his ship to dip, swing, and then spin uncontrollably. This was the end. *Lord Commander, forgive me.* Dizziness overcame him as the Earth reached out with her swirling black and grey arms to deliver the inevitable crushing hug.

CHAPTER TWO

The pain from Novah's sprained ankle was severe, and he figured a shot or two of bourbon would ease it. The mostly-empty bottle of bourbon was the only luxury item he had found in the trailer, and if ever a man needed or deserved a little luxury, this was the time.

Swirling the brown, iceless liquid in his blue plastic mug, he cast a wary eye towards the western horizon. The forecast called for clear, warming weather throughout the weekend, yet as the afternoon slipped casually into evening he noticed menacing clouds far off in the distance. A thick black blanket was heading his way so his thoughts now centered on preparing his camp trailer for rain. He'd have to roll the awning up, make sure the generator was sheltered, and close the windows. He'd thought of throwing the heavy tarps over the trailer and the truck for good measure, but knew he'd be unable to do that on only one leg. His ankle was throbbing enough already.

Novah Burns was the only child of Greg and Sasha Burns, normal American parents living an average American life before The Fall. There was nothing else to call that pivot point in history, really, except The Fall. All of human prosperity was chattering along like a china cup on a table on a train, inching closer and closer to the edge through the early 21st century until it finally fell off and shattered into a hundred fragments of hopelessness. Novah remembered his father talking to him about it often before it happened. He told Novah to prepare, because the signs all pointed towards inevitable economic collapse. Too much national debt, too few jobs, economic policies that hurt business, new social programs that required higher and higher taxes to fund them, terrorists pouring in over open borders, and on and on and on. Novah's dad was one of the few that hadn't put his head in the sand pretending that everything was going to be okay. Novah rolled his eyes whenever his parents would talk about preparedness. He was totally unconcerned with economics beyond finding enough money to buy video games and gas. That didn't stop Greg from stockpiling – hoarding, as it would eventually be called – firearms, ammunition, canned goods, dry goods, gasoline, and bullion. He'd bought the twenty-five acres of remote forest land as a bug-out location, a place to take his family and start new when the inevitable collapse happened.

While his parents were wrapped up in their world of doom and gloom preparation, Novah was busy failing in school. His grades had been good until his junior year in high school and then he found it much more convenient to stop doing homework or studying. Why bother? If the world was going to come crashing to and end anyway, what difference did it make what his grades were? It was a convenient excuse, plus it was so much easier to fiddle with his phone all day texting his friends and playing games. In spite of failing grades he was passed to his senior year. This did nothing other than to validate his thinking that school didn't matter, and thus he continued to do nothing until his phone, car, and basically everything else was taken from him by his parents in order to incentivize him. He grudgingly did just barely enough to graduate in 2017.

Novah – through connections his mother had – got hired on that spring as a janitor at the school district administrative headquarters, which was a sprawling, aged complex filled with vacant hallways that always needed mopping and trashcans that rarely needed emptying. He passed the idle hours at work talking with Juan, a slightly older Mexican guy who worked hard, ate well, and wouldn't stop talking about his dream of bringing his mother up from Mexico. "I just need a little more money," Juan would often say. Money was the only obstacle, and Juan needed enough to pay for her train ticket, a car, and a bigger place for them both to live in. The border with Mexico was essentially open now, and people from every continent on earth were pouring into and dispersing across the United States with impunity. For three years Novah listened to Juan say "just a little more."

~~~

Novah downed another swig of bourbon, mustering up the courage to tackle the painful task of sealing up the trailer. Twenty minutes later he sat at the table with his ankle elevated on the opposite bench. The dark clouds were drawing closer and announcing themselves with the low, distant rumbling of thunder. He didn't bother to turn on a light, content to sit in the darkness of the trailer, and of his thoughts. The sixteen months or so since the fall were rougher than even his dad had predicted. His dad had been proven right in many unfortunate ways, including the whole "go to prison if you steal" thing. "You're too pretty to go to jail, son." Novah had just rolled his eyes.

Novah lost his janitor job due to The Fall. Almost everyone he knew had, within the span of a week, collapsed into economic ruin. Novah didn't understand what happened. It seemed few people did. He heard that the stock market crashed because of something to do with China and Russia, and that dollars weren't worth anything anymore. Seemingly overnight gas went from five dollars a gallon to fifty. A day later all banks were closed for a two-day bank holiday, which stretched into four days, which stretched into a full week. Nobody was being paid so many people stopped working. The few that still had jobs couldn't work because they couldn't get to their jobs. Soon there was no gasoline to be purchased at any price – federal, state and local emergency and law enforcement agencies claimed it all. Because no gas was available, no food could be trucked to supermarkets. Store shelves were quickly emptied, mostly by lawless looters the police couldn't contain until they started shooting people, which made things worse.

The same sequence played out in every city. Little time passed before someone killed someone else. Sometimes it was the police shooting a looter, sometimes it was a looter stabbing a cop, and sometimes it ended up being a formerly middle-class mother, desperate to feed her starving child, bashing in another desperate mother with a tire iron to steal food or diapers or whatever was available. Gunfire was regularly heard in every formerly-peaceful suburb as those that were armed and had something of value were constantly fighting off diverse mobs of upper-middle-class socialites and welfare recipients eager to take both the weapons and the food. The mobs almost always won, overrunning homes by sheer numbers like a fast-moving locust swarm. Once the mobs became armed pure anarchy ensued. The scents of smoke and death became commonplace. The veneer of civilization had been rubbed off until it was raw, leaving behind a bleeding wound of hunger, fear, rape and murder.

On the tenth day after The Fall began, streets were filled with military vehicles from every Federal agency in existence. Government seized just about everything – hospitals, schools, and every store that still had anything of value. The plug was pulled on the internet. Radio and television were nationalized. Martial Law was declared, which didn't go over well in some parts of the country. Civil war broke out but was over in a matter of weeks as the government military utterly overpowered any resistance. Agencies went house by house, apartment by apartment, simply taking whoever was on their list of resisters or even possible resisters. In most cases some government vehicle would pull up in the dead of night, enter a house without permission, and confiscate three things: weapons, food, and the men. A wailing trail of wives, children and girlfriends were left in the government's wake. Rumors circulated that the men were taken to distant internment camps, but in reality, most of these "Constitutionalist rebels" were thrown in railcars, shipped to some undisclosed location, gassed, and then dumped into mass graves.

Novah remembered the flashlight beaming its rude awakening at him in the middle of the night. He couldn't see his dad while rubbing his eyes, but he certainly heard his urgent whispers.

"They're coming," he had said. "You need to get out of here. Your mom and I are going to hide in the crawlspace. We're too old to make a run for it, and too outgunned to fight."

Novah groggily grabbed the small bug-out-bag his dad had made for this occasion and fled out the back door into the darkness, tears and confusion mixing with the cold February rain. He saw three sets of lights pull into the driveway, then the shadows of many well-equipped invaders. Novah ran deep into the ravine behind the house, stumbling downhill as wet unseen cedar branches colluded to slow his adrenaline-fueled escape. He fumbled in the dark up the floor of the ravine into the more rugged areas where nobody would likely follow. He crawled, soaked to the bone, into a large drainage culvert. He sat shivering in six inches of cold, fast-flowing runoff for hours, his teeth chattering, filling his ears with the imaginary sounds of the pursuit which never came.

Novah didn't return to his house – he knew his dad would want him to stay away. He made his way up the ravine to the next road, cold and more afraid than he thought he'd ever be. He walked along the road, just inside the tree line, headed south, drinking rainwater collected into his water bottle and eating the meager trail mix rations he had in his pack. Three miserable and soaked days later, prune-skinned and starving, hunger forced him to walk into town.

He wandered into what had been a Safeway grocery store, now a generic, nationalized food distribution center, heavily guarded by local police armed with heavy weapons and wearing thick military-grade armor.

There, on a shelf not twenty feet inside the main entrance, taunting Novah's gurgling stomach, was a small rack containing half a dozen Butterfinger candy bars. He had no money, and even if he wanted to steal one, he couldn't, because right next to the shelf stood a burly, middle-aged King County police officer, the name Clarke engraved on the brass nameplate under his badge. Novah looked at the candy, then looked at the officer, then back at the candy. The officer shuffled over to him, his mobility slightly hindered by the comprehensive body armor bulging out of his uniform, and spoke in a hushed voice.

"Do you want a candy bar? You look half starved."

"I don't have any money," Novah replied.

The officer put his arm over Novah's shoulders and smiled. "I can see you're hungry. I'll tell you what. Just follow me over there. When I turn my back, just slip one into your pocket. Nobody will be the wiser."

A little voice inside his head warned him – *don't take the bait*. Yet the power of hunger compelled him. He followed Officer Clarke back to the shelf, snatched a candy bar, crammed it in his pocket, and ran. He ran as fast as he could, leaping over the wooden checkout line barriers and out the door where he was met by the wiry tentacles of a taser fired from one of the officers stationed outside. The two metal prongs dug through his wet clothing and into his chest, delivering their charge with cruel efficiency. Some unknown amount of time later he found himself propped up against the interior window of a squad car, his pants soaked with his own warm urine. He helplessly watched Officer Clarke turn to him and devour the last of the Butterfinger with a satisfied and malicious grin.

Novah was taken to the King County Mall at Cedarwood Heights, otherwise known simply as "the Mall." Before The Fall, the Mall was a classy, three-story bustling hive of economic activity. After, it had been hastily converted into a makeshift prison/holding facility. It was well guarded, but only on the outside. Inside was basically a free-for-all which is exactly what made the Mall a place nobody wanted to go to. If the rumors were true, only five in ten completed their sentences and were released alive – alive being a relative term. Sure, their hearts were beating, but they could be blind, maimed, or simply broken beyond repair. Once each week the nearby streets and fields had to be swept by the Corpse Retrieval Units, as they were littered with the festering bodies of the recently released who had simply given up and found various ways to shed their mortal coils. With no jobs, homes, or transportation, the only way to survive on the outside was to resort to theft or worse – the same things that got them put in the Mall in the first place, and they were *not* going back.

The attending officer, seated next to Officer Clarke in the passenger seat of the cruiser, exited the car and then dragged Novah out of the back seat by the hair. He was roughly led by the scalp to the processing station where the officer stated unemotionally Novah's crime and sentence: "Grand theft of food. Multiple witnesses. Guilty as charged.

Sentence is one year in the Mall." Novah's left arm was pressed to the table, forearm facing upwards, and a wide swath of dark-blue ink was painted across it. The processing attendant adjusted the pins in the tattooing stamp – usually used for marking farm animals – and then placed it over the blue ink on Novah's arm. With a thump of her palm, and a high-pitched yelp from Novah, the tattoo was painfully stamped in. The bored facilitator then absently brushed a fallen blonde lock of hair from her face, talking to her assistant while placing the stamping unit into a well-used container of inky alcohol. "Recorded as FEMA Region Ten, Kingco sub, inmate 353834. Burns, Novah J. DNA recorded and cross-referenced." Each tiny pinhole making up the numbers 353834 in Novah's arm began to bubble with tiny droplets of blood. The assistant sloppily bandaged the markings on Novah's forearm with three loops of wide medical tape, saying nothing.

Novah's numb mind vaguely remembered the days – or was it just a concept? – when trials determined if a person was guilty, convicted by a jury of peers. Those days were gone though and he was unceremoniously shoved through the main entrance of the King County Mall, reeking of mildew and his own urine.

It turned out that pissing his pants was the best thing that could have happened to him. His stench allowed him a luxury most new inmates never received – time. Time to hide. Time to gather his thoughts. Time to come up with a plan to survive in the state-sanctioned anarchy of the Mall. The various roving gangs of criminals and miscreants within the Mall's walls mocked and laughed at him, but never closed to within arm's length before their noses crinkled. More than a few choice words were exclaimed regarding his rancid smell yet nobody touched him. Novah slowly slunk away into the shadows trying to get as far away from the main entrance as possible. The further he could get away, he figured, the better his odds of staying safe.

He eventually discovered and followed the painted arrows to the stations within the sprawling complex designed to meet basic prisoner needs. The basement floor of Sears had been converted into a prisoner clothing distribution center. A surprisingly courteous prison worker handed him a shrink-wrapped package containing a pair of clean underwear, socks, a plain white t-shirt, and dark blue coveralls. Novah took them gratefully. He asked if there were any other places he should know about and was informed about the infirmary on the main floor at the Apple store, and that meals were served in the food court. There were no cells or designated sleeping areas. People slept where they could, gathered in small groups for their mutual protection.

As Novah looked around for a place to change his clothes, he caught the eye of a tall, thin, dirty brunette, visibly shaking, her eyes darting around as if expecting to be struck by an invisible hand at any time. He averted his vision but she slowly stepped towards him, stopping once she caught a good whiff of him.

"Dude, you stink really bad," she offered. "You piss your pants or something?"

Novah nodded, embarrassed, but made note of her violently melodic voice. The quaking under the surface lent it a subtle vibrato. "It's been a rough few days," he said. Her eyes darted around the area.

"Come with me, I know a place you can clean up."

He followed obediently as she casually – yet carefully – walked around the corner into the Build-a-Bear store. Near the back was a wood-paneled door that blended in with the paneled walls. She looked around, pressed in, and it swung inwards.

"Hurry!" she whispered urgently.

She grasped for her nose and closed the door behind him.

"In dair," she gulped, pointing to a small restroom. Novah discerned that he was in the back office of the store where the manager had probably hidden out and done nothing. He was closing the bathroom door as a thin arm darted in, holding an empty plastic garbage bag. He took it silently and finished closing the door.

Novah looked at himself in the mirror, his cheeks much more hollow than he remembered but filled with stubble from many days left unshaven. He pulled off his shoes between reluctant breaths, barely able to stand his own stench. He peeled his jeans and underwear off and crammed them into the garbage bag and then sealed it. He stripped off his shirt and soaked it in the sink, surprised that there was actually running water. It wasn't hot but he didn't care at that point. He washed himself as best he could with the shirt before putting on his new prison uniform. He tied his shoes, looked in the mirror, shrugged, and exited the washroom. Gazing around the small office area he saw the scrawny-yet-could-be-pretty girl fidgeting in a chair.

"Thank you," he said quietly. "I'm Novah."

Her voice crackled somewhere between exhaustion and friendliness. "I'm Penny." She tried to provide a painful smile and failed.

"Is this place yours?" Novah asked.

Her sad green eyes fell to the floor. "Well, as much as any place can belong to anyone here, I suppose. It actually belonged to Kara."

He knew better than to ask, but did anyway. "What happened to Kara?" Novah watched as Penny's body stiffened, her fingers curling into her palms to steel herself against what was obviously a bitter memory.

"She's dead. She died five weeks ago."

She then told the story of how she and Kara were caught and raped by three guys in the hallway behind GameStop. Kara had pleaded – *no no, please, not again* – to no avail.

"They finally let us go, but Kara was broken. She jumped off the third floor. I snuck back here." Tears streamed down Penny's face. "Kara was the smart one."

A cold chill went up the back of Novah's neck. "How many…"

"Four times in three months," she replied, pre-empting the question. "It was Kara's seventh. Everyone in the mall gets raped eventually, unless you're a good fighter or part of a good group." Her voice quivered.

Novah was confused. "Why did you help me? How did you know I wouldn't just rape you?"

Penny snorted, and a spray of tears and snot blew out from her face as she laughed. "You? You pissed your pants. You're too scared to do anything." She sobered. "And I needed to find someone new to partner up with. To start my own group. It's the only way we'll be safe."

Novah nodded.

"Don't be getting any ideas though. I ain't your girlfriend, and I ain't anything to you but someone who's back you watch and who watches yours. I don't want to see another dick in my life, much less have one in me."

"I understand," he said. And he did. His father's voice echoed in his head – *you're too pretty for prison.*

During the next couple of days Penny showed Novah the ropes of the Mall. Where and when to get fed, what stores to avoid, the names of the main gangs, and most importantly, how to be sneaky. Penny hammered into his head repeatedly that getting caught meant getting raped. Boy, girl, it didn't matter. He took her very seriously. The atmosphere of angst pervading every hallway underscored each word Penny said. So did the random screams heard often throughout the Mall.

At night Penny slept on a narrow cot in the office. Novah slept on clear bags of white bear stuffing piled up in the corner near the bathroom. The office door was barred from the inside to help deter any unwanted company. Penny always fell asleep before he did, usually with sniffles and light sobs. He tried to empathize in his mind, knowing yet not *really* knowing the suffering she had so far endured in this forsaken Mall. Novah comforted himself by thinking of more pleasant thoughts, imagining the pair of them in a different world, hypnotized by watching her breathe and admiring her curled-up curves. He found himself growing fond of Penny. Perhaps, together, they'd be able to make it through this ordeal, and maybe she'd soften up in time.

One evening four days later, as the pair were sharing their capture stories, there was a light, patterned knock at the door. Novah shot to attention. Penny waved dismissively at him. "Don't worry, that's just John and Jacob. They're friends. They know the secret knock."

Penny slid the bar off of the door and in barged two larger-than-average, heavily bearded guys, closing the door behind them. The room shrank uncomfortably.

Penny was shivering as the larger man bent down and gave her a healthy, hard kiss before dismissing her with a shove of her chin.

"Who's your friend, Penny?" he asked, burning a hole in Novah with his eyes.

Penny spoke softly. "This is Novah, Jacob. He's a good guy. Eager to learn."

"Is that true, Novah? You like to learn stuff?"

Novah stared at the hulking Jacob with steely, defensive eyes. "I suppose it is. Penny has taught me a lot since I arrived."

John curled the corner of his mouth upwards and gave the slightest of nods. "That's good, boy. We have something new to teach you."

Before Novah could react the two men overpowered him and wrestled him down, face first, onto the cot. Jacob pulled sections of rope from his pocket and tied Novah's hands to the cot frame while John worked to rip open Novah's coveralls. Novah struggled until he could struggle no more. He cried out with painful wailing sobs as Jacob and John took turns raping him while Penny watched, expressionless.

When he woke up, he was still tied to the cot, his ass bare, bleeding and cold. Penny was kneeling down next to him with a small but very sharp and shiny knife pointed at his eye.

"Now here's the way it is," she started, "It was either you or me. You see, Jacob and I have a deal. I provide him and John with fresh meat every week or so, and they make sure I don't get raped. I ain't never getting raped again. You hear me Novah? I ain't *never* getting raped again. I'm going to untie you. You're going to drag your sorry, bleeding ass out of here and you ain't never gonna come back. If you do, you're dead. I'll make sure of that! You get me, Novah?"

"Yes," he croaked through his hoarseness and cracked, bloody lips.

"Good." She untied his hands. He put himself together as best he could, barely able to walk. "Get OUT," she hissed.

It was still dark as he inched his way out of Build-a-Bear. Walking was an exercise in torture, his hind quarters burning with every small step. *Just get to the Apple store* he kept telling himself. *Just. Get. There.*

He prayed nobody was watching. He had no shot of outrunning anyone. He used all of the stealth tricks he learned, sticking to the shadows, pillars and planters as he made his way down the mall. The Apple store wasn't too far. The entrance, which had once been glass from floor to ceiling, was now a barricade of concrete. He banged on the single steel door which was marked with a red cross. It rang cold and hollow.

The noise caught the attention of a pair of men who were resting just two stores down near the Starbucks.

"They don't open at night," yelled one. They both stood up.

"You ought to come back in the morning," said the other. They split, predatorily, fifty feet away, attempting to block any exit Novah might have. They knew his condition, though. They'd watched him limp up.

"You sure are pretty," the first said with a toothy grin. "And it looks like you've been broken in. It's a shame to see you out here all by yourself." The second guy laughed, and they both stepped closer.

"Don't be going anywhere now… we ain't gonna hurt you… much." They leaped at him just as the door opened. Someone grabbed his arm and yanked him inside just before the other prisoners caught him.

"You can't stay in there forever, boy! We'll be waitin'!"

The infirmary was the closest thing to normal civilization that he'd seen in a very long time. Bright, white, and sterile. The doctors and nurses were civilians, dressed in blue and white clothing and showing appropriate compassion on their faces.

A tall, greying nurse in traditional white greeted him with concerned eyes. "That was close. You're very lucky."

"I don't feel so lucky," Novah groaned.

The nurse helped Novah to a table, noticing his torn open coveralls the thin trail of blood dripping down his thighs. She let out a heavy sigh of familiarity.

"Rectal hemorrhage, table three!" she shouted out. A head poked out of a nearby cubicle. "What was that, Alice?"

"Rectal hemorrhage, I said! Bring the usual!"

Novah hurt too much to feel shame and complied with requests to undress and reposition as best he could. He didn't know what the nurses were doing *back there* and he didn't want to know. All he wanted to do was cry himself to sleep. The prick of the needle that slipped into his arm was barely noticeable against the backdrop of other activity.

Sometime later, he awoke. He tried to move.

"No no," a pleasant voice chided, "just be still. Stay on your stomach. You need time to heal."

As his eyes focused, he thought he recognized the nurse. "Alice? Is that your name?"

"Yes, that's my name," she said politely. "And you're Novah – at least according to the number on your forearm." Novah nodded, rubbing his cheek up and down the cool sheets. "We cleaned that up a little, too. Those heathens in processing have no concept of sanitation. It says in your file that you were added to our fine community nine days ago. Surprising really."

"Surprising?" Novah queried.

"Yes. Surprising you made it so long without coming to visit."

Three days later, Novah was discharged from the infirmary. Walking was still difficult. His diet, while purely liquid, had rejuvenated him to a degree. Nurse Alice escorted him to the alternate entrance which was a hallway that ran behind the Baskin & Robbins in the food court. It was lunchtime and he could blend into the crowd.

"Try not to come back, okay?" Alice said with a smile.

"I hope I never see you again," Novah replied with a smile to reflect Alice's.

They had given him a fresh set of prison clothes, and in spite of his ordeal, he felt relatively confident in his mobility as long as he didn't have to run.

Days passed and Novah felt better physically though not mentally. Deep down inside festered a seething boil of hate, growing daily. He struggled to control it. *Let it go* he kept telling himself to no avail. His mood became blacker even as his ability to survive in the Mall increased. He'd become adept at the art of stealth. He'd learned how to live solo. He'd found an access point that led up to the roof, where he'd fashioned a makeshift shelter from whatever he could scrounge up. It sucked on the windier, rainier days, but dealing with the wet was a small price to pay for the comfort of sleeping in relative peace.

Every few days he'd find a concealing vantage point outside of

Build-a-Bear to see if he could catch a glimpse of Penny or her conspirators. Jacob and John would appear once every week, always at night after the mall lights had been turned off. They'd knock, enter, and leave after an hour or so. Soon thereafter a hapless soul would stumble wretchedly out of the hidden office, always in tears, always struggling to walk. The hate within Novah waxed every time. He would simply watch for a couple of minutes, and then swoop in silently, lending a shoulder to the shell-shocked victim, escorting him or her through the darkness to the infirmary. Some of those he tried to help fought him, scratched him, kicked at him, whatever their primal resistances could muster. Novah suffered their weak assaults. He suffered their wretchedness and wailing. He suffered the heavy reminders of his own unforgettable pain. Darkness filled his soul.

After a few weeks Nurse Alice noticed the pattern and was always on hand to open the infirmary door. She even posted guards to protect Novah's approach. He would simply help the victim to a cot, nod grimly at Alice, and leave through the back door.

As the months passed, every once in a while he would recognize the face of one of the people he'd helped. Some were obviously still broken, eyes glazed and hopeless, and some were slumped by the weight of the same burdensome hate Novah was carrying. He'd helped fourteen. He'd seen, by his count, seven of them since, here and there around the Mall.

After Novah deposited number fifteen on a cot, Alice pulled him aside.

"Aren't you going to do anything about this?" she asked.

The words poured out of Novah like hot lava, sizzling with every syllable. "Just what the hell am I supposed to do? It's all I can do to drag the victims here. I have no weapons. No 'kung fu'. Both of those guys are much bigger and stronger than I am."

Nurse Alice cocked her head sideways, staring at him with a look of incredulousness.

"Novah," she said with an irritated smile, "use your head. Think. Who else might want these monsters dealt with? Don't think you have to do it by yourself."

Novah pondered for a moment. He leaned in to Alice with an urgent whisper.

"Sure, I might be able to convince some of the other victims to join me, but we can't kill them, Alice…as much as I want to. If I…any of us…get busted for murder, we're in here forever. I don't *want* to be in here forever."

Alice looked at him, triple-blinked in astonishment, and grabbed him by the shoulder. "Come with me," she said.

She led him deeper into the infirmary, beyond the surgery unit and the recovery cubicles, beyond the supply room, to a solid, cold steel door. She opened it and they both stepped inside. It was cold and their breath plumed out in white swirls. The twenty foot by twenty foot room was home to many black body bags, stacked like cordwood along the right hand wall.

"These are this month's victims, Novah. Twenty-seven of them so far with a week to go. They all end up here. Once a month a government truck shows up and takes them god-knows-where. There are never any questions. Never any police. Never any relatives. They are trash, Novah. Nobody cares. It's anarchy in the Mall by design. There is no law. There is no "getting busted" except by your fellow inmates. There's no penalty for taking matters into your own hands. All you have to do is survive until you're released." She paused to let the words sink in. "Now let's get out of here before we freeze to death."

Novah followed her out of the freezer, reflecting on what Alice had just told him. A plan began to form in his mind. Not a fancy plan, not anything elaborate, just a simple plan that would probably work. He warmed himself on the growing fires of potential revenge.

"Alice, we have nothing out there. I'd rather not rely on chance and have to figure things out as I go. Is there anything you can give me? A knife? A gun? Anything?"

Her answer was sympathetic, yet definitive. "No."

Novah pressed on. "Nothing? Can I at least get some paper and a pen?"

"Well, I suppose I can do that much," she said. She went to her desk with Novah in tow. She pulled out a dusty, unused 4x5 prescription pad and a pen, and handed them to him. "What are you going to do?"

He stared into her cool blue eyes with urgency. "If anyone shows up with one of these… prescriptions, you have to let them in. They have to stay here until I come. All of the people who bring one will be a victim. They'll know they are safe here. They'll trust you. Can you keep them here until I arrive?"

Alice furrowed her brow. "Alright."

"Good. I don't know when it'll happen yet. It'll take me time to figure this all out. Just be ready." Alice nodded.

Just then, a voice yelled out. "Nurses to station. Looks like three wounded near the door."

"I have to get to it, Novah. Show yourself out. Good luck." Before he could thank her, she was rushing to the front of the infirmary to tend to the fresh wounded. When she was out of sight he quickly opened her desk drawer and stole the unused roll of surgical tape that was there. On his way to the back door he pilfered a scalpel out of a supply cabinet.

The plan was simple. Get a posse together and ambush the rapists when they came out of hiding to do their dirty work. He believed the ambush would be easy provided he could manage the much trickier posse-building part.

Novah didn't think about it too much and instead just went to work. He didn't think about the odds of finding victims of Penny's evil plan, of finding solemn, broken needles in a dangerous haystack. He just worked to find them, slowly and methodically, store by store, aisle by aisle, hour by hour, day by day. When he found one, he didn't judge, he didn't guess as to whether or not they'd want to participate, he simply handed them a prescription note and walked away. He never looked back to see if the person even read it. He just counted on enough people having enough thirst for revenge to show up at the infirmary at the appointed day and time.

At the end of the three week window he'd given himself prior to gathering everyone together Novah had handed out twelve sticky notes. He didn't like that number, thinking it was too few. It would take a good group to take down Jacob and John. If, in the end, only a handful agreed to participate, things would get very dicey indeed. Perhaps even fatally so.

Two evenings later Novah danced with the shadows and made his way to the infirmary. Alice met him at the door.

"How many?" he inquired as he slipped inside. She smiled at him. "Twelve."

The twelve had been quietly shepherded to the hallway near the side exit and looked uniformly uncomfortable in the cramped space. Their eyes were filled with flinching uncertainty as Novah grabbed a folding chair, placed it near the head of the hallway, and sat down. He slid the duffel bag he had pulled out of the supply cabinet under his chair and pulled a prescription note from his pocket and held it up.

"Over the past few weeks I sought each of you out and handed you one of these," he began. "It simply says 'If you want justice, meet at the infirmary the evening of January 23rd.' The fact that you are all here is great. I know how you have suffered. I have suffered the same shame and harm at the hands of Jacob and John. But I must be honest with you. In my heart, this is less about justice, and more about revenge. What I offer you is not an arrest or a trial. Neither of those things matter here. What I'm offering is retribution. To be absolutely clear, I mean to rid this prison of Jacob and John forever. To kill them."

Nobody moved. Nobody even flinched. All eyes and ears were locked on Novah.

"It won't be easy," he continued, "both of them are bigger and stronger than any one of us. But we have numbers. If we strike like a pack we can overwhelm them."

A timid hand half raised into the air, followed immediately by a thin but determined female voice.

"How will we find them?" she asked.

"They have a pattern," Novah explained. "Once a week they visit Build-a-Bear and rape someone new. It's almost always every seven days. Last night was six days. That means they will probably show up tonight. Our objective is to intercept them before they get to the Build-a-Bear. Either that or wait for them to come out."

There was a bubbling murmur of "nooooooo." Waiting meant that there would be a new victim stumbling into the darkness an hour later. Nobody wanted that.

"Okay then. Intercept it is. They always come from Nordstrom's. That's about a fifty yards down the wing. There are eight large planters along the way. We need to hide behind them as best we can, and at the signal, strike and strike hard. No mercy. We must be fast and we must be brutal. As brutal as they were to us. They have to die. There's no law here. Nobody is going to get in trouble. Once the deed is done just finish out your sentences as if none of it ever happened, if you can."

"How can we kill them?" a male voice asked. "We have no weapons."

"We have these." He reached down and unzipped the duffel bag under his chair and pulled out a two-foot section of a broken broom handle. Alice had ordered a case of brooms, which nobody questioned, and while Alice pretended not to know, Novah used them to fashion the weapons. One end of each was wrapped in a thick layer of surgical tape, serving as a handle, and the other was simply the ragged, splintered pointed break. He handed the weapons out. "Stick them with these. Over and over, in the chest, back, neck and eyes." His audience looked at the weapons in their hands, then looked at each other. Another voice spoke.

"I…I don't think I can do this," said a lean man with dark hair. "Doesn't this make us as bad as them?"

It was the question Novah knew was coming. It was the question he'd struggled with himself. He took a deep breath to support his reply, but was interrupted.

"Don't be a fucking pussy!" snapped a high, female voice belonging to the smallest member of the group. She looked no more than twenty years old, and maybe weighed a hundred pounds soaking wet. "Those guys raped me! They raped me *over and over and over!* They raped all of us! They are going to keep on raping until they are stopped! Grow some balls and help us kill these bastards!"

Lowering her voice, she erased the four cramped feet between herself and the objector. She pressed a thin, pointed finger into his chest and stared up at him into his eyes.

"If we don't do this," she whispered, "the next person that hobbles all broken and bloody out of that store is on *you*. It's on *you*, man. And every person after that is on *you*. Every black eye, every ripped up asshole, every bruise, every wounded pussy. It's. On. You." She jabbed him with her finger at each of the last three words.

The hallway was silent, shocked by her language and her ferocity. Novah slowly stood, walked two steps, and pressed himself between the pair.

"What's your name, miss?" he asked. He'd made a point of never asking names when he dragged them to the infirmary. Most were in shock and badly hurt. Names didn't matter.

"Jamie," she replied.

"And yours?" he asked, turning to face the man.

"Carter."

"Jamie. Carter. This isn't how this is going to work," Novah said in a smooth, steady voice, surprising himself with his own calm. He looked at Jamie. "If his heart isn't in it now, no amount of shaming is going to convince him differently. Some people just aren't willing to kill. That's okay. I am prepared to kill these guys. It looks like you are too. Carter isn't. We'll have to live with ourselves and he'll have to live with himself."

He turned to Carter, trying to hide his own personal disgust behind a veil of cool compassion. "You'll have to stay here until it's done. We can't risk that you'd jeopardize the plan by doing something stupid like telling them we're coming in exchange for protection."

Carter flushed and was about to protest, but realized he'd be safer waiting in the infirmary and so kept his mouth shut. Shame was a small price to pay for survival.

"Is there anyone else who has any sort of objection, moral or otherwise, to snuffing those two clowns?"

Silence.

"Be sure. After the training, I'll ask once more."

Another voice piped up. "Training?"

26

"Yes. We're going to have a training session right now, with these weapons, on real human flesh. We need to know how much force is needed. It probably takes more effort than we think to cram a broom handle into someone's torso. We're going to use one of the bodies in the morgue."

"Hey," Alice protested, "I didn't sign off on *that*. What the hell, Novah!? No!"

Novah did his best to keep his emotions in check, though his words still came out as if each one had been stamped from a sheet of steel. "We need to practice. We won't get a second chance if we screw it up. If we do, we're dead, and those guys will continue raping others. I don't want to die. I don't want anybody here to die. *You* don't want to stack up any more bags in your freezer. We're going to practice, and we're going to kill those rapists." He pointed a broom handle weapon towards the back of the infirmary and looked at Alice. "Now we're going back there, and you're going to point us to the freshest corpse, and we're going to take turns stabbing it. Unless you've had a change of heart and like stitching up holes every week."

Alice stood silent for a moment before responding. "You're right, Novah. Better two more corpses in the freezer than a dozen."

Novah casually issued a waving gesture. "Let's go, everyone."

They walked as a group the thirty paces to the freezer door, where Novah told them to wait. He then stepped inside the freezer where Alice stood shivering from the cold.

"Here's one that was dragged to our door very early this morning. Rigor mortis has already set in pretty good," she whispered clinically, trying to distance herself emotionally from what she was tacitly approving.

Novah pulled the body bag off of the pile with a thump, dragged it flat, and opened the zipper. It was an adult male, mid-thirties. A little smaller than Jacob and John, but it'd do. Novah tried to ignore that half of his skull was caved in, but in the end realized he couldn't. Neither would his posse.

"We need to bag his head." Novah thought for a moment, unbuttoned the front of his coveralls and then peeled off his t-shirt.

He tied the neck hole in a knot, pulled the shirt over the dead man's head, and then used the long sleeves to tie it firmly around the neck. Novah's body shuddered at the chill, or at least that's what he attributed it to.

He pulled the fully-clothed body from the body bag and out into the hallway. Almost everyone there had seen a dead body before so it wasn't a complete shock to them. The Mall had hardened them, numbed them.

"Alice says this guy was also a rapist," Novah lied. "He picked on the wrong person, though, and ended up getting his skull bashed in. Too bad, so sad. Now he's going to be our practice dummy." Novah dragged the corpse a few feet down the hallway, and with great effort hoisted it up onto a pair of coat hooks that were screwed into the wall. The dead man's feet dangled about an inch off the floor.

"They'll be standing so we'll start out here. If we do it right, they'll be on the ground in no time, which will make it easier to stab them because the ground will add resistance. Who wants to go first?"

Nobody moved.

Novah knew it wouldn't be easy. He just didn't think it would be this *hard*. He pointed to the closest person, a forty-something, chubby, dirty-haired woman who was still nursing a black eye.

"You, what's your name?" he asked.

"Molly."

"Ok Molly. Take your weapon and stab this rapist."

Molly looked at him, looked at her weapon, and looked at the corpse. Novah could almost see her replaying the movie of her rape in her eyes, which narrowed angrily. She took her pointy, broken-off broom handle and jabbed the corpse in the heart. The tip barely penetrated the coveralls and t-shirt.

"And this is why we're practicing," stated Novah. "We're using primitive weapons against lightly-armored people. It's going to take more force than we think."

Molly, embarrassed, snapped "let's see *you* do it!" The others gave a vocal second to the motion.

Novah was no expert on killing. He'd never expressed physical violence towards anyone since middle-school. If this plan was going to work, though, he needed to be the leader. He needed to stop faking it and really show the determination he felt. He needed to muster in himself the steely resolve he was asking of everyone else. He honestly had no idea how much force it would take to cram a broomstick into a human chest, but he had to do it. He scanned in his head scenes from every war and marital arts movie he'd ever seen, gathering up courage and what he hoped was useful knowledge.

"Alright," he said. "First, grab your stick like this. Put your dominant hand over the end. There's lots of tape, so you won't hurt yourself. Use your other hand and grab the stick halfway down. You want to shove the stick *through* them. Put your body behind it. If you are stabbing from the front, you want to try to touch their spine with the tip. The belly will be softer, because it's not protected by the ribs." *The moment of truth.*

Novah crammed the stick deep into the corpse's intestines with every bit of strength he had. He felt the tip jab against the concrete wall. He then withdrew the stick, pulling out a gooey, wretchedly-smelling trail of congealed bodily fluids. He stoically ignored it even as the others turned a bit green.

"However," he continued, "we want these guys to go down fast. We don't want them to get a chance to fight back. So we have to go for the vital organs. The heart and the lungs."

The corpse made a sickening *ka-chunk* sound as Novah's stick skewered the corpse at an angle through its left chest muscle. The tip drove in about three inches, which was plenty to reach the heart.

"A few of those and that's that. Don't go for the middle of the chest – the breastplate is too hard. Go off to the side like I did here." He pulled his broom handle out, then pointed it back at the corpse. "Now, Molly, stab that rapist!"

A half an hour later each of the eleven had taken a couple turns and the corpse was riddled with holes. A few of the holes even looked deep enough to reach a vital organ.

"Good work, everyone," Novah said as he scanned the group. "Head back to the area we were before. I'll take care of this rapist and be right there."

The group shuffled off, and Novah crammed the slowly oozing corpse back into its sack. He gave the corpse a parting gift, finally releasing the vomit that had been banging at the back of his throat. He wiped off his mouth on his sleeve, zipped up the body bag, and pushed it up against the existing pile of bodies. *There's no turning back now*, he told himself.

"Alright everyone," he stated authoritatively as he rejoined the group, "now is your last chance to decline. Speak now, or forever hold your peace."

Novah knew which two would raise their hands even before they did. Their hearts weren't into it during practice. They only participated out of peer pressure. Sure enough, two hands waved halfheartedly out of the crowd.

"I'm out," said a tall, lanky fellow, who still looked a bit green from corpse-stabbing.

"Me too," said a shorter, balder man. "I just can't see myself doing this. I hope you get them, though."

Novah nodded, again hiding his internal disgust. *How could they just wuss out like that? Did they forget they were raped?* "Very well, you two will have stay here and keep Carter company. The rest of you, take five. We'll meet back here to discuss the details."

The group didn't really have anywhere they could go, so mingled quietly amongst themselves. Novah pulled Alice aside, pressing his lips very close to her ear. "They can't leave, you know. Think you can keep them here?" he whispered.

She looked up at him with narrowed eyes. "I don't like it," she replied, "but I'll keep them here. I'll sedate them if I have to. I'll do some lab work close to the side door."

"Thank you, Alice. I know this has turned out to be a bit more real than maybe you thought."

She nodded softly and turned away.

The time quickly passed and Novah gathered everyone in an elongated huddle.

"Ok team, here's how we'll play this. There are ten of us total. We need to ambush them both simultaneously, so five for each." He took a quick glance around the circle, dividing the group into two in his mind in an effort to build two groups of equivalent strength. He repositioned people in the circle, dividing them into two groups. He explained his reasoning while he did it and everyone seemed satisfied that the division was reasonable.

"Ok, group one here on my left will take out Jacob. Group two, John. If you don't remember who was who, Jacob is the taller one."

Novah pulled out a prescription note on which he'd drawn a rough map of the general area near Build-a-Bear. He pressed it out on the floor for everyone to see, kneeling like a quarterback in the huddle.

"They always come from Nordstrom's, usually around eleven p.m., two hours after the lights turn off. We'll want to be in position by lights-off at nine so that we don't miss them. They might come early. Or they might be later. We'll just have to be ready." Novah pointed at the paper. "There are eight large round planters cemented to the floor here. You've all seen them. At lights out, group one will hide behind these four, and group two the other four. When they reach the midpoint between the planters we strike. Strike hard, fast, and repeatedly.

"Remember what they did to you. Remember what they did to the person next to you. Know that if they aren't stopped, they will do it to someone else. Summon up all the pain and fear and anger you have, and deliver justice. Let's go."

Jacob and John didn't see it coming, and the ferocity of the group's attack was primal. Jamie had to be forcefully removed from Jacob's corpse as she appeared to have no "off" switch. She just kept stabbing, and stabbing, and stabbing, long after he was done for. When it was over, and everyone stood above the two dead bodies panting in a blood-soaked, adrenalin-fueled fury, only one question was left to be answered, and it was asked by Molly: *what about Penny?*

Yes, what about Penny? Novah had been gnawing on that question for weeks. What was he going to do?

"I'm going to deal with Penny myself," Novah said. "You all have done enough. I'll finish this once and for all."

31

The group grumbled in protest, and Novah raised a conciliatory hand, and spoke with his own short-breathed, shaky voice. "I know, I know. You want a piece of her too. You deserve it. I'm asking you, though, to let this belong to me. I put this group together. I built the plan. I taught you how to execute it. I ask for nothing but Penny. Let me do this. Please."

There were more under-breath murmurs, but in the end, they granted Novah his request.

"We'll wait out here," growled Molly.

"Thank you. Thank you all," replied Novah.

He wiped his broom handle off on the leg of his coveralls and casually walked around the corner to the entrance of Build-a-Bear. He knew the secret knock, and also knew he would have to act fast once the door cracked open. He summoned up his second wind.

When Penny unlatched the door and let it swing inward, Novah rammed his shoulder into it opening it fully, knocking Penny backwards. He then followed with a powerful, crunching right hand directly into her face. She crumpled to the floor, dazed, blood gushing from her upper lip. Before she could gather her wits, he picked her up, slammed her on her back on the cot, pinned her down, and quickly taped her wrists to the frame. Penny choked on her blood as she tried to scream. He tied down her ankles, and then crammed a sock into her mouth and taped it over. Just as he was finishing this, he noticed a pair of shocked, silent eyes staring at him from the corner of the room. The young Hispanic woman there holding her knees tried to speak, scared out of her wits, but nothing came out. Novah calmed himself, even as Penny began to come to, struggling and grunting fruitlessly.

"Don't be afraid. I'm not going to hurt you," Novah said looking at the woman. He slid slowly into Penny's now-vacant chair. "Penny is a very bad person. Tonight, two of her friends were going to come here and rape you. My friends and I caught them. We killed them. They had raped all of us. Penny set us all up. She offered us all as sacrifices for her own protection. She was going to do the same to you. She picks out new inmates, befriends them, and then turns on them."

Still, nothing but wide, frightened eyes from the woman in the corner.

"You should leave. My friends are outside, around the corner towards Nordstrom's. They'll protect you. Please. You don't want to be here." He reached out his hand, and the woman shrunk away in abject fear.

"Ok, I'm going to move over here by the bathroom. That gives you a clear path to the door. I won't move until you're gone." He stepped away, framing himself with the entrance to the bathroom.

"Go on!"

Faster than a cat the woman dashed out of the office and into the blackness of the mall. Novah moved the chair to the side of the cot, where he was met with furious, tear-filled eyes. As he poked the door closed with his broken broom handle, Novah said in a soft, steady voice, "Hi Penny, remember me?"

Penny tried to scream through her gag.

"Oh, I know you do. The last time we met, it was me tied to the cot, and you in this chair." He ran the broken broom handle slowly down her leg, making sure she could feel it. "Do you see this stick? I just used this stick to kill Jacob and John." He held it up to her eyes. "That's their blood on it." Penny's eyes shrieked at him as she continued to scream through the gag.

"You traded my ass for your own protection, Penny. It hurt like hell." He used the stick to hook the bottom of her shirt, pulling it upwards to bare the bottom of her heaving abdomen. She froze in fear.

"I've been thinking about this moment for a long, long time." Novah dragged the tip of his stick slowly across Penny's naked belly. "I've been debating what I should do. Should I rape you? Should I kill you? Should I do both?" His voice was low and even, almost fatherly. "My friends outside – others who you helped get raped – want me to kill you. They never want you to victimize anyone ever again. I know how they feel. I don't want you to trap anyone ever again."

Novah sat silent for a minute, just staring at Penny, honestly unsure of what he was going to do. Staring into her eyes he saw something new. The rage had transformed into pure, hopeless fear. Her tears magnified the pity Novah felt.

"Okay Penny. I don't think I'm going to rape you. I'm going to take that sock out of your mouth and we're going to have a conversation. If you start screaming again I'm going to shove the sock back in. Do you understand?" Penny nodded.

Novah peeled back the surgical tape, drawing the bloody sock out of Penny's mouth.

She gathered a breath, her chest heaving, before bellowing "you motherfucker!"

Novah's hand pressed the sock back towards Penny's mouth. She reconsidered her tone.

"No, wait!" she pleaded. "I'm sorry! Please don't gag me again."

"One more outburst and the sock goes back in," replied Novah. "Got it?"

"Yeah, I got it," Penny said.

"Ok then," said Novah, "tell me why I shouldn't just kill you here and now."

"Maybe you should," she said weakly. "I'm tired of living every day scared."

That wasn't the answer that Novah expected. He relaxed his tone further, struggling to find the balance between the vengeance he needed and the blossoming compassion he was feeling for her.

"Everyone here lives every day scared. Yet you do worse to people. You gain their trust, and then *betray* them. You turn their trust into pain. You promise to help and then do nothing but hurt them."

"I know," she replied softly. "But it's all I know how to do."

"Learn something else then," chided Novah. "You have the skills to make friends. Gather friends. Don't cash them in for safety. The more friends you have, the safer you'll be. You know that! And with Jacob and John gone, there's no reason you can't start fresh."

"Are they really dead?" she asked.

"Yes. A gang of ten of us took them out just before I came here."

Penny grew silent for a few seconds before the flicker in her eyes reignited. "Perhaps I can start fresh then," she said.

Novah began to untie her bindings. "You can, Penny. Promise me you won't hurt people like this anymore. Tell me I can tell the others it was the right thing to not kill you."

Penny sat up on the cot, rubbing her wrists, tear and blood stains on her face. "I promise, Novah." She leaned over and gave him a chaste kiss on his cheek. "I hate you, but I promise. Thank you for not killing me. Thank you for not raping me."

"Don't make me regret this," Novah said as he stood and opened the door.

"I won't," promised Penny. "As long as you never come back."

"Deal," he said as he walked out the door and back into the mall.

Novah spent the next half an hour making his case to the others. Penny wasn't cruel. She was doing what she thought she needed to do to survive. The real rapists were now dead, unable to rape anyone ever again. Penny had good in her and deserved a second chance. Some of his posse spat at him. Some swore to get their own vengeance on Penny. Some understood. In his heart Novah believed he'd made the right decision no matter what the others may have thought.

Six weeks later he watched two men and a woman leave Build-a-Bear in the dark of night. An hour later, a young, thick black woman came stumbling out, broken and bloodied. After some coaxing she let Novah help her to the infirmary.

"Nature abhors a vacuum, Novah," Alice said. "With John and Jacob gone, someone else had to rise to the top of the scum-chain. That's the way it has always been. That's the way it will always be."

"But Penny promised she'd stop," Novah replied.

"Penny is doing the only thing she knows how to do."

"I should have killed her," said Novah, seething. "Every new person raped because of her is my fault."

Alice gave Novah a motherly hug, but said nothing else.

~~~

Lightning crashed bringing Novah back momentarily to the present. He counted to ten before the thunder echoed through the valley. The wind was picking up, rocking the trailer when it grew particularly stiff. He poured the remainder of the bourbon bottle into his plastic cup, disappointed that it only filled an inch of it. With the next sip his mind drifted back to the past three days. He was free now, and counting his blessings.

At the end of his sentence Novah exited the Mall with fresh clothes, identification, and a $50 food voucher which would feed him for maybe two days if he was very careful. Within the protective barricades surrounding the main towns something akin to normalcy had begun to take shape in the past year. There were noticeably less people and significantly fewer cars on the streets, and anarchy no longer reigned. Plain white tractor trailers moved goods into the protected zones. It was still dangerous outside these zones, however, with groups of roving gangs picking clean society's corpse outside of the heavily militarized areas. Drones dealt with particularly large or unruly groups, and occasionally the military would do a sweep, killing or capturing the few remaining insurgents.

Novah assumed that his parents had been killed, captured, or sent away. He had nowhere else to go, though, so decided to walk the fifteen miles home. Perhaps someone was still there. Perhaps he could find a meal and a warm bed. Perhaps he could find something of use to help him get by. His dad had been a smart man. A clever man. Chances are that something might have escaped the government's grasp. It was a thin hope, but it was the only hope Novah had.

The weather was unseasonably nice, the air clear and crisp. He noted with curiosity that Mt. Rainier, far in the distance, was steaming, sending white tendrils curling up into the blue sky. Novah stared for only a couple of minutes before turning and beginning his long walk. He set a brisk pace, walking through the night, and by the middle of the next day he found himself back home. The house was empty, boarded up in places, and overrun with rodents. As Novah stepped up onto the creaky, weathered deck at the front of the house he noticed bullet holes dug into the splintered cedar siding. The metal door lay crumpled on the ground, its frame ruptured at the deadbolt.

He quietly looked for signs of occupation, slowly peeking into each room, discovering that the house was indeed empty except for rats and mice. A putrid smell of mildew and rodent urine rose up from the carpets, permeating the air. He walked through the hall and noticed that the door to the hall closet was still intact. Opening it, he found the hinged entrance to the crawlspace where his mom and dad had hidden. It was undamaged, indicating that it hadn't been forced open. It gave him hope that his parents were still alive somewhere.

Walking out of the ruined kitchen into the garage where his dad had stored their supplies, he was shocked at the thoroughness with which the place had been looted. There was nothing left. The thousand-pound safe had been ripped right out of the garage's cement floor. The large standup freezer was gone. The circuit breaker panel was gone. Even the shelving was gone. Novah stepped over the torn-out metal garage doors into the driveway. The small storage shed was not only empty, it was burned to the ground. He picked through the charred and molten rubble but there was nothing even remotely recognizable.

The greenhouse was simply missing. The ten by twelve foot cement footprint was all that remained. There was no wood, no glass, no metal. It was as if a giant hand had simply reached down and plucked it effortlessly from the garden. Novah sat down on a charred railroad tie that was once part of the elevated planter boxes and pondered. He reflected on the "good years" in the house. How he'd mastered *Madden 2020* on his dad's old Xbox One. How he'd chased their yellow lab, *Orbus*, through the yard. How he'd sneak off to the treehouse and watch porn on his smartphone...

"The treehouse!"

He hadn't climbed up into the treehouse since well before graduation, as more important things had eaten up his days, then the years, and then he'd simply forgotten its existence. Perhaps it had not yet completely succumbed to the weather which eventually rotted everything.

Looking around and not seeing anyone, Novah walked to the far point of the back yard and hopped over the short wooden fence that separated the yard proper from the deep forested ravine behind it, the same ravine that had allowed his escape more than a year earlier. The ravine was filled with cedars, madronas, and many varieties of shrubs, ferns, and vines. It looked exactly as it had for years.

Stepping carefully several yards down the blackberry-infested hillside, he came to the large madrona tree where the small treehouse still remained, perched a good twenty-five feet up. The wooden ladder strips that had been nailed to the tree were gone, much to Novah's consternation – which in short order turned to delight. *This has dad's fingerprints all over it,* he thought. *There must be something here. Why else would dad make sure nobody came across the ladder by accident?*

Sure enough, with some searching of the surrounding area, he found the lumpy stack of wood pieces shoved under a particularly gnarly blackberry bush. The pieces still had the nails in them and at the bottom of the pile was a rusted hammer.

Novah looked at the rotting wood and the rusty nails with concern, worried that they wouldn't hold his hundred and sixty pounds. He couldn't think of any other options, however, so carefully made his way up the tree, hammering in the ladder piece by piece as quietly as he could, which wasn't very quiet at all. His paranoia informed him that it wouldn't be long before someone came to investigate no matter how far away the nearest human might be.

Pulling himself up into the inside of the small four by eight foot treehouse he found it completely empty. It usually was, even in his childhood. He knew, though, that his dad had hid something here, and he knew exactly where. When they'd built the treehouse together his dad had hollowed out a small area of the trunk of the tree, an area just about big enough to put a brick in. As he was covering it with a wall board, nailing it to the tree, his dad said *if something ever goes wrong, and I'm not around, remember this place.* Novah had, of course, forgotten until now.

It was silly. It was simple. It was genius. He was so glad he remembered. With some effort he pried the board off of the tree. Inside the carved out area was a piece of white PVC pipe, 2.5 inches in diameter, eight inches long, and covered at both ends with a generous amount of duct tape. Novah was shaking with cold, hunger, and excitement as he peeled open one end of the tube. He pulled out a small plastic sandwich bag that had a folded piece of paper in it. Deeper inside the tube he found two keys, a small knife, and twelve silver liberty coins.

Sitting down on the floor of the treehouse, he read the note contained in the sandwich bag:

Son,

If you are reading this, things have taken a bad turn. I am likely dead and/or gone beyond rescue. Your mom and I managed to escape detection the night I sent you out, but I have no doubt they'll be back. I'm certainly on their list, and your mom and I are not inclined to run. We talked about it, and next time, we're going to fight. We're too old to live life on the run. You'll need to fend for yourself.

The keys are to units 17 and 18 at the Ajax Boat and RV Storage Center. You know where it's at – tucked away behind the closed school where they used to store the unused school busses. Find Charles. Hopefully the contents of the units are still there. Take them and get away. You know where to go.

Find a way to make your way. Live every day. Read. Learn. Keep an open mind. I wish I could be there for you now.

Don't seek revenge. Simply seek to live a peaceful life.

Love,

Mom and Dad

Novah wiped the tears from his eyes and put all of the items in his pockets. He put the board back for no other reason than to make the treehouse whole. There was still enough daylight left to make it to the storage place so he decided to get going.

On his way down the tree one of the ladder pieces gave way and he fell fifteen feet to the ground, the sound of his impact a mixture of his scream and a heinous *SNAP*. Pain exploded through his left ankle.

He sat motionless in the damp dirt and held his ankle with both hands, gritting his teeth. As he slowly removed his hand he expected to see bone sticking out, but didn't. In fact, though he'd very obviously sprained his ankle badly, and it hurt like hell, it didn't *feel* broken. To his relief he discovered that the snap he heard was just a dried madrona branch.

Walking was an exercise in gasping breaths, tears, and frequent rests. Novah quickly learned that trying to hop back up the blackberry-infested, slippery slope of the ravine was a fool's errand. He decided to work with gravity instead of against it following the stream downhill.

Deer had made a narrow path along the stream which made it easier for him to gingerly hop from tree to tree. Time was against him now and every heartbeat echoed a painful throb in his foot. He needed to get to the storage place before dark, which meant he had about three hours. He knew he could follow the ravine down to the main road that bisected it at the bottom. That'd take about half an hour at his current pace – it wasn't far. Then a mile along the highway going west, then a quarter mile south to the old school. He was hungry, thirsty, and crippled, yet believed he could make it before night fell. The hope that the storage units were still intact motivated him. He clung to that hope like the crutch he wished he had to help him walk.

Just as dusk settled in Novah limped up to the aged, off-centered double gates of the storage facility, his fingers entwined in the chain links for support. A light was on in the main office so he hopped the remaining hundred feet to the rusty door. Exhausted, weak and nearly weeping in pain, he turned the knob and stumbled in. A tall, thin, black man with short white hair and a surprised expression greeted him, an eyebrow arched questioningly.

"Well now, what interesting visitor has dusk thrown through my door? Please, young man, hobble over to that fine upholstered chair and regain your breath." Novah obliged with a nod, barely hearing or understanding the words, still panting from exertion.

The black man went to the water cooler and filled up a small paper cup. "Here. Drink this, and then tell me how I may assist you."

Novah took the water gratefully and chugged it down in a single swallow. "I'm here to get my stuff from a pair of your storage units," he said through a pained wince.

The black man nodded, went back behind the counter, and pulled out a thick brown ledger and opened it up while grabbing the black-framed glasses dangling by a silver chain around his neck.

"Very well then...which units?"

"Seventeen and eighteen."

The man dragged a long finger along one page, then another, then another.

"Hmm. You'll excuse me for saying so, sir, but you don't look like

40

the man who these units are assigned to, and though I'm sure you are a fine, upstanding citizen, I'm afraid that without a change in circumstances, our transaction can proceed no further." Unseen, the man reached underneath the counter feeling for the sawed-off shotgun hidden there. He placed his hand on the stock but otherwise didn't pull it out.

"They are my dad's. Burns. Greg Burns."

"Please pardon my skepticism. I knew Greg Burns. He came here now and then." The man cocked his head slightly, squinted, and looked carefully again at Novah. "Though, somewhere under that hideously unruly beard and hair of yours might be a face I recognize. You do carry his countenance, and though you've grown taller since the last time I saw you here, I do believe you may be his son. Yet I don't know if I can trust these fading eyes of mine, and find myself compelled to seek further proof. Do you possess any identification?"

Novah nodded, reached into his pocket, and pulled out his government-issued I.D. card.

"Please bring it up here. I know you are injured, yet I must insist." He re-gripped the shotgun with a sweaty hand.

Novah understood the man's caution. This was a dangerous world in which anything even resembling the shadow of trust had to be earned. He was pretty sure the old man had a gun behind the counter and wouldn't hesitate to use it. Novah pushed himself up off the chair, and made three ginger hops to the counter and placed his I.D. on the journal. The man picked it up.

"Mr. Novah Burns. Welcome, and please forgive my insistence." He let go of the shotgun, and made his way back around the counter. "I'll help you back to the chair. I'm Charles. Charles Alexander."

"Pleased to meet you, Charles. I vaguely remember you, but never knew your name." Charles guided Novah back to the relief of sitting.

"What happened to your parents, Novah?" asked Charles.

"I don't know. They could be alive, they could be dead. I haven't seen them in over a year," Novah replied.

Charles' brow furrowed. "That's unfortunate. There is little sense in speculating on their condition or whereabouts, however. We'll just have to assume they are doing the best they can." Charles motioned to the chair.

"Please sit and rest here. Business hours have concluded and I need to go lock the front gate. I'll return in five minutes and then we shall discuss these circumstances." Charles shuffled out the door. Novah closed his eyes.

Three hours later Novah awoke, startled and confused about where he was. It all came back quickly as his ankle throbbed painfully. Charles looked over the rim of his glasses, setting aside the paperwork he was doing at the counter.

"You were sleeping by the time I returned, and I decided it was best for you to get some rest. You may sleep here the night if you are so inclined. It appears that you've been through a bout of unfortunate circumstances, and you're likely half starved. Follow me to my living quarters. Use those crutches I found."

Charles nodded at the corner behind Novah's chair where a pair of old wooden crutches stood, most the gray foam long eaten off of the support points. Novah took them and awkwardly followed Charles around the old wooden counter and out a different door which opened into a modest living quarters which smelled of pot, dust, old books and leather. Charles pointed to an aged, brown easy chair. "Please sit. Pull the lever and raise your feet. Let's evaluate the extent of your injury."

Charles slid over the ottoman, sat on it, and struggled to remove Novah's left shoe and sock. The room was dimly lit but even so they both could see how bruised and swollen the ankle was. The bruising extended all the way to Novah's toes.

"A nasty sprain indeed. Perhaps even some ligament damage. I wish I had some ice, but I don't. All we can do is wrap it up and stabilize it. I'm afraid you won't be able to put your shoe back on."

Charles wrapped Novah's ankle with a used roll of elastic medical cloth, securing the end with a pair of small clips. "Sit back and relax, Mr. Burns. I will see what I might be able to rummage up in the form of sustenance."

Novah leaned back into his chair, jostling the small table next to it with his elbow. A stack of old National Geographic magazines, piled on the shelf at the bottom of the table, tumbled onto the floor. He reached down and pushed them back into place. A dusty picture frame capped the stack and Novah's curiosity got the best of him. He wiped away the thick layer of dust and read the certificate hiding underneath:

Massachusetts Institute of Technology
Upon the Recommendation of the Faculty
Hereby Confers on
Charles Lloyd Alexander
The Degree of
Doctor of Physics
Given This Day Under the Seal of the Institute at Cambridge
September 20, 1983

Novah was admiring the calligraphy as Charles walked back into the room, a plate of biscuits and beans in each hand.

"You're a doctor, Charles?" Novah asked.

Charles frowned and handed Novah a plate. "I earned a doctorate degree," he said quietly, as if saying it any louder would somehow invoke demons he'd rather not wake. "Such trophies are a relic of a time long passed."

"What happened? Why have you been working here all these years? Shouldn't you be off winning a Nobel Prize or something?"

Charles stiffened briefly, as if shocked, then relaxed as he sat down in a brown folding chair near Novah. "I nearly did, once," he said reflectively. "I discovered and mathematically proved a particularly interesting electrical phenomenon which…" Charles shook his head. "Nevermind. All of that is of no consequence now."

Novah read something in Charles' body language. "You got screwed, huh?"

A smirk crossed Charles' face. "I suppose that would be a colloquial way of stating what transpired, yes. I simply say I was "Tesla'd."

Novah gave Charles a quizzical look. "Well now you *have* to explain."

Charles chuckled lightly. "Nicola Tesla, one of the greatest minds of the last century, discovered a way of siphoning electricity straight out of the ionosphere. It would have provided free, unlimited electricity to everyone. Unfortunately, Mr. Tesla's contemporary and former associate, Mr. Thomas Edison, allegedly bribed Tesla's financier to shut down the atmospheric electricity harvesting tower. There was much more money to be made in regulating Edison's direct current electricity model. Money talks, so Edison got rich while Tesla died in poverty. Just as tragically, Tesla didn't write down much of what he discovered and his knowledge was lost to the ages. By chance, I rediscovered how to harvest electricity from the atmosphere. To make a long story short, my life was threatened. I was told I'd be killed if I published the research. I presume the same type of crony monopolistic entities that broke Tesla's will decided to do the same to me. That evening, I erased all of the data in my laboratory, burned the paper copies of my discovery, left Chicago, and came here. Some might say it was an act of cowardice. I assert that any society that won't allow science to freely provide for the betterment of all mankind does not deserve such advances. I withdrew my mind and abilities from a society that wanted to abuse it. Now eat your dinner."

Novah didn't press the issue any further, and the hot meal of biscuits and beans made him feel better than he'd felt in well over a year – ankle pain notwithstanding. The pair of puffs on the joint Charles offered after dinner helped ease the pain and allowed Novah to drift off contentedly.

Novah's ankle felt *very* bad in the morning when he awoke but there was nothing he could do about it. He was stiff and still tired, trying to hoist himself out of the chair when Charles walked in with a plate of fried eggs and handed it to Novah.

"My doctorate isn't in medicine, but if it was, I'd probably insist that you avoid putting pressure on your ankle for a few days. I am unable to board you for that long, however. The challenges of maintaining even this simple existence for myself are already difficult. Mine is a solitary life. I tolerate the rare customer but open and close this place out of habit more than necessity. I find that the routine helps keep me from wallowing in despair. I've been living the last few months off of the contents of these storage units, bartering items of perceived value with local farmers. We all work to maintain a low profile. If we live quietly, the government won't bother us, or so we choose to believe."

Charles saw Novah's panicked look. "Relax, Novah," he said with a smile. "I haven't opened up seventeen or eighteen yet. I began at one-twenty and am working my way backwards. I'm only at unit eighty-five. Finish up your eggs, and let's go see what your father left for you."

Novah gulped down the eggs and three glasses of water. A few minutes later, he crutched his way outside, slowly following Charles along the dirt and gravel avenues between the storage units.

"Seventeen and eighteen are at the end of this row. They are my largest units. I know what they contain, but I'm content to keep it a secret," Charles said with a teasing grin.

They reached unit seventeen, which had a roll-up door twelve feet wide and eight feet high. Novah fumbled for the key labeled "17" and unlocked the heavy lock. Charles bent down and heaved the reluctant door upwards in spite of its rusty screech of protest. Daylight flooded in, revealing a large brown tarp which was covering a large object. Charles grabbed the front edge of the tarp and dragged it away out into the open revealing a blue, spotless, mint-condition Ford F-150 pickup truck. It was an older model but immaculately maintained. Novah hobbled around the exterior, mouth agape.

"It hasn't been started in well over a year, and the gas has probably separated, so don't get your hopes up too high," cautioned Charles. Novah didn't really hear him though. He was busy taking inventory of the truck. Tow package. Four-wheel drive. Matching canopy. He opened the canopy and caught the faint whiff of gasoline. Fifty gallons worth in ten five-gallon jerry cans, strapped solidly to the bed of the truck. He hoped the fuel was still usable. There was also a cardboard box filled with various spare parts. Belts, hoses, clamps, a case of oil and a pair of filters, and a few other things he didn't recognize. There was also a medium-sized steel toolbox.

"Wow...this is great!" he blurted out. Charles chuckled to himself. "Wait until you see what eighteen contains. I predict you'll be equally pleased."

Novah crutched himself back out into the daylight and over to the next similarly-sized door that hid the contents of unit eighteen. He unlocked it, and again Charles hoisted up the door. It was a twenty-something foot travel trailer, blanketed by a form-fitting cover.

"Amazing" was all Novah could say as Charles carefully peeled the tarp off. Novah wondered when his dad had bought these and how he managed to stash them without giving away the secret. This setup wasn't cheap. He figured his dad thought the fewer people that knew, the better.

What was even more amazing is that the truck actually started on the first key turn.

"Your father must have supplemented the fuel by adding some stabilizer to it. Quite smart!" Charles noted. All Novah could do was grin and be thankful that it was his left ankle and not the right that was sprained. Driving would have otherwise been nearly impossible.

"Will you help me get this hooked up to the trailer?" asked Novah.

"I'd be delighted," replied Charles, smiling broadly.

In no time they'd hooked up the trailer and pulled it out into the daylight. It was packed with everything needed for an extended camping trip. Food, canned goods, a water purifier, two cases of bottled water, thirty gallons of propane, and a massive first aid kit. What it didn't contain, much to Novah's surprise, was any weaponry. Nor was there any other communication left from his dad. The only other item of note was a map on the counter of the kitchenette. It was a map of the state with a route to the remote property lined out in red. It avoided major highways and towns wherever possible. Novah knew what he should do, and dared to think that perhaps his family was waiting for him there. He decided to leave that evening. Charles pulled out an old air compressor and made sure all the tires were inflated. He added fresh water to the tank, then double-checked the hookup to the truck, giving the whole outfit a complete walk-around. Novah hobbled around inside the trailer for the remainder of the day taking inventory. Everything appeared to be in order.

Shortly after the sun had set, Novah shook hands with Charles, and pressed three of the silver pieces into his hand.

"Thank you, Charles. Take care of yourself."

Charles took the coins, admired them with a smile, and replied. "Same to you, Novah. Good luck. I don't know what potential hazards exist beyond this area, so proceed cautiously."

Novah was paranoid. He had no idea what was out there on the open road. Were there government checkpoints? Roving gangs? He figured the only traffic he might see would be government vehicles and supply trucks, as they were the only ones with access to gasoline or diesel. The last thing he wanted was to be seen. Somehow he had to drive this large vehicle three hundred miles without getting caught.

He studied the map carefully and decided not to make a run for it. He'd use the same tricks he'd learned in the Mall. Stay away from crowded areas. Hide in the shadows. Move slowly. Focus on situational awareness. He would drive with no lights on, and only for an hour before he couldn't see any longer and an hour after he could first see in the morning. He'd be able to see the road, if just barely. He'd go slow, along the side roads, and hide his rig under the heavy spring foliage. He had plenty of gas so could take whatever route he wanted without fear of running out.

Novah managed his daylight and route smartly. He wished he could fish along nearby streams during the day, but with his ankle the way it was, he could barely hobble from the truck and trailer far enough to fertilize a tree when his bladder commanded him to do so.

He always kept an eye out for drones and other aircraft, and froze like a deer in headlights whenever he heard a vehicle. Thankfully, that was rare, and nobody ever saw him – or so he chose to believe. The spring foliage was ample enough that he was able to hide his rig with relative peace of mind.

As dawn broke on the third morning he was far enough from the last major town that he felt comfortable in finishing the journey. He was certain that someone, somewhere, had seen him in his travels. He assumed they had bigger fish to fry and he took comfort in the fact that he was miles away from the nearest *anything*. He didn't expect to be bothered as he slowly backed his trailer into a flat spot near a medium-sized creek on his dad's secluded forest land, a good mile from any road.

~~~

The rain grew more intense, thumping with authority on the trailer's roof, waking Novah from his recollections. After a few minutes he shook the last few drops of bourbon into his mouth, shrugged his shoulders, undressed, and crawled into the small bed at the fore of the trailer. The deep rolls of thunder echoed through the valley with increased violence, growing closer with each passing minute. Flashes of the lightning bathed everything in bright light for split-seconds, causing Novah to pull the covers over his head. Over and over, for hours, the storm pummeled the trailer with furious noise. Around four in the morning he was awakened by the loudest thunderclap he'd ever hear. It sounded like the whole of the earth cracked, and the trailer moved with it. It gave him chills. The rain pounded until the storm faded, and the last thought he had before he fell back asleep was *I'll need to see how close that strike was when I wake up tomorrow.*

CHAPTER THREE

W hat does V'kath mean, D'kob is gone?" S'heil M'har D'leem asked, infuriated.

V'kath twitched, cursing his luck. His tri-dice had never failed him before. He and his companions had decided that the fairest way to determine who would tell Admiral S'heil of D'kob's escape was to let the six-sided, multicolor dice decide. The eight of them used a tournament format, rolling against each other in pairs. The first to roll all blue faces on their three dice moved to the next round. The tournament lasted two hundred and twelve minutes with V'kath emerging as the unfortunate victor.

V'kath sighed. "Admiral, V'kath does not know how D'kob escaped. D'kob's cell was simply empty when checked." V'kath left out the details of *when* D'kob's cell was last checked, an omission not missed by S'heil.

"How many hours?" asked S'heil with his trademark smoothness, the warning that the answer better be the one he wanted to hear.

V'kath sighed again, and silently prayed. "Seven."

"SEVEN?!?!"

"Yes, Admiral."

"S'heil is most displeased. Does V'kath know what happens now?"

"Yes, Admiral, however V'kath wishes..."

The draw from S'heil's holster was so fast that V'kath barely had time to gasp. The kinetic bolt fired by S'heil instantly drilled a hot hole right between V'kath's wide, surprised eyes, leaving a dark dime-sized and smoldering burn.

"Wrong, V'kath," S'heil stated with disgust as V'kath slumped dead to the cold, sterile floor of the bridge. "Escaped. The most important prisoner of the last four thousand years, and V'kath let D'kob escape."

S'heil yelled at nobody in particular. "A Khamek must find out how, now!"

Several members of the Khamek species headed for the exit door, more to escape S'heil's wrath than to investigate the escape. The total number of Khamek that S'heil had shot in the face in the last year was now seven and nobody wanted to be the eighth.

S'heil paced angrily back and forth across the bridge of his frigate. As he was prone to do, he found himself regretting shooting V'kath so quickly. He didn't get any information about how D'kob had escaped, or when. The where was obvious – the planet the Humans called Earth was the only habitable planet in four light-years, and it was also the suspected location of the R'ptyr, though the specific location was unknown to all Khamek except D'kob.

The R'ptyr was critical to S'heil's mission. The designated time for the culmination of the agreement made with Human leadership sixty years ago was near. S'heil was not about to let sixty years of planning and negotiations go up in nuclear fire because the R'ptyr – and the codes to access it – were missing. S'heil was utterly perturbed. Only D'kob knew the information S'heil desperately needed. Now D'kob was missing. Without D'kob the arrangement with the Humans was doomed, and therefore S'heil's place in Khamek history.

S'heil continued to pace. He could think of no other option than to explain the circumstances to the Humans and plead for their help. Perhaps they would understand. The Khamek needed the Humans. Without them, S'heil would never be able to return home to V'jima Prime for the parade S'heil knew he'd receive. Being the first Khamek to reach V'laha, even if he couldn't return home, would have to be enough.

1942.54 years S'heil has been stuck in this forsaken backwater planetary system, thought S'heil, *this is S'heil's only chance to earn S'heil's deserved adulation.*

He debated continuing on to the planned rendezvous with the remainder of his fleet near N'ala 5, but ultimately thought that fruitless. He needed to keep this minor setback as private as possible. If word got back to V'jima Prime, he'd be recalled and stripped of command. The only way S'heil could save his hide and place in history would be to capture D'kob. Seven hours had already passed which would put him a full day behind schedule if everything went well and they were able to locate D'kob immediately upon arrival back at Earth.

"Helm, position."

"The *L'ghorsk* has just crossed the orbit of N'ala 4," replied the helmsman.

"All stop and reverse course. Head back to N'ala 3, best possible speed."

"Yes, Admiral. Stopping and reversing course, destination N'ala 3. Arrival in five-point-three hours."

S'heil pressed a soft, glowing blue spot on the palm of his four-fingered left hand. "K'jahl!"

A clear voice replied through S'heil's tiny neural implant. "Yes, Admiral?"

"Khamek of *L'ghorsk* are returning to N'ala 3. Arrange a conference with the Humans. S'heil will speak to the Humans face to face at the earliest possible convenience."

"Yes, Admiral. K'jahl will make the arrangements."

K'jahl had been making such arrangements for the last sixty Earth years, ever since the first discussions of the deal with the Humans. In order to avoid a war – which the Humans through their history had proven quite adept at – the Khamek had made a bargain: fifty thousand select humans would be protected in exchange for 7.5 billion humans. Every five years, a meeting was held between the Khameks and the Humans to discuss the progress. The endgame was near and both sides were nervous. The numbers simply weren't there. The arrangement had to be completed by Earth year 2023. The key to the deal – the *R'ptyr* – was still out of their grasp, with only a year remaining. Once they arrived back at Earth, K'jahl would send the appropriate signals to the appointed Human leaders to meet in two days at what the Humans named the Bilderberg Hotel in the country called the Netherlands.

S'heil tried to calm himself as he once again pressed the comm button embedded in his palm. "S'lace."

S'lace answered in her usual cool, professional tone. "Yes, Admiral S'heil. S'lace is listening."

"S'heil needs S'lace to take an armed scout ship to Earth's surface and capture the escapee named D'kob. S'heil must speak with D'kob, so D'kob must be alive and mostly unharmed. Contact S'heil once S'lace has completed capture. Complete this task, and S'lace will be well rewarded."

"Understood, Admiral," S'lace replied. She broke off communications and immediately set about the gathering a hunting party. She'd captured D'kob before and new she could do it again.

S'heil hopped up into his command chair, his short, thin legs swinging like pendulums. He cursed the engineer of the chair every time he sat in it. The Khamek were all of similar height, and yet some engineer had signed off on having a swiveling command chair that no commander could swivel because their feet couldn't reach the floor.

CHAPTER FOUR

Thick purple blood was dripping into D'kob's eyes, and as he instinctively raised his hand to wipe his vision clear, he noticed two things. First, he was upside down. Second, his right arm was broken. The upper part of his canopy had shattered in the crash, and his craft sat inverted, the nose burrowed into the ground and the aft end lodged in the broken remnants of a pair of thick pine trees. Wincing, he used his other hand to wipe his eyes clean and look for the source of the blood. He found a significant cut right under his chin. Had it been much lower it would have likely cut his carotid artery and he'd have never awakened. He looked around and could see nothing but broken branches and wet pine needles. His head was about five feet off the ground. His harness had kept him from flying out, thankfully, because otherwise he'd have surely suffered misadventure. All in all, in spite of his wounds and the pain, he felt gloriously fortunate.

It was morning and he was grateful for the cool, fresh breeze sweeping up from the wide valley below. D'kob knew he didn't have time to just hang around so began thinking of how to extract himself. Gravity, unfortunately, continued to be his enemy. If he simply released his harness, he would freefall the remaining distance to the ground, on his head, with only one arm to potentially cushion his impact. It was risky but he didn't see any other choice. He reached up with his functioning left arm and found the release mechanism. The tension on the mechanism fought against him, but after a focused effort he managed to get the button pressed. Immediately upon doing so he wished he hadn't. As predicted, he fell – but he didn't hit the ground. His legs tangled in the harness, and while his fall was broken, he was left dangling with the top of his head about six inches from the ground. He twisted in the breeze, bloodied, broken, and now dizzy, with his broken arm dragging back and forth in the dirt. He tried in vain to do a mid-air hanging sit-up but he was just too weak and tired. There was nothing left to do but pray to the Prime, so that's what he did.

Morning crept into noon and there D'kob hung, as patient as his many centuries had disciplined him to be. Logic dictated that he would either be captured, rescued, die of thirst, or be eaten by some hungry N'ala 3 mammal. He was mentally prepared for any of the four outcomes. He had a preference, of course. He hoped his prayers would be enough.

D'kob meditated quietly, his head thumping with his pulse. He listened. In the distance he heard the gait of a peculiar creature. It was coming towards him slowly, and he assumed it was a predator of some sort. He heard the same heavy repeating pattern – *creak-whump, creak-whump, creak-whump*. Eventually he could hear the creature panting. It was coming closer. Shortly a Human, propped up by a pair of supplemental slender appendages, appeared in his inverted field of vision. The Human caught sight of D'kob and froze, eyes wide and mouth dropped open.

Novah stood cemented in place, head cocked to one side, not quite believing what was there before his eyes – a comically tragic cocktail of the impossible highlighted by the absurd. An alien – a true, honest to goodness alien, dangling helplessly out of a shimmering, upside-down UFO.

The ship looked just like the old black and white photos he'd seen a long time ago – except that instead of being flat and circular, it was flat and triangular, probably twenty feet from point to point with a width of perhaps six feet at the middle, tapering to no more than a handful of inches at the outer edges. It was metallic, but shimmering in an odd dance with the shadows cast upon it by the trees and noon-time sun. Novah made a quick, amazed mental record of the craft, then returned his full attention to the creature before him swinging gently in the breeze.

Had he seen an alien simply standing there Novah might have been more scared. This alien, though, appeared utterly harmless and helpless, and wounded – its scrawny right arm hung in a completely unnatural fashion with what appeared to be a bit of bone poking out of impossibly-pale skin. Purple blood was splattered all over its skin and pure-white flight suit. The alien looked just like pictures he'd seen on TV – thin, short, and pale, with an inverted-triangle-shaped head and large, black, almond-shaped eyes. It had no ears he could see, no discernible shape to the nose apart from a pair of pencil-diameter nostrils. Its mouth was thin and lipless.

Novah took a cautious step closer, resting on his crutches. The alien simply stared at him swinging ever so slightly in the breeze. Yes, it was clearly injured. He couldn't very well leave the creature hanging there, so decided to make a friendly overture.

"Hello," Novah said. "I am Novah." He pointed to his own chest, and poked it twice.

"S'nakl zofredu kralkalka," replied D'kob, the vibrating, high-pitched tones utterly incomprehensible to Novah.

"I am sorry. I do not understand."

D'kob's voice sounded wheezy and worn.

"S'nakl zofredu kralkalka," he repeated, slowly raising his left arm, pointing to the harness in which he was entangled.

Novah laid his crutches aside, and very gingerly limped towards the craft with his hands to his side and open in what he hoped was a universal gesture of good will. He approached slowly and spoke in a soft, calm voice.

"Ok, I'm going to cut you down from there. I'm going to pull out my knife. Don't be afraid."

Very carefully, Novah stepped to the side of the craft, bracing himself against it. He slowly drew out the menacingly-large tactical knife with an eight-inch, razor-sharp blade that was attached to his belt.

He reached down with his left hand, slid his fingers into the inside of the alien's suit at the collar, and gripped the material tightly. It was unlike any material he'd ever touched before. It seemed to pulsate in his fingers. With his other hand he reached up into the broken cockpit and quickly sliced through the restraining harness at two points. The alien, while heavy, wasn't unmanageable, and Novah was able to set him down gently. He slipped his knife back into its hard plastic sheath immediately and then positioned the alien with difficulty upright against the large trunk of a snapped-off tree.

"There you go. Now let's see about those wounds."

"Z'lathl mofflet ghakkaan," said the alien in what Novah took as an urgent, yet not angry, tone. Again, the thin alien arm reached up and pointed into the overturned cockpit. Novah discerned that the alien wanted something from inside.

Novah rebalanced himself against the craft and stared up into the cockpit. He wasn't sure what he was looking for, but assumed that whatever it was would be located in a box or some small compartment. He looked for latches. Near what would have been the pilot's right leg, just barely within his reach, he found a small circular indentation. He pressed against it and a clear bag the size of a folded-up t-shirt fell out. He caught it, ducked back out of the cockpit, and showed it to the alien.

"This what you are looking for?"

"M'kathl," hissed the alien, nodding.

Well, he knows about nodding...I hope it means what I think it means, thought Novah. He sat on the wet pine needles at the alien's feet, handing it the bag. The alien placed it beside his left hip and opened it. It was clearly looking for something. A few seconds later the alien pulled out a cream-colored canister no larger than a tube of lipstick. He held it out to Novah, who took it.

"Ok, I take it there's something in here you need." Novah examined the container and discovered that it opened by simply twisting off the cap. Novah poured the contents – fifteen or so dime-sized discs of assorted colors – out into his palm. He spread them out as best he could and extended his hand towards the alien. "One of these?"

The alien reached out, and with his two smallest of his four fingers, grabbed the blue disc. Novah carefully placed the remainder back in the container. The alien held out the tiny blue disc to Novah. Novah took it and gave the canister back. The alien stashed the canister back into the bag and motioned for Novah to move closer. Novah complied, sliding up beside the alien. Novah giggled at the absurdity of the moment as the alien stared at him with curious yet pained eyes.

"Ok, now what do I do with this?" He suspected the alien wasn't understanding his words but figured the intent would be obvious to any sentient being.

The alien held out his hand, palm facing upward. Through its translucent skin Novah could see a faintly pulsing pattern of green and blue lights. The alien curled its short index finger into its palm, tapping a place directly to the left of the blue glow before re-extending the finger. Looking closely, Novah could see the thinnest of scars – or what looked like a scar – in the alien's palm. Novah looked closer, squinting. The scar was perfectly straight and just slightly longer than the diameter of the tiny disc in his hand.

"M'kathl," the alien said, nodding at Novah, and then at Novah's hand which held the tiny blue disc.

Novah held the disc by its edge and pressed the opposite edge against the alien's scar. In a flash the scar grabbed the disc, pulled it under the alien's skin, and resealed. Novah stared in astonishment as the blue light pulsated very quickly for about three seconds before resuming its normal state.

"Hello, Human," spoke the alien in a pleasantly-pitched metallic voice – not quite robotic, but not quite human. Startled, Novah let out a little yelp to accompany his sideways butt-scoot.

"Do not be afraid. The blue disc is the Human language protocol disc. The Human language protocol disc allows D'kob to communicate with the Human in the Human's native language. Is the Human understanding D'kob?"

"Is D'kob your name?"

"Yes, D'kob is D'kob's name. D'kob expresses D'kob's thanks for the Human's help in cutting D'kob down from the entanglement."

"I am Novah. Novah Burns. I have never met an alien before."

"D'kob is only alien to Novah Novah Burns. D'kob is member of Khamek species, widely known in galactic sector seventeen. D'kob is also suffering from broken right appendage, deep cut on anterior portion of mandible, and assorted other non-fatal yet inconvenient contusions. Appendage break requires painful realignment. D'kob is prepared. Novah Novah Burns will realign."

This guy gets right down to business, thought Novah.

"First, just call me Novah. Second, I have never set a bone before. I really have no idea what I am doing, and it's really going to hurt."

"Acknowledged. D'kob is prepared for pain commensurate with Novah's inexperience and the injury's nature." D'kob reached back into the bag and pulled out a long, thin object that looked like a flattened straw. He waved it in front of Novah. "Appendage immobilizer. Realign appendage, unwrap, press against fractured area, and pull tip."

Novah couldn't see how that would possibly work but took the object and nodded.

"Ok then, let's do this," Novah said.

Novah positioned himself next to D'kob's broken arm and winced as he took a closer look. The yellowish bone was protruding about a quarter inch out of the skin about midway up the forearm. He thought a minute, quickly referring to what he'd seen on TV in what seemed like a lifetime ago. *I can do this*, he thought to himself.

He reached down and grabbed D'kob's arm, one hand on the alien's elbow, and the other grasping its hand. As Novah began to slowly stretch out the arm, D'kob instantly did something Novah didn't expect – the alien passed out cold.

Novah was relieved, grateful that he didn't have to deal with the drama of a screaming or weeping alien. With D'kob passed out he was able to clumsily set the arm without distraction, pulling on the alien hand until the bones resumed what Novah hoped was their normal position. He wasn't overly bothered by the blood – he'd seen lots of that at the Mall, and royal purple blood was a novelty he was more fascinated with than grossed out by. He peeled the thin clear plastic off of the *appendage immobilizer* and pressed it against the inside of the broken forearm. As instructed, he pulled on tip. Instantly, a light blue force field circumnavigated the broken arm. It hummed ever-so-slightly. Novah reached down and grabbed a pine needle, then touched the field. Nothing happened – the needle simply bent just as it would against a normal plaster cast. He then felt brave enough to tap it with his finger. Nothing happened. It was completely solid and harmless, protecting the alien's entire forearm.

"Whoa," Novah exclaimed in awe.

The afternoon sun had passed the trees and was now beating squarely on the odd pair. Overly warm, Novah peeled off his jacket and outer shirt. With the shirt he fashioned a sling, positioning D'kob's broken arm in the traditional place across the chest, with the wrist higher than the elbow. He noticed the cut under D'kob's chin but saw that it had stopped bleeding so decided to leave it alone. The trails of purple blood that had drained down D'kob's face had dried to a crusted black in a pattern that looked like thin zebra stripes.

Novah gingerly rubbed his own swollen ankle. In the excitement of the past half an hour he'd forgotten about his own pain. Now that his adrenaline level had normalized the familiar throbbing came roaring back.

D'kob appeared to be sleeping peacefully, so in spite of his pain Novah picked up his crutches and made his way back to the trailer. Once there he packed a few essentials into a small blue backpack – some water, a little food, a fleece blanket, and a brown, wide-brimmed hat. He also reached into the bathroom medicine cabinet and found a couple Tylenol which he gulped down with half a cup of water. When he returned to the crash site twenty minutes later the alien was right where he left him, snoozing peacefully.

Novah covered D'kob with the blanket from the neck down – not because it was cold, but because insects were starting to discover that alien meat was a tasty treat. Additionally, Novah thought it wise to cover the alien's exposed skin as the sun would surely turn this white creature a distinctly pink color in short order. Novah took the hat and covered D'kob's face, cowboy-style, then stood back and basked in the sheer ridiculousness.

Novah wanted to explore the craft and the rest of the crash site a bit more thoroughly but naptime was calling him as well. He nestled himself against a nearby fallen log and dozed lightly until late afternoon. The shadows again reached towards them, their dark fingers once more shielding the alien from the yellow sun. Looking over towards the alien Novah was relieved to see that he had at least changed positions. D'kob's chest was lightly moving up and down.

As evening settled in Novah cursed under his breath. He clearly couldn't go back to camp and leave the alien alone all night. He'd have to stay here and guard him until he woke up. That meant both of them would be shivering by morning.

"Screw that," Novah muttered. He swung himself over to the sleeping alien and gingerly tapped on D'kob's leg with the tip of one crutch.

"D'kob...wake up. It's getting dark."

Nothing. Novah tried again.

"D'kob. Time to wake up." Novah swept the hat from D'kob's face and pulled aside the blanket. The alien stirred.

"Arise, alien," Novah stated with a flourish.

D'kob awoke, blinking his large, dark eyes in what Novah thought to be a very human fashion.

"The Human day is ending. D'kob has slept too long. D'kob and Novah must leave current coordinates." D'kob looked down at his arm, resting in the primitive sling.

"Gratitude for the realignment. D'kob will be fully healed in three days."

Novah knew better than to be amazed. This alien race was clearly advanced well beyond human knowledge. At that moment he also realized that he was in a position perhaps unique to all of mankind. He wasn't sure what D'kob had in mind, or what D'kob would ask him to do. All he knew is that he wanted to help. To do something unique with his life. To have a companion. They might be scared, hurt and lonely, but they could be those things together. As long as D'kob's mission wasn't to destroy the whole of the human race, Novah was on board.

D'kob lifted himself to his feet and used his good arm to brush off the dirt and pine needles.

"Ok then, let's go," Novah stated firmly.

"No, two tasks first before departure. Remain still."

D'kob walked to the overturned ship, reached his good arm up, and did something that Novah couldn't see. The alien then walked over to Novah. There was a beeping coming from the ship.

"Ship-destruct sequence initiated. Remain calm."

There were ten beeps followed by the frightening, screeching sound of metal compressing. D'kob's craft was collapsing upon itself. Within ten seconds it had fallen out of the trees in which it was wedged. In thirty, the craft was no larger than a deck of cards. D'kob swept some pine needles, branches, and other debris over the shrunken mass.

"Task one completed. Please sit for task two."

Still awestruck by the amazing shrinking ship, Novah sat down on a nearby stump. D'kob picked up his bag and walked over to Novah.

"D'kob will now repair Novah's damaged appendage."

D'kob sat on the ground and lifted Novah's ankle onto his lap, running his good hand over the swollen flesh. He bowed his head, and, much to Novah's surprise, began to sing. The song was unrecognizable yet beautiful. Novah felt a burst of warmth followed by the glorious sensation of all pain fleeing his body growing fainter with every note. D'kob finished his song and released his grasp on Novah's ankle.

"Task two completed. Is appendage repaired to Novah's satisfaction?"

Novah twisted his foot left, then right, then in a circle.

"Yes! This is amazing! Thank you! How did you do that?"

For the first time, Novah thought he saw what amounted to a smile on D'kob's ultra-thin lips.

"The Z'korz," D'kob said, as if it was the most obvious thing in the world. "Now, Novah and D'kob must evacuate coordinates. S'heil has undoubtedly sent searchers to capture D'kob. Capture will result in misadventure."

That doesn't sound very promising. "Ok, ok. We'll leave. I have a vehicle at my camp just down the trail. But I must ask one question first." Novah choked on the silliness – the cliché-ness – of the question he felt compelled to ask.

"Initiate query."

"Do you come in peace?"

D'kob stared at him with a blinking of eyes and a head-tilt that emoted exasperation.

"D'kob does not come as an emissary. D'kob comes for the R'*ptyr*."

.

CHAPTER FIVE

P resident Alberto Hernandez had the historically unfortunate timing to be President of the United States when The Fall happened. The economy had been sputtering on lethargically for two decades, slowly dying like an untended campfire. As such things happen, the die-down was gradual. The extinguishment was sudden.

Shortly after his election he ordered the Federal Trade Commission to investigate and subsequently reduce the influence of all digital currency, the largest and most impacted being Bitcoin – the computer generated, untraceable, unbacked currency that was gaining traction, particularly in black and underground markets. The drug trade was operating almost exclusively through bitcoins, and before long, bitcoin transactions were happening for arms deals. World governments had developed a long history of "following the money" to track their adversaries, and since bitcoins were very difficult to follow, fear echoed down the corridors of power. Bitcoin had to be stopped.

Reams of rules and regulations were put into place to govern digital currencies. These rules and regulations, as designed, intended to strangle them out of existence, since the rules basically forbade trading "imaginary" currency for any sort of real item.

Three years into the process Alberto had made a grievous tactical error, believing he could give the final death stroke to digital currencies. In a nationally televised address he railed against bitcoin and its separation from government control, and hence its rampant use by terrorists and drug cartels. He bragged that soon the rules and regulations would become so comprehensive that digital currencies would become extinct. What he didn't realize – what none of his advisors had mentioned – is that in spite of the new regulations bitcoin use had encroached too deeply into the early adopter portion of the "S" curve. Regular people around the world were using them for everything from buying books to cars. The public backlash was terrible, and since it was an election year, Alberto caved. He rescinded the regulations – much to the horror of Europe – and narrowly won reelection. By that time bitcoins were all over the place presenting a grave danger to the U.S. Dollar. Bitcoin *had* to be stopped. So Alberto issued an Executive Order – in secret – to have the Federal Reserve buy every bitcoin it could find. Unlike dollars, bitcoins couldn't be printed out of thin air. It took months to mint a bitcoin due to the security algorithms. That was part of the appeal of bitcoins – there wasn't an infinite number of them, which meant they had value, and digits on a thumb drive were much easier to carry and exchange than gold.

So the Federal Reserve, and soon thereafter most of the world's central banks, began secretly purchasing bitcoins. The price of bitcoins shot through the roof and the central banks just kept on printing more money to buy them up. Near the end a single bitcoin was selling for ten million dollars. People eagerly gave up their bitcoins for the mother lode of cash. These folks then went out and bought things, but since there was so much cash flowing in the system, merchants upped their prices. And upped them again. And again. Hyperinflation took over as people soon came to realize that they'd been suckered. The value of dollars had been diluted to the point of near worthlessness.

In a matter of weeks faith in the dollar crumbled completely and the economy collapsed. People were still bringing home their pre-Fall salaries, yet inflation pushed gas up to $50 a gallon and bread was $25 a loaf. People stopped going to work because it didn't matter. Suppliers stopped shipping goods because there was no money in it. Farmers stopped growing crops. China stopped selling their goods to

Americans, unwilling to ship home cargo containers full of worthless dollars. The Chinese then joined the Russians and Brazilians in forming an actual gold-based currency which most of the rest of the world eagerly adopted. That was the final straw for the U.S. Dollar.

Within three days store shelves were bare, and after a week a deep, unfamiliar hunger struck the nation with a merciless slap. Normally decent people did things they'd never thought they'd do just to feed their families. Roving gangs of middle-class suburbanites started breaking into homes looking for food. Parents sold their daughters' innocence for a can of chili. Starvation became too much to bear for many, so they found less time-consuming paths to ease their suffering families – and themselves – into the grave.

Factories, farms, and homes burned across the nation. Alberto was forced to institute Martial Law. The armed forces were mobilized and sent to the cities and enforced a nine p.m. curfew which was violently resisted. Gun battles erupted all over the country. Many American soldiers switched sides and started supporting the populace, attacking food and fuel depots that were reserved for government use. Alberto had asked the United Nations for help but most other nations were having similar uprisings.

Alberto knew the nation was in deep trouble. Everyone would end up dead one way or another if he didn't get the populace and economy under control. It was time for even more drastic measures. He pulled the plug on the internet. He signed an Executive Order nationalizing all farms and factories. The farmers and transportation owners who refused to work for the government for free were shot. He had to get food back into the system. The food voucher program was expanded and used as an incentive to work, and in a few weeks trucks and trains once again started delivering supplies to the cities. Unfortunately, millions had died in the upheaval from starvation, lack of medical care, and general violence. Those that continued to resist were added to the *insurgent terrorist* list and hunted down. Some of the captured were thrown into boxcars and shipped by rail to secret prison camps. The rest were shot and left to rot as an example to others. Fear reigned supreme.

Alberto looked at the single briefing page in front of him and slumped in his Oval Office chair. The year that it had taken to get things under control had cost a staggering 112 million American lives. This was a huge problem. He had a quota to meet and now he knew there wouldn't be enough people to fulfill his end of the deal. He suspected the leaders of other nations were sitting at their respective desks with the same worries. Without the deal, there was no telling what those damned aliens would do.

Alberto unlocked the drawer of the Resolute Desk and pulled out a thick, green file folder. This folder had been handed down personally, from President to President, since Eisenhower. It was the second item on the handoff checklist right after the "nuclear football." It was that important.

He opened the folder in front of him like he'd done dozens of times before in the past six years. He remembered the private conversation with his predecessor as if it had happened yesterday. *Aliens are real. We've been working together since the 1950's. In this folder are the details of the deal we made with them. Read this. Honor this. The fate of humanity depends on it.*

Alberto selected the yellowed, typewritten page that was simply entitled "The Deal with the Khameks." The deal was only a single page long. No legalese, no infinite list of conditions or appendix of fine print.

This document constitutes a contract between the Humans of Earth and the Khameks of V'jima Prime. In exchange for 7.5 billion healthy, living humans, 50,000 Humans – to be selected by the Humans – shall be granted the following: The starship R'ptyr, which is sufficiently large to hold in modest comfort 50,000 Humans, one dozen Khamek volunteers to act as technology advisors, and passage to A'ala, the nearest uninhabited Earth-like planet on which to establish a new Human colony. Furthermore, the Khamek agree to provide limited technology at Khamek-determined intervals from this point to the Earth year 2023, when the deal will be culminated. Additionally, the Khamek hereby swear that they will serve as Eternal Protectors of the new Human colony, guarding them as is technologically possible from extraplanetary threats.

Should the Humans not fulfill their end of this agreement, all of humanity on Earth becomes forfeit and will be destroyed.

It was signed by President Eisenhower. Next to Eisenhower's signature was an intricately designed stamp signifying the name *S'heil M'har D'leem* which was typed immediately below.

The second page in the folder described how the 50,000 chosen people would be identified. The Khamek had provided two large cases of specially-made sigils. Each case contained 25,000 of the drink-coaster-sized sigils. Each sigil was made from what looked to be blue crystal and gold, with thin gold lines and circles traversing the face reminiscent of crop circle designs. The swirling blue webs of energy within the cool blue crystal made each sigil seem alive. They were utterly impossible to counterfeit. Only those that presented a sigil would be allowed on the ship.

Of course, there had been much ado among the Eisenhower administration about who would be given sigils. Eisenhower rightly calculated that there was no way the United States alone could provide billions of humans. That meant that the rest of the world would have to be involved, especially considering that there were less than three billion people on earth total at the time. There were only sixty years to well more than double the planet's population.

Page three was a fading, handwritten note written by President Eisenhower:

I hate this deal. The idea of negotiating the assumed destruction of the vast majority of humanity repulses me. Yet the Khameks very sternly warn that all of humanity will be destroyed without this "deal." I've seen their technology. There's little doubt they can destroy us as we can destroy an anthill. Now I have to figure out a just way of deciding who gets a sigil – none of whom will be alive to use one. May God have mercy on my soul. – DDE

Alberto went to the next page. It outlined what Eisenhower's decision was regarding distribution of the sigils. He decided that every member of his cabinet would get one – and only one. They would all be dead long before 2023. They could will the sigil to whomever they pleased. He kept one for himself. He counted the years until 2023 and divided by four, then threw in an additional five as insurance. These would be reserved for future Presidents, to hopefully ensure their cooperation with the deal. Then he multiplied that by a dozen to set aside for the various cabinets.

Eisenhower noted that he had considered giving some to every Nobel laureate of the past decade, but realized that would be silly, as they'd all be dead. He knew that the survival of humanity depended on the best and brightest minds of the time, so he set aside five thousand to be distributed in the years 2021 and 2022 by the American President of that time.

Alberto was that President. Those five thousand sigils were secured in a thick steel box under the floorboards directly under his feet. Sometime soon he had to get them dispersed.

Eisenhower had called a secret summit of world leaders and explained the deal to the incredulous audience. They simply didn't believe him – until Eisenhower introduced them all to a Khamek named K'jahl who, after displaying modest Khamek technology to the group, assured them all that the deal was real. Eisenhower ended up dividing one case between the Soviets, Indians and the Chinese, even though it rankled him and his advisors. The simple fact of the matter is that those countries had large populations and room to continue growing. He divided the remainder evenly amongst the other leaders in attendance. He left as they squabbled. Eisenhower gave out another hundred, mainly to bankers, captains of industry, and key media stakeholders. It was unanimous amongst everyone who knew that this was the most secret of secrets. It stayed a secret – mostly.

He left the remaining almost-half of a case to his successor, President Kennedy.

Alberto went on to the next page in the folder, which was handwritten by President Kennedy:

If I didn't meet this K'jahl alien myself, I'd have never believed this. I will not scrap this "deal," but I'll be damned if I'm going to let the majority of mankind go meekly into the night.

The next day, Kennedy gave an impassioned speech to the nation, jumpstarting the U.S. space program.

Kennedy left only one additional note in the folder, dated October 31, 1963:

I was visited by a delegation from global banking concerns yesterday. They were demanding 5,000 sigils for their brethren across the United States, Europe, and South Africa. I didn't insult them by playing dumb. I told them to go screw themselves. I'm worried that the secret is leaking. If it does, there will be a panic, and we won't be able to meet our end of the deal.

A month later, Kennedy was dead. His successor, Lyndon Johnson, left a single notation in the folder:

I gave 5000 sigils to a group of bankers who visited me today, a robust economy being vital to population growth.

Alberto continued to read pages, thumbing through President after President, most of whom were unceasingly wordy in their opinions of the deal. When he reached President Reagan, he smiled at the simplicity of his single entry:

I met K'jahl today – he seems like a nice fellow.

After Reagan's note, once again the notes became droning pages of opinion, each President trying to outdo the previous one in length. Alberto made a habit of skipping the last 75 pages in the folder.

The first thing Alberto had done upon being reelected in 2020 was to take a small number of sigils and give them to his closest family and friends. He said nothing other than to not lose them, that they were each worth more than everything they owned combined, and that they'd know what to do with them when the time came.

Alberto noted it in the folder just for completeness. If the Khamek were right, it wouldn't matter, as there would be no further Presidents.

Because of the deal, and the nearness of its culmination, every country had invested heavily in the infrastructure necessary to count every citizen. Algorithms were put in place to estimate population growth based on local diet and conditions. It was all remarkably sophisticated and manifested itself as a single number on Alberto' smartphone. He hit the refresh button, and the number 5.78B displayed in red. Well short of what was needed. The global civil war had pretty much doomed them all.

"Goddamn Bitcoin."

His desk phone rang. "Yes Margery?" Margery had been the secretary to four Presidents. She knew everything there was to know.

"Mr. President, I have K'jahl for you on line one."

Oh shit. Here it comes.

"Thank you, Margery. I'll take it from here. Oh, and can you please have some flowers sent to Ramona? Today is our anniversary and…"

"Already taken care of, sir," replied Margery.

"Thank you, Margery. You're the best."

Alberto picked up the receiver and pushed the blinking red button.

"K'jahl. It's always nice to hear from you. How may I help you?"

"President Hernandez, K'jahl is commanded by S'heil to arrange a meeting with President Hernandez and other Human leaders at the Bilderberg Hotel in two days. S'heil will address Alberto and other Humans personally."

Alberto slumped in his chair. "Ok, K'jahl. I'll be there," he said heavily. "Can you tell me what this is about?"

K'jahl measured his words, unsure of what he should divulge.

"Recent events are causing S'heil concern, and S'heil wishes to be transparent with S'heil's concerns."

Alberto gulped. "Very well, K'jahl. I look forward to hearing S'heil's concerns. I'll see you in two days." He hung up the phone, went to the large wooden globe to the right of the American flag, opened it, and poured himself a long, straight shot of scotch. Margery walked into the Oval Office.

"Should I make flight arrangements, Mr. President?" she asked quietly.

"Yes Margery. Arrange for the planes to be ready to depart tomorrow morning for the Netherlands. Myself, the VP, cabinet, and joint chiefs. Follow the usual protocols."

"Yes sir. I'll get right on it." She left the room.

Alberto swirled the scotch and stared blankly out the window into the garden.

CHAPTER SIX

S'heil stood staring eye-to-eye with D'kob, sneering at him through the glass in the containment area. He tapped the thick glass half expecting D'kob's clone to flinch. The clone did nothing but breathe silently in its warm, foggy capsule. S'heil then giggled. He should have told D'kob that he had his clone when D'kob was captured, but it had slipped his mind. D'kob escaped not realizing that his clone was in the room across the hallway from his cell. S'heil spoke to the glass.

"If D'kob had only been patient, if D'kob had only given S'heil the *R'ptyr*, D'kob would be enjoying life in D'kob's clone. No need to travel back to V'jima Prime."

K'jahl ignored S'heil's one-sided conversation, moving to a position alongside the Admiral, and spoke to the glass as well.

"S'lace has completed the analysis of D'kob's crash site. No body was found and the ship was destructed. There was Human interference. If not for the seven hour delay in the report of D'kob's escape D'kob would likely be in custody now. With this much of a head start, however, D'kob could be anywhere on N'ala 3."

"If K'jahl mentions the seven hour delay again, K'jahl will need K'jahl's own clone," snapped S'heil.

"Apologies, Admiral. Is S'heil prepared to depart for the conference?"

"Yes. S'heil did not affix all of S'heil's shiny medals to S'heil's chest

71

for nothing."

"K'jahl is certain that the Humans will be impressed," replied K'jahl dryly.

They made their way to the flight deck and entered the triangle-shaped shuttlecraft, which was promptly jettisoned out the bottom of the *L'ghorsk*. The Khamek craft cloaked and entered European airspace in the wee hours of the morning, with no lights or radar signature, landing on the roof of the Bilderberg Hotel. They were met there by their human attendants and ushered into the massive northeast section of the hotel which had been hurriedly readied for the Summit for Sustained Global Economic Restoration – or so it was described in the news stories.

The main ballroom had been converted into a massive conference room complete with a huge circular table. In front of each chair was a printed seat assignment. The world leaders began to shuffle in at around nine a.m., seating themselves alphabetically around the table as assigned. At precisely 9:59 a.m., S'heil and K'jahl took their two seats between Kenya and Kiribati. S'heil gave K'jahl an angry glance, irritated that he had to sit in a seat of equal stature to the humans.

At ten a.m. a warm tone echoed throughout the chamber and everyone grew silent, looking over at the alien presence in the room. Everyone there had met with them before but there was still a sense of wonder – and unease.

S'heil spoke in English, and those that didn't know the language placed their translation headsets on.

"Greetings, Human friends. S'heil will not speak overly long, nor couch S'heil's words with undo formality. S'heil has called for this conference to discuss the progress of our deal."

Alberto, sitting almost exactly across from the forty-foot-diameter table as the alphabet would have it, felt S'heil's glassy gaze. *Here it comes*, he thought.

"Khamek have monitored Human events on Earth for many Human years. Khamek have noticed the recent violent upheavals that have left many hundreds of millions of Humans dead or weakened. Khamek calculations show that Earth is currently well short of the agreed upon number required."

The collective gurgling mumble of the room indicated to S'heil that he better get on with it. S'heil raised his four-fingered hand to settle everyone, privately delighted that he could control these Humans with a mere gesture.

"The data clearly show that it is impossible for the required number to be reached. Little time is left before the appointed time. Certainly not enough to generate the difference."

More murmurs.

"The deal clearly states that all of humanity will be forfeit and destroyed should Humans fail to meet the required quota."

S'heil waited patiently for the rancor to die down before continuing.

"However, Khamek are willing to alter this deal in exchange for cooperation that is of utmost importance to Human interest. K'jahl, please read the new arrangement."

K'jahl pressed a button on his data pad.

"K'jahl has broadcast the text to each Human's data pad so that each Human may read along." K'jahl then read the words aloud, as instructed.

"The agreed terms between Khamek and Humans shall be amended such that Humans provide *every available* human apart from the previously agreed 50,000 humans as designated by ownership of Khamek Sigils. In return for this decrease, Humans agree to assist in the search for the spaceship *R'ptyr*, suspected to be hidden on Earth. Without the retrieval of the *R'ptyr* humanity is forfeit and doomed to destruction."

The chamber was again filled with quiet whispers.

"Admiral S'heil," boomed Alberto's voice across the room, "I think the time has come for you to tell us what the hell is going on. For sixty years, humanity has borne the weight of this Khamek threat to destroy us. You are extorting us for the greatest portion of our species for an unstated cause. I believe I can speak for all of us here when I say that we want and deserve the big picture. If you don't, I swear that I'll nuke every last city on this planet before we hand over a single soul to you."

The room fell silent, and every eye stared at the pair of Khamek who sat unmoving. After a few seconds, S'heil replied.

"S'heil understands and will explain. Khamek were mistaken not to explain the circumstances around this arrangement at the time of arrangement's beginning." S'heil took a moment to stare Alberto in the eye.

"For the record, President Hernandez, no statement of Human destruction by Khamek was ever mentioned."

S'heil let his gaze linger a bit on Alberto before resuming a conciliatory posture and addressing the room.

"For many thousands of Earth years, Khamek have been engaged with Humans. In the earliest Human times, Khamek contact was very direct. Khamek made no effort to hide. Human forbearers saw Khamek as gods and Khamek did nothing to correct that assumption. In exchange for modest technological improvements, Khamek accepted many, many Humans for Khamek needs. Humans prospered and Khamek received what Khamek needed in return. As millennia passed such arrangements continued. Only one time did the arrangement leave Khamek and Humans dissatisfied, for which the Khamek take responsibility. In an effort to increase Human productivity, Khamek gave Humans *advanced* technology. This was limited to one specific group of Humans on one part of Earth. When Khamek came to collect on the arrangement two hundred Earth years after the introduction of advanced technology, Humans reneged on the deal. Khamek scout ships and personnel were met with violence by the group of Humans known as Atlanteans. Several Khamek ships were destroyed. All of Atlantean defenses were destroyed in retaliation. Khamek forcibly extracted the agreed-to number of Humans, and then destroyed the remaining aggressors with a kinetic-disruption bomb, completely destroying the continent. Khamek are deeply regretful, as the deployment of this bomb was not approved by the Khamek Grand Council. Admiral V'nelaka, who was in command during the skirmish, independently ordered the bombing. He was recalled to our home world, tried, and executed for genocide. Sadly, the bombing had residual effects across your planet, and many earthquakes and volcanic eruptions occurred in the years immediately after due to Earth's crust filling the gap made by the bomb."

S'heil took a long breathe and looked around the table. Every Human was perfectly attentive. He continued.

"After the destruction of the Atlantis continent Khamek changed policy regarding contact with Humans. Only a very small number of humans were contacted openly. Most other scientific and diplomatic missions were indirect, mostly through remote illusory projections. The policy of limited technological trade was reinstated. Khamek were patient, allowing Humans to grow at their own pace. Khamek ships often protected Earth from external destructive elements. One comet in 5 BCE would have destroyed all Humans were it allowed to impact. Khamek intercepted and destroyed this comet."

S'heil let this sink in as he sipped some water.

"Again, in Earth Year 1961, Khamek saved your species as Human nation known as Soviet Union attempted to launch pre-emptive nuclear strike on nation known as United States. Khamek targeted and disabled these missiles immediately before ignition."

The table turned their collective gazes to the Russian delegate, who shrugged indifferently.

"Humans will observe," S'heil continued, "that Human well-being is important to Khamek. We have twice saved Humans from global catastrophe, and many times over saved smaller groups from more minor catastrophes. When Khamek approached President Eisenhower in Earth year 1951, it was known that this would be the last deal. Khamek were – and are – deeply vested in ensuring Human prosperity."

S'heil smirked slightly. "Now, there are logical questions on all Human minds. S'heil will attempt to answer these questions before the questions are asked. The first question is *why do you require so many humans?* The short answer is that we need them to fuel our main ships. Humans produce a quantum field known to Khamek as a *Z'korz Envelope*, named after its Khamek discoverer. I will not attempt to explain the physics. The Z'korz Envelope inherent in each Human is a specific energy source that can only be provided by highly sentient beings. A set quantity of Z'korz energy is needed to open a wormhole, which is a necessity for interstellar travel. The more Z'korz energy, the farther the wormhole can reach. It takes twenty thousand living, healthy humans, preferably adults, for a Khamek frigate or cruiser to return home. Over the millennia Khamek have been able to modestly increase the Z'korz yield from each human. Spare Humans – and other sentient species – are preserved in great comfort on the moon N'nava near our home world until needed. And yes, those designated to sacrifice their Z'korz energy are physically destroyed."

The room let out a collective gasp. S'heil raised his palm in a calming gesture.

"Understand that if there was any other way to fuel Khamek ships, Khamek would. Also, Khamek have been scientifically prudent in Human selection in accordance with very strict guidelines too numerous to go into here. Finally, this final deal is an attempt to save the Earth Human species from utter destruction. Earth is, and has been, inherently instable. Khamek have been able to protect Earth from outside forces but are unable to protect from inside forces. Khamek have been monitoring Earth for thousands of Earth years. All studies have concluded that a tremendous cataclysm is about to happen. Khamek cannot stop it. All Humans will perish, except those 50,000 who Khamek have agreed to save. Unfortunately, even that small number cannot be saved without locating the R'ptyr. The R'ptyr was specially designed and provisioned for Humans. No Khamek ship can accommodate more than a few hundred Humans. Without the R'ptyr, Humans become extinct."

A cacophony of questions erupted from the room. Alberto let loose a loud bellow. "Quiet! Let him finish."

S'heil nodded politely. "As per the original agreement the R'ptyr is to transport 50,000 Humans to the planet A'ala, a nearby, Earth-like planet capable of sustaining Humans for the foreseeable future. There are no sentient beings on A'ala. The planet is slightly larger, but has a nearly identical atmospheric composition. Khamek engineers have recently completed a city in a beneficial location capable of housing and feeding Humans. The R'ptyr holds enough raw provisions for the voyage, plus gardening areas so that Humans can establish complete sufficiency. Khamek vow to forever only observe and study A'ala and never to interfere in its governance. Nor shall Khamek ever again take Humans for fuel."

S'heil paused and sipped some water. He wasn't used to talking this long.

"So, as Humans can see, it is the last chance for Human species. Sadly, it is also the last chance for Khamek. Khamek have not taken or stored enough Z'korz to travel to V'laha. V'laha is where our god lives and Khamek are commanded to come or be destroyed in fiery wrath. Only with the Z'korz from billions of Humans can Khamek generate a wormhole large enough to reach V'laha. V'laha is simply too distant otherwise. To summarize, Khamek will save the number of Humans possible to save, and the remainder – which would surely die in the cataclysm to come – will be spared needless suffering. Those Humans will perish to save Khamek from destruction by our god. Khamek save Humans, Humans save Khamek."

"The next inevitable question you have is *what is the nature of the cataclysm that is coming?*" S'heil nodded at K'jahl who projected a large transparent three-dimensional globe rising above the center of the table.

"Khamek have been monitoring Earth's plate tectonics very carefully, especially after the disruption caused by V'nelaka's treason. The data clearly shows that there will be multiple, simultaneous cascading earthquakes and volcanic eruptions beginning in Earth year 2023 and continuing for many years. The Yellowstone caldera, Long Valley caldera, Valles caldera, Toba caldera, Taupo Caldera, Aira caldera, Phlegraen Fields, Laacher See, Tambora, and many other smaller volcanos." K'jahl simulated these eruptions on the projected sphere, which appeared as red, then black explosions.

"There will be immediate widespread loss of life. Those that might survive the eruptions will undoubtedly starve to death as the plumes and atmospheric contamination darken the planet such that no sunlight can reach the surface. Crops will not grow. Water will not flow, as the planet will mostly freeze. So even those not directly in the blast zones will suffer. Humans have amusingly been concerned about global warming for the last twenty Earth years, yet in the end, it is global cooling which will cause Human extinction. Earth will not be habitable again for hundreds of years."

S'heil expected his pause to be greeted with great commotion, but instead the Humans largely mumbled quietly to themselves.

Kazahiro Tanaka, the Japanese president, spoke through a translator:

"Thank you for explaining this to us, S'heil. Japanese scientists have been studying these volcanos as have our counterparts across many nations. We know it is a matter of when, not if, these caldera erupt. Of course, humanity's doom is not something often discussed. It is clear we must face it now, and if not for the Khamek, all of humanity would surely be destroyed. We are grateful for the opportunity for a few of us to begin anew as painful as the loss will be."

Other voices around the table, briefly presenting their own country's findings, compiled a clear and irrefutable picture of the coming doom. Each country had a piece to the puzzle, and only here, only now, did they all fit together in the context of S'heil's declaration. The gratefulness of the Japanese was echoed nearly unanimously.

"The Khamek are grateful to humanity as well. Such gratefulness cannot be overstated," replied S'heil. "However, the problem of locating the *R'ptyr* still remains. Khamek ask Humans to marshal all available resources to assist Khamek in searching for the *R'ptyr*, which Khamek believe is hidden somewhere on Earth."

Alberto piped up. "I gather we're talking about a very large ship. How did you lose it? How come, with all of your advanced technology you can't do an 'Earth scan' or something and find it easily?"

"The *R'ptyr* is equipped with advanced stealth technology. The hull completely nullifies all scanning efforts. This was done at great expense to the Khamek so that Humans would be safe on the journey to A'ala. Other space-faring species exist and Khamek believed it would be best to ensure an invisible migration. So, Khamek cannot scan for the *R'ptyr. The R'ptyr* was stolen from orbit around Titan nearly 2000 Earth years ago. Khamek do not know why it was stolen. Khamek began a sector by sector visual search of Earth and every place else in N'ala system. No wormhole was created, so the *R'ptyr* must be in the N'ala system. Eventually, Khamek captured one of the thieves. This thief knows the location and has the access codes for the *R'ptyr*. This thief escaped captivity two days ago and is on Earth somewhere. It is this thief, named D'kob, Humans must help find. The ship D'kob escaped with crashed in the Pacific Northwest portion of the United States. D'kob somehow survived and is undoubtedly heading for the *R'ptyr*. S'heil believes D'kob intends to destroy the *R'ptyr*. Such an event is contrary to the interests of Khamek and Humans."

K'jahl moved his fingers along his data pad, and in an instant everyone at the table could see the dossier on D'kob, complete with photo and last known coordinates.

Alberto eyed his data pad. "Ah, with these coordinates, we can find the tax records and owner of this property. It could be that the owner was there when D'kob landed. We can find the owner easily once we know who it is. That shouldn't take more than a few hours. We'll round up all the owners on the surrounding properties as well. Your alien might have wandered."

Alberto turned his head to catch the eye of the Canadian Prime Minister. "This is close enough to the border that he may have slipped into Canada. Do you have the resources to investigate?"

"Our resources are at your disposal," replied the Prime Minister. "In this matter, all jurisdictional issues are waived. Feel free to pursue as appropriate through Canadian territories. We will of course assist as best we can."

Thus began the largest alien hunt in human history.

CHAPTER SEVEN

Novah wished he had paid more attention in school. The amount of technology D'kob had in his little bag was astonishing. Novah was at a loss to fathom how it was possible to fill up the gas tank with a tiny pill or to make the truck and trailer invisible with nothing more than a magnet no larger than a credit card affixed to the roof. D'kob had covered the truck's headlights with something that blocked the light, yet still enabled Novah to see everything in front of him while driving. When he'd ask D'kob to explain how this stuff worked, D'kob was delighted to explain it, but all of the terminology was beyond Novah's understanding.

They had made their way out of the mountains and were heading south.

"So where are we headed?" inquired Novah.

"South. D'kob and Novah must head south with best possible speed. The distance is great and time is short."

Novah tried again. "How great? Oregon? California? Mexico?"

"D'kob will give no specifics. If D'kob and Novah are captured it is best that Novah does not know specifics. Khamek thought extraction processes are 99.89% effective on Humans."

Novah gripped the wheel, staring off into the dark in frustration, yet couldn't deny D'kob's logic. He'd agreed to go on this adventure yet so far it wasn't adventurous at all. Just boring. He had a thousand questions yet could understand none of the answers. The one thing he knew, though, is that he didn't want to get caught. Novah had no desire to go back to prison or worse, and worse was what surely would happen now that aliens were involved. One anal probing in his lifetime was enough.

"There will likely be checkpoints at major bridges and borders, D'kob. We're invisible to satellites and the casual observer, but I don't think we'll be able to keep this rig hidden."

"True. The likelihood of reaching our destination undetected is small. Humans and Human technology is avoidable. The methods of the Khamek recovery teams are what D'kob must mitigate. D'kob suggests dealing with problems as they arise, for it does no good to conjecture."

"I understand that, yet there are concrete realities we must face, roadblocks being one of them."

"Roadblocks are of no consequence as roads will very soon become obsolete. D'kob and Novah will utilize a human flying vehicle." D'kob pointed to a marker on the truck's GPS. "Here."

"Do you even know how to fly?" Novah regretted the question the moment the last syllable parted his lips. The alien mustered as much exasperation as his limited facial muscles could conjure, staring at Novah disappointingly.

"Ok, ok, dumb question. Sorry. This whole alien....thing...well, it seems like a dream. I'm trying to stay calm and go with it. I'm not as smart as you. I'm going to say things and do things you are going to think are stupid."

D'kob eased his posture. "D'kob understands. It may take D'kob a few seconds to familiarize with the comparatively primitive aeronautics systems, but D'kob has no worries about effectively flying any Human aircraft."

Novah didn't doubt that. He peeked at the GPS marker D'kob had pointed to which was a small airport along the Columbia River, a mere half hour drive at their current pace. There hadn't been another car on the road in the ninety minutes they'd been driving. He didn't expect any issues reaching the airport.

A half an hour later, D'kob removed the cloaking devices and

Novah drove the truck and trailer through the airport's main gate. The lights of the airport illuminated the vehicles completely – there would be no more sneaking around.

"Are we just going to steal the plane?" questioned Novah.

"No. While D'kob has stolen before, there is no need to steal here. Novah shall buy the aircraft."

"I forgot my credit card," retorted Novah sarcastically.

D'kob waved his four fingers dismissively. "Do not worry about the payment. The payment will become evident. Go now and find the attendant, who D'kob believes maintains the plane contained within this hangar. When Novah returns, Novah will understand. D'kob will hide.

Novah hopped out onto the warm tarmac and walked through the muggy night towards the main airport office. Their arrival had been noticed so he was met halfway by a scrawny, bespectacled man. They shook hands politely but with the wariness that the times commanded. The airport attendant made no effort to hide the sidearm he was carrying. Novah spoke first.

"Hey there. I'm looking to buy a plane. Do you have anything in that hangar I can make an offer on?"

The attendant rubbed his chin. "I've only got two planes here these days, and they aren't mine to sell. The hangar rent is late, though, and the owners haven't been around for nearly a year. For all I know, they're dead or in jail somewhere. It's hard enough to eat these days without getting paid."

"So is that a yes?"

The attendant let out a heavy sigh. "I don't have the titles."

Novah thought for a moment. "Well, what if I just rented one?" Novah used air quotes with the word rented. "It's not like titles or property matter much anymore anyway. I just want a plane." Then the light bulb ignited in Novah's head. "I'm willing to trade you straight for that Ford and trailer, plus all of food and fuel that are in them, apart from what I'll need for my trip."

The attendant's eyes widened, and then narrowed as he squinted through the runway lights at Novah's setup. He smiled. The wheels were clearly turning. After spending ten minutes examining the truck and trailer, the attendant reached his decision.

"Alright. I'm sick of this furnace of a runway anyway. Let's do it!" A grin widened on his face, and he walked over to the hangar door, pulled a lever, pushed a button, and watched as the massive door was rolled up to reveal a dual-prop six-seat Beechcraft and a single-prop two-seat Cessna. "Which do you want?"

"I'll take the big one," Novah replied.

"Figured you might. It'll fly three hundred miles further. Tip-top shape, too. Only fifteen hundred hours on it. I'll pull it out and fuel it up while you get what you need from the truck."

Keys were exchanged half an hour later. D'kob had managed to stay hidden through it all, eventually sneaking onto the plane while the attendant was distracted by Novah.

"She's all yours," said the attendant, "good luck."

"Good luck to you too," Novah replied. The attendant wasted exactly no time pulling away, headed north. Novah wondered how long it would be before some drone sighted the vehicle.

D'kob hopped up out of hiding. "This aircraft is exceptional for the purpose. Good job, Novah."

"Thanks. I'm glad I thought of the idea of trading the truck for it."

D'kob gave him a slight smirk. "Do not underestimate the Z'korz."

"I have no idea what that means. Care to explain?"

"Some other time," replied D'kob, "D'kob and Novah must depart. Time is against D'kob and Novah."

D'kob stepped down the stairs out onto the tarmac, opened up the fuel tank, and deposited four tiny pellets into it. He then sealed it back up, entered the plane, and pulled up the stairs behind him.

"Refueling will not be an issue. The destination is now reachable without stopping," D'kob commented.

"And where, exactly, are we going?" inquired Novah.

"To a land mass known to Humans as Antarctica."

"Antarctica?? That has to be thousands of miles! It's going to take us days!" exclaimed Novah.

"Ten-thousand, one hundred and thirty-two point six miles. At three hundred and eleven miles per hour, D'kob and Novah will arrive in only 32.58 hours. So, not days. Novah's planet is not so large."

"Smartass."

"Where?" inquired D'kob, looking around. "D'kob does not notice any intelligent crossbreed equine in the area."

"Never mind," said Novah.

"Did the smartass disappear?"

"No," Novah sighed, "apparently only Humans can see it."

"D'kob is concerned about Novah. Novah should rest. Hallucinations are abnormal."

Novah sighed, oblivious to the fact that D'kob was toying with him. "No, you'll need help flying this plane. I don't know much about flying, but I'm pretty sure you're going to need two hands, and you only have one to work with."

"Novah makes a good point," D'kob replied somberly. "D'kob will need Novah's assistance during takeoff and landing. Beyond that, this craft will require only minimal flight adjustment, which D'kob can complete easily even with one arm."

With that, D'kob hinged open the plane's side window, placed the thin cloaking generator against the side of the plane, buttoned the window back up, and settled back into the pilot's seat. Three minutes later they were airborne, flying fast and low into the darkness, heading 180.0 degrees. D'kob engaged the auto-pilot.

"Novah may rest now."

"You should rest too," replied Novah. "Your arm still needs to heal."

D'kob looked down at his arm and shrugged. "Only two days until full functionality is restored."

"How come you couldn't just heal yourself like you did for my ankle?" Novah inquired.

"Z'korz field nullification. The Z'korz energy cannot be refocused on the source of the energy. Nullification ensues. Zero results."

"So you create some sort of energy?"

"Z'korz energy. Quantum energy. All sentient beings create it. Some beings can focus Z'korz energy to alter physical properties.

D'kob altered the physical properties of Novah's wounded flesh to make it healthy flesh," replied D'kob.

"It's like magic," Novah offered.

"No!" replied D'kob fervently. "Not magic at all. Science. Quantum physics and dimensional channeling. The Lord Commander taught me this. Novah will meet the Lord Commander soon."

"Well it's a cool trick anyway," growled Novah.

"No!" repeated D'kob. "Z'korz quanta is not a trick! Science! Mathematically proven and modeled."

"Ok, ok, I get it," replied Novah with a sigh. "I was never any good at science."

"D'kob suspects Novah merely wasn't very good at studying. Science is bound by rules and formulas. Science is easy. *Philosophy* is hard."

"Whatever!" snapped Novah. "Just fly the plane."

"The plane is flying itself," D'kob replied. "Autopilot."

"Aarrrghh!"

CHAPTER EIGHT

Te acceptance of the new proposal met with less than expected resistance," K'jahl observed once the Khamek party was back aboard their shuttle to the *L'ghorsk*. "Though I don't recall anything in the Great Teachings that states Khamek will be destroyed if Khamek do not meet The Prime on V'laha."

S'heil nodded. "A little exaggeration to evoke Human's natural sympathetic tendencies, linking Khamek and Humans together in a common cause of self-preservation. As has been studied and documented, Humans, especially these particular humans, value self-preservation above all else. These humans also crave the recognition of being chosen. S'heil was nervous when Alberto threatened the use of nuclear weapons. Unlike in Earth Year 1961, Khamek cannot stop every possible missile. Human missile proliferation exceeds current Khamek orbital capacity to intercept. Fortunately it appears such an unfortunate turn of events has been avoided."

They sat in silence for the remainder of the ascent, and only when the shuttle had fully docked did S'heil speak again.

"What is the status on the search for D'kob?"

"D'kob has not yet been located but the search is narrowing. S'lace reports that Humans are cooperating in the search. All air travel has been suspended and all borders closed. Personal records have been retrieved and indexed. The owner of the property on which D'kob crashed has been in containment for many months, while the son of the owner was recently released from incarceration. A GPS tracking device embedded in a truck owned by the property's owner was activated three days ago. Logic concludes that the son acquired the truck. The current location is not far from the crash site. S'lace will have it within minutes," reported K'jahl.

"Excellent," replied S'heil. "Keep me informed of S'lace's progress. S'heil wants to know the moment this vehicle is captured. Even if D'kob isn't in the vehicle, this Human may have seen something."

"Of course, Admiral." K'jahl nodded as they parted, each taking a separate corridor towards their respective quarters.

CHAPTER NINE

Novah drifted off to sleep to the comforting hum of the airplane's engines, awaking several hours later. D'kob was still sitting contentedly in the pilot seat.

"How much further?" asked Novah.

"D'kob and Novah must still fly for another twenty-six hours. Not long."

"I'm sorry for before," said Novah sincerely. "I know I'm not that smart. I know I never applied myself. It is frustrating to struggle to understand things."

D'kob nodded with understanding. "Novah is so very young. When D'kob was Novah's age, D'kob could not even speak complete sentences. Only after a full century of training did I master Khamek language. Several more centuries of training were needed to train D'kob's mouth and vocal cords to accommodate Human Language Protocols. D'kob understands frustration."

"How old are you?" asked Novah.

"Five thousand three hundred and seventeen Human years," he replied.

Novah shook his head in disbelief. "No way."

"This is my third body. It is nearly identical to the previous two. As Khamek reproduction in the traditional sense is unreliable, most Khamek commission clones. Within thirty minutes of death, or if the existing body shows signs of unsatisfactory performance, Khamek consciousness and Z'korz energy can be transferred into a clone. Upon transference and consciousness reactivation, a new sample is taken from the body and a new clone is grown. The clone grows in a growth tube until maturity is reached, then is suspended in state until needed. Some Khamek are very old. The oldest known has transferred twenty-three times. Most clones degrade beyond usefulness by the fifteenth generation, however, so twenty-three is an anomaly."

"Amazing!" replied Novah. "Do you have a clone frozen somewhere?"

"Yes," replied D'kob. "On the Khamek home world of V'jima Prime. D'kob's current body is weakened and frail. D'kob was promised by the Lord Commander that upon completion of this mission, D'kob may return to V'jima Prime and transfer. D'kob's current body may not last another hundred years. D'kob strongly desires to transfer to D'kob's clone before the structural integrity of D'kob's current body fails completely."

"You still seem quite spry to me," offered Novah.

D'kob smiled his thin alien smile. "Novah would not say this if Novah could see D'kob in a fresh clone. The performance difference is substantial."

The pair passed the time in conversation, with Novah asking non-science questions, mainly about D'kob's life and mission. D'kob was intentionally vague in many ways, not wanting to disclose too much. Both seemed to understand that there were places the other didn't want to go and were respectful of that. The confinement was tolerable because each was tolerant.

It was a long twenty-some hours to Antarctica. Novah napped between conversations. It wasn't until it became cold – really cold – with frost growing thick on the plane's windows that Novah became shiveringly aware of just how far south they'd come. He suspected time wasn't on their side, however. S'heil's minions would likely be closing on them shortly. D'kob brushed away any anxiety Novah had about this, simply stating that once inside the *R'ptyr*, everything would be fine.

"The *R'ptyr* is utterly impenetrable. Only D'kob has the key codes. No manner of force can break through *R'ptyr* shell. Only were the

R'ptyr to be flown into a star or black hole could it possibly be destroyed. Such is the crowning achievement of Khamek civilization," D'kob lectured.

It was early autumn in Antarctica and the sun hung low in the sky. D'kob had landed the plane effortlessly on a nondescript patch of the eternal ice, and both realized soon afterwards that they were woefully underdressed. The bitter Antarctic wind cut through them as if they weren't there.

"Novah and D'kob will be warm soon enough," said D'kob through tiny, flat, chattering teeth.

"Soon enough may not be soon enough," Novah retorted through blue lips while hugging himself tightly.

"Watch and see," D'kob said. From his bag he pulled out a tiny black sphere no larger than a marble. He held the sphere between two fingers, squeezed it, then tossed the sphere onto the ice.

"Hyper-magnetic homing ice-drill," stated D'kob proudly. "Stand back."

The sphere began to expand until it was the diameter of a manhole cover. Once it reached that size, the color began to change from black to orange. Just as Novah was beginning to enjoy the warmth radiating from the sphere it vanished effortlessly through the ancient frozen ground, a billow of steam shooting skyward behind it and out of the newly-created hole. Novah shook his head in amazement even though he knew he shouldn't be amazed at this point. He bent down to peer into the hole, but D'kob quickly grabbed him.

"Unless Novah wishes to meet with misadventure, D'kob suggests not putting Novah's face into a boiling steam cloud."

A minute later the steam dissipated leaving only a darkening hole that angled downward like a slide at a waterpark. Novah knelt and stuck his head in the hole but could see nothing but blackness.

Staring off towards the horizon, D'kob could see the quickly approaching Khamek scout ship headed directly for them. Somehow they'd been tracked.

"Come, there is no time to spare," said D'kob, who shoved an alien boot against Novah's rear, sending him plunging face-first into the abyss. D'kob seemed amused by Novah's echoing, fading scream.

There was no sense in trying to hide the plane or the hole. Their pursuer would figure it out soon enough and undoubtedly had their own ice drill. That didn't keep D'kob from buying a little extra time, however. He tossed out another black sphere with coordinates completely opposite of the first hole. It would drill for miles along a slowly descending and meandering slope. He walked back to the first hole hoping that the distraction hole would sucker the hunters. As he slid in and began his plunge into the Antarctic shell, he saw the familiar triangular form cast its long evening shadow above him.

Novah sat soaking wet and dumbfounded on a warm rock just outside the hole from which he had gently slid. The drill had enough sense to level out the last several hundred feet so that when Novah finally popped out onto a shockingly green mass of lichen his speed was no faster than that of a child's playground slide. Before him was the largest cavern he'd ever seen in his life, or even seen in pictures, lit up by the soft glow of lights marking the outline of what had to be the *R'ptyr*. He guessed he was staring at the nose of it, which he thought looked remarkably like the nose of a 747, only easily twenty times larger. He estimated the ship to be more than two hundred yards wide. He sprinted along the lichen in order to get a view of the length and stood motionless as he discovered he could not see the end of the craft. The crystalline hull just kept going and going and going, to a vanishing point. It was just one large, very long tube, sparkling like a blue diamond. No wings, and no windows that he could see, just the long, steady stream of white lights that lit up the glass-like hull every few feet. Refractive rainbows were everywhere.

The cavern was warmed by the geothermal vents that gave off a sulfur smell. Steam rose high, then condensed in the cold, falling back as a light mist. Novah was wet from the slide, wet from the steam, and wet from the mist, but the fires of his imagination warmed him from the inside.

A few seconds later, D'kob popped out of the tunnel.

"Hurry, Novah, there isn't much time. The pursuers are very near." D'kob made haste towards the very nose of the craft. Novah leaped after him urgently.

"And now… the codes!" D'kob reached out with his now-healed right arm and touched the ship. A panel flipped open, and he entered what Novah thought was a fifty-digit code. A seal was soon broken and a door-width section of the nose collapsed inward, becoming stairs. "Hurry," D'kob beckoned. Novah scrambled up the stairs behind him. They stepped up onto a small platform and the stairs folded back out to once again become part of the hull.

"Welcome, Novah, to the *R'ptyr*," said D'kob with a happy sigh. "We are now safe. Come and see." Novah followed D'kob up a long and dizzying twisting gangplank to what he assumed correctly was the bridge. It was massive. D'kob went to a console and the white exterior walls of the bridge became transparent at the touch of a view screen's icon. They walked to the front of the bridge reaching the clear window just in time to see S'lace and her companions pop out of the tunnel. They lost sight of their pursuers immediately due to the bulk of the *R'ptyr*, so D'kob switched one of the consoles to a ground camera view. Knowing she was too late, S'lace simply put her hands on her thin alien hips, shook her head, and sighed. She then yelled up at the craft, but neither occupant could hear what she was saying through the hull's thickness. D'kob pressed a yellow square on a display, enabling an intercom.

"Hello, S'lace," D'kob stated triumphantly.

S'lace cackled back in her natural Khamek tongue something unsavory, judging by D'kob's response.

"Please, there's no need for inflammatory language. If S'lace wishes to converse, D'kob would request S'lace insert S'lace's Human Languages Protocol chip so that Novah may understand what is being said."

S'lace fiddled with her palm for a couple of seconds, then spoke. "Congratulations, D'kob. D'kob has signed S'lace's death warrant."

"Nonsense," D'kob replied. "D'kob has authority from the Lord Commander to rescue S'lace from S'heil's wrath. All S'lace must do is renounce S'heil and submit to imprisonment on the *R'ptyr* until the rendezvous with the Lord Commander."

S'lace considered her options. She could return to S'heil and be shot in the face, or submit to imprisonment and the Lord Commander. She went over the options with her two companions. After a brief conversation, the three of them dropped their weapons and walked towards the ship. "S'lace, V'kol and N'dim surrender. S'lace, V'kol and N'dim will comply peacefully."

"Very well," replied D'kob. "Please proceed to the foremost starboard entry bay and enter the *R'ptyr*. D'kob will see that Khamek are provisioned. Please proceed immediately. Departure is imminent." He turned to Novah.

"The *R'ptyr* is a Human ship, designed for Humans. Everything is built around Human needs and comfort. However, the *R'ptyr* was built nearly two Human millennia ago. The *R'ptyr* requires a neural update to conform to Novah's modern language structures and to calibrate the displays to interfaces Novah and other Humans will be comfortable using. The update will take some time. Please be patient."

Novah nodded, and once again D'kob snatched a small chip from his bag of tricks – the disc that had been taped to his tray the day of his escape. He walked to a console and inserted the disc. Ten seconds later, he turned back to Novah.

"The neural update is complete. On behalf of the Lord Commander and the Khamek species, D'kob presents to Novah, representing Earth's Humans, the Interstellar Spacecraft *R'ptyr*." D'kob stretched his arm and hand out in a flourish, waving it in a wide arc across the *R'ptyr*'s bridge.

"D'kob," spoke Novah, "this is the single greatest thing I've ever seen or experienced in my life. Thank you for bringing me along on your mission."

Novah then fell silent, a bit overwhelmed by what was happening. Here he was, a young convicted felon, a thief, a conspirator and a murderer, now in the driver's seat of the greatest technological gift in the history of humankind. The crushing weight of guilt and the fact that he could let his guard down and relax for the first time in ages weighed down on him more heavily with each breath. It pushed him to his knees, and then he wept, his withheld suffering gushing forth in wailing sobs. Tears rained into his palms. Ragged breaths forced themselves out of his lungs with liquid coughs. D'kob stood silently, unsure of what to do, waiting for this uncomfortable turn to end.

After a few minutes Novah was able to compose himself. He managed to shut off his distressing thoughts in a locked-away corner of his brain and refocused on the adventure at hand.

"What do we do now, D'kob?" he inquired softly.

"D'kob does not know how much time will pass until S'heil realizes that S'lace has stopped reporting. S'lace was undoubtedly tracked. In short order, S'heil will know where the *R'ptyr* is. Though the *R'ptyr* is impenetrable, logic and caution suggest moving the *R'ptyr* from Antarctica as soon as possible. Once moved, Novah can begin the necessary orientation process. The *R'ptyr* is a massive ship and there is much to learn. Novah must also meet the Lord Commander."

Novah had questions but thought it wise to concentrate on getting the ship moved. The questions could be asked later. As impervious as the *R'ptyr* was said to be, he didn't relish the thought of S'heil testing it.

"I presume this ship has some sort of cloaking device? Once we get out from under all of this ice, we'll be out in the open and visible – and this ship isn't small."

"Novah's presumption is correct," replied D'kob. "The *R'ptyr* is designed to ensure Human safety in all conditions. The *R'ptyr* can be made invisible to all varieties of detection with a simple setting." He walked to the command chair pressed a release mechanism. A small drawer slid open, and D'kob withdrew the small black band inside. "Hold out Novah's left hand," D'kob commanded.

Novah held out his left hand, palm up, and D'kob placed the thin, inch-wide black band around his palm, encircling his hand just below the knuckles. The band tightened automatically, conforming perfectly with his palm.

"This is Novah's command module," stated D'kob. "Novah will notice four small circles on the palm side of the module. The leftmost circle is the power engagement button. The remaining three are projection and interface components. Please press the power engagement button."

Novah stared at his left palm, then used his right index finger to depress the leftmost button. Instantly, a large holographic black frame formed in his left hand surrounding a screen projected by the module. It was a photo of Earth and it was as clear as if he was holding a computer monitor. He waved his right hand back and forth through the display just to make sure it wasn't material.

"This is incredible!" gasped Novah. "It's clearer than any TV I've ever seen! And weightless!"

"The module is completely customizable as well," continued D'kob. "Grab the lower right hand corner of the holograph and pull."

Novah did, pinching his right thumb and index finger together until they touched. He moved his hand to the right, and the holograph increased in size. He moved his hand towards the left, and shrunk the display to no larger than a credit card.

"This is so neat!" Novah exclaimed. "What else does it do?"

"All of the R'ptyr's systems can be operated from this interface," said D'kob. "The rest of the consoles you see on the bridge are simply for status monitoring. The ship itself is designed to be controlled almost effortlessly. Touch the planet on your interface."

Novah complied, and the ethereal screen instantly changed to a control panel with digital icons.

"Hey! How did it do that? I just pushed my whole hand through this a minute ago, and now I simply touch something on this and a new screen shows up?"

D'kob nodded. "Command modules are an extension of the R'ptyr, which is designed with advanced situational logic and biometric analysis protocols. The R'ptyr can interpret Novah's intent based on eye focus, hand and finger position, micro-fluctuations in blood pressure, previous behaviors, learned preferences and other metrics. Novah intended to press an input, so R'ptyr's Natural Intent Command Language Interface protocols reacted appropriately. The more Novah uses the system, the greater the R'ptyr's understanding of Novah's intent. With time, the Natural Intent Command Language Interface protocols will learn to accurately predict Novah's next intents.

"The settings you see on the display are based off of the Natural Intent Command Language Interface's assessment of the current environment and circumstance. Other options can be accessed through the interface menu, and are customizable to Novah's needs. All of these advanced instructions can be learned later. For now, though, Novah should move R'ptyr away from Antarctica."

Novah stared at the holograph extending from his left hand and read the colored boxes on it. There were only two. A blue one said "cloak," and a green one said "start engines." He pressed the blue square, and immediately an airy female voice echoed politely through the bridge – occaeco absolutus. When Novah heard the voice it sent a chill up his spine. It was beautiful and perfect, even if he didn't understand the language. It didn't sound artificial at all. The lighting inside the bridge changed subtly from a pure white to a slight blue hue – a visual cue to match the icon he pressed to indicate the ship was cloaked. He couldn't keep himself from grinning.

"Apologies, Novah," said D'kob. "The current audible language reply configuration is set to a prominent Human language at the time the R'ptyr was completed. This should have been repaired by the neural update. There appears to have been an oversight. Human language has changed, so D'kob will now update the language protocol." He walked over to a console, altered a few settings, then returned. "Audible language protocol updated. Novah may proceed."

Novah pressed the "start engines" button. He heard nothing but the lovely voice say engines started. No rumble, no hum, no vibrations, no indication whatsoever that anything was different other than each of the consoles on the bridge lighting up with a thin band of amber light. Instantaneously, the choices on his holograph changed. The cloak and engine boxes slid to the right side and shrank. In the middle of the screen appeared six directional arrows.

"I'm not sure what to do next, D'kob," confessed Novah. "Which way should we go?"

D'kob gave him his alien smirk. "Why do you ask D'kob? Ask the Natural Intent Command Language Interface protocols! Be natural. Remember, R'ptyr is designed for human interaction."

Novah thought for a minute. "So, the ship can listen to my voice as well?"

"Affirmative," D'kob confirmed. "Simply tell the Natural Intent Command Language Interface your wishes."

Novah took a seat in the formidable command chair directly in the center of the bridge. The chair adjusted automatically so that his feet touched the floor perfectly. Novah grinned.

"Show me a map of our current position," Novah commanded. Nothing happened.

D'kob looked at Novah quizzically. "Command directives must be issued to the Natural Intent Command Language Interface directly."

"You mean I have to call it by name? I have to say all of that each time I want to talk to the ship?"

D'kob nodded. "Affirmative."

"That's quite a mouthful," observed Novah. "Is there a way to shorten it?"

D'kob thought for a moment, confused by Novah's laziness.

"D'kob presumes the identifier can be remapped to a name of Novah's choosing simply by asking."

Novah sat and thought, staring at the header across the top of his command module hologram. Natural Intent Command Language Interface. *Natural Intent Command Language Interface*, he thought. *Surely there is something simpler I can name you. NIC...no, ships should have girl names. NICL.....NICLI...no...hmm...*

"Aha!" he blurted triumphantly.

Novah looked up towards the ceiling and spoke. "Natural Intent Command Language Interface, can I change your name?"

The answer floated down like butterflies into Novah's ears.

Affirmative. What would you like to name me?

"NICOLE," Novah stated, speaking the modified acronym.

Warning. Only one alternate identifier may be assigned to the Natural Intent Command Language Interface. Are you sure you wish to make this identifier NICOLE?

"Yes," stated Novah.

Rename complete.

Novah grinned. "NICOLE, please display our current position."

Current position now displayed on starboard display screen and on your command module hologram.

The display screens showed a simple, white map of the continent of Antarctica, with a ship-shaped icon showing the *R'ptyr*'s location therein. He touched the icon of the *R'ptyr*, and the map zoomed in. No further details revealed themselves.

Novah thought back to the last map he had seen, the forest service map of his dad's property in the trailer. He assumed that there would be mountains and valleys all over the place under all of the Antarctic ice. For all he knew, this entire ship was tucked under some giant mountain range. Even he could see that trying to move a ship this large blindly was silly.

"NICOLE, can you overlay topographical data focusing primarily on the area between the ship and the closest ocean?"

Affirmative. Map adjusted. The current distance from the R'ptyr to the Pacific Ocean is 376.2 miles.

"This is so cool!" exclaimed Novah. D'kob nodded.

"NICOLE, can you tunnel through ice?"

Affirmative. Engine exhaust heat can be directed to melt the ice. For maximum efficiency, tunneling in reverse is suggested.

Novah giggled. "NICOLE, how long would it take to tunnel through the 376 miles and reach the ocean?"

Compensating for terrain with the necessary course corrections, the Pacific Ocean can be reached in 7.4 minutes.

Novah turned to D'kob in disbelief. "How is that possible?"

D'kob shrugged. "Melting ice is a trivial exercise. The engines create enough heat to basically eliminate ice as a variable. Tunneling through ice then equates, within a few percentage points, to traveling through air. Any non-ice obstructions will simply be vaporized by the massive amount of energy and pressure created."

Novah looked upward and spoke to the ship again. "NICOLE, what are the three deepest points in Earth's oceans?" The response was immediate. NICOLE put the data on the displays and read it:

Challenger Deep – Mariana Trench
Hawai'i Mapping Research Group Deep – Mariana Trench
Galathea Depth – Philippine Trench
Locations displayed.

Novah sat back and thought. If the goal is to stay hidden and deceive this S'heil guy, a little misdirection would be smart.

"Ok, here's the plan. We're not going to tunnel. We're going to go straight up through the ice. S'heil will think we went into space somewhere. That would be the logical thing to think. Once we get above the ice, we make straight for the ocean, dive in, and assume a position in the Galathea Depth. S'heil will be up in the sky hunting, and we'll be down here out of the way." He turned to D'kob. "What do you think?"

D'kob stared at him with sympathetic eyes. "Novah's plan is a fine plan. D'kob would alter the plan slightly, yet this is Novah's command."

"How would you alter it? I'm no tactician. I'm grateful for any help you can offer."

D'kob was relieved. "D'kob would suggest tunneling to the ocean as Novah originally thought. Once at the ocean, leave the planet. Space is infinitely larger than Earth's tiny oceans. S'heil will count on Human nature to stay close to home. S'heil will see the tunnel as validation of this assumption. Plus, with S'heil concentrating S'heil's efforts on searching Earth, D'kob and Novah will know where S'heil is."

Novah frowned, disappointed with himself. "Yes, your plan is better. I told you I was no tactician."

"Novah and D'kob should proceed then. S'heil will soon be wondering what happened to S'lace."

Nodding, Novah once again spoke to the *R'ptyr*. "NICOLE, please proceed with the tunneling. Once we are in the ocean, we'll leave Earth."

Destination?

Novah glanced at D'kob. "Suggestions?"

"Not too far away," replied D'kob. "There is business yet to conduct on Earth. D'kob suggests, perhaps, hiding in the clouds of N'ala 2. Venus, as N'ala 2 is known to Novah."

"Sounds great. NICOLE, proceed to the ocean."

Affirmative. Engaging.

Novah could barely feel the movement of the massive ship, yet could sense the speed from the perspective of the view screens which filtered through the billowing steam showing the ice melt explosively in all directions as the ship tunneled effortlessly through the Antarctic ice.

CHAPTER TEN

N'kul lay dead on the floor sporting a circular burn between his eyes from which a tiny grey wisp of smoke twirled slowly upward and then disintegrated in the ship's draft. He had lost the tri-dice tournament, and as expected, S'heil didn't take the news of S'lace's disappearance well. K'jahl approached, paused, looked indifferently once at the body, and then continued. He silently wondered how it was that he had managed to avoid his own circular burn for all these centuries.

"Is it true there is no sign of S'lace, K'jahl?" S'heil inquired.

"Yes, Admiral. S'lace's last reported position is Antarctica. Tracking was then lost and not regained. A search party found S'lace's craft and a drill hole leading to a massive cavern in the ice."

"S'heil presumes a thorough search of the cavern is underway?"

"Indeed, Admiral. A crew of twenty Khamek began forensics a few minutes ago. An update is expected soon."

S'heil nodded, visibly irritated. *Patience, S'heil,* he told himself.

"Logic defines only three possible choices," S'heil said calmly. "One, S'lace is still in that cavern somewhere. Two, S'lace found the *R'ptyr* and is onboard either as a conqueror or a prisoner. Three, S'lace has suffered misadventure. S'heil prefers one of the first two options."

K'jahl's palm pulsed red. "Excuse K'jahl, Admiral…the communication K'jahl is now receiving may be important."

S'heil nodded, and K'jahl brought his left palm to his ear. After a couple of minutes, K'jahl closed the conversation – during which he'd been completely silent – with "K'jahl will be in contact later."

"Admiral," K'jahl continued, "That was President Hernandez stating that a pair of United States submarines patrolling in the South Pacific ocean have picked up extraordinary anomalies. The submarine commanders could not identify any mechanical sounds, but could not mistake the displacement wave. A logical conclusion is that the *R'ptyr* is moving through that ocean."

"Have the submarines been able to plot a projected course?" inquired S'heil.

"Yes, Admiral. The track points towards the Galathea Depth. This Depth is a highly logical place to hide a large craft."

"Excellent," beamed S'heil. "Please express S'heil's gratitude to President Hernandez after K'jahl has dispatched reconnaissance craft to the Galathea Depth."

"Yes, Admiral." K'jahl hesitated.

"What troubles K'jahl," asked S'heil.

"It is obvious that D'kob and D'kob's human companion have captured the *R'ptyr*. The *R'ptyr* is designed to be impenetrable. The *R'ptyr* can be found, the *R'ptyr* can be observed, but no Khamek will be able to capture or destroy the *R'ptyr*. K'jahl wonders what S'heil's plan is."

S'heil focused his broad, dark eyes on K'jahl. "To negotiate, of course. There is a common Human saying – every Human has a Human's price. S'heil intends to discover the price, and to pay the price. K'jahl and S'heil must remember the mission."

K'jahl nodded. "Of course, Admiral."

He hesitated again.

S'heil sighed. "What troubles K'jahl?"

"What is S'heil's plan to deal with the Lord Commander? The Lord Commander has no doubt made note of S'heil's insubordination."

S'heil stared harshly at K'jahl. "S'heil has told K'jahl never mention the Lord Commander." K'jahl nodded, turned on his heel, and set off to his tasks.

S'heil sat in the command chair, brooding as his feet dangled. *S'heil wonders if K'jahl knows how close S'heil came to shooting K'jahl in the face.*

Sooner or later, S'heil knew, he'd have to deal with the Lord Commander, that pesky Human who insisted on interfering with all of S'heil's plans.

CHAPTER ELEVEN

D'kob watched with mild amusement at the delight at which Novah took to learning the controls of the *R'ptyr*. Novah had taken manual control of the ship shortly after popping out into the Pacific. He experimented with all of the directional controls, often causing the ship to shudder in the sea. After a few minutes, he gave control back to the *R'ptyr*.

"NICOLE, continue a course to the Galathea Depth, and when we are close, let's leave this planet and get to Venus," Novah instructed.

Affirmative. Course plotted.

Novah sat in the command chair, basking in the echoes of the comforting voice, and D'kob sat in the chair to the immediate right. D'kob didn't have to wait long for the questions to begin.

"Ok, D'kob," began Novah. "We're safe, we have the *R'ptyr*, and we're on our way. It's time to cough up some answers."

"D'kob will try to answer Novah's questions adequately, and without unnecessary phlegm. D'kob will also defer some questions as some questions will be best answered by the Lord Commander, whom Novah will meet soon enough."

"Sounds fair," replied Novah. "Now then, this is a humongous ship. I haven't even been able to look through the entire floor plan yet, much less have a walking tour. Why is this ship so large? What is its purpose?"

D'kob provided his answers in a matter of fact fashion, because his answers were, in fact, a matter of fact.

"The *R'ptyr* was created to save the Human species. In order to provide enough genetic diversity to ensure long-term human survival and prosperity, Khamek scientists estimate that 50,000 Humans are sufficient. The *R'ptyr* is designed and provisioned to sustain 50,000 Humans for the time needed to transport Humans to a nearby, pre-selected world compatible with Human survival."

"Save the human race from what?" inquired Novah skeptically.

D'kob then related the evidence and projections of Earth's geological instability, painting a most thorough picture of the certain doom awaiting the planet in the very near future.

"Human survival on Earth will be impossible," D'kob concluded. "Only those on the *R'ptyr* will survive."

"So you're telling me everyone not on this ship is going to die?" asked an incredulous Novah.

"Affirmative," D'kob replied.

Novah slumped in the command chair, lost in thought. He replayed his life in his head, thinking back on people he'd met, the movies he'd seen, and the girls he had secretly observed but never asked out. He thought about the stack of National Geographic magazines back at Charles' place, of all the countless sights and cultures contained in those pages, pages he'd never read, places he'd never get to go. He thought about Charles, and Juan, people he knew were oblivious to what was coming. He thought about all of those cat and dog videos on the internet, all of the music and the musicians, and all of the time he'd spent doing nothing, believing there would always be time. He thought about Penny, noting that if the world was going to end, at least that little bitch would end with it. Most of all, though, he thought about his parents. He remembered his mom bringing freshly baked cinnamon rolls up to him each birthday morning. He remembered his dad teaching him to read, to drive, and chewing him out about using the same bucket to wash both the wheels and the car itself. Memory after memory flooded into his mind until his mind was full. Then the memories flooded out of his eyes.

D'kob, trying to learn to make the best of these awkward moments, made a fumbling gesture of sympathy, placing his hand on Novah's shoulder. He tried to find words to comfort Novah.

"Thousands of planets die every day in the galaxy. Gamma ray bursts, asteroids, orbital shifts, supernovas. Such tragedies are normal. In the end, Earth is just another planet."

"But it's MY planet!" yelled Novah. "Everything I've ever known or ever seen is going to be gone! How can I just dismiss that?"

"Because Novah must," D'kob said simply. "Humanity is forfeit otherwise."

"Is there nothing...*nothing* that can be done?" pleaded Novah.

"No."

Novah gripped the arms of his chair. He wanted to run, but there was nowhere to run to. Furious rage welled up within him, washed over him...and then, somehow passed into a tranquil, even burn. *All things end*, his father had told him. *How we choose to face those endings is just as important as how we face beginnings.*

Here he was, staring both a beginning and an ending square in the face. Him, not somebody else. A position unique in human history. He could either embrace it or reject it. He could either step up and lead or lay down and wallow in a pitiful misery that wouldn't change anything. That didn't mean this new reality didn't hurt. He pushed the pain into a compartment inside him to be dealt with later. He relaxed his hands, wiped the tears from his face, and stood up.

"So what's the plan then?" he asked.

"D'kob does not know. Novah's question is best answered by the Lord Commander."

"Are you sure I'm the right human for this mission, D'kob?"

D'kob smiled. "Novah is the only human currently available."

"Oh hogwash," replied Novah. "It would be simple to swoop down on the Pentagon or someplace and grab a general or something."

"Perhaps," replied D'kob, "but the primary mission is to secure the *R'ptyr* and to rendezvous with the Lord Commander. The Z'korz was kind enough to deposit D'kob's crash near Novah, as the Lord Commander predicted. D'kob is happy to accept the gift of survival and appreciates Novah's role. Novah has a greater role yet to play, of that D'kob is certain. What D'kob is uncertain of is what porcine cleanliness has to do with this situation."

Novah sighed, in no mood for D'kob's weak attempts at humor.

"Again with this Z'korz thing. You say its science, but you talk about it more like a religion."

D'kob sighed. "The Z'korz is both religion and scientific fact. Human history has illustrated that Humans are largely incapable of understanding this duality. The Lord Commander can explain the Z'korz better. The Lord Commander knows the Z'korz better than any Khamek."

"It sounds hokey to me," said Novah.

"Apologies, Novah, the word 'hokey' does not align with a suitable substitute in my version of the Human Language Protocol. Please explain."

"It means it sounds crazy," Novah replied.

"Novah has much to learn," D'kob said with a cool edge.

"Well, let's get this ship to Venus so that I can talk with this Lord Commander of yours," ordered Novah. "NICOLE, how long until we arrive at Venus?"

Three hours replied the soothing voice.

"That should give me just enough time to finish scanning the floor plans of this ship. I still can't believe how large it is," stated Novah.

"Very well," replied D'kob. "D'kob will take this opportunity to deal with a private matter."

"Umm…speaking of private matters, where is the bathroom?"

D'kob pointed to large, metal bench against one of the bridge walls, out in the open. It had a dozen melon-sized holes punched in it. "D'kob is afraid that the waste evacuation facilities are commensurate with those at the time of the *R'ptyr*'s completion. Shall D'kob attempt to find Novah a sponge-stick?"

"You're kidding, right D'kob? Please tell me you are joking. You want to have 50,000 modern humans use open toilets and… sponge-sticks?"

D'kob stared at the floor. "There are no resources on board to retrofit the *R'ptyr* to modern Human standards."

"How do Khamek… evacuate waste and…well…wipe?" asked Novah.

"The same way most advanced known species do. The three seashells."

Novah stared at D'kob blankly. "What the f-…"

"I'll fetch a set for you," D'kob interrupted, and quickly entered a small antechamber near the toilets, returning and handing Novah three shell-like items. They appeared to be made from porcelain.

Novah looked at the 'shells' in his palms. "What...wait…how…?"

"D'kob must attend to a private matter immediately. Good luck, Novah." D'kob walked away quickly. As he entered a private room, D'kob heard Novah: "NICOLE, how do I use these three shells?"

…

D'kob dealt with his personal matters, and then pressed a finger into his left palm. Communication was instantaneous.

"Lord Commander. D'kob has acquired the R'ptyr. D'kob has a Human companion named Novah, as well as three S'heil operatives in custody. Destination is N'ala 2, estimated arrival in 2.75 hours."

"Excellent work, D'kob," replied the Lord Commander. "I could not be more pleased. You have done very well indeed. What is your impression of Novah?"

D'kob was careful. The Lord Commander had a habit of asking probing questions, gleaning answers well beyond the scope of the question being asked.

"Novah is civilized but troubled," D'kob replied. "Events of Novah's past haunt Novah. Novah has confessed to a myriad of crimes yet has shown no violence towards D'kob. Novah also understandably struggles with Earth's impending doom."

"This is to be expected. Earth's destruction is not an easy situation to deal with," replied the Lord Commander. "I would like to meet Novah. Once the R'ptyr has been hidden in the clouds of Venus, bring him to me. I'll be on the fifth deck of section forty-seven, in the main amphitheater."

D'kob was astonished. "The Lord Commander is on the R'ptyr? D'kob is confused."

"I have been on the *R'ptyr* for a few weeks now," replied the Lord Commander. "I have been waiting and preparing. There is much work to do. If S'heil were to capture you and force you to disclose the location of the *R'ptyr*, and compel you to unlock it, which he no doubt would have, he would have needed to be dealt with."

"Lord Commander…"

"Yes D'kob?"

"How did the Lord Commander gain access to the *R'ptyr*?"

"I know the key codes. Remember, I was the one who provided them to you." replied the Lord Commander.

D'kob sighed, embarrassed. "Of course."

D'kob ended the communication and walked back out to the bridge. Novah was sitting in the command chair watching the swirling brown sphere of Venus grow closer and closer through the view screen.

CHAPTER TWELVE

"Did Novah find success with the three shells?" inquired D'kob.

"No," replied Novah bitterly. "Let's not talk about it."

"As Novah wishes. The Lord Commander wishes to see Novah once the R'ptyr has reached Venus."

"The Lord Commander is on Venus?" asked Novah incredulously.

"No, the Lord Commander is on the R'ptyr. Please save questions regarding the Lord Commander for the Lord Commander," sighed D'kob.

"Is the Lord Commander as important as his title says he is?" asked Novah, ignoring D'kob's request.

"The Lord Commander is the most important being D'kob has ever known."

"Well then," replied Novah, "I could sure use a shower and a shave. And perhaps a change of clothes."

"I will show you to the bath area," said D'kob. "While Novah bathes, D'kob will dispose of Novah's clothing. The R'ptyr is not provisioned with modern Human clothing selections so D'kob offers Novah a choice – toga or command uniform?"

"I'd rather not wear a sheet," Novah replied.

D'kob nodded and turned. Novah followed him to a pocket door at the back of the bridge which slid open with a swoosh. Beyond the door was a small, white room, with a softly-pulsing blue circular area about six feet in diameter and slightly raised in the middle of the floor.

It reminded Novah of a gel insert that could be inserted into shoes for extra comfort. They stepped up onto it and sunk slightly into the sponginess.

D'kob spoke one word. "Baths."

Instantaneously, the pair were teleported to a similar small room. The door opened to a stunning Roman bath house. Marble columns surrounded large, waist-deep pools. Steam billowed upwards to the brick domed top which was intricately decorated with colored cherubim. It was if the whole room was plucked from a Roman villa and set inside the ship.

"D'kob took the liberty of warming the water when D'kob and Novah departed Earth, predicting Novah might wish to cleanse. The temperature is set to 312 degrees Kelvin," D'kob stated matter-of-factly.

Novah stood in silent sensory overload for several seconds.

"Did we just teleport or is this some sort of revolving door trick?" he asked.

"Teleportation," replied D'kob. "Khamek teleportation platforms allow completely safe teleportation of any material for a distance of up to five Human miles provided that a matching platform is at the destination. D'kob and Novah teleported one quarter of one mile aft of the bridge. The *R'ptyr* is two miles long. Any teleportation attempt beyond five Human miles would result in misadventure."

Even though he'd lightly perused the floor plans of the *R'ptyr* it was still difficult for Novah to wrap his mind around the sheer scale of the ship. While the ability to teleport wherever in the ship he wanted might make the ship seem small, there was no doubt that this was a serious vehicle with a serious purpose. It was clearly designed for humans. The ship could have likely been a third of its size and accomplished the same mission but human comfort focusing on larger spaces and places to roam was a clear priority in the design.

Novah looked in awe at the baths, and at the same time wondered how practical they would be for a modern society of 50,000 people. Bathing is a private matter these days. Would humanity regress in this regard and feel comfortable bathing together in one of these steamy pools that could easily hold fifty? And the toilets! Some other solution would have to be figured out. How many other ancient amenities would have to be adjusted to?

Novah peeled off his stiff, sticky clothing and slid into the comforting water of the bath, paying no heed to D'kob who gathered the clothing and then disappeared.

It had literally been years since Novah had last taken a bath and the reintroduction to the sensation of immersion pleased him greatly. He slid under the surface, holding his breath for as long as he could before coming back up. He used the wool cloth at the side of the bath to scrub himself top to bottom. He scrubbed himself red and raw, and while all of the dirt came off, he couldn't wash away the guilt of his crimes and regrets no matter how hard he tried. He was thankful that this new and exciting adventure provided enough distraction that he could avoid thinking about the Mall.

Thirty minutes later D'kob returned with a pair of white wool towels and a two-piece, light gray jumpsuit with a pair of similarly colored deck-shoes.

"Why D'kob, I didn't know you were so handy at laundry," Novah teased.

"D'kob does what needs to be done," he replied, obviously lacking the context to appreciate Novah's teasing. "Novah should dress and then D'kob will remedy Novah's follicular challenges."

"Follicular challenges? What are you talking about?" Novah asked.

"Novah's hair and beard. The hair and beard must be dealt with as Novah appears more like an orangutan than a Human."

Indeed, Novah hadn't had a haircut in over a year and his already long hair now extended beyond his shoulders. He especially noticed it when it was wet, heavy, and pulling on his scalp. His face hosted similar growth, tangled and uneven.

"Good idea," replied Novah. "Do you have a barber on board?"

"No," stated D'kob. "D'kob will have to suffice."

Novah dried, dressed, and followed D'kob to one of a score of small alcoves off of the main bath area. D'kob pointed to the simple wooden chair where Novah took a seat.

"Remain still. D'kob will be finished in four minutes."

D'kob worked with an efficiency and precision that surprised Novah. D'kob had no scissors or traditional clippers. Instead he held a black, palm-sized rectangle with a green-glowing light at the top. Large swaths of wet hair fell all around Novah. D'kob then ran the device along Novah's face, rendering it smooth as silk.

When it was all over, exactly four minutes later, Novah ran his hand along his face.

"That's one hell of a razor! Where can I get one of those?"

D'kob smiled, and handed the device to Novah. "Do not expect D'kob to continue Novah's follicular maintenance in the future."

Novah smiled and pocketed the techno-razor. He looked at the floor, amazed at how much of his dark brown hair had been removed.

"Is there a mirror?"

D'kob went to the near wall and pressed an imbedded blue square. The wall then ignited in reflection, floor to ceiling. Novah looked at the strange person in the mirror – thin, clean cut, and with a mouth that tasted like ash. It had been days since he'd brushed his teeth.

"You don't happen to have a magic toothbrush, do you?" Novah inquired.

"Magic is an imaginary construct," replied D'kob. He pointed to a small, translucent canister on the nearby countertop. "D'kob suggests Novah place a dental wafer on Novah's tongue."

Raising an eyebrow, Novah opened the canister and pulled a dime-sized green wafer from it. He placed it on his tongue. A rush of cool carbonation filled his mouth, bubbling for about fifteen seconds, then dissipated. There was nothing to spit, nothing to swallow. His mouth was fresh and clean.

"Amazing!' exclaimed Novah.

"The time is near when Novah and D'kob must meet the Lord Commander. Novah and D'kob should eat first as the meeting may be long."

"That sounds great!" Novah's belly rumbled in agreement. "Is there a steakhouse somewhere on board?"

D'kob stared at Novah blankly. "Khamek do not eat meat. In fact,

Khamek eat very little." He handed Novah a pair of pills that Novah thought resembled multivitamins. "Nutrition enhancement tablets. The pair contains all of the calories and nutrients required for optimum Human efficiency and maintenance. The tablets will also expand in the Human stomach, providing a sense of fullness. Novah will not require additional tablets for seventy-two hours. D'kob suggests consuming the tablets with water."

Novah stared into his palm realizing with sadness that it would likely be a very long time before he ever ate a steak again. He washed the pills down with a glass of water, full but unsatisfied.

"Now Novah and D'kob go to the Lord Commander," D'kob continued. There was a noticeable trace of nervousness in D'kob's voice. They walked back through the baths to the teleportation platform.

"Main theater, deck five," spoke D'kob. In less than half a blink the pair were teleported to the foyer surrounding the main amphitheater complex. Scores of teleportation pads surrounded the complex, obviously to accommodate many people arriving concurrently.

Deck five was the top deck of the R'ptyr and the high, arching ceiling in the theater area had been made transparent. Looking up, Novah witnessed the violent swirling of the Venusian atmosphere. He also heard a deep, rumbling thumping in the distance. The main entrance to the amphitheater was seventy five yards away and with each step towards it he could hear the *boom boom boom* of a beat grow more distinct. Then he heard crowd noise, loud and enthusiastic. As he and D'kob stepped through the marble doors and walked around a brick dividing wall, the arena opened up before them – a giant amphitheater with the main stage far below, easily cutting down through two decks of the ship. Thirty thousand screaming fans were cheering with delight at the band playing on stage. Novah recognized the sound and the song, thundering mercilessly as it concluded. It was AC/DC playing *Back in Black*. A classic.

The song ended as D'kob and Novah made their way towards the stage. As they came closer Novah realized that the band sounded like AC/DC, but were not. He didn't recognize any of the band members.

The crowd continued to cheer as the lead singer, clad in tight-fitting black leather, spoke into the microphone, his voice pure and booming.

"Ladies and gentlemen! Please welcome our special guests, D'kob and Noooovaaaaahhhh!"

The audience cheered enthusiastically and all of the lights went out on the stage except for one, which highlighted the rhythm guitarist. He began to play, and as each subsequent instrument joined in, a new light beamed down on them. The sounds from each instrument layered on each other flawlessly. The resulting music was a song Novah had never heard before, yet felt he had. It was hard, rhythmic, loud, and perfect. It sent chills up his spine. The audience sang along and Novah found himself singing along as well, even though he *thought* he didn't know the words. It was like magic – the words popped into his head and out of his mouth.

The song ended in a crescendo of guitars and a fitting drum smash, and the crowd went wild. The lead singer shouted a heavy "thank you and good night!" before hurrying off of the stage.

D'kob awoke Novah from his trance in the aisle. "Come with D'kob. Hurry."

Novah obeyed, following D'kob down along the front of the stage and to the right, into a side door. He thought it odd that there were no yellow-shirted security personnel. A few steps later they were behind the stage in a small, dimly-lit room, inside of which was a smaller-than-average-sized, thirty-something year old man with long hair and a red bandana, his face and body drenched with sweat. Novah immediately recognized him as the lead singer.

The rocker removed the towel from his face. "Novah! D'kob! Welcome! We've got one more number…one encore. Novah, you're going to join me on stage." The man handed him a Gibson guitar. "What do you want to play? Pick anything. Hurry though."

"But I don't know how to play this thing!" exclaimed Novah.

"You do today," replied the singer. "Trust me. Now pick something. Something suitably rocking." The man smiled at Novah through bright, perfect teeth.

Novah thought he'd blow a synapse. He suffered from complete sensory overload. He worked to focus, trying to remember songs, trying to play snippits of them in his head to find something sufficiently "rocking." His response came out more as a question than a suggestion.

"*Won't Get Fooled Again*, by The Who?"

"Perfect! Let's go!" The singer pressed a palm into Novah's back, guiding him up a small set of stairs onto the stage. The crowd went wild. The lead singer nodded to the band member at the keyboard, who, seemingly without any sort of knowledge beforehand, began playing the introductory keyboard riffs. Novah stood on the taped X on the stage that the singer pointed at, and at the perfect point, Novah felt a surge of musical knowledge and power erupt in his nervous system. It was like seeing a sunrise for the first time after a year of darkness. He was playing the part of Pete Townsend. It wasn't fake. He could feel the sting of the strings on his fingers as he crunched through the song. He found himself completely ad-libbing a guitar solo as if he'd been playing guitars since birth.

The lead singer was perfect, with a voice raw and true, making the original Roger Daltry sound pale by comparison. The drum solo came and went, the keyboard filled it in, and afterwards the spine-shattering *yeaaaaaahhhhhhhhhhhhhh!!* was delivered in absolute perfect primality. The band wrapped it up with a suitable vibrating, face-melting finish.

"Thank you! God bless you all! Goodnight!"

Sweaty and invigorated, Novah followed the lead singer back off stage and down the steps, completely awed by what had just happened. The man closed the door behind him sealing off the crowd noise. D'kob was gone. It was just the two of them.

"Awesome, wasn't it?" the man stated as a foregone conclusion.

"Beyond awesome. I've seen a lot of amazing things in the past three days but this takes the cake," Novah panted.

The man handed Novah a towel. "This is one of my favorite hobbies," the man said. "It's been awhile since I've had the time and the facilities to do it, so I'm making up for lost time. Music makes the universe go 'round." He pulled off his headband, and to Novah's surprise, most of his hair. It was a wig. Underneath was a cleanly-cropped, professional cut of slightly-mussed, dirty-brown hair that matched his similarly colored goatee. The wig had also hid a multitude of thin scars which extended down the man's forehead and scalp. This man had clearly seen battle.

He tossed the wig aside, dried off his hands on the towel, then extended his hand to Novah.

"I'm the Lord Commander," he stated clearly. His tone, grip, and posture left no doubt about the man's authority, in spite of his smaller than average stature. The four words came out with a smile, though, setting Novah at a respectful ease.

"I'm Novah, but you already know that," Novah replied shaking the Lord Commander's strong, warm hand.

Novah had been tired after a long, exciting day, but the music had invigorated him. The Lord Commander's presence invigorated him too. He was surprised, but pleased, that the Lord Commander was human. He felt in his bones that the Lord Commander was a great man, even though he couldn't find the words in his own head to explain why.

"Thanks for joining me on stage, Novah. We have much to talk about, however, and it is time your patience was rewarded with proper explanations. Let's get cleaned up first. Out the door to your left is a dressing room complete with a primitive shower. As much as I appreciate a good bath, there's something to be said for a shower. There are some fresh clothes for you there. Once you're ready head back to the bridge. I'll meet you there in thirty minutes. Is that enough time?"

"Yes, sir." The *sir* just popped out of Novah's mouth naturally.

"Very well then. See you in half an hour."

They parted company and Novah headed to the dressing room. The shower was pleasingly warm and even though he'd bathed less than an hour earlier the shower felt needed after the on-stage session of adrenaline and hot lights. He washed his hair, removing the tiny remnants left over from his haircut. He dried himself off with the large, wool towel, and found a fresh set of clothing folded up neatly on the counter. The trousers were black, and the pull-over top was a thick, white, long-sleeved garment of a material that he thought was the same as what D'kob wore. It was tastefully form-fitting, and gave a look of formality. The collar was snug around the circumference of his neck. Looking at himself in the mirror, he was pleased. *Certainly better than blue coveralls*, he noted to himself.

He walked back the way he came, and since he had a few minutes to spare, opened the stage door and went back up onto the stage. The stage, formerly filled with amps and instruments, cables and set pieces, was now simply a flat black platform devoid of anything. The theater was completely empty. There wasn't a trace of human existence. There was no trash. There was no clue that a concert had ever happened less than an hour ago. Novah walked back up the stairs to the back entrance of the theater. There was nobody. Where had all the people gone? He thought for a moment, then snapped his fingers.

"NICOLE, where did all of the people in the theater go to?"

The response was immediate and just as soothingly pleasant as always.

There were no people except for you and the Lord Commander. All in attendance were independent holographic projections.

Holograms! Novah shook his head and made his way to the closest teleportation chamber. "Bridge."

Seemingly before the word was completely out of his mouth Novah stood on the bridge platform. The door opened and he stepped out. The Lord Commander and D'kob stood together expectantly. The Lord Commander was in a uniform very similar to Novah's, only all-white. A thick blood red stripe was embroidered on his shirt extending diagonally from his left shoulder to right hip. He looked every part a commander.

"Right on time, Novah. Please join us in the tactical lounge," said the Lord Commander, pointing to a thin door thirty feet behind the command chair.

Novah nodded and followed the pair into a reasonably-large-but-not-cavernous room. It, like the bridge, was brightly lit and futuristic, in stark contrast to the strange retro-Roman feel of the rest of the ship. The room was appointed with modern, leather chairs and a significant white oval table about twenty feet long and six feet across at the widest point. D'kob pressed a hidden button under the table causing the table to telescope upon itself from all directions until its size was a more intimate four-by-eight. The Lord Commander sat on one side, while D'kob and Novah sat across from him.

"Now then," began the Lord Commander, "I'm going to talk a lot and explain many things. Some things you will understand immediately, some things you will not. This will amount to a long history lesson though I will leave out parts that have no bearing on our purpose. I know that D'kob has told you some of this, but I will re-emphasize it. There are also things I will say that even D'kob does not know. Shall we begin?"

Novah and D'kob both nodded.

The Lord Commander interlaced his fingers in front of him on the table. He spoke with clarity, narratively, in a warm, easy tone.

"The Khamek have an ancient and rich history dating far back before humanity on Earth. One of the pillars of their faith centered on the Prime Single. The Prime Single was a thing of legend and rumor for thousands of Khamek years. The Khamek tradition states that the Prime Single, or K'vlo'ki in their language, is the DNA of God. The legend further states that the Prime Single is *not* Khamek but instead aligns with some other species – a species with which the Khamek must partner with in order to reach V'laha, the Khamek name for Paradise."

D'kob nodded as the Lord Commander spoke, giving his silent agreement.

"It wasn't until the Khamek achieved interstellar travel capabilities that the legend became anything more than a traditional story," continued the Lord Commander. "Once the Khamek began explorations they found artifacts that referenced the Prime Single, and eventually were able to divine the location. Buried deep beneath the ruins of the planet named X'los 5, which had been rendered uninhabitable by its expanding, dying star, was a magnificent cavern full of ancient writings which included the galactic coordinates of V'laha. More amazing than that, a single small cryogenically frozen test tube was prominently displayed in the center of the cavern. It was the paramount find of the Khamek civilization. X'los continued to slowly expand and the Khamek scientists determined that the star would continue to expand for only a few more years before collapsing and going supernova. However, the Khamek scientists were reluctant to remove anything from the cavern, as it and all of what it contained was considered a sacred place. So, in an engineering feat still marveled at, the Khamek decided to remove the entire cavern from X'los 5. Over the span of a three years, deep, careful cuts were made into the planet's surface. Finally, on a day that has been celebrated since as Recovery Day, in yet another masterpiece of physics and science, two-thousand of the largest Khamek ships gathered in orbit. Massive cabling focused from space to the planet's surface and below, and in a process that took a little more than a day, the entire carved cube, roughly half a mile on each side, was lifted out of the surface of X'los 5. The cube was brought to the Khamek home world, set down carefully, and cordoned off for study by every branch of science and academia. For another century Khamek scientists studied the cavern and the cryogenic device. Entire universities were built around the study of the inscriptions found there."

The Lord Commander tilted his head toward D'kob. "Do I have this correct so far, D'kob?"

D'kob nodded politely. "Yes, Lord Commander." D'kob appreciated the courtesy, but both he and the Lord Commander knew that it was a silly question. The Lord Commander's memory had never faltered.

The Lord Commander continued. "Eventually, the great Tome of the Prime Single, the scientific summary of the knowledge gained from the cavern, was published. The summary conclusion stated unequivocally that the contents of the cryogenically frozen test tube amounted to a single spermatozoa. Most of the inscriptions discovered outlined the genome. A genome aligning most closely with a species the Khamek had first contacted many hundreds of years earlier, the Humans of Earth. The genetic architecture was a 99.13% match. The Prime Single had a pair of extra chromosomes that the Earth humans didn't have, but the purpose and function of this extra pair was not captured in any of the inscriptions. The instructions, however, were perfectly clear: to reach V'laha and their god, this seed was to be planted on Earth. There were explicit instructions about what age, size, genetic profile, and general temperament the host incubator – or I prefer to use the term host mother – was required. So the Khamek had a mission: find the right human woman, impregnate her with the Prime Single, and do everything they could to make sure the pregnancy came to term and the child was born. This child was promised to be what the Khamek call the *L'kos Vzzekk*, or The One Who Shall Guide."

He paused once more. "Still with me?" Both nodded, totally engrossed by the story and the storyteller. The Lord Commander went on. "I'll skip ahead a bit."

"Roughly two millennia ago a woman meeting the requirements was found after a global search. Khamek visited her shortly after she grew to child-bearing age. The finest Khamek psychologist appeared to her, calmed her, and assured her that she was special, and had been chosen to give birth to a special child. She was then sedated, taken aboard a Khamek medical craft, and artificially inseminated. She was returned and once again it was explained that she was now carrying a child that would be a glory to a whole civilization. She carried to term and gave birth to a healthy son."

The Lord Commander paused, looked at D'kob, and then at Novah. "I am the L'kos Vzzekk. I was that child."

D'kob reverently placed his forehead down on the table. "D'kob hails L'kos Vzzekk."

A chortle came out of Novah's mouth. "D'kob, don't believe this silly story. You're smart – do a little math. There's no way he's over two thousand years old. If he's human he'd be long dead by now."

The Lord Commander turned to Novah and smiled. "You are correct, Novah, yet I have been dead already." The Lord Commander rolled back the cuffs on his sleeves, and laid his arms, palms up, out on the table towards Novah. "Do you see these dime-sized scars on both sides of my wrists?" The Lord Commander rotated his forearms to show the scarring. "Much of the imagery you are accustomed to is wrong with regards to these scars. The Romans did not nail those doomed to crucifixion through the hands. They nailed through the wrists." He paused, driving a stare from his bright blue eyes into Novah's green ones. "To Khamek, I am L'kos Vzzekk. To humans, I am known as Jesus Christ."

CHAPTER THIRTEEN

It wasn't long before S'heil realized that the *R'ptyr* wasn't on Earth. The displacement tracking failed just before the Depth. No submarine, ocean buoy or other technology was able to discern anything abnormal.

"There must be a method of locating the *R'ptyr*," he stated calmly as K'jahl walked up to him.

K'jahl stood stone-like, mentally calculating the odds of S'heil's response to his coming question. He finally mustered the courage to ask.

"What if the *R'ptyr* is beyond locating?" K'jahl asked.

S'heil lowered his voice to a near whisper. "A contingency plan must be formed. If the *R'ptyr* cannot be located, Khamek must resort to involuntary harvest."

Involuntary harvest. The two words caused K'jahl's eyes to widen.

"Admiral, involuntary harvest is prohibited. S'heil would be recalled and executed," whispered K'jahl.

S'heil nodded slightly. "The humans will not tolerate any alteration of the deal. Humans would self-misadventure before submitting voluntarily. S'heil sees no other option. S'heil's mission is to capture the *R'ptyr*, yet the greater mission is to reach V'laha. Without the fuel, there is no chance. Without the Humans, there is no fuel. Without N'ala 3, there are no Humans, and N'ala 3 is doomed. Better to save one species than lose both. Besides, recalling S'heil from V'laha would be a difficult task."

"Involuntary harvest is prohibited. Also, S'heil has already noted that it is impossible for Khamek to intercept the Human nuclear arsenal prior to massive misadventure. K'jahl can think of no way to mitigate this. However, there may be another, simpler, permissible option," stated K'jahl. "S'heil could attempt to contact the Lord Commander and have the Lord Commander command D'kob to S'heil's cause."

S'heil's right hand went to his holster with habitual efficiency. Before he could draw, however, K'jahl had closed the distance and placed his own hand over S'heil's.

"Admiral," spoke K'jahl softly, "K'jahl does not wish to transfer to K'jahl's clone quite yet. Please do not draw S'heil's pistol. Remember, K'jahl's role is to advise Admiral S'heil. Sometimes that advice may seem unsavory." K'jahl slowly withdrew his hand. S'heil did the same.

"S'heil is impressed with K'jahl's reflexes," S'heil said somewhat sheepishly.

S'heil paced back and forth along the bridge, his hands clasped behind his back. *Would the Lord Commander consider ordering D'kob to fulfill S'heil's obligation? After all, the obligation wasn't S'heil's, really, it was a Khamek obligation. Surely the Lord Commander would understand. Saving humanity was the preferred option. Would the Lord Commander let his ego — his title of L'kos V'zzekk stand in the way? How much does the Lord Commander know about the deal anyway?* To S'heil's recollection the Lord Commander was never involved in any of the negotiations with the Humans.

He continued to pace trying to piece it all together.

The Lord Commander commands D'kob, who has the R'ptyr. A great deal of effort was invested to keep S'heil from acquiring the R'ptyr. Why? S'heil's intentions are not outside the scope of the deal. Everyone with a sigil gets saved. Khamek receive the remainder for the needed fuel to get to V'laha. Either the Lord Commander wants all Humans to die, has another plan for extraction, or....

"K'jahl," spoke S'heil, "is there *any* possible way, apart from the use of the *R'ptyr*, that enough Humans can be extracted from N'ala 3 that would secure sufficient genetic diversity?"

"No, Admiral," K'jahl replied, "there are no other Khamek ships in range capable of supporting more than a hundred or so Humans. There are only a dozen Khamek ships of marginal size that could be at N'ala 3 before its destruction. Most of those ships could only hold a few tens of Humans.

S'heil frowned. "How many Humans can the *R'ptyr* truly transport?"

K'jahl did a quick mental calculation. "The *R'ptyr* is designed to carry 50,000 Humans in great comfort for the four year journey to A'ala. With less comfort, the number of Humans could be increased to the intersecting line between ship space and extra supplies needed to sustain the population. Water is the main issue. Human requirements for water are high. Extra water would take up considerable space. K'jahl estimates that an additional 50,000 Humans could be transported on the *R'ptyr*, though with a significantly decreased comfort level."

S'heil rubbed his temple. "Perhaps the Lord Commander will listen to a compromise solution. The Lord Commander is Human, therefore logically would not desire Human extinction. The Lord Commander has no other means to extract humans, else the Lord Commander would not have worked so hard to acquire the *R'ptyr*. The only logical conclusion for the Lord Commander's actions is that the Lord Commander has issues with the agreed upon method of Human selection."

"The sigils?" inquired K'jahl.

"Yes, the sigils. The Lord Commander must know of the terms of the deal yet is unwilling to accept those terms. The Lord Commander wants to select *different* Humans. This is understandable. However, S'heil still has an advantage over the Lord Commander that might force compromise."

K'jahl nodded. "A tactical advantage."

"Yes," beamed S'heil, "the *R'ptyr* must return to N'ala 3. The *R'ptyr* must land for extraction. The *R'ptyr* must also de-cloak in order to allow boarding. During this phase S'heil could make boarding very difficult. S'heil cannot damage the *R'ptyr* but can certainly cause misadventure for any Human attempting to enter the *R'ptyr.*"

"Shall K'jahl send out the system-wide communication beacon?" asked K'jahl.

"Yes," replied S'heil, "Khamek will wait at N'ala 3. The Lord Commander will answer. The Lord Commander knows a reply is required. Send the following: Lord Commander, please respond. S'heil wishes to negotiate a peaceful solution to Human extraction."

"As S'heil wishes," replied K'jahl, who set to the task immediately.

S'heil stood on the bridge in contemplation, hopeful but uncertain. *S'heil must still pursue other options*, he thought to himself.

CHAPTER FOURTEEN

*T*he Jesus? From the Bible?" asked Novah incredulously. "I don't believe it."

The Lord Commander turned to D'kob. "It is always the same with humanity, D'kob. They do not believe until they see. Some do not even believe *after* they see. I have always been bothered by this. The math would be much easier if belief was a constant."

He turned back to Novah. "Yes, the very same. Born of an artificially-inseminated virgin, died on the cross, and came back to life shortly thereafter. Extra chromosomes have their privileges."

Novah struggled to parse the turn of events. His thoughts were like wheels spinning in the mud of his mind unable to move forward. Every time he believed he might have something to say the words slipped away. He stared blankly at Jesus, his mouth perpetually caught between speaking and remaining silent.

"The sooner you get the belief thing out of the way the sooner we can get on with the mission," Jesus said with a smile.

Novah continued to sit there, silently dumbfounded. Tears began to stream down his cheeks. He couldn't face the man across the table. His soul burned with shame and confusion. Jesus and D'kob waited patiently. Novah finally wilted under the pressure of Jesus' eternal stare and managed to speak in a quiet, shaking voice.

"I don't know if you are really Jesus or not, but I do know you are a very powerful and important man. I can feel that in my bones. I just don't want you to be Jesus, because if you are, I might explode in shame. I have stolen. I have lusted. I have murdered. I have inspired others to murder. If you are who you say you are, and all of the Sunday-school stories are true, you are going to send me straight to hell. Do not pass go, do not collect two-hundred dollars, do not get to ride on a fancy alien spaceship."

"You're not going to hell, Novah," replied Jesus with a smile and light sigh. He turned to D'kob. "Will you bring two glasses of water, please?"

"Certainly, Lord Commander."

After what seemed like an eternity to Novah, D'kob returned with two glasses of water and put them before the Lord Commander. The Lord Commander pushed one to Novah.

"Have a sip of water, Novah."

Novah's shaking hand reached out, took the glass, and took a sip of the water. It was cold and pure, and tasted really good. He set the glass back down and Jesus reached for it.

As Novah watched through watery eyes, Jesus swirled his index finger in the glass. Instantly, the water turned a deep, rich red. "Have another sip."

Novah took the glass again and sipped, discovering that the water had changed to wine. It was the best thing Novah had ever tasted.

"That isn't a miracle, Novah. It's physics. You've seen amazing technology in the past couple of days. It's all science. Just because you can't understand it doesn't mean it is magic or divine. Every miracle is applied physics. Even this."

With snake-like quickness, Jesus reached out and snatched Novah's hand. With his other hand, Jesus took the other glass of water and splashed it right into Novah's face.

Novah felt the hand, felt the water, and then for the briefest period of time felt nothing. It was if his mind and body were rebooting. As the water trickled down his face, it felt as if he was shedding his skin. His shame and angst melted from him. All of the guilt was gone. He felt reborn.

"My Lord!" he exclaimed.

"Lord Commander," replied Jesus. "Let's leave the deity stuff aside, at least for now. Lord Commander or Jesus is fine. I suffer the Lord Commander title because the Khamek insist. This is technically a military mission after all."

"All of the feelings I was feeling...they are just gone?!" asked Novah. "What's the physics in that?"

Jesus smiled. "I have just reversed the polarity of your negative Z'korz."

"Z'korz again! I have so many questions," Novah blurted.

"Yes, I know. They will all be answered in time. I'll take a few more minutes and continue on with the history lesson. You'll understand more. Then you shall sleep, and tomorrow we shall speak a little more. Then I'll give you your mission."

Novah was intrigued. "Okay," he said simply.

"When I was five years old," Jesus began, "I started to realize I saw things differently than other people. I *literally* saw things differently. I could *see* more. I could see, for the lack of a better term at the time, a glowing particulate cloud around every person. Sometimes thin sections would drift off and touch something, or touch someone else, or join in a river of multiple sections. It appeared random. I didn't know what to make of it. After much meditation, I saw that this vision allowed me to piece together how seemingly disparate parts of life fit together. I could see how actions caused reactions sometimes weeks later." He sipped some wine.

"When I turned thirteen, I was alone in an olive orchard early one evening thinking, as I am prone to do. That's where I had my first contact with the Khamek. I wasn't afraid. I was told that I could learn about what I am seeing – what the Khamek call Z'korz. I was told that I was very special and that I had talents no other human had. They asked me to come with them. I told them I would after I said goodbye to my parents, who were remarkably understanding. The next evening I boarded a Khamek craft and departed the earth." Jesus paused for another drink of wine. Novah and D'kob sat in rapt attention.

"I was taken to a Khamek science vessel where I studied for the four years it took to return to the Khamek home world. Once there I was given my own laboratory. The Khamek see Z'korz as sort of a random cloud, like I did at first. They sense it, and have instrumented it, and to a primitive extent can control it – yet they have absolutely no clue about its true nature. To the Khamek, the Z'korz is an important construct mainly because they learned to harness it for interstellar travel and later for Z'korz transference to clones. The impact of Z'korz to interstellar travel provided the means to reach V'laha. I was able to figure out what the Z'korz really is."

"And what is it?" Novah interjected.

"Complicated," replied Jesus, "extraordinarily complicated. It is quantum physics which by its nature is difficult to explain. Human science has only recently began discovering the mysteries of the quantum universe. Most of the quantum universe is invisible to humans. It's hard to study what you can't observe. Most quantum mechanics cannot be observed by humans – yet at least – because much of it is interdimensional. There are more than three dimensions – or four if you count time as you do currently. There are actually eleven dimensions. The Z'korz particles span seven of them. It took me three years to figure that out."

"So you're not really holy – you're just a scientist!" exclaimed Novah.

"I'm a physicist. My earthly 'holiness' derives from being able to do things that others find impossible. I can use the physics of the Z'korz to manipulate matter. That being said, I have seen too much to discount the existence of God. Humans are more advanced than apes. Khamek are more advanced than terrestrial Humans. I am a Human more advanced than Khamek. My genetic father – as indicated by the Prime Single – is human-like and more advanced than me. At each level the scope of what can be seen and controlled increases, into multiple infinities," Jesus explained. "I have mathematically proven the existence of the ultimate, big-G God. But as I said let's not get all hung up on the deity conversation. I need to explain the nature of Z'korz to you."

"I take it this Z'korz thing is very important," Novah observed.

"It is," replied Jesus. "There is nothing that I've found in my studies that has greater impact on the lives of sentient creatures. I'll explain it, but keep in mind that this is highly advanced quantum physics. I'm going to grossly simplify things so that you will understand. Do not be offended. Even the most intelligent person on earth would not be able to conceptualize the true nature of the Z'korz."

Novah and D'kob nodded in unison, both eager to hear what the Lord Commander had to say.

"Z'korz particles are created by thought. Z'korz particles come in two flavors – positive and negative. As you might suspect, positive thoughts create positive particles, and negative from negative. At the beginning of each and every thought neutral Z'korz particles are created. I use the term "created" to indicate that they appear. They always existed but explaining that is beyond the scope of this conversation. Anyway, the particles are created, and the nature of the thought determines the spin of the particles. Think of the thought process as a pipe angled toward the ground and each Z'korz particle as a marble. The top of the pipe is the thought genesis, and the exit of the pipe is the thought endpoint, which may or may not end with an action. A negative thought will create a forward spin on the marble so that it rolls through the pipe faster. A positive thought will create a backspin on the marble. It is slightly slower to move through the pipe but because it takes more effort, the marble is larger, and thus exits with the same energy. Negative thoughts are easier thoughts. Negative Z'korz are created quickly and easily. Positive thoughts require more effort so are slower to create, yet each positive Z'korz contains the same energy as a negative Z'korz – with one notable exception. Hyper-Z'korz can be created through the overpowering of the original Z'korz spin. If a negative thought is turned to a positive one prior to the resulting action the energy of the new positive Z'korz is greatly increased. Are you with me so far?"

"I think so," replied Novah.

"Yes, Lord Commander," D'kob replied in kind.

"Ok then, let's see what you have learned. Novah, there is a cul-de-sac with four families in it. It becomes known that one of the families has no food and is starving. One neighbor ignores the situation. One neighbor immediately rushes over and provides food. The third neighbor ignores the situation at first but eventually decides to also provide food. Which neighbor has produced the highest energy Z'korz?"

"If I understand correctly," answered Novah, "the neighbor who chooses not to care produces negative Z'korz. The neighbor who rushes over to provide food produces positive Z'korz. But the energy of each is the same. The third neighbor, who changed his thought from negative to positive prior to the action, creates the Z'korz with the highest energy."

"Very good, Novah," replied Jesus. "There are multiple variables even in that sample case but you have learned the general principle. The meta-point is that the act of *overcoming* negative thought is the most beneficial in terms of positive Z'korz production. Other types of thoughts and actions that generate positive Z'korz are prayer, music, belief, and love.

"Now we move up a level. Each Z'korz particle is part of a Z'korz field, an energy envelope which surrounds all sentient beings. The charge associated with this field is dependent on the dominate charge of the Z'korz particles. If most of the Z'korz are positive, the field charge is positive, and vice-versa. These fields continually build. There are two levels – a person's primary Z'korz level, and a secondary. The primary builds much slower than the secondary over the span of a lifetime. The primary field has a very narrow quantum envelope – it stays very near the body and never strays. It can never mix with any other Z'korz. The secondary, however, builds much more quickly, and unlike the primary, will expand around a person in a much, much more nebulous field. This Z'korz field is also highly elastic – it can stretch over vast distances. Imagine a ball of taffy. That is a person's secondary Z'korz field. Pieces can be pulled and stretched outwards. They can blend with other Z'korz fields from other people. Those are called Z'korz anchors. They can also anchor on inanimate objects. Any person at any given time could have thousands of Z'korz field anchors. Every action you take creates a Z'korz anchor, either to a person or object. Anchors to persons are stronger than anchors to objects, just like a magnet can be attached strongly to another magnet, or weakly to a regular piece of metal."

"But what do these Z'korz fields do?" asked Novah.

"Z'korz fields are quantum energy. They allow for the transformation of matter. Manipulation of Z'korz is how water can be transformed into wine, milk, mercury, whatever. Molecular structures can be realigned and the forces within them. Quantum forces trump Newtonian forces in most cases. By manipulating Z'korz energy I can change the surface tension of water to that of concrete, allowing it to be walked on. Z'korz fields also determine if positive or negative things happen to you. Whenever you talk of 'coincidences,' 'luck' or 'karma,' you are actually talking about the impact of Z'korz fields and anchors. The formula surrounding the forces involved with the manipulation of Z'korz energy are extraordinarily complex. The formulas surrounding non-purposeful Z'korz interactions are several orders of magnitude more so. I had to invent a whole new branch of mathematics to explain it."

"So there's no such thing as luck?" asked Novah.

"Correct. Many results in a person's life, though not all, are a result of the Z'korz field they generate and how that field interacts with the rest of the world."

"How come good things happen to bad people, and bad things happen to good people then?" Novah inquired.

"Good things and bad things happen to everybody because everyone has good and bad thoughts and do good and bad things. Plus, Z'korz works outside the bounds of time. Humans tend to view cause and effect very narrowly and in time terms. Z'korz doesn't work that way. For example, a person may make a habit of doing bad things for a long time, generating a sizeable negative Z'korz field that is anchoring to people and things all around that person's life. Then, for whatever reason, that person decides to change, to become a better person. They could become a completely wonderful person, building positive Z'korz, but that does not wipe out the negative Z'korz they created before, nor the anchors. Eventually the math dictates a breakage in the secondary negative Z'korz. Breakages are the energy conservation mechanism. The Z'korz breakage might manifest itself, through all of the interconnected forces of all of the negative Z'korz in that person's life, as a tree breaking in a windstorm and smashing into the person, injuring or killing them. Because humans view cause and effect in a narrow time window the reaction is *He was such a good person. How could this have happened? It makes no sense...life is random.*"

Novah grew skeptical. "So then, you're telling me that if a nun gets raped, she had it coming?"

"I made no mention of proportionality. A nun is still human and has had negative thoughts and taken negative actions. Your typical nun has a mathematically very small chance of her negative Z'korz manifesting itself as rape. What you must remember is that the Z'korz does not govern *all* things that happen to you. A nun could be raped simply because her path crossed that of a rapist. She was not to blame."

Novah sighed. "This all sounds very complex. How can you control this Z'korz?"

"First of all, I can see it. Seeing it gives me the opportunity to study it. To understand it. This is a quantum leap – no pun intended – of understanding far, far beyond a terrestrial human. To humans, the Z'korz is simply coincidence or luck. To Khamek, the Z'korz is known as a scientific fact, and can be controlled in only the crudest, simplest ways. To me, the Z'korz is an amazing tool. It took me ten years of study to formulize the Z'korz and to learn how it worked. It took me several years beyond that to learn how to reliably control it and bend it to my will in simple ways. By the time I returned to Earth, I could control Z'korz fields to the point where I could control matter and the perception of life and death. It has taken me all of the time since I left Earth after my crucifixion to master it, and even with that I am sure I do not understand all of the special cases."

Jesus took another sip of wine. "The extra pair of chromosomes I possess gives me the ability to see Z'korz fields and gives me the intelligence to understand them, in addition to accelerated healing and significantly enhanced longevity."

The middle section of the table transformed into a flat view screen.

In the middle flashed a small green square with the word "answer" under it. The *R'ptyr*'s voice spoke.

Incoming communication from S'heil sent via broad-system transmission.

"Thus ends the lesson," said Jesus. "We'll talk more tomorrow."

The green square continued to flash.

"Are you going to answer that?" Novah asked.

"No. S'heil can wait. Meet me in the library in the morning."

D'kob showed Novah to his quarters, one of the several rooms just aft of the main bridge along the port and starboard sides. Novah slipped into the narrow bed exhausted from an exciting day. His brain hurt from trying to process everything. He thought he would never get to sleep. That was his last thought prior to awaking the next morning.

As he dressed the recollection of the previous day flooded back into his brain. He felt overwhelmed. He left his quarters and stepped into the teleporter room directly across the hall.

"Library," he said.

Novah stepped out of the teleporter into a small circular marble foyer which had a single regular wooden door opposite him. He walked forward and opened the door, utterly shocked at the great three-level library that spread out before him. Marble columns supported the elevated floors above and matching marble staircases climbed to his left and right upwards to the higher levels. The ceiling was softly curved above the entire canyon of stacks, appearing as one giant source of light, beaming down upon the rows and rows of bookshelves with a warm and pleasant ambience. At the very far end of the library, a good two hundred yards away, he saw a tiny figure who appeared to be sitting at a desk. Novah began walking towards the end, eyes cast upward, soaking in the pure majesty of the collection. It would not have surprised him to learn that the library contained the whole of human knowledge and understanding. At the end of his walk he found Jesus reading a thick, intricately hand-written book. He looked up to meet Novah.

"Good morning," said Jesus.

"Good morning," replied Novah. "What are you reading?"

"I'm reminiscing a little. This is a mid-15th century version of the

Bible."

"Is everything there as you remember?"

Jesus chuckled lightly. "It aligns pretty well historically, though selective editing has taken some of the flavor out of it. It comes across as more of a severely editorialized and abridged version of history. That's to be expected given the myriad of personal and organizational agendas present in the creation of this manuscript."

"There are some that would call that blasphemy were it to come from any other mouth but yours," noted Novah.

Jesus nodded. "Of course. People are deeply invested in their beliefs. People gasp and moan and throw out the words blasphemy and heretic when belief systems collide, or when new data is found that forces a person to question or reconsider their beliefs or conclusions. It is this type of inflexibility that has led to burnings at the stake, imprisonments, and even wars. The science camp and the religion camp of humanity have eternally been at odds with each other with only a very few enlightened people ever discovering that they must coexist and grow with each other. Science grows with discovery. So does faith. A lack of growth is stagnation. Stagnation leads to rot, which leads to death. Faith and science have both been strangled by those who grip too tightly to the status quo, fearing that learning something new, particularly from the opposite side, will undermine their beliefs. They hide this fear in every variety of language, using words as a blindfold to keep from accidentally seeing something they don't want to reconcile with their beliefs or data model.

"I could return to Earth right now, turn water into wine through Z'korz manipulation as I showed you, and many if not most Christians would still insist that it is a holy miracle no matter how much of the science I showed them. That which can't be understood is most often termed miraculous. To a dog, turning on a light bulb is a miracle. To a terrestrial human, turning water into wine is a miracle. It all depends on how deeply the physics of the universe is understood. I could also spend hours lecturing the best and brightest scientific minds on the mathematics and proofs of God's infinite existence, but because they wouldn't understand it, either by choice or through not comprehending the science, it would be dismissed. Such is the way people are and have always been. Reconciling the two belief structures is difficult if not impossible for most."

"Are there things *you* don't understand?" asked Novah.

Jesus let forth a great chuckle, genuinely bemused by the question. "Oh goodness, of course! The universe is a massive and miraculous thing. The planet V'laha is a miracle in my eyes. The entire planet is a planet within a planet, the interior one a shifting quantum chamber, phasing from dimension to dimension. Travel there in a craft and one day it'll appear to be a normal planet, but on most days it will appear to be an empty shell. V'laha can only be reliably reached at the correct intersection of space-time and quantum Z'korz phases. This is what S'heil doesn't understand. He believes it is simply there like any other planet. He's going to do awful things to reach V'laha only to find it isn't there. I have told him this many times, yet he refuses to believe. Only through me can V'laha be reached. Only I can see the correct Z'korz pathways to V'laha's current quantum phase. I don't understand at all how the planet moves between phases – I can only track it. Beyond that little miracle is the surface itself which I can't even begin to describe other than as a great honeycomb of embedded concurrent realities. Worlds within a world. It is within these worlds that souls spend eternity."

"My brain hurts already," sighed Novah.

Jesus nodded. "Understanding these things is not easy, particularly when you don't know what questions to ask."

"Since you mentioned souls, I presume, then, that souls are real?"

"Yes. The term soul, however, is simply an unscientific name for an individual's Z'korz primary envelope," Jesus replied.

Novah let out a heavy, frustrated sigh. Jesus smiled, and continued.

"I'll try to simplify it for you," he said. "Just as soon as the brain starts firing conscious thought in the womb a person's Z'korz field begins to accumulate. As we covered before, this field is created through thought – is the product of thought. Thought is what makes sentient creatures who they are. You are what you think by definition. You grow and your Z'korz grows with you. Your Z'korz *is* you. When your body dies your Z'korz remains for a couple of hours until it realizes it is no longer being fed by new thoughts. At that point your primary Z'korz floats up – literally – into the sky until it reaches the planetary Z'korz quantum shell.

"The what?" said Novah, struggling to understand.

"A place that isn't Earth but isn't paradise. Limbo. While there is a sense of identity there is no sense of time. Furthermore, there is a sensation of being part of a greater whole. There these Z'korz wait until I can take them to V'laha where they will reconstitute as quantum beings and feel as if no time has passed whatsoever."

"If you're humanity's greatest teacher, I must be humanity's worst student, because I'm still not getting it," Novah whined.

"It has always been the case that explaining concepts to those without sufficient context for understanding is difficult. In the old days I used parables to show things in contexts that people could understand. People still rarely understood. Every parable can be misinterpreted, particularly as society and the meanings of words change. That's why I love science as I do. There's very little room for interpretation for those looking to find a real answer."

Jesus stood up and pointed at a row of seventeen books on the shelf behind him, each volume roughly three fingers thick, bound in deep red leather with gold lettering on the spines.

"These volumes contain everything I've discovered about the Z'korz. Most of what they hold is formulae and proofs. There are parts, however, that explain the things I talked about yesterday and today in much, much greater and significantly more complex detail. I've also thrown in some philosophy and other topics as spice to break up the math. There's even some autobiographical information in them you might find interesting. Read them, if you wish, when you have the time. Or do not. There are principles in these books which will cause you to question your very existence and purpose – particularly the discussion and mathematics around Z'korz anchor breakages."

"Sounds difficult to understand," offered Novah.

"Oh, it is. I'll give you a quick, simple example anchor breakage you can relate to and you will see that what you think is random is just the result of very complex Z'korz anchor breakage mechanics. Do you remember that valentine's card you wrote to Susan when you were a freshman in high school?"

Novah blushed. "Yes. Susan Cortez. She was a senior, stuck in my lab class for some reason. I never gave her the valentine though. How did you know about that?"

"Volume 6, Section 43," Jesus said with a smirk. "Look it up sometime. Anyway, you threw the valentine away because you were afraid of being rejected. Yet in writing it and in the sincere, teen love you expressed in it, you created a strong Z'korz anchor with Susan. What you don't know is that even though you threw it away she found it anyway when she tossed out a milk carton at the end of the class. She never said anything. She didn't really like you but didn't want to hurt your feelings. Over the years that anchor grew in mass because you would sometimes think about her and that valentine, and she would sometimes think of you. Well, a little over a year ago, the anchor achieved enough mass to break. Susan worked as a stocking clerk at a grocery store. One day, distracted by the call she received from her doctor that morning telling her she had cancer, she made a mistake. She placed a box of chocolate bars near the door of the store, something she had been told not to do. A certain someone we both know was tricked into stealing one of those candy bars. Susan was fired. Sick and saddened, she wanted to go home to Missouri. Her husband, Lawrence, asked for and received and transfer to Fort Leonard Wood. However, even though the anchor broke, you still sometimes think of her and she still sometimes thinks of you. A new anchor has formed and shall continue to grow until she dies, which will be soon."

"What will happen to the anchor when she dies?" Novah asked grimly.

"It will break, and math will happen, and you will understand why I told you this instead of scratching your head like you are doing now."

"I don't think I'll ever really understand," said Novah.

"Perhaps not," said Jesus. "Regardless of whether you understand or not, though, I've talked far too long and the time has come for you to take over."

"What do you mean, take over?" asked Novah.

"I have other matters to attend to. I am field-promoting to you Captain. This ship is yours. Your orders are to proceed to Earth, deal with S'heil, and collect 50,000 humans of your choosing. You will then transport them to A'ala and colonize that planet."

Novah's mouth dropped open and flapped closed a couple of times before he managed to find words. "But…but… I'm not qualified! I'm not a military guy! I don't know who to choose! I just happened to be the one who found D'kob. You should pick someone else…*anyone* else. I'm just…a nobody."

Jesus smiled at him, yet spoke in a calm, firm voice. "It was not coincidence D'kob crashed where he did. It was not by luck that you happened to be there. You are here because I chose you to be here. You will do as I command. You will make mistakes and you will learn from them. If you'd have paid any attention in Sunday school you'd have learned that I have a penchant for choosing regular people. You are not a nobody. You are one of the most important somebodies in all of human history now. I am counting on you to handle your mission with wisdom and care. I expect you to succeed. You *will* succeed."

Novah lowered his eyes.

"Look at me," ordered Jesus. Novah complied, trying to withstand the stare, trying to believe.

"The mantle of leadership now rests upon your shoulders. D'kob will be your first officer. Listen to him, for he is wise in all things Khamek. Yet you will crave human input as well. Since I will not be here personally I shall leave with you that which is most dear to me. Follow me to the bridge."

They walked out of the library and took the teleporter back to the bridge. Standing to the left of the command chair was the single most beautiful woman Novah had ever seen in his life. Long blonde hair framed an oval face highlighted by a pair of beaming blue eyes and delicate lips, which opened in a broad smile when she saw the two. Long legs carried her shapely frame to meet them half-way. She was dressed in uniform, only hers was a form-fitting light blue instead of white. When she reached Jesus, she embraced him.

"Grandfather," she said in NICOLE's voice much to Novah's surprise. Jesus grasped her shoulders and held her at arm's length.

"*Sangreal*, he said with a smile. "You grow more lovely each time I see you." She blushed lightly. "It was only last night, Grandfather!"

Jesus turned her to his side, an arm lovingly draped over her shoulders. He spoke to Novah.

"Captain Novah Burns, I would like to introduce you to Rebecca, my one hundred and first and last living descendant grandchild. The vessel of my blood and your companion on this mission."

Suddenly all of the meekness and insecurity in Novah was gone. He wanted this woman. He wanted to impress her even more than he wanted to impress the Lord Commander. He searched to find in himself a different level. *Jesus believes in me. I'll make her believe in me too.*

"It is my sincere pleasure to meet you, Rebecca," Novah said with a polite nod. "Welcome to the *R'ptyr*. We are honored to have you as our guest."

The woman raised an eyebrow. "I am not your guest, Captain. I am your assistant, at your service in the operation of the *R'ptyr*. I know this ship better than any human except Grandfather. You will notice that the *R'ptyr*'s voice is actually mine. Grandfather insisted." She playfully stared at Jesus through narrowed eyes. "I've spent the last two years here alone apart from Grandfather's occasional visits. I'm delighted to finally see another human face." The door to the teleporter opened and D'kob walked out, somewhat surprised to see yet another human. She turned slightly to face D'kob.

"V'ledz kozzilk mek logrank'la Khamek," she spoke with a broad smile.

"Zaklaz," D'kob replied with a deep bow, impressed with her greeting and her knowledge of native Khamek. Jesus introduced the two formally.

"Now then," spoke Jesus, "S'heil would likely wait around forever but we have missions to complete, so you must see what he wants, Novah. I am off to meet my fleet." He held out his hand, which Novah took. "Good luck, Novah," he said with a smile and ironic wink. "Oh,

I almost forgot! I left a small box in your quarters, the contents of which you might find useful."

"What's in it?" asked Novah.

Jesus leaned in and whispered into Novah's ear. "Blood and the world."

Confused, Novah stood silent.

"I'll be monitoring your progress," Jesus continued. "D'kob, I'm counting on you, too."

"The Lord Commander will not be disappointed," D'kob said.

Jesus then went to the teleporter room, turned with a wave, and vanished.

"Orders, Captain?" asked Rebecca.

That voice...oh that voice.

Novah's eye caught the flashing green button. S'heil's call was still unanswered.

"D'kob," asked Novah, "how long do you really expect S'heil will wait for a reply?"

"D'kob believes S'heil will wait until S'heil decides not to," D'kob replied unhelpfully.

"I want to think for a little bit before dealing with this S'heil guy. He can wait a little longer."

"A wise decision," said D'kob. "S'heil will be angry. Preparation will help."

"Ok then," said Novah. "I'm going to head to my quarters and think for half an hour. I'll see you both in a little bit."

Three and a half hours later Novah woke up, shocked he had accidentally slept so long. He jumped out of the thin yet comfortable bed. He took inventory of himself in the mirror. His uniform was wrinkleless much to his pleasure. His hair, however, was rustled. There was a comb in one of the small drawers and he was able to recompose his hair in such a way that he felt like he could be seen in public. By in public, he meant by Rebecca.

Jesus, what have you done to me? He thought quite literally. *You gave me arguably the most important job in human history yet provide quite possibly the greatest distraction in human history.* He would have to address this head-on. Later. Right now, S'heil needed to be dealt with. He walked out of his quarters to find D'kob and Rebecca chatting on the bridge.

"Captain on the bridge!" Rebecca snapped, assuming a straight, riveted posture, eyes forward. D'kob mimicked her, facing Novah.

Novah rolled his eyes. "At ease," he said. "Please don't do that again. D'kob, you are my friend, and Rebecca, I hope you will be my friend too. This military stuff isn't necessary."

"Yes, Captain," stated D'kob. Rebecca put her hand to her lips to suppress her grin.

"Stop it! No titles, at least not when it's just the three of us. Do you understand, or should I make it an order?"

"Understood, Captain," Rebecca said with a sparkle in her eyes.

Novah laughed. He couldn't help it. He was rested and the way Rebecca carried herself was intoxicatingly delightful.

Recovering, Novah remembered the task at hand. "Ok, let's see what…" Three Khamek came walking through the teleporter door. It was S'lace and her two associates. They were dressed in black *R'ptyr* uniforms.

"Captain," began S'lace, "the Lord Commander spoke with S'lace, V'kol and N'dim last evening and told S'lace, V'kol and N'dim of Captain Burns' mission. The Lord Commander took the oaths of S'lace, V'kol and N'dim, swearing absolute loyalty to the Lord Commander and Captain Burns. S'lace, V'kol and N'dim are most grateful, beg for the Captain's forgiveness, and wish to be used in whichever way the Captain sees fit."

Novah raised an eyebrow and turned to D'kob. "The Lord Commander vetted them? I don't have time to deal with double-agents. Wouldn't it be safer to keep them confined?"

"The Lord Commander told D'kob that the Lord Commander would speak with the prisoners and secure cooperation. D'kob trusts the Lord Commander and advises that Captain Burns do so as well."

"That's good enough for me," said Novah, relieved. "S'lace, V'kol, N'dim… D'kob is First Officer of the *R'ptyr*. The lovely woman next to him is Rebecca, granddaughter of the Lord Commander and my…" He paused for a moment. "What would you like to be, Rebecca?"

"Chief Engineer," she replied.

"Chief Engineer," continued Novah. "You will address them both as Commander."

"Yes, Captain," the three said in unison.

"Commander Rebecca, what roles would you advise for these three?"

"Captain, I do not know. I have only just now met them. May I interview them, learn their skillsets, and assign them roles afterwards?"

"Of course," replied Novah. "In the meantime I confer upon S'lace the rank of Lieutenant, and V'kol and N'dim the rank of sub-Lieutenant. Welcome aboard."

He wanted to ask Rebecca more question, just to get her to talk more. He refrained. He talked to the R'ptyr instead.

"NICOLE, please move us out of the atmosphere and into clear space. I don't want any interference in the picture when I talk to S'heil."

Engaging thrusters. The R'ptyr will be clear of Venus in thirty-seven seconds.

Novah looked at Rebecca, smiling. She winked.

CHAPTER FIFTEEN

S'heil sat patiently in his command chair. K'jahl would come by every few minutes like a comet on a slow orbit around his sun. They exchanged glances, each wondering when the hail would be answered, as they knew it would. Thirty hours after the original transmission was sent a reply finally came.

"On screen," S'heil commanded. The image appeared instantly but it wasn't the Lord Commander. It was a human and standing next to him was that vile creature D'kob.

"Admiral S'heil," said the human, "My name is Captain Novah Burns, commander of the *R'ptyr*. You have been hailing us for some time so I thought I'd see what it was you wanted."

Captain Burns? CAPTAIN? It took S'heil a dozen years at the Academy plus another 250 years of service to earn that title...and this...Human...had been handed the title for nothing. S'heil choked back the bile and tried to be pleasant.

"S'heil was expecting the Lord Commander," S'heil stated flatly.

"The Lord Commander has more pressing issues to attend to," Novah stated, completely oblivious to the fact he was insulting S'heil. "As the object of your long search has been the *R'ptyr*, the ship which I command, I am the one you want to talk to anyway."

Very well then, thought S'heil.

"*Captain*," S'heil bit off, "S'heil thanks the Captain for returning

S'heil's hail. There is much to discuss."

"What is it you would like to discuss?" inquired Novah.

As much as S'heil wanted to say *your terms of surrender*, he knew better. "S'heil would like to discuss the possibility of saving more human lives."

"Go on," replied Novah with a measured tone.

S'heil decided to be blunt. "An agreed-to arrangement with the Humans of earth has been in place for sixty years. Humans were given 50,000 sigils to dispense as deemed appropriate. The sigils indicate who among the humans would be allowed to board the *R'ptyr* for migration to A'ala. Khamek are an honorable species. S'heil desperately wishes to fulfill the agreement with the Humans. Since S'heil cannot fulfill the agreement without the *R'ptyr*, S'heil asks that Novah fulfill the agreement instead."

"Is that all?" asked Novah.

"Yes," replied S'heil.

"Oh, you said there was much to discuss. I was expecting more. I will consider your proposal and reply in twenty-four hours," Novah said.

S'heil seethed internally but simply nodded and cut off the transmission.

"The *R'ptyr*'s location has been pinpointed," spoke K'jahl.

"Good," replied S'heil, "though the location is irrelevant at this point. The Human will bring the *R'ptyr* to N'ala 3. The absence of the Lord Commander concerns S'heil, however."

S'heil paced back and forth across the bridge. "Recall the fleet. S'heil wants all Khamek ships in the vicinity of N'ala together at N'ala 3."

"Yes, Admiral," replied K'jahl.

"When will the extraction regiments arrive?" asked S'heil.

"Concurrent with the boarding of the Human sigil holders, if everything continues according to schedule," replied K'jahl.

S'heil sat in the command chair and pushed a glowing square on the small display on the arm. In a few seconds President Hernandez appeared on the screen.

"Greetings, Admiral. Do you have some good news?"

"Greetings," replied S'heil. "The *R'ptyr* has been located and is heading back to Earth. S'heil is negotiating to secure Human transport, per the deal."

"Negotiating with whom?" asked Alberto.

"The *R'ptyr* is commanded by a human named Novah Burns. Novah is young and inexperienced at command."

Alberto rifled through some paperwork on his desk. "That name sounds familiar," he stated. "Ah. Here it is. It looks like Novah is the son of the property owner where D'kob's ship crashed. Novah Burns. Recently released from a rehabilitation facility near Seattle. He was incarcerated for theft."

"Novah's rehabilitation appears to have been inadequate," stated S'heil dryly.

"Can you take the ship?" asked Alberto.

"Not by force as the *R'ptyr* is virtually impregnable and indestructible. All hope rests in successful negotiations," replied S'heil. *Well, most hope, anyway.*

"Perhaps I can help in the negotiations," offered Alberto. "I'm his President. He will listen to me."

"Novah said to expect a reply in twenty-four hours. When Novah responds S'heil will include Alberto in the discussion," S'heil replied.

"Very well," replied Alberto. "I'll clear my schedule."

S'heil nodded and cut off the transmission.

Alberto turned to his chief of staff. "Clear my calendar and get me every scrap of information on this Novah Burns I don't already have. Locate his parents if they are still alive."

"Already done, sir," replied a nondescript, grey-suited man. "Novah Burns' entire dossier is uploaded to your account. His mother is dead. His father is in a FEMA camp in Alaska. No other living relatives."

"Bring his father here. Today. Now. Get him out of that camp, cleaned up, shove him in an F-22 and have him in this office within twelve hours."

"Yes Mr. President!" replied Alberto's chief of staff who hurried out of the Oval Office.

Alberto sat down in his chair. High above and behind the moon, S'heil sat down in his. All they could do for the time being was wait.

Meanwhile, Novah met with his crew in the tactical lounge.

"Thoughts?" asked Novah.

Everyone started speaking at once. Novah lowered his head and pressed his palms flat against the table. He let the din die down naturally. When all was silent, he went around the table in order.

"Rebecca?"

"We should depart for Earth immediately. Whatever you decide, we'll need to be at Earth."

Novah nodded.

"D'kob?"

"S'heil is clever. S'heil will try to take the *R'ptyr* somehow. D'kob does not know how, yet does not underestimate S'heil's persistence and intelligence. D'kob advises great caution."

"S'lace?"

"S'lace agrees with D'kob. S'heil is ruthless. S'heil always gets what S'heil wants. S'heil wants to be the Khamek to lead the first interstellar expedition to V'laha. S'heil will also find great displeasure in negotiating with a young Human."

Novah tapped his fingers on the table in thought.

"NICOLE," he finally said, "take us to Earth. Keep the cloaking device engaged."

Course plotted. Estimated arrival in three hours.

"S'lace, I'd like you to come up with an inventory of all alien craft in the solar system. I want to know where all of S'heil's ships are, their sizes, and their capabilities. I figure you'd have the best knowledge of this."

"Yes, Captain." She stood up and exited the room quickly.

"D'kob, I'd like for you to do some thinking about S'heil. Write up a quick biography. Work with S'lace. I want to know how he thinks, what he likes, everything about him."

"Certainly, Novah," he said with a smile, and left.

The door closed behind D'kob, and Novah turned to Rebecca, his heart beating a hundred beats per minute. Nervously, he reached out and took her hand.

"I need to address the elephant in the room, Rebecca," he began. "I'm very attracted to you. You're the most beautiful woman I've ever seen. Your voice melts me. We've known each other for less than a day yet I feel like I've known you a lifetime. I want to get to know you better. I'm saying these things because they need to be said. I can't keep them inside as they will distract me from thinking about the other stuff."

Rebecca looked at him with a sharp yet disarming smile. "Did you just call me an elephant?"

Novah recoiled in horror. "No...no...that's not what I meant...I..."

"I know what you meant, and I have to say that's a pretty lame approach to the topic, Captain," she said. "How many girlfriends have you had in your life?"

Embarrassed, Novah dropped his eyes to the table. "None."

"None. No wonder you're rushing headlong like a bull at a red cape," Rebecca replied. "You think you're in love, and it's cute. I certainly appreciate the compliments. It's more likely that you're simply in love with the *idea* of being in love, having had no real experience in the subject."

Novah's sat silently, his ears burning hot, angry at himself for stepping into this mess.

"I didn't say I was in love..."

Rebecca, seeing his discomfort, laughed and squeezed his hand. "It's ok, Novah. I like you too. Don't think that grandfather had the *complete* say as to who would get picked for this mission." She winked. "But since we're being open and honest it's only fair that I tell you that I know just about everything about you. Your file is quite comprehensive. You have no secrets I don't know about."

Novah sat back, both curious and panicked. Rebecca hurried to put him at ease. "Yes, Novah, but please don't worry. I know what you've done, and why, and you have been forgiven, utterly and completely, by my grandfather, and by me."

Novah was suddenly confused. "Why would I need *your* forgiveness? I don't think I've done anything bad to you."

She slid her chair to his side of the table and took both of his hands, holding them tightly. Tears welled up in her eyes and her voice softened. "I had a younger sister. She was a cunning and deceitful person. I tried to warn her that one of these days she was going to get herself into real trouble. She never listened. When mom died, she got even worse, did stupid things and ended up in the Mall. A three year sentence." She held Novah's hands even tighter. "Her name was Penny."

With those words the dark cloud that Jesus had instantaneously swept away came creeping back, enveloping him in guilt and anger. His voice was barely audible and cracked.

"I didn't hurt her," said Novah. "I thought about it…I wanted to – I had planned to – kill her. I just couldn't do it. I just threatened her is all." Old anger found renewed vigor in Novah. "She promised she would stop luring people to rape but she didn't! She lied! I let her live and she just kept on doing to others what she did to me. I could have ended it. I *should* have ended it. Maybe *then* you'd have something to forgive me for."

He started to shake and the tears began to form in his own eyes.

Rebecca spoke quietly. "Even the purest of flocks can have a black sheep. Penny was an awful person."

"Was?" asked Novah.

"She's dead, Novah," replied Rebecca, her own voice beginning to crack. "She jumped from the upper level like her friend Kara did. Grandfather says the guilt of breaking her promise became greater than the pain of being raped and she couldn't bear to be raped again. She saw no other way out."

Novah wrestled with the conflicting emotions of guilt and glee, the mixture of which only came out as more anger.

"So let me get this straight. Penny made me a promise, broke it, felt guilty, killed herself, and somehow it's my fault she's dead? I need forgiveness for *that?*"

Rebecca shook her head. "Grandfather forgives you for everything you've ever done that you feel guilty for. That's the way he is. It has nothing to do with Penny. My forgiveness of you is different, in a way

Grandfather likely wouldn't approve of." She breathed in and stared hard into Novah's eyes. "Penny lived a horrible, tortured life in the Mall. She suffered emotional and physical pain you cannot imagine after that night you tied her up. It would have been merciful to have done what you originally wanted to do, but instead, she was forced to each day carry the burden of shame that she could not wash away."

Her nostrils flared, and she spoke with trembling words in the closest tone to anger that Novah would ever hear from Rebecca.

"What I forgive you for is *not* killing her."

Novah sat dumbfounded, his mind swirling in confusion. He tried to speak but Rebecca interrupted him. Her voice soothed him, even if her words did not.

"Let it go, Novah. We are just being open with each other, right? The past is the past, and we have to move forward into the future. Accept your role and accept mine as your friend and partner."

Novah sat silently, closing his eyes. *Let it go*, she says. *How the hell am I supposed to do that?*

"I don't know if I can let it go but I'll set it aside for now until I figure out what to say," he stated, pausing another couple of seconds. "Partner, huh?" he inquired.

"Yes. Your partner and confidant, for as long as you will have me," she replied sincerely.

"That almost sounds like a proposal."

Rebecca laughed lightly. "There you go again getting ahead of yourself. We can talk more about *that* later. For now, we have bigger questions to ask."

"Such as?" asked Novah.

"Why, the most important question of all, Novah! What sort of people are you going to choose for the new human colony?"

At that moment Novah truly began to grasp the significance of his mission. He needed to figure out who, out of billions of people, to choose, and that thought alone was enough to rip him back out of the past and into the present. He would decide who lived and who died. Or would he?

"If we agree to honor S'heil's arrangement the people have already been chosen," stated Novah.

"True," Rebecca said, "but are those the right people? Are they the best and the brightest? Are they capable of supporting a new civilization, building from scratch? All we know is that they have a fancy sigil. Possession of a trinket doesn't mean anything in the big picture."

Novah thought for a moment. "You are as wise as you are beautiful, Rebecca," he said. "It sounds like we have two tasks. We need to figure out the criteria we're going to use to select people, and we need to figure out a response for S'heil."

"Do we really care about S'heil's bargain?" asked Rebecca. "What happens if we just tell him no?"

"We should ask him," replied Novah. "I think there are pieces to this puzzle we're not seeing yet. We need to get all of the information we can."

"Perhaps some insight into this deal from the human point of view would be helpful," Rebecca suggested.

Novah smiled broadly at Rebecca. She smiled back.

"NICOLE, please place a call to the White House."

Connecting.

On the third ring a human voice answered. "White House switchboard."

"Hello, I'd like to speak to the President please. My name is Novah Burns."

"Please hold."

Three minutes later the voice returned. "Patching you through to the President, Mr. Burns." There was a barely audible click, and then a new voice.

"Mr. Burns." spoke Alberto, "Thank you for calling. This is an unexpected surprise. I've been wondering when we'd get a chance to talk."

Novah thought that he shouldn't be surprised that the President knew who he was but was surprised nevertheless. He refocused himself, remembering that he was a captain, not a nobody.

"I'll cut to the chase, Mr. President," said Novah. "I've spoken to

S'heil about this deal of yours and now I want to hear the human side. Tell me what's going on."

It had been years since Alberto was on the receiving end of orders, but he was wise enough to understand the gravity of the moment. He had a chance to secure the deal right here, right now.

"It's quite simple," started Alberto, "50,000 humans get saved from the imminent destruction that will soon befall Earth. Every human with a sigil, per the original agreement signed by Eisenhower sixty years ago, gets passage aboard the *R'ptyr*. The remainder of humanity is to be fuel for the Khamek. Humanity gets saved and the Khamek get what they want. Billions of people will die no matter what. It's a tragedy, but we must be pragmatic. Saving our species must be the priority."

Fuel? What's this talk about fuel? thought Novah. *Something else is going on here!* He took a breath to refocus.

"S'heil has asked me as the commander of the *R'ptyr* to honor your sigils. I'm trying to figure out why I should. Why should I let sigil-holders on instead of choosing others?"

"Mr. Burns," Alberto said slowly and clearly, "this is an agreement decades old. If you break it, there's no telling what the Khamek will do. I *can* tell you, though, what I will do. I have your father. If you do not comply with the deal, I will kill him. If that doesn't work I will nuke the entire planet. There will be nobody left to take."

"You have my dad? Where is he? Why would you kill him? Why would you kill *everybody*?" yelled Novah.

"Because for humanity to survive it needs leaders. It needs people with experience in government. People that know how to take care of other people. Shepherds for the flock. People others can rely on for protection and guidance. Government is just another word for things we choose to do together. We have to stay together, to work for the common good. Without that, humanity won't survive anyway," chided Alberto. "Besides, you can't expect farmers and lumberjacks to govern successfully. Let them do what they do best. Let me do what I do best."

Novah heard everything he needed to hear.

"Thank you for your input, Mr. President," stated Novah. "You'll have my answer within a day. Goodbye." NICOLE ended the communication.

Novah turned to Rebecca. "I have this feeling in my gut that he is less concerned about survival and more about losing power," he said.

"I honestly believe he thinks humanity won't survive without...how should I put it...*adult supervision*," she replied. "Government is the adult, and everyone else are the children."

"If the key point to remember is human survival, I don't see how his plan works. How will entitled bureaucrats, who don't even know how to cook their own meals, survive? I bet that every single sigil-holder is of the 'elite' class – bankers, lawyers, career politicians and the like," said Novah. "People who have grown up having other people do everything for them."

"I suspect you are right, Novah," replied Rebecca, "but we'll have to find some sort of compromise. I believe him when he says he will kill your father and nuke the planet."

Novah nodded. "And what's this fuel thing? The President said S'heil is going to take people for fuel. Everybody! Including, likely, my dad, who he said is still alive!"

"I don't know, Novah," answered Rebecca. "At least we have more information."

"It's time to gather a little more," stated Novah. "NICOLE, hail S'heil."

Hailing.

Within two seconds S'heil appeared on the view screen. "Greetings, Captain. Twenty-four hours have not elapsed. Has the Captain reached a decision early?"

"No, not yet," replied Novah. "I simply have a question."

"Please ask," said S'heil cordially.

"What will you do if I simply ignore you? The President says he'd sooner nuke the entire planet than allow the deal to be altered."

"Rest assured, Captain, S'heil will do everything in S'heil's power to prevent President Hernandez from engaging in such a counterproductive act," replied S'heil. "S'heil would instead insist upon S'heil's approach to changing Captain Burns' mind. S'heil knows that in order to collect humans for transport the *R'ptyr* will have to land. Doors will have to be opened to allow entrance to passengers. S'heil and human leadership will simply post ships and personnel by each door, and cause misadventure to any human attempting to enter the *R'ptyr*. Furthermore, S'heil will simply walk through the *R'ptyr*'s open doors and take the *R'ptyr* as the Captain does not have the personnel to stop me."

S'heil grinned mockingly. "At that point," he continued, "S'heil would honor the original deal."

"Thank you for your candor, S'heil," stated Novah icily. "I'll be in touch." NICOLE disconnected the call.

Novah rubbed his temples. "He's right. We don't have any way of protecting our open doors once we land. He and whatever army can just waltz right in," he said.

Rebecca reached over and grasped his hand but said nothing.

He pressed the intercom square on the table. "D'kob, please come to the tactical lounge."

Within seconds D'kob arrived and took a seat opposite Novah. Novah recounted the two conversations with D'kob, who listened patiently. At the end Novah came to his question.

"Do you believe that S'heil will leave the *R'ptyr* alone if we honor the deal?" he asked D'kob.

"S'heil is primarily concerned with S'heil's legacy. S'heil wants to be the first Khamek to V'laha. S'heil wants to honor the deal with the Humans. Both together enshrine S'heil in the Khamek Hall of Legends. S'heil will seek to eliminate risk. So long as S'heil believes Novah will honor the sigils, D'kob believes it is likely S'heil will not interfere. However, S'heil's perspective of risk often changes. D'kob suggests exercising extreme caution."

"It sounds like we have little choice," said Novah. "Pissing off S'heil will only make things worse."

"There are always choices," offered Rebecca. "We just have to find them."

Novah nodded and then looked back at D'kob. "Changing subjects, what's this business about humans being needed for fuel. What's the story there?. Can you explain?"

"Certainly, Novah," said D'kob, who fiddled with some settings on the table until a flat hologram, essentially a very large piece of paper, appeared. "First, D'kob will demonstrate interstellar travel." He used his finger and drew two dime-sized dots on the hologram, about two feet apart. "This is Earth," he said pointing to the first dot, "and this is A'ala," pointing to the second. "Both systems are similarly sized. The distance between them is 36.3 light years. This means that light – the fastest particle that can exist – would take 36.3 years to travel between the two worlds. There currently exists no technology that can approach light speed. Therefore, rapid interstellar travel between them, travelling in a straight line, is extraordinarily time consuming. In order to travel such a vast distance in a much shorter time span a wormhole is created." D'kob began manipulating the holographic paper, placing a finger on each dot, and moved his hands together until his fingertips touched. A large upward bowing in the paper was created. "The plane is space-time, and you see how space-time now bends. The key point, however, is D'kob's fingertips." He moved his fingers away, yet the hologram remained as it was, with the representations of Earth and A'ala pressed paper-thin against each other.

"The touching of the two systems represents the creation of a wormhole," D'kob continued. He fiddled with the table controls again and a small representation of a ship appeared in midair. "Once a wormhole is created, travel between two systems is instantaneous." He pushed the tiny ship through the hologram where the two systems met – first it was on Earth's side, then it was on A'ala's. Using his hands he then stretched the bowed sheet back flat against the table. "So, with wormholes, Novah can see that interstellar travel takes much less time."

"Then how come it takes four years to travel between the worlds?" Novah asked.

"Ah," replied D'kob. "Wormholes are high energy, high mass objects. One does not snap fingers and have a wormhole appear. Massive quantities of energy are required. The quantity of energy required to open a wormhole is such that were a wormhole to be opened within a star system immense gravitational forces would disrupt the system. Planets would be flung from orbit. Intra-stellar wormhole creation is strictly, strictly forbidden. Therefore, all wormhole creation must take place at a safe distance outside of star systems so as not to cause perturbations. For Earth's system the safe distance is 1.5 light years. Most systems are surrounded by a large sphere of comets and asteroids. Wormholes must be opened and closed well outside these spheres. Travel between systems is instant, yet the travel to and from the wormhole location to the final destination still takes many, many months of time using normal fusion propulsion."

"I understand," Novah said.

D'kob nodded. "Good. Now comes the Z'korz science. Z'korz fields are high energy fields. Very high energy fields. Most of this energy is contained in quantum dimensions outside of current human understanding. The Lord Commander knows the math much better than D'kob does. If enough Z'korz fields are extracted and properly focused, the energy is such that a wormhole is created. The larger quantity of focused Z'korz, the larger the wormhole. The distance that can be travelled is directly proportional to the size of the wormhole. S'heil requires the number of humans S'heil does because the distance between Earth and V'laha is very, very great. Billions of Z'korz fields are required."

"How are the human Z'korz extracted for energy?" asked Novah.

"For large ships sentient beings are contained in a large rotational chamber. Once a specific rotational velocity is achieved, the chamber is ignited. The beings are vaporized, and the Z'korz fields are centrifugally pushed out holes along the rotational chamber's walls, funneled down channeling tubes, and then focused into a series of batteries until needed. For smaller ships, extraction teams are sent to planet surfaces to extract Z'korz directly using a Z'korz extraction beam which terminates the Z'korz supplier as the supplier's Z'korz is transferred to a containment device carried by the extracting Khamek. These containment devices are then collected and dispersed to larger satellite batteries tethered to the ships. When called upon the Z'korz energy from the batteries is focused in multiple beams at a single point. Where the beams meet in front of the ship a wormhole is created. The longer the beams last, the greater the wormhole grows. When the beams stop the wormhole begins to decay. The decay is exponential. Decay starts very slowly, but accelerates over time. A ship or fleet has plenty of time to pass through the wormhole and reach a safe exit distance."

Novah didn't know what to think about D'kob's totally casual explanation about vaporizing humans. He stated things as they were as if there were no consideration about anything other than the facts. Novah discovered that he didn't really mind D'kob's detachment. He asked for data, he got data. One question did trouble him, however.

"D'kob, what is the plan to fuel the *R'ptyr* for interstellar travel to A'ala?"

D'kob blinked at him as if Novah was being stupid. "The *R'ptyr*'s batteries contain enough Z'korz to reach A'ala. Eighty thousand of the species known as Argints were divested of their Z'korz before the *R'ptyr* left V'jima Prime. Less than half of the Z'korz supply was consumed to bring the *R'ptyr* to Earth. The remainder is sufficient for the rest of the journey."

"Thank you, D'kob, that will be all," said Novah. D'kob nodded and left the tactical lounge.

"What are you thinking?" asked Rebecca.

Novah leaned back in his chair and took a deep breath. "I wonder how many worlds the Khamek is farming for Z'korz."

Rebecca just shook her head.

"See you later?" asked Novah.

"Of course," Rebecca said with a smile, trying to lighten the moment. Just as she was about to step through the door out into the hallway she paused and looked over her shoulder.

"Novah?"

"Yes?"

"Next time, try bringing flowers."

CHAPTER SIXEEN

N ovah made his decision. The *R'ptyr* was capable of containing 100,000 humans. He would honor the deal while selecting 50,000 more for migration. Precisely twenty-four hours after his first call to S'heil, Novah reopened communications.

"S'heil is very pleased that Captain Burns has seen reason," opened S'heil after hearing of Novah's decision. "Very pleased indeed. S'heil and the Captain should contact President Hernandez. S'heil will add him to this transmission."

A minute later, a harried looking Alberto joined the conference.

"Apologies for my tardiness. San Francisco was levelled by an earthquake two hours ago. Estimates put the dead at fifty thousand. Untold numbers more are missing," reported Alberto.

"Sad news indeed," replied S'heil. "S'heil is afraid that this earthquake is but the opening act. Many more earthquakes will occur in the near future."

Novah piped in. "S'heil, how long does Earth have? How long until all hell breaks loose?"

"Khamek scientists have been monitoring Earth for centuries. Enough data has been gathered to provide an accurate extrapolation. Khamek scientists believe, with 97.5% certainty, that only fourteen earth months remain until the ultimate cataclysm. Periodic tragedies, such as the occurrence in San Francisco, will increase in frequency until then."

Novah, Rebecca, and Alberto all turned white. The reality of what was going to happen was finally sinking in.

"Ok, here's the plan," said Novah. "I will honor the original deal, as I've said. Every person with a sigil will be welcome aboard the R'ptyr. Additionally, 50,000 additional humans, of my choosing, will come aboard. It will be painfully cramped, but we'll have to make do. Do either of you have a problem with that?"

"That's fine by me," replied Alberto.

"An extra 50,000 is essentially a rounding error for Khamek purposes," replied S'heil. "S'heil accepts these terms."

Novah addressed Alberto. "Mr. President, in one week, I will broadcast to all of Earth that humans are not alone, that the Khamek have given us a ship, and that I am seeking 50,000 volunteers to begin a new colony on the planet of A'ala. This is going to be a big deal. It will be humanity's first public confirmation that we are not alone in the universe. My hope is that humanity is ready. If it is, it is, if it isn't it isn't. That'll be your problem to deal with. I will not mention the deal with the Khamek. You will have to arrange for those with sigils to be prepared. I will also not mention the coming cataclysm. That will only cause people to freak out. Twelve months from my announcement, I will land the R'ptyr at the location of your choosing, hopefully a secluded one. At that time everyone with a sigil will be boarded. Two days later, the next 50,000 will be boarded at a location of my choosing."

"Agreed," replied Alberto. "That's more than fair."

"There are a couple more things," stated Novah. "First, you must realize that aboard the R'ptyr, I am in command. Not you. What I say, or my officers say, goes. Is that understood?"

"Yes," replied Alberto. "I understand. I will not seek to usurp your authority, and I will do my part to make sure none of the other sigil holders cause problems."

Novah nodded. "Secondly, and this goes for you too, S'heil, if there is *any* interference with the R'ptyr during either boarding phase...any interference at all, I will destroy the R'ptyr. There are to be no troops or aircraft of any kind within fifty miles of the *R'ptyr*. Any attempt to commandeer this ship will result in its destruction. Am I clear on this?"

"Yes, Mr. Burns," replied Alberto.

"Agreed, Captain," replied S'heil.

"There's more, Mr. President," said Novah, working to contain his anger and stay on task. "I'm sure you have an extra sigil or two laying around. I expect you to give one to my dad. I expect that he will be treated well for the next year. I expect that you will explain to him all of this, and I expect you to apologize for your actions in having him taken prisoner. Tell him I'll be back for him. God help you if he's harmed."

"I'll make sure he's well taken care of," replied Alberto.

"And finally," concluded Novah, "over the next year, I will be providing a list of provisions necessary for our journey. The *R'ptyr* will need extra supplies and some retrofitting for the extra people. I will provide regular lists to you, Mr. President. You will coordinate with S'heil times and places at which these supplies will be given to the Khamek, who will retrieve them, and then transfer them to the *R'ptyr* by teleporter."

"Whatever you want or need," replied Alberto. "The last thing I want is to starve to death halfway to A'ala."

"This arrangement is well-thought, Captain Burns," stated S'heil. "S'heil is impressed, and assures Khamek cooperation. All parties are satisfied."

"Mr. President," said Novah, "I think you will agree that the time for the imprisonment of political adversaries has ended. There are bigger fish to fry. I strongly suggest that you open the gates to all FEMA camps and other incarceration facilities, and let those people go back to their homes."

Alberto thought for a moment. "No, Mr. Burns. It is going to be difficult enough maintaining order with the increase in the number of natural disasters plus preparing for departure. I can't afford to just open up the floodgates and let thousands of people who want to do nothing but continue to disrupt things have free reign."

"I understand," replied Novah, sensing it was smarter to take the deal he had and not push it further. "I'll be in touch." He closed communications.

"That went well," said Rebecca.

"Indeed," offered D'kob.

"Well enough," sighed Novah. "Now comes the hard part. We have a year to pick 50,000 people, and a week to come up with the criteria. Choosing who lives and who dies won't be easy."

Once again, D'kob stared at him as if he was an idiot. "Novah doesn't need to choose. If the criteria are set, the humans will choose themselves."

"D'kob is right," offered Rebecca. "We build the right criteria, and see who fits. The hard part will be drawing the line at 50,000."

"We need to write down what we need, and fill those roles as best as we possibly can. We'll start working on it tomorrow," said Novah. "I'm wiped out. You guys must be tired too. Let's get some sleep."

They both nodded in agreement, and the three of them parted ways heading towards their respective quarters. Novah was asleep before his head hit the pillow.

Sometime deep in the night, Rebecca tiptoed down the hall and entered Novah's room. Silent as a cat, she approached his bed. She leaned over and gave him a brief, silent kiss on the cheek. The next morning, when Novah saw Rebecca, he remembered. He thought it was a dream, but from Rebecca's blush, he knew it wasn't. He smiled.

The next few days were long. Novah and Rebecca focused on writing Novah's speech to be delivered to the world, while D'kob and S'lace did provisioning calculations and logistics. The first item on the list, at Novah's insistence, was toilet paper.

Novah was amazed with Rebecca. She was a master of tone, volume, and facial expression. When Novah suggested something she disagreed with, she pushed back, but in a light, friendly way. She never crossed the line, always leaving the ultimate decision to Novah on an issue. This endeared her even more to him, solidifying their bond. They discovered that there was very little they disagreed on after talking things through.

The bulk of their conversations centered around the selection of the 50,000. There was simply no way to avoid hard, seemingly cold choices. They struggled to keep themselves emotionally detached – because that was the only way they were able to make concrete progress. They agreed in short order to dispense with the concept of fairness. None of this was fair – a mantra they repeated to each other frequently. Somebody – a great many somebodies – were going to get left behind. They were glad to be insulated from the judgment of the masses, as every single criteria they discussed would enrage some group or another. Trying to stay principled, they focused on what they believed were the most important things – compatibility and survival. Some basic general principles were penciled out:

- All of those brought aboard must be completely healthy and normal. Nobody would be allowed who has health issues or genetic disorders. This was the easiest, least controversial principle. For humanity to survive the healthiest population had to be gathered.

- All men must be under the age of 60. Building a new human civilization would take youth and strength. The drawbacks of supporting the elderly, with their growing infirmities and waning strength were greater than the potential benefit of their increased experience. As they believed the fundamental role of women on board, apart from their professional duties, was procreation, they capped the female age at 40.

- All must speak English. Everyone had to be able to communicate with each other. Sure, English might not be the most dominant language on the planet, but that's what Novah and Rebecca spoke, so they were naturally biased.

- No homosexuals or people who were sterile. Rebecca and Novah had no issue with homosexuality per se. Survival, however, meant encouraging procreation, early and often.

- All must be willing to do whatever job was asked of them. There would be no 'parasites' who benefited from doing nothing while others worked.

- All must have good character. Novah and Rebecca spent two whole days trying to define what that was.

- All must be able to provide a useful service. Extra consideration would be given to farmers, doctors, hunters, scientists, soldiers and tradesmen.
- Families consisting of two adults and any number of children up to the age of 18 could be brought as a group, assuming that each individual member met the other criteria. They agreed that common-sense judgment would be applied. For instance, if a forty-five year old father was selected, they wouldn't say that his forty-one year old wife would have to stay behind, provided she was otherwise healthy.
- All must be physically fit. Perfect fitness is not required, but reasonable accepted strength and weight guidelines would be adhered to.

They agreed that exceptions could be made on a limited basis based on common sense. To make sure that exceptions were limited, they agreed that they each could have ten personal exceptions to give out.

They made the conscious decision to write down a list of things that would *not* exclude candidates:

- Race wouldn't matter.
- Religion wouldn't matter, provided that the religion did not advocate tenets contrary to human survival, such as wanting to kill others for believing differently. Rebecca suggested that one, much to Novah's surprise.
- Educational level doesn't matter (though intelligence does).

They decided that they would create a comprehensive application form. They expected millions of applications to be submitted. They would require submission via secure email to the servers D'kob would set up for the purpose. The *R'ptyr's* computers would catalog and categorize all applications and build the needed databases.

At the end of each day, the crew would gather for a meal in the tactical lounge to discuss progress. After the fourth day, Novah could tell that everyone – human and Khamek alike – was exhausted. There was no way the six of them would be able to maintain this pace.

During one of the periods of silence Novah asked D'kob a question.

"D'kob, do you think S'heil would give us a couple of small scout craft?"

"For what purpose?" D'kob replied.

"I think waiting for a year to get everyone boarded could be a mistake. It might be better if we bring the slam-dunk candidates on early. They could help with the preparations, and we could manage their transition better," said Novah.

"If the term slam-dunk equates to strongly acceptable, D'kob concurs with the Captain's thinking. D'kob believes S'heil would give support, if stated in terms of relieving some of S'heil's responsibility for supply transport. The less S'heil has to do, the more S'heil will like a plan," said D'kob.

"D'kob is correct," added S'lace. "S'heil prefers to be responsible for very little. S'lace believes S'heil would lend scout ships."

D'kob spoke to S'heil that evening, one result of which was S'heil's agreement to lend four scout craft. Each was thoroughly scanned to make sure there were no explosives or other threats, and their control systems were completely replaced in order to be sure that S'heil couldn't assume control of them remotely.

Alberto was quite amenable as well, working with D'kob to provision the *R'ptyr*. Whatever was asked for, Alberto saw to it that it was made available at the prearranged times and locations.

After dinner, Novah would work on his speech. When he was too tired to think he went to bed and fell fast asleep. Every night Rebecca would sneak in, plant a kiss on his cheek, and slip out.

It was agreed that Alberto would speak first as a means of introduction. Alberto had privately communicated to all of the world's leaders what was happening, and a what time the speech would begin, and to have translators ready. Every television channel, every satellite, and every radio station would broadcast the address to every corner of the globe.

Novah paced the tactical lounge nervously. The appointed time came, and his view screen crackled to life. He sat down to watch Alberto, though he wasn't really paying attention. He was concentrating on what *he* was going to say.

"My fellow Americans," Alberto began, "citizens of the world, friends, enemies, and all. Today marks a historic occasion in all of human civilization. A great secret shall be revealed, something that your governments have kept from you for a long time. The time for honesty has come. I and the other leaders of the world are taking a gamble, hoping that the rest of the citizens of the world are ready for the news we have to share.

"Since the dawn of time, we have all, at one time or another, looked up into the night sky and wondered if there was anybody else out there, or if we are really alone in the universe. Today, I officially announce that we are not alone. Your governments have been communicating officially with a species known as the Khamek for sixty years. We have shared our cultures and they have shared technology and knowledge. We have treated and trusted each other as friends. I assure you that they mean no harm. I would like to introduce one of them now."

The camera slowly zoomed out, until both Alberto and K'jahl were in the picture.

"My alien friend here is named K'jahl. He is the representative of the Khamek that we have been working with for some time. As you can see, he looks very different from us. The Khamek species is an ancient species. They have travelled this part of the galaxy for many thousands of years. They can speak our language. Say hello, K'jahl."

"Hello, Humans," said K'jahl uncomfortably. "K'jahl and all Khamek are delighted to finally address all Humans. Khamek have learned to appreciate Humans greatly."

Alberto took over again. "The Khamek understand the importance of planetary diversification, that is, not having all of their species in any one solar system. They have colonies on many worlds. Rest assured, however, that they are not interested in Earth. It is too far from their home. In fact, sometime in the next couple of years, the few Khamek here will leave Earth completely to go off and explore other worlds. Because the Khamek wish humanity to diversify as well, and to learn the joys of interstellar exploration, they are leaving us with a gift. To explain this gift, I would like to introduce one of humanity's own, Mr. Novah Burns."

That was Novah's cue, so he gathered himself and spoke directly at his view screen.

"Thank you, Mr. President," began Novah. "My name is Novah Burns, and I am the captain of a space ship called the *R'ptyr*. This ship is a gift to humanity from the Khamek. It was designed and built specifically for humans. The *R'ptyr* is about two miles long, and 250 yards in diameter. It's basically a giant cruise liner. The purpose of this ship is to transport people to a distant world known as A'ala. It is a world slightly larger than Earth. It circles a young, stable star in an orbit that provides diverse environments quite similar to that of Earth. There are no sentient species on A'ala. It is ours to explore and study. It is a world filled with undiscovered wonders and unknown dangers. It will take four years to get there.

"I am looking for 50,000 volunteers from all walks of life and backgrounds to join me on this mission of discovery. If that sounds exciting, that's because it is. It is also very strenuous and dangerous. Colonizing a new world will take special kinds of people. Farmers, hunters, doctors, scientists, and other critical specialists. We need people that know how to do things, how to build things, and how to adapt to ever-changing and unknown circumstances. I also need to tell you that this is not an equal-opportunity situation. The choosing of the colonists will be highly selective. I'm sorry, but that's the way it has to be in order for the colony to survive and grow. We will not, however, discriminate based on race, color, creed, religion, or education level. The website shown at the bottom of your screen contains details and the application. If you wish to apply, simply fill out the application and hit send. Applications will be evaluated and ranked based on your qualifications and the role you are specialized in. If you qualify, you will be asked to take a health exam. Only healthy, disease-free people can be part of this first wave of colonists. The *R'ptyr* will land on Earth exactly 368 days from today to pick up those that qualify. A very small number of skilled specialists will be selected and brought aboard earlier to help prepare the *R'ptyr*. Everyone who applies should be ready to leave at a moment's notice, so have your affairs in order.

"This is an exciting time in human history. We are not alone. We have friends in the universe. Soon we will be an interstellar species. I look forward to the adventure, and so should you. Thank you, and welcome to the new era of humanity!" Novah switched off the view screen. The next thing he saw was Rebecca, beaming at him.

"You did great, Novah!" she exclaimed giddily. She gave him a tight hug. He hugged her back, breathing in her intoxicating scent.

"Thank you," he breathed into Rebecca's ear. His heart thumped heavily.

"Captain," D'kob interjected, "the number of access requests to the application server are staggering. Over one million already."

"I would guess that nobody on earth is going to sleep tonight," replied Novah. "Any reports of rioting? Mass suicides? Crazy stuff?"

"Not yet, Novah," answered D'kob. "D'kob believes the planet is still in shock."

The next day, the applications starting rolling in in vast numbers. NICOLE automatically sent back applications that were incomplete. The database was beginning to build rapidly.

At dinner that evening, Novah announced a slight change in plans.

"I don't want to wait until the last minute to board our 50,000," he said. "I want to select them and get them on board as soon as possible. We know the kind of people we want, and the roles they need to fill. As soon as we find them, we should bring them on board. Quietly, as part of the supply runs. I don't want S'heil or the President knowing we're pre-boarding. They're okay with a specialist here and there, but will likely balk if they were to know I'm getting people on board more quickly. They have been cooperative thus far...*too* cooperative. I still think they have something up their sleeve. I want numbers on our side in case they try to pull something." The crew agreed.

Rebecca and Novah sat in the tactical lounge, overwhelmed by the volume of applications to be sorted and decided on.

"Are we smart enough to do this?" asked Novah, feeling a bit panicked. "How can we possibly keep up? This is beyond the ability of two people to do!"

"You're right," replied a similarly-overwhelmed Rebecca. "Maybe we should take D'kob's advice and let NICOLE do the sorting and ranking. We can spend our time spot-checking instead of trying to categorize and rank everything by ourselves. I just hope our principles are right."

"Maybe NICOLE can recognize our intent and think of things we haven't thought of to help make sure the right people are selected," Novah offered.

"Maybe," replied Rebecca. "Though, as they say, the road to hell is paved with good intentions. I don't see any other way around it, though. We'll just have to be diligent and do the best we can."

Novah addressed the *R'ptyr.* "NICOLE, please analyze the application database and rank applicants based on the application criteria and needs of the ship and crew going forward." NICOLE's response was immediate.

Processing complete, Captain. Applicants are sorted by category and ranked based on my assessment of their applications and my analysis of your intentions. I have cross-referenced from all known Earth databases to ensure accuracy of application responses.

Novah and Rebecca blinked at each other in surprise.

"NICOLE," asked Rebecca, "how did you do that so fast?"

Per your conversation, in which I was twice invoked, I reached the logical conclusion and began the categorization immediately.

"Amazing," whispered Novah.

Novah and Rebecca looked at the first results. NICOLE had filled all 50,000 slots and had ranked them by specialty. Skeptical, Novah called up the application of the last person in the lowest ranked specialty group – an archaeologist named Frank MacDoughall from Whitefish, Montana.

Name: Frank James MacDoughall
Age: 28
Occupation: Archaeologist, specializing in large dinosaurs
Sexuality: Straight
Wife and/or children: None
Height: 6 feet 2 inches
Weight: 212 lbs
Health issues: none

Allergies: none, apart from mild seasonal symptoms

Novah scanned the rest of the lengthy application, finding nothing that would even cause him to raise an eyebrow. Then he got to the final page, which was an essay question.

Please write why you want to go to A'ala.

His answer was succinct: *Because I want to be free, and there's no place left on Earth where a man can truly be free.*

Novah turned to Rebecca. "This is the last person on the list, and he's perfect," he said. "but he's likely not going to make it on board. It's only the first day. NICOLE will keep taking applications and ranking them. Mr. MacDoughall will likely get pushed off before lunch."

Rebecca took his hand. "We knew this would happen, Novah. A great many good people are going to be left behind. But look at the bright side – everyone we take is going to be great."

"You're right, of course," he said. "I just have to shut my mind to it."

"It's not your mind," said Rebecca softly, raising her open hand and pressing it to his chest, "it's your heart. And it's why I've grown quite fond of you."

Their kiss lasted for a full minute before the need for oxygen – and D'kob's curious stare – forced them apart, panting.

"Please pardon D'kob's interruption," D'kob stated plainly. "When should Human boarding begin?"

"As soon as possible," replied Novah. He looked at the rank list. "Start at number one on the list, Dr. Katyrina Annikov. Take a scout ship, find her, administer the health test, and if she passes, bring her up. Keep working down the list in order. Do it in shifts with S'lace so that you aren't exhausted. I want it done quickly, but I don't want you guys endangering yourselves with fatigue."

D'kob nodded and exited the room.

CHAPTER SEVENTEEN

D r. Katyrina Annikov was a second-generation Russian-American in charge of the infectious disease investigation unit at the Centers for Disease Control in Atlanta. Her father, a former Soviet rocket scientist, immigrated to the United States with his lovely bride and managed to get a job at the Marshall Space Flight Center in Huntsville, Alabama. A year later, that's where Katyrina was born, developing a quirky southern drawl with Russian flavoring. She tested into advanced classes throughout her schooling, eventually graduating at the top of her class from the University of North Carolina School of Medicine. Nobody was more dedicated to medicine that Katyrina, which explained why, at age thirty-two, she was unmarried, unattached, and sitting alone at her desk in the CDC offices at eleven p.m. on a Friday evening, working to whittle down the unending pile of administrative paperwork that had accumulated during the week. She spent as much time, if not more, in her office than she did in the lab or hospital these days which created a slowly-growing seed of discontent in her heart. So much paperwork. So many regulations. So much bureaucracy standing in the way of medicine.

Dr. Annikov rubbed her eyes with the heels of her pale hands, then rested her forehead on her cool metal desk. Just as she closed her eyes she heard a knock on her office door.

Christ Almighty, I told the janitors to leave me alone.

"Go away!" she yelled with irritation. "I told y'all to just ignore this office wh…"

She froze mid-word as she looked up and realized that it wasn't a member of the cleaning staff standing in the doorway, but a pale, almond-eyed creature of clearly extraterrestrial origin.

"Dr. Katyrina Annikov?" asked D'kob.

"Yes, I am Dr. Annikov," Katyrina replied instinctively, still not sure if what she was seeing was real or a bit of undigested beef mixed with fatigue.

"D'kob's name is D'kob. D'kob is here to escort you to the *R'ptyr*. Is Dr. Annikov prepared?"

"I didn't expect you so soon! I…I didn't expect you at all," replied Katyrina.

"Regardless," stated D'kob, "Time is short and Dr. Annikov is to be taken aboard the *R'ptyr*. Does Dr. Annikov wish to remain behind?"

"NO!" she blurted out, surprised with the tone of her own urgency. "I'll come!" She grabbed her purse, jacket, and the small bag of extra clothes and bathroom supplies she kept in her drawer in case of all-night stays at the office. "Ok, let's go!"

"Health check first," replied D'kob, who walked up to her and held a small, clear test tube up to her face. "Please blow into the health evaluation crystal."

Katyrina raised one of her auburn eyebrows but did as she was told, leaning over to blow a warm breath into the tube, causing the clear glass to fog and then crystallize into a bright green.

"Health check passed. Congratulations." D'kob turned back towards the door with the doctor following him close behind. She reached to the wall and turned off the lights on her way out, not giving a second thought to the life she was leaving behind.

Twelve minutes later a new human set foot upon the *R'ptyr*. D'kob guided a wide-eyed Dr. Annikov to the tactical lounge where she was greeted by Novah and Rebecca.

"Captain, D'kob presents Dr. Katyrina Annikov."

"Thank you, D'kob," replied Novah. He turned his eye to the doctor. She was an athletically built with short red hair and green eyes, wearing a white lab coat over a red shirt and blue jeans. She oozed intelligence and independence and was clearly amped up on adrenaline.

"Welcome aboard, Dr. Annikov. I am Novah, and this is Rebecca, the *R'ptyr*'s chief engineer."

The doctor took a deep breath and blinked twice before responding.

"I'm…well…this all has happened so fast! I sent in my application last night, and here I am today. I half thought all of this was a joke until your little alien friend here dropped by the office. The world is so different today than it was yesterday," she said. Her voice was confident and excited, which emphasized her drawl.

"Indeed it is," spoke Rebecca. "You are the very first colonist selected. Are you prepared for the journey of a lifetime?"

"I think so," Dr. Annikov replied. "I don't have much…just what I had at the office. He…you're a he, right sugar?" she said looking at D'kob, "expressed great urgency. I haven't even really had time to think about what's happening. One minute I'm sitting at my desk, the next I'm blowing into a test tube, the next I'm sitting in a snot-fast UFO, and now I'm here. I'm just rollin' with it."

"I know how you feel," said Novah. "Dr. Annikov, I am appointing you to be the *R'ptyr*'s chief medical officer. For the duration of our journey to A'ala all medical personnel will report to you. You report to me. Please hold out your left hand." She did, and Novah fastened a blue command module wrap around her hand and showed her how to use it. "You'll learn everything you need to know using this. It describes the *R'ptyr*, shows where your quarters are, and the three main medical facilities. It also goes through the basics such as how to use the teleporter system. If you get stuck just ask the *R'ptyr* herself for help."

Dr. Annikov, wide-eyed, nodded.

"We chose the best and the brightest," continued Novah. "I know you have a lot to absorb, yet we need you ramped up and on station as soon as possible. All additional medical personnel – and there will be a lot of them – will be funneled directly to you and you'll have to tell them what you want them to do. You have full authority to handle your doctors and nurses however you like. Whenever a new person to be assigned to you is selected their file will be uploaded to your module for you to review. This will give you time to read it before the person arrives so that you can get them off and running quickly."

Rebecca added her instructions. "We have a staff meeting every night over dinner. As chief medical officer you'll be expected to attend whenever possible. It's in this room at seven p.m."

The more instructions she was given, the more the smile on Dr. Annikov's face broadened. Her smile was accompanied by a single sparkling tear that streamed down her face.

Novah reached out and touched her shoulder. "Are you ok, doctor? I know it's a lot."

"Oh, I'm fine," she replied with a sniff. "I'm just... well, I'm happier than a puppy with two tails. I'm finally in a place where I know I'm going to spend ninety percent of my time making a difference instead of filling out paperwork."

"Yes, you are," said Novah with a smile. "Now off you go."

She saluted. "Yes, Captain. And thank you!" She was gone before Novah could tell her a salute wasn't necessary.

Back on Earth, S'lace had landed her cloaked scout craft on the roof of an apartment complex in Springfield, Missouri. Carefully, she made her way unseen down the stairs to apartment 710. She knocked on the door which was soon answered by a very large human.

"Captain Lawrence Tines?" she asked the visibly-surprised man.

"Y...yess," the man stuttered.

"May S'lace come in?"

Captain Tines stood aside and S'lace entered the apartment. He closed the door behind her. There was a heavy odor of marijuana. "Are you a Khamek?" he asked.

"S'lace is Khamek, yes. S'lace is here to take Captain Lawrence Tines to the R'ptyr. Is Captain Tines prepared?"

A weak, wheezy voice called out from another room in the apartment. "Larry...who's there?"

"You better come out here," Larry said. "And bring the kids."

Larry's wife, Susan, hobbled out of a side bedroom. Behind her followed two children, Hobbs, age five, and Erin, age three.

"An alien!! An alien!!" squealed Hobbs. "Mom, it's a real alien!"

"Yes, it appears so," wheezed a surprised Susan. Erin was coupled to her leg, visibly frightened. "Larry, why is there an alien in our living room?" asked Susan.

Larry turned to look again at S'lace. "Apparently, I've been selected to be one of the colonists."

"You filled out an application? You said we'd talk about this first!"

"I didn't think I'd get chosen, Susan," said Larry, sullen. The room grew quiet.

Susan turned to S'lace. "I need to speak to my husband alone for a couple of minutes. Can you watch the children?"

S'lace blinked, unprepared for this situation. Before she could respond, Susan bent down and placed Erin's hand in Hobbs'. "Go on. Your father and I will be right back. Please be nice to the alien."

Erin hid behind Hobbs, and Hobbs took a pair of tentative steps towards S'lace, who stood motionless, not knowing what to do.

Susan took Larry's hand, led him into the bedroom, closed the door, and firmly, with what little strength she had and as much violence as she could muster, slapped him across the face.

"You bastard!" she hissed in an angry, quaking near-whisper. "You said we'd talk first! You filled out that application...you knew! You knew I couldn't go, and you did it anyway!" She slapped him again, hard, tears flowing down her weathered face. "What were you thinking? You can just leave me behind? I'm broken, I'm dying, but I'm still *your wife!*"

She slapped him again, and he retreated, pressing his back up against the old wooden dresser. She pursued, her breath shaken and rattled. She clenched her fingers into fragile fists, pounding them repeatedly into Larry's chest.

"You bastard! You bastard! You bastard!" she repeated with each set of blows, accompanied by coughs and tears. Larry absorbed each blow like a dagger in the heart until Susan's strength and voice withered. Larry wrapped his arms around her and she collapsed into him. "Larry...oh Larry...why?"

Larry rested his chin on the top of Susan's head, tears in his own eyes, holding her tight. He spoke softly, sincerely. "You're dying, Susan, and soon you will be gone. I have to think of the kids now, and what will be best for them. Without you, this world turns dark, and will be full of ghosts, ghosts that will haunt them – and me – forever. Up there there will be excitement and distraction and a whole new world of things to learn. A chance for Hobbs and Erin to grow without limits."

He pushed her back slightly and lifted her chin until they were looking eye to eye.

"It's the right thing to do," he said with quiet conviction.

The blush of anger fell from Susan's face, yet didn't fade to her sickly pale. She stepped back from Larry, holding his hands together at her breasts, standing straight and strong for the first time in months. The wheezing of her breath eased, and while still ragged, her tone and demeanor solidified. She didn't bother to wipe away her tears, and simply smiled at her husband through them. After half a minute, she spoke again.

"Thank you, Larry," she said. "Thank you for reminding me yet again why I married you. No matter what, you always try to do the right thing for the family. Thank you for being strong for me. Thank you for being strong for all of us." She kissed his hands, and then kissed his lips.

They were holding hands as they opened the door and walked back out into the living room. To their surprise, Hobbs was sitting on the couch, a coloring book in his lap, pretending to read to S'lace snuggled on his left side, and Erin, pressed against his right.

Relieved, S'lace stood, eager to relinquish babysitting duties and resume her assigned task.

"Is Captain Tines prepared?" S'lace asked again. "S'lace must administer the health test."

"My kids can come, right?" inquired Larry.

"A spouse and all natural-born children under 18 years of age are eligible, provided each passes the health test," replied S'lace. Larry sighed, squeezing Susan's hand tightly.

"Susan is very sick," Larry said.

"What is the nature of Susan's sickness?" S'lace asked.

"I have terminal stage-four lung cancer," Susan said weakly.

S'lace looked at Susan, looked at Larry, then again at Susan. "S'lace is unable to remedy terminal cancer. S'lace regrets to inform Susan that Susan is disqualified." S'lace paused, then looked Susan in the eye. In a quieter tone almost resembling sympathy, S'lace offered something else.

"S'lace can, however, help Susan….sleep." There was no mistaking what S'lace meant.

Larry looked at Susan, heartbroken, losing his resolve. Before the words could form on his tongue, Susan interrupted him.

"Don't even say it, Larry," said Susan mustering as much authority as her shriveled lungs could manage. "You're going, and you're taking the kids. There's nothing for you here. We're broke. The Army doesn't pay you jack. I'm no help to you, only a strain." She softened her tone. "Go, Larry. Make a new world. Let our kids be part of a new, wonderful adventure. Name a flower for me or something," she said, choking up.

The family embraced, tears flowing freely.

"Hobbs, Erin, you two obey your father. The spaceship is going to be fun. You're going to get to do things that no other kids have ever been able to do before. I'll be fine here on Earth," Susan told her children. She turned again to Larry.

"I'm so, so proud of you," she said through her sincere tears.

"Time is short," stated S'lace.

Ten minutes later, having passed the health tests, Larry had packed a backpack for each of the three travelers. They said their final tearful goodbyes. S'lace looked back at Susan, and ever so subtly tilted her head to one side in inquiry. Susan nodded a single time.

"Ascend to the roof via the stairs," S'lace instructed Larry and the two kids. "S'lace will follow shortly."

Larry held Susan tightly. She held Larry's face in her hands and kissed him for the last time, then ushered her family off with a smile and a stoic wave. Larry shut off his emotions and grabbed his children by their two tiny hands and led them up the stairs. S'lace closed the door behind them, then turned to Susan.

"Is Susan certain?" asked S'lace.

"Yes," she replied.

S'lace guided Susan back to the bedroom and Susan laid on her back at S'lace's instruction. S'lace blindfolded Susan with a t-shirt.

"Susan will feel no pain," said S'lace, "only a sensation of warmth."

"Thank you," said Susan, shaking.

S'lace withdrew a small, curved blade from her belt. It was a ceremonial blade, carried mostly as decoration, and used only for killings of mercy. For Khamek it was an honorable thing to mercifully end terminal suffering. The blade was coated with an anesthetic that acted instantly so that there would be no sting. S'lace placed a large cotton towel over Susan's throat and held it down with her left hand. Her right hand slipped beneath the towel, and then drew the blade deftly along a two inch length of Susan's carotid artery.

"Sleep now," said S'lace.

Blood channeled out rapidly and Susan felt nothing but a warm wash down her right side. Five seconds later, the towel was soaked through, and Susan lost consciousness. In less than a minute she was gone. S'lace drew the sheet over Susan's face, wiped her hands and the blade off, and refocused on her mission.

She found the three on the roof, their eyes widening as S'lace uncloaked the scout ship. It was a tight squeeze, but they all managed to snug themselves in. In seconds, they were airborne. A minute later they were high above the earth much to the gasping delight of S'lace's younger passengers. Soon thereafter they landed in the *R'ptyr*'s docking bay. S'lace escorted them immediately to the tactical lounge.

"Captain," stated S'lace, "presenting Captain Lawrence Tines, and Captain Tines' two children, Hobbs and Erin."

"Thank you, S'lace," said Novah. "Get some rest. You look exhausted."

"Yes, Captain," S'lace replied gratefully. As she turned to exit the room, Erin touched her leg. "Bye Sayce!" the little girl said. S'lace, not knowing how to respond, simply patted the child on the head and left.

Novah and Rebecca went through the introductions, working from the same script as before with Dr. Annikov. By the time Captain Tines left the room with his kids in tow and new title of chief security officer, he was invigorated with purpose, which helped to cauterize his grief.

"Children already!" exclaimed Rebecca. "We may have to alter the order and have a teacher or two brought on board. It's hard to expect anyone to do their jobs with kids to watch all day. I must confess, I do love seeing children though. It reminds me of what we're doing and who we're doing it for, as if I needed any reminders."

"I wonder where their mother is," said Novah.

"There will be plenty of time to learn everyone's stories," responded Rebecca. Novah, in a fit of bravery, drew her close, placed a finger under her chin, and lightly kissed her on the lips. Her smiling lips didn't resist.

S'lace and D'kob averaged six new colonists each per day. Novah insisted they work no more than twelve hours. V'kol and N'dim focused solely on the provisioning runs. After six days, ninety-eight new colonists were on board. Novah gave the crew Saturday off, and called for a ship wide gathering in the R'ptyr's main banquet hall. The banquet hall could seat ten thousand, so the tiny group of 104 seemed insignificant. There was no agenda. It was just a mixer so that people could get to know each other. The R'ptyr was so huge that running across someone else was rare outside of normal duties.

Five thousand of the passenger slots were reserved for various military and security roles. One out of every ten new colonists was current or former military. Protecting the new A'ala colony was a top priority.

The first ninety-eight filled almost all of the major positional leadership roles with immediate subordinates. Tines had a crew of twenty reporting to him, which he had broken down into shifts and set up assignments for. Dr. Annikov had a solid crew of nine doctors and nurses reporting to her after the first week. The farming crew was busy in the greenhouses planting crops. Other specialists found their places on the R'ptyr and worked to organize their areas. Twenty spouses and forty children were put to work doing whatever they could to assist.

Everyone was remarkably polite and courteous. Orders were followed mostly without question, yet when they were questioned, a clear and thorough explanation was offered so that they orders were understood.

A pleasant routine was in place by the third week. Novah and Rebecca would meet at six a.m. each morning in the tactical lounge, have a cup of coffee, and basically talk about whatever was on their minds. At seven a.m., the first ship would return from Earth with passengers. S'lace and D'kob would escort them to the appropriate crew chief after on-board processing. Rebecca and Novah would go on rounds together, teleporting all over the *R'ptyr* to check in on the various chiefs and to ask if they had everything they needed. They'd take notes and adjust the provisioning requests accordingly. Every evening at seven, the crew chiefs would gather in the tactical lounge over what they called dinner even though food was very rarely served. Each chief would give a brief summary of the day's actions and a personnel report. The dinner wrapped up at nine, and Novah and Rebecca would spend an hour on the observation deck chatting. At ten, they would depart to their quarters with a single, quick kiss. In the deepest dark of the night, as always, Rebecca would sneak into Novah's quarters, kiss him gently so that he didn't wake, and then go back to bed.

CHAPTER EIGHTEEN

A month later the manifest of the *R'ptyr* listed four-hundred and sixty-three people. It was glaringly obvious that at the current pace only around five thousand of the 50,000 would be pre-boarded. There were no reasonable options available to increase the rate of boarding. S'lace and D'kob were already working their brains out.

Security Chief Tines was tireless and masterful at his craft. Nearly every occupied corridor of the *R'ptyr* was patrolled regularly. His men and women made a point of being friendly and helpful, a reflection of their chief. Chief Tines spent the occasional on-shift hour monitoring a large series of grids at the station on the officer's quarters deck. A softly flashing red dot indicated where each security person was. Blue dots indicated the rest of those on board, except for Novah, Rebecca, S'lace and D'kob, who were designated as yellow dots. Anyone monitoring this station could see where everyone was all the time. Open doors lit up red as well, then gradually faded after a few seconds.

Tines had volunteered for the night shift, telling Novah that it would be smart to have at least *one* chief on active duty at all times. He arose at three p.m. to welcome Hobbs and Erin from school, attended dinner at seven, worked through the night and returned to bed at nine a.m. after Hobbs and Erin went to school. All of the other chiefs worked a normal day shift, though close subordinates kept all of the critical stations open continually.

Every night and around three a.m. Chief Tines walked by the security station to check on things, and watched the yellow dot exit Rebecca's quarters and move down the hall to Novah's. At first this set off an alarm at the security station – nobody should be sneaking into an officer's quarters. He spoke with Novah about this privately and was assured that it was fine, and didn't restrict Rebecca's access codes. Rebecca's dot lingered in Novah's quarters for a few seconds before returning back to where it belonged. This always happened between three and three-thirty in the morning. He looked forward to seeing this movement of her dot during the night. It made him feel less lonely.

It was three a.m. and Chief Tines stood at the security console waiting for the yellow dot to move. Instead, to his surprise, the red doorway indicator to Captain Burns' room flashed. There was no corresponding dot. A cold chill gripped his spine. Novah's dot was still in bed. Rebecca's dot was just now stirring. The red doorway flashed again. Then again, as if the door was trying to open but refused. Something was wrong. He started his fifty yard sprint to the Captain's quarters.

Tonight's the night, Novah thought. *Tonight's the night I finally stay awake. I'll be dog tired tomorrow, but I'm going to be giving the kiss for a change.* He lay still in his bed, back to the door, eyes closed, waiting, working hard to keep from nodding off. He finally heard the door open with its gentle swoosh. He heard the soft pitter-patter of feet head towards him. He was giddy. He sensed Rebecca's approach. *Just a little closer....just a little closer.*

He popped upright in bed to snatch Rebecca, but the surpriser became the surprised. Instead of Rebecca he saw the reflection of two large Khamek eyes in the low ambient light, and the lightning-fast flash of a small, curved blade streak towards his neck.

"S'heil hates risk. Novah has now suffered misadventure but this is a mercy compared to what S'heil would do."

Novah heard the voice but the words didn't register. Blood was spurting out of his neck in violent, uncontrolled spurts. He tried to apply pressure. The room spun and faded, then turned to black. At that moment the door to Novah's quarters opened fully and the bright lights of the hallway ignited a door-wide pillar of vision that highlighted a wide-eyed, blade-wielding Khamek and a gruesomely-bleeding Novah.

Rebecca shrieked. A split second behind her was Chief Tines.

"Oh my God," said the Chief.

"Tines!" Rebecca squealed, "Kill this Kha..!"

The report from Chief Tines' pistol drowned out everything else. The .45 caliber hollow-point streaked and created a crushing hole between D'kob's eyes before exploding out the back of his skull. D'kob fell to the floor instantly, his ceremonial blade clanking to the floor. Before the echo had time to fade Tines pressed his fingers into the doorway intercom system. "Medbay! All available medical personnel to Captain Burns' quarters...NOW!!"

Rebecca rushed to Novah's bedside and was applying pressure to the wound, her heart racing and her ears ringing. "Please...oh please God...let him live. Grandfather help me!" she pleaded.

Within seconds, medical personnel had arrived and were taking control. "He's lost a lot of blood. We need to get him to the operating room *now!*" Dr. Annikov had heard the gunshot and ran from her quarters. She stood at the doorway in her bathrobe and bunny slippers, panting.

"Operating room A1! I'll scrub!" she said, vanishing into the teleporter across the hall. Two med-techs lifted Novah onto a gurney quickly and wheeled him to the teleporter. They were gone in a flash. A third med-tech spoke urgently. "If he's to survive, he's going to need blood, right now. Do you know his blood type?" he asked Rebecca.

"No," she whimpered. Then she suddenly became more hopeful. "But mine will work!" She rushed across the hall into the teleporter and was gone.

Others started to arrive. Chief Tines blocked access to Novah's room and stationed two guards. "Nobody enters this room without my explicit say-so," he ordered.

"Yes chief!" the pair replied in unison. The Chief then turned to another man.

"Rawlson, I want S'lace, N'dim and V'kol rounded up for questioning. Yesterday!" he yelled. Rawlson hurried off.

"S'lace is here," she said appearing seemingly from nowhere. "What event has transpired?"

Tines worked to regain some civility even as he restrained S'lace's hands with a pair of zip-ties. "D'kob has just attempted to assassinate the Captain and the odds are that he'll be successful," he said ruefully. "D'kob knew right where to cut him. He's lost way too much blood."

"Where is the Captain now? S'lace has knowledge that might help save the Captain," she said urgently.

"Medbay One. Jones, take her. Don't let her out of your sight."

S'lace and Jones rushed into the teleporter chamber.

Operating room A1 was a display of controlled panic and urgency. Novah was on the operating table with Dr. Annikov working diligently to sew up his neck wound. She had tossed her thick, cumbersome robe aside and was operating in only her white panties and white tank-top, each stained with Novah's blood. Nobody cared.

"He's AB negative!" shouted one of the techs.

Dr. Annikov finished closing the artery and pointed two her two surgical assistants. "Keep him alive." She turned to Rebecca and assumed a compassionate, whispered tone.

"He's going to die. There's nothing I can do. He's lost too much blood, and his type is AB negative, the rarest there is. We'd be lucky if two people on this ship had that type, and there isn't time, and there wouldn't be enough."

"Mine will work," cried Rebecca. "Please!"

"It doesn't matter, Rebecca," said the doctor. "Even if your blood could somehow match, you don't have enough to save him."

"Please!" Rebecca begged. "Trust me! We have nothing to lose!"

S'lace ran quickly up to the two human women. "S'lace knows a way. Find the blue canisters."

Katyrina pointed at the nurse nearest the supply closet. "Kendra! Third shelf on the right hand side, blue canister about the size of a gallon of milk. Get it now!"

"Yes doctor!!"

"Generic hemoglobin," stated S'lace. "Mix with three parts warm water. The mixture also needs one part of the appropriate blood type."

"Mix it!" yelled Dr. Annikov. "Rebecca, roll up your sleeve. This is a one in a million shot, and we're out of time. I need half a pint as fast as your little heart can pump it out. George, Alexis…start a central line in the right subclavian! Get some defib patches on him!"

Five seconds later, Rebecca's blood was pouring out of the clear tube inserted into her left arm and into the mixing container. She was squeezing and releasing her left hand as fast as she could. "Hurry," she repeated in a whisper, "hurry… hurry."

"He's crashing!" someone cried out. Monitors were beginning to go crazy.

Dr. Annikov grabbed the container and handed it to George. "Pump it! Now! Keep that heart going!" George and Alexis immediately began the forced transfusion.

"Cardiac arrest!"

"Charge it to 300!" yelled the doctor. "Don't you go dying on me, Novah. Give this blood a chance. Clear!" Novah's chest convulsed with the voltage sent through his system.

"No response doctor!"

"I can see that, damn it! Charge to 360! Clear!"

Novah's chest convulsed again with no response.

"I'm not losing my first patient on this ship! Clear!"

She shocked him again, with no response. "Epinephrine! Now!" the doctor bellowed as she climbed up on the table, straddling him, locking her elbows and administering CPR. She kept pumping her palms into his chest. Fifteen times. Twenty times. "Live, damn you! Live!" Thirty times.

"There's no pulse, doctor," said a voice in the room. Katyrina kept pumping, and then one of the nurses reach for her arm. "He's gone, doctor."

Dr. Annikov's shoulders slumped. The room grew silent except for the heart monitor's monotone squelch. Katyrina paused, clenching her teeth to keep from crying.

"Call it. 3:12 a.m. I'm so sorry everybody," she said as she climbed down, heartbroken.

The mournful wail from Rebecca roared with such fright from her throat that for the rest of their lives, nobody who was there to hear it ever forgot it. It echoed through their souls for ten seconds, and only as Rebecca inhaled in anguish for a brief second did everyone hear the beep.

"Respirator!" yelled Dr. Annikov through her own tears. "Respirator!!"

She was the first one to reach the large bag-valve mask dangling loosely from Novah's intubation tube and began squeezing it urgently, rhythmically. Novah's heartbeat wasn't steady but it was there. A few seconds late, he started breathing on his own. The doctor turned to Rebecca.

"He just might make it. I don't know how, but he just might make it," she said through tears equal parts fatigue and amazement. The two hugged, and the rest of the room cheered.

"Ok, everyone who doesn't need to be here, get out," Annikov commanded, pulling herself together. "We need to make sure he's stable and then move him to intensive care. Good job, everyone."

Only Dr. Annikov and four nurses remained with Novah. Everyone else was pushed out of the operating room. They spoke nervously amongst each other. There was no certainty in Novah's survival and everyone knew it.

S'lace stood guarded by Jones in the waiting area and before long, Rebecca sat down beside her. She reached out and grabbed S'lace's long, thick fingers, then looked at Jones.

"Cut these off," she commanded, nodding at the plastic wrapped around S'lace's wrists.

"Ma'am, she's a suspect in…"

"I said, cut…these…*off.*"

The knife-sharp stare from Rebecca convinced the reluctant Jones to comply, and he sliced through S'lace's restraints with a small pair of cutters.

"I'm not so sure…"

"Your dedication to duty is duly noted, Jones. You can tell Chief Tines I compelled you. Now return to duty."

"Yes, ma'am," replied Jones, visibly angry as he left the medbay.

Jones gone, she regained a softer face and spoke to S'lace who was rubbing her wrists, but otherwise acted as if she'd never been restrained.

"Thank you, S'lace," Rebecca said.

"Rebecca is welcome," S'lace replied. "S'lace is fortunate to have remembered about the powdered hemoglobin."

Rebecca's fear and anguish was turning back to anger. "S'lace," she said, "I need you to find out why D'kob did this. Whatever you need to do, wherever you need to go, find out. I'll inform Chief Tines and have him give you all the support you need. You need to prove yourself to him, too. This will give you that chance."

"So S'lace is not to be banished?" she asked.

"Banished! Why would you be banished?" asked an incredulous Rebecca.

"D'kob was Khamek. S'lace is Khamek. Logic suggests that all Khamek be banished to protect Humans. Chief Tines is right to be skeptical of Khamek."

"S'lace," asked Rebecca, "did you have anything to do with the attack on Novah?"

"No!"

"Then there is no reason to banish you. Because D'kob was bad doesn't mean all Khamek are. Khamek each make their own choices, just as humans do," concluded Rebecca. "You are our friend."

S'lace leaned over and gave Rebecca a clumsy but sincere hug.

"S'lace thanks Rebecca," S'lace whispered.

Rebecca held S'lace by her thin shoulders, and stared into her large, dark eyes. "Just find out why he did this, ok?"

"S'lace will," she swore.

Rebecca returned to her quarters and changed out of her blood-soaked pajamas into regular clothes. She did her best to clean up, straighten her hair, and make herself presentable. She was in charge now, at least – and hopefully – temporarily.

Suck it up, Rebecca, she told herself. She made her way back to Medbay One.

Dr. Annikov had covered up her bloody undergarments with a long white lab coat, though her bunny slippers still poked out from the bottom. She met Rebecca at the door.

"He's stabilized," reported the doctor. "He will likely be unconscious for several days though. There may be some brain damage as well. It's just too early to know anything for sure. He could still slip away."

"I understand," said Rebecca. "When can I see him?"

The doctor shrugged. "You can see him now, I suppose. There's not much to see though, since he's knocked out colder than a Christmas goose."

"Thank you, doctor," Rebecca said.

"You're welcome," she replied.

"No," said Rebecca with utmost sincerity, "I mean *thank you*."

Dr. Annikov smiled warmly. "Thank me tomorrow."

Just as the doctor said, Novah was sleeping and Rebecca could see nothing but the regular, comforting bleeps on his monitor and his chest rising slowly up and down.

Rebecca made her way back to the officer's deck. Chief Tines was coordinating the investigation. She walked up behind him and put her hand on his shoulder.

"Thank you, Larry," she said wearily. "You were amazing. I'm glad you were here. If not for you, I'd be in the Medbay as well...or worse."

"We got lucky," he replied. "How's the Captain?"

"He's alive, if barely. We'll know more tomorrow."

The chief nodded. "There's not much to report here. That's clearly D'kob. The blade on the floor over there is the one that dropped from his hand. I don't understand the motive, though. I'd have never thought D'kob of all..err.. officers would do something like this."

"I've asked S'lace to help out. She has insight into the Khamek, obviously."

"Do you trust her?" he asked.

"I do," Rebecca replied.

He raised an eyebrow. "I'm not sure that's wise."

"If you are concerned, that's all the more reason to have her work with you in the investigation. I don't think she's any more involved in this than Hobbs," she said.

Tines frowned. "Maybe not, but my job is to be paranoid. I think we are in a lot more danger than you or the Captain realizes. S'lace and I will get to the bottom of this."

Rebecca made her way to the bridge. She looked at the empty command chair but refused to sit in it. She sat instead in her usual spot to its right. There was nobody else around.

"NICOLE, initiate order 3C," she commanded.

Order 3C initiated, replied the ship. Order 3C locked down the *R'ptyr*. No ships could come or go, and no communications could go in or out, without Rebecca's approval.

"NICOLE, display all communications logs for the past twenty-four hours."

Displaying.

The log listed all incoming and outgoing communications over the past day. Rebecca looked through the entries line by line. There was nothing out of the ordinary – only scout ship departure and arrival notices.

She sat and tried to think, her brain clouded by fatigue and stress. Nothing coherent came. She was worried about Novah. The vision of his spurting neck haunted her. Tired as she was, she wondered if she would ever sleep again.

Three hours later she was awakened with a gentle nudge by Jones, his demeanor noticeably softened from when they last exchanged words.

"Apologies, ma'am," he said quietly, "Dr. Annikov would like to see you in Medbay One."

"What time is it?!" Rebecca asked.

"Oh-seven-thirty, ma'am."

Too soon, Rebecca thought. She ran for the teleporter.

The Medbay One teleporter door opened, and Dr. Annikov was there waiting for her. She grabbed Rebecca's hand.

"Come with me," she said urgently, pulling her purposefully to the intensive care area. They entered the room and Dr. Annikov slid the curtain aside. Novah was in his bed, his head and shoulders elevated, beaming a smile at Rebecca as she entered.

"Novah!" said Rebecca, rushing to his side.

"I'm going to be ok," he replied somewhat weakly.

Dr. Annikov closed the door. "Someone better tell me what the hell is going on here," she ordered. "By all rights, *you* should be dead," she said pointing to Novah, "and if not, certainly still asleep." She turned and looked at Rebecca. "I ran your blood type. It's not compatible with AB negative. It should never have worked." The doctor was exasperated.

"You better tell her," said Novah, "or should I?"

"Oh, this should be interesting," said Rebecca, "considering you don't know jack." She smiled sweetly at him, holding his hand.

Novah looked at the doctor. "Pull up a chair, doc. I still can't speak very loudly." Dr. Annikov wheeled over a stool and sat near the head of the bed. Rebecca sat on the bed next to Novah's legs.

"Have you heard of the Holy Grail?" asked Novah.

"Sure," Dr. Annikov said, "the cup of Christ, from the last supper, or so the legend goes. Some big fancy gold cup that is supposed to have magical properties. Are you telling me you drank some magic potion from the Holy Grail?"

"No no no," replied Novah. "The whole cup thing is just a legend. A substitute. A distraction. A way of keeping danger away from the real Holy Grail – the *Sangreal*. A 'holy' vessel of an entirely different kind."

"You're losing me, Captain," said the doctor impatiently.

"It's a very long story, doctor, so I'll cut to the chase. Jesus Christ is a hybrid human. Is, not was, because he is still alive. He married and had children. Rebecca is his sole surviving heir, his 101st-generation granddaughter. She is the *sangreal*, the 'holy vessel' which contains his special blood. Of course the blood isn't 'holy' in the religious sense. Jesus carries an extra set of chromosomes, one byproduct of which is accelerated healing. Rebecca's genetically altered blood, passed down for generations, accelerates healing."

Rebecca and Dr. Annikov both looked at Novah in silence for a few seconds.

"How do you know all of that?" asked an amazed Rebecca.

"Your grandfather told me," replied Novah. Rebecca raised an eyebrow.

"I don't know if you're crazier than an outhouse rat or not," spoke the doctor, shaking her head. "I suspect you're still a little off from the trauma you've gone through. I'm highly skeptical about this whole granddaughter-of-Jesus thing." She continued to shake her head. "All I know is that you should be dead, and if not dead, certainly not have recovered so astonishingly quickly. It's medically unprecedented. It either has something to do with the Khamek powdered generic hemoglobin or Rebecca's blood. I looked at them both under the microscope and couldn't find anything odd. That being said, a month ago I didn't believe in aliens. I'm going to keep an open mind," she concluded. She turned to walk out of the room, made it to the door, then stopped.

Staring at Novah, smiling, she said "I'm glad you're alive, whatever the cause." She then turned to Rebecca, her smile hardening just a bit while she extended her index finger, pointing.

"And you...I want you in here every six weeks to donate. If you do have some magical properties in your blood, I want to have plenty on hand."

"Yes, doctor," replied Rebecca courteously. Dr. Annikov left them alone together.

Rebecca squeezed Novah's hand, tears in her eyes. "I'm so glad you made it. I was so worried."

"I didn't want to come back," Novah confided sadly. "It felt like I was gone for hours. I saw everything. I learned everything. I understood everything. Then Jesus ordered me back. Walked right up to me, put his hand on my chest, and gave me a shove saying *you're not done yet.*"

"Why do you sound so sad?" Rebecca asked softly.

"Because now it's almost all gone. It's like having an awesome dream but forgetting the details when you wake up. All I know is that for a little bit I saw and knew *everything*. Now most of that knowledge is gone. I remember the part about your blood, and maybe a couple of other little things, but for the most part I feel empty inside."

Rebecca raised his hand to her mouth and softly kissed his knuckles. "You should rest," she said. "We have lots to talk about once you've fully recovered."

"You're right," replied Novah. "I'm really tired. Everything okay on the ship otherwise?" he asked.

"I have S'lace and Chief Tines working to figure out why D'kob tried to kill you."

"I doubt you'll get far with that," replied Novah. "Just go to the source. Talk to S'heil. He's the puppet master."

Rebecca nodded. "Yes, that makes sense."

"You also need to talk to the President, right away," said Novah. "Let him know what happened. Try to find out if he was involved."

"I can't stand that man," confessed Rebecca. "He ruined so many lives. But I'll talk to him. I won't like it, but I'll do it."

Novah smiled at her, exhausted. "Thank you, Rebecca," he said. "I love you."

It caught her completely off guard, but she knew it was true. She could see it in his eyes. It had been true since they first met and only now did she recognize and embrace the emotion. A warm glow filled her, spreading out to every part of her being.

"I love you too, Novah," she said with a smile and a chaste kiss on his lips. "Get some sleep. I'll visit again in a few hours."

Novah drifted off before she could even close the door.

CHAPTER NINETEEN

Rebecca made straight for the bridge and was surprised to find S'lace there waiting for her. Rebecca sat in her usual seat. She could see that S'lace was eager to tell her something.

"Commander, S'lace has discovered D'kob's personal log."

"What does it say? Does it say he planned to kill Novah?" asked Rebecca.

"D'kob's log is comprehensive. Regarding the attempt on the Captain, D'kob states clearly that D'kob's clone is held by S'heil. S'heil coerced D'kob to kill Novah and Rebecca in exchange for D'kob's clone."

"Why would he do that? Why would he betray his friends?"

S'lace paused, considering the question. "The Khamek imperative of Khamek-preservation is deeply ingrained in all Khamek. S'lace believes D'kob, perhaps due to D'kob's heightened awareness of D'kob's mortality while being hunted for centuries, had an even greater focus on Khamek-preservation."

Rebecca seethed. "Thank you, S'lace," she said. "Take D'kob's log to Chief Tines."

"Yes, Commander," said S'lace, who quickly left the bridge. Rebecca returned to the task at hand.

"NICOLE, call the White House. Skip the switchboard. Connect me to the President directly."

Connecting, said the *R'ptyr.* Rebecca made a mental note to have NICOLE's voice changed. She knew Novah liked it, but she couldn't grow accustomed to hearing her own voice come out of the *R'ptyr*'s speakers.

NICOLE had patched in to the phone at Alberto' location, which was the office where he held his meeting with the Joint Chiefs three days a week. The Chiefs were all there. Alberto saw the emergency button flashing, and hit "answer" on the speakerphone.

"This is the President with the Joint Chiefs. To whom are we speaking?"

"Mr. President, I am Rebecca Carpenter, Chief Engineer aboard the *R'ptyr.* I must speak with you urgently."

"Certainly, Miss Carpenter. I'm turning on the video feed. The Joint Chiefs all know what's going on," Alberto said pressing the appropriate icon on the phone's digital display to bring up the video. The dark circles under her eyes and disheveled hair and clothes let him know that something was wrong. "What's the matter?"

"I thought you should know that the Khamek known as D'kob attempted to assassinate Captain Burns. D'kob is dead, and the Captain is in intensive care. His survival is uncertain," she lied.

"That's horrible news," replied an aghast Alberto. "Who commands the *R'ptyr*?"

"I do," replied Rebecca. "D'kob was an agent of S'heil, attempting to steal the *R'ptyr.* An investigation is ongoing. It would be most unfortunate if we were to discover that you were involved in this conspiracy to kill Captain Burns."

Rebecca tried to mask her tone, and her anger, to no avail. Alberto was keenly aware of just how upset Rebecca was. He tread carefully.

"Miss Carpenter, I can assure you that my administration has nothing to do with the attempt on Mr. Burns' life," he said. "The last thing I want to do is to jeopardize our arrangement."

"That's good to hear, Mr. President," Rebecca bit off. "I am ordered to fulfill the arrangement and pick up your 50,000 at the appointed time regardless if the Captain lives or dies, so long as the investigation validates your claim. If the investigation reveals any part of your administration in this conspiracy, the deal is forfeit."

Alberto smiled, leaning forward, and folded his hands together. "Miss Carpenter," he said with obvious condescension, "We had nothing to do with this assassination attempt. Investigate until your heart is content. I will remind you, however, that this deal is irrevocable. If you refuse to pick up the sigil-holders I will see to it that every city on this planet is vaporized. It's an awful, terrible chip to play, but you see, it's the only one I have. It's the sole perk of being the most powerful man on the planet. If S'heil somehow manages to keep you from arriving on time, I'll nuke the planet. I suggest you remind him of that. You two can have whatever kind of orbital war you want up there. I don't care so long as the *R'ptyr* shows up on time. We've been filling your requisition requests faster than you can transport them to your ship. We're doing our part. Make sure you do yours. Good day, Miss Carpenter." He ended the call.

Flushed and angry, Rebecca struggled to maintain decorum. She knew he was right, and she believed he'd push that big red button if it came to it.

"NICOLE, jam all outbound communications from Earth," Rebecca commanded. She wanted to be sure to talk to S'heil before Alberto did. She cursed herself for not doing that first.

Communications jammed.

"NICOLE, hail S'heil."

Hailing.

S'heil's white face filled the view screen. "Hello, S'heil," spat Rebecca.

S'heil cocked his head slightly to one side, his eyes slightly narrowing, confused.

"Hello, Rebecca," he said casually.

She suppressed the surprise that S'heil knew who she was. "Why did you have D'kob attack Novah? We agreed to honor your deal!"

The response was surprising. She was fully expecting excuses, but instead received frankness.

"D'kob's mission was to kill Novah, kill you, and kill however many Humans necessary to take control of the *R'ptyr*. S'heil offered D'kob a

Vice-Admiralship, a ship of D'kob's own, and assorted privileges and riches impossible for any Khamek to refuse. D'kob, being a particularly stubborn Khamek, refused anyway. Not until S'heil informed D'kob that S'heil had D'kob's clone did D'kob agree. Novah's – and your – inexperience in command and logistics represents a risk to the deal. S'heil's task is to eliminate risk. To ensure the success of the deal. S'heil has no confidence that Captain Burns would follow through. S'heil is required to take whatever actions are necessary to increase the odds of success. S'heil had to try to take the *R'ptyr*. Were the roles reversed, S'heil believes Novah would have attempted the same. Now, however, since D'kob's mission has failed, S'heil is out of options. S'heil must sit idly by and see what Humans do."

"I intend to make sure you no longer try to interfere," said Rebecca.

"NICOLE, target S'heil's ship. Fire on my command."

Ship targeted.

S'heil's eyes grew even wider than they already were. Claxons rang aboard his ship as sensors picked up the weapons lock from the *R'ptyr*. S'heil's cool and collected nature collapsed into something more urgent.

"Stop! Stop!" he pleaded. "Please! S'heil surrenders!"

"S'heil," stated Rebecca, "I am forgiving and merciful. With a word I can destroy you, but I shall not, for the sake of your crew. Do not mistake my mercy for weakness. If you try again to interfere, in any way, you will be eliminated. You have become a threat to the deal. A risk. You are not the only one who seeks to eliminate risk."

"S'heil understands," he replied.

"D'kob is dead," continued Rebecca. "Do you have any other agents aboard the *R'ptyr*? If so, they will be returned unharmed."

"No," replied S'heil grimly. "D'kob was the only agent." *Technically*, he thought to himself.

"I advise you to 'sit idly by,' as you put it. It is a dangerous game we play, S'heil, with our civilizations at stake. If you attempt anything else, you will never reach V'laha. If the *R'ptyr* doesn't collect the sigil-holders, Alberto will nuke the planet. If anything interferes with the boarding of the additional 50,000, we will destroy the *R'ptyr*. If everyone remains patient and calm, everyone will get what they want," she concluded.

"NICOLE, stand down."

Weapons disengaged.

S'heil relaxed, his narrow shoulders slumped in resignation.

"S'heil will not interfere," he promised.

Rebecca ended the transmission. S'heil grinned devilishly as he pressed a small button on the arm of his command chair.

An hour or so later, Rebecca called Chief Tines and S'lace to the bridge.

"You can stop your investigation. S'heil admitted to blackmailing D'kob to get him to kill Novah and me. That plus D'kob's own admission in his log is enough to satisfy me that we know what happened."

Chief Tines frowned, and S'lace lowered her head in shame.

"Apologies," offered S'lace, "on behalf of all Khamek, S'lace carries D'kob's shame."

"Nonsense," retorted Rebecca. "S'heil carries the shame, not you. I want you to resume your shifts bringing people on board. Without D'kob, we'll only be able to bring half as many on, but half is better than none."

"S'lace can work longer each day," S'lace offered.

"No," replied Rebecca, "you'll maintain your normal shift. N'dim and V'kol will continue to ferry supplies. Nothing changes."

"As Rebecca wishes," said S'lace. "S'lace shall continue at once."

"Thank you, S'lace. Chief Tines, please dispose of D'kob's body if you haven't already and have his quarters cleaned out. Keep whatever looks interesting, but otherwise destroy everything. I'd like those quarters sterilized and ready for a new occupant tomorrow."

"No problem," he replied. "I already found his command module tucked in a drawer. That's how come his security dot didn't show up."

Rebecca frowned. "That doesn't seem terribly secure," she noted.

"It isn't," Tines replied, "yet as concerned as I am with security, I don't know that we want to live in a world where everyone is tracked every hour of every day. I feel like a voyeur watching the board and seeing everyone's movements."

"I didn't even know about the tracking station," Rebecca said. "Have you been watching my dot?"

"I watch everyone's dot," he replied with a look that let her know that he knew exactly what she did in the wee hours of the morning.

"We should talk about it when Novah's back on his feet," she said. The chief nodded.

D'kob's quarters were directly adjacent to Novah's on the starboard hallway of the officer's deck. Rebecca's quarters were directly opposite on the port hallway, a fair distance away. Since D'kob would no longer be needing his quarters it only made sense from a logistical point of view to move in next to the Captain. Or so she justified to herself.

The next day Novah was dramatically improved and checked himself out of Medbay One. Dr. Annikov's instincts rejected the notion at first but after he passed all of her tests with flying colors she saw no reason to keep him.

He made his way back to his quarters, and as he did, he walked by D'kob's. The door opened as he pressed against it. It was sterile and empty. He left it and went next door to his own.

"NICOLE," he said, "seal D'kob's quarters. Lock the door. Nobody enters without my permission."

Quarters secured.

Novah changed his clothes and made his way to the baths. After a long soak, he shaved, working carefully around the stitches on both sides of his neck, and did his best to regain his former bearing. He then made a point to visit several of the stations on the ship, hopping around via teleporter, to see how things were going. The ship still felt hollow and empty except for the small bands of scientists or craftspersons busily working in their areas. On the architecture deck he walked up to a burly black man named Richard Cohagen, the man in charge of architecture and design aboard the *R'ptyr*. Cohagen recognized Novah immediately.

"Captain! What a pleasant surprise!" he said sincerely.

"Hello, Chief Cohagen. I have a couple requests. One falls outside the normal scope of your job description, the other is a necessity that

I'm not sure if you've put on your list yet."

"Let's hear 'em, Captain."

Novah smiled. "As you may have noticed, the lavatory situation on the *R'ptyr* is less than modern."

"Oh, I've noticed," Cohagen replied with a nod. "Right out of ancient Rome. The ship is big enough that a person can usually find a row of toilets with nobody around, but that won't last long."

"I'd like you to address that issue," continued Novah. He walked to Cohagen's table and called up the *R'ptyr*'s floor plan. He swiped through the decks until he found the one he wanted.

"Here," he said pointing. "Section 12 on Deck 3. The Hall of Justice. It's a large, round structure, surrounded by a dozen teleporters. I don't expect that we'll be needing a courthouse this large for quite a while, so I want you to convert it into proper bathrooms. Half male, half female, plumbed right, with stalls, doors, sinks, and showers. Get me a list of the supplies you need and I'll adjust the acquisition table accordingly. It doesn't have to be fancy, just functional. Cram as many stalls in there as you can. Think you can have it done in three months if you start getting the supplies this week?"

Cohagen chuckled. "Captain, I don't mean to burst your bubble, but this ship has a built in sewer system, and all of it is piped through the existing toilets. I could build you the Taj Mahal of bathrooms in that building, but it wouldn't matter because there's no connection to the existing sewer system. The best I can do is set up some partitions on the existing facilities. I can make them nice. Full walls with doors, like you'd see in a high-class office building. It's not perfect, but folks will have some privacy. As far as showers go, well, the best we can do is convert a couple of the bath areas. One for ladies, one for gents. I can plumb some shower heads in and it'll be just like a health club locker room."

Novah frowned. "Well, how fast could you have that done?"

Cohagen smiled. "I don't know what kind of sorting algorithm you used to select who is on board right now, but I have seven people working for me. They are, by far, the best, hardest-working, most adept, most adaptable and intelligent work crew I've ever known. I always thought I was the best at what I did. Half the folks working for me…well, I should probably be working for *them*. If you could get me all of the materials tomorrow, we'd have it done two weeks later. We'll go through the supplies faster than you can get them to us though. That's a boatload of partitions and pipes we need. We're gated on how fast you can get us materials. So realistically, we're talking two to seven weeks to completion. It won't be ideal, but it'll work. What was the second thing?"

"A special project," replied Novah. "A little remodeling."

He gave Chief Cohagen the details, they shook hands, and Novah continued on his rounds.

Rebecca made her way to Medbay One, and after Dr. Annikov informed her that Novah had checked himself out, she headed towards the bridge figuring that's where he'd be. He wasn't. He wasn't in the tactical lounge. He wasn't in his quarters. He wasn't at the baths, which had become one of his favorite places.

He's probably just wandering, she concluded. She could easily ask NICOLE where he was, but figured she'd let him return to normal life at his own pace. She went back to her quarters and filled a medium-sized box. She didn't have much at all – nobody did. One box contained her entire life. She picked up the box and walked to D'kob's old quarters. The door didn't open when she touched it, much to her surprise. She sat the box down and pressed on the door again. No response.

"NICOLE, unlock D'kob's old quarters," she commanded.

Access denied.

"NICOLE, command override alpha one one. Unlock D'kob's old quarters."

Access denied.

"NICOLE, access denied by whom?"

Access restricted by Captain Burns.

"That's odd," she said out loud to herself. She picked her box back up and returned to her quarters.

Eventually they found each other in the tactical lounge. It was shortly before seven, and all of the officers offered their hands to

Novah as they trickled in, wishing him well, saying they were glad he was alive and similar courtesies. The reports offered nothing new or substantial, apart from S'lace's new colonist report, which was now half of the usual number. After dinner everyone went about their way. Rebecca took Novah's hand. He seemed distant.

"Are you ok?" she asked.

"I'm fine," he replied. "In fact I actually feel really good. I'm just...distracted."

"Distracted by what?"

"Just thoughts. Thoughts about life, about what we're doing, where we're going, how little time is left, that kind of thing." She assumed he was talking about their mission.

"Do you want to talk about it?" she asked with a soft smile.

"I do," he said much to her surprise. "Let's go to the observation deck. I like looking out at the Earth and stars."

They walked in silence to the observation deck, a smaller version of the theater area – round, with a large clear canopy overhead covering the area like a bowl. It was dark except for the Earth, the stars, and a single candle flickering on a white tablecloth at the very center of the room.

"What's this?" Rebecca asked.

"Dinner," replied Novah. "I hope you don't mind a real meal."

"Heavens no!" she exclaimed with delight.

They walked to the small round table and sat down. The candle flickered, highlighting real plates, real silverware, and real glasses. Out of the darkness a man approached dressed to the nines in the finest waiter-wear complete with a white cloth draped with precision over his left arm. He stood there, and with a wide smile, said "Good evening." His French accent was thick, but his English was easily understood.

"Rebecca, may I introduce Chef Leguiliamme, the *R'ptyr*'s Master Chef."

"Please accept my apologies for my attire," the chef said with a smile. "I play two parts this evening, that of chef and waiter. I find the waiter outfit provides better immersion, no?"

Rebecca smiled. "It's delightful, Chef Le..leghu..."

"Leguiliamme," he stated politely.

"Leg-you-lammey," she tried to say carefully.

He smiled at her, ignoring her pronunciation, and continued. "I'm afraid tonight's menu is quite limited. It seems that real food, especially meat, is difficult to come by. I can only offer you a delicious salmon steak on a bed of dark rice with lemon, or an equally delicious filet mignon with a baked potato, seasoned and grilled to your preference."

"I'll have the salmon," said Rebecca, "and the Captain will have the steak. Medium."

"Medium?! Are you sure?!" protested the chef.

Before Rebecca could respond, the chef shook his head rapidly. "No no no...medium will not do. I shall prepare the steak properly. Now then, shall I bring the wine? I only have one, so the pairing will not be ideal."

"Yes please," replied Novah. "I'm sure the pairing will be fine." He winked at the chef.

"Indeed, sir. I will return shortly." The chef retreated, mumbling *À point, bien sûr...*

Novah squinted at Rebecca. "What makes you think I want the steak?"

Rebecca smiled. "It's been a long time since we had real food. If he's going to offer two kinds of meat, I figured we should strike while the iron was hot and get both!"

"So I suspect you'll be wanting to taste my steak?"

"Mmmhmm." She batted her eyelashes, her chin resting on her hands.

The chef returned with the bottle of wine. He was as pale as a ghost.

"Captain, you said there was a bottle of wine in the box you gave me beforehand, but I did not bother to look at it. You must have some very special friends to get this particular bottle..." his voice trailed off.

"What is it?" inquired Rebecca.

Leguiliamme regained his waiterly posture, holding the bottle along his left forearm, label out. "Madame, this is a 1945 vintage of Chateau Mouton-Rothschild. It is quite possibly the perfect wine. It is extraordinarily rare and expensive."

"Pour some," said Novah.

"Indeed, sir," said the chef, "though I suggest letting it air for a few minutes. When your dinner arrives, it should be ready."

He filled the pair of glasses and retreated to the kitchens. Novah picked up his glass and held it out towards Rebecca.

"Cheers," he said.

"He said to wait!" protested Rebecca.

"Oh come on," said Novah, "do you really think I have the ability to tell the difference between an aired-out wine versus straight out of the bottle?"

She smirked and raised her glass. "I know I don't!"

Their glasses were half empty by the time dinner arrived. Chef Leguiliamme was aghast. "You didn't wait!" he exclaimed.

"It is delicious nonetheless," stated Rebecca.

The chef placed the plates before them. The three of them salivated, the aroma of the meats wafting upward towards their noses – the first meat they'd seen in months. Novah picked up his fork and knife.

"I'm afraid you won't be hearing much from me in the next four minutes," he stated, digging in.

"Save some for me!" she squealed.

The chef rolled his eyes and refilled their glasses. As he turned away, Novah stopped him, his mouth still full of steak.

"Wait," he mumbled, trying to swallow. He reached over and grabbed the third-full bottle of wine and handed it to the chef. "Take this. Enjoy!"

"Merci!" exclaimed the chef.

The pair rapidly consumed their dinner, both feeling a little guilty as the last bites dropped into their stomachs. Novah wiped his mouth with his napkin.

"Ok, so maybe that was a little rushed. But it was so good!" he said.

Rebecca giggled. "I suppose dessert is out of the question?"

Novah sighed and nodded. "I'm afraid so," he said. "Let's walk this off."

He pushed his chair back, stood up, and grabbed Rebecca's hand as she did the same. They walked to the port side of the *R'ptyr*, where the Earth slowly rotated below them.

"It's hard to believe everything down there is going to be dead in a few years," he whispered. "Every animal, insect, tree and person."

"Something will survive," offered Rebecca. "Something always does. This won't be the first time nearly everything has been wiped out. Remember the dinosaurs?"

"That was a bit before my time," he jested. "Perhaps we should ask your grandfather?"

She nudged him in the shoulder playfully. "That was well before his time, even!"

"Anyway," continued Novah, "we're never going to see Earth again after we leave."

"No," she whispered sadly. "Our lives will continue on A'ala. I'll miss Earth, but at least we'll be alive."

Novah nodded, and reached into his pocket withdrawing a small, hand-carved wooden box. "I have something for you," he said. "Happy birthday." He handed her the box.

"But it's not my birthday," she said absently, taking the box. She cracked it open, gasped, then closed it again. Tears welled up in her eyes, and she reopened the box.

"Oh Novah!" she cried, "It's…it's…"

"Astonishing, isn't it?" he finished for her.

"Yes!" she exclaimed. She pulled the ring out of the box, holding it between two fingers, admiring it in what little light there was. It was a thick, crystal ring with a round stone about a centimeter in diameter set in the middle, recessed half-way into the body of the ring. The stone was actually a sphere-within-a sphere. The inner sphere was a model of Earth, with the outer sphere designed to be clouds. The inner sphere floated in the ether of the outer one independently, giving the illusion of a moving atmosphere swirling over the planet.

"Where did you get this?!" she asked.

"A friend," he said, taking the ring and sliding it on her ring finger. "I know it's not a diamond but I hope you'll accept it as a substitute." She barely heard the words, utterly mesmerized by the tiny blue and green world swirling in clouds nested on her finger. Novah took her hand, covering the ring, breaking the spell.

"Rebecca," he said, "will you marry me?"

She worked to focus through the tears in her eyes, the pounding of her heart, and the happiness bursting inside her. She withdrew her hand from Novah, then placed both of hers against the sides of Novah's face.

"Novah," she said, "I've been married to you since we met – in my heart. Before we met, I had my doubts. Reading your file, knowing the troubles you've been through, I didn't know what to think. Grandfather asked me to see beyond, to open my heart to who you really were inside. When I saw you in the flesh, I knew. I knew I would spend the rest of my life with you. So yes, Novah Burns, I will marry you, though in my heart, it's only a formality at this point."

She drew his face close and gave him a kiss to melt the world.

"When?" he asked after regaining his breath.

She shrugged. "Whenever," she replied. "It doesn't matter to me when the official paperwork is done… if we even need to do that anymore. I think it's more about ceremony at this stage than anything else. Do we even have anyone on board who can officiate?"

"I highly doubt it," Novah replied. "But I agree that there's no real need to hurry with the formality. When we can, we will. I'm yours in my heart, too." Rebecca beamed.

"I have one more present for you," he continued. "Follow me."

She followed Novah to the observation deck teleporter. "Officer's deck," he commanded.

The door opened and they were on the officer's deck, directly across from Novah's quarters. They took a right and walked a few scant feet down the hall to the locked door to D'kob's old quarters.

Rebecca was just about to say something, but Novah "sshh'd" her.

"NICOLE, unlock officer quarter two. Code to Rebecca's palm signature."

Access granted.

Novah gestured to the door. "Go ahead!"

She pressed her hand against the door and it slid into its pocket. Walking in, she saw that D'kob's quarters had been completely redone.

Metal had been replaced with wood in places. The thin mattress on the bed was replaced with a thick, comfortable one, covered with an orange down comforter. A rich, deep blue shag carpeting covered the floor, offset by the lime-green walls. Bits of metal and glass still remained, poking out from knobs, tables and drawers in sterile protest to the colors now surrounding them.

"These are your quarters now," stated Novah. "I want you closer."

She leapt into his arms. "This is wonderful!" she exclaimed. "It's beautiful! How did you do this?"

"Chief Cohagen had some guys whip this up. Didn't take them long. Getting the carpet on board was the hardest part. It had to be cut in several sections to fit in the supply ships." He led her deeper into the room.

"And over here," he said pressing a button on the wall, "is a new feature." A door swished open, revealing an opening that lead directly into Novah's quarters. "If you get mad or sick of me, you can just close the door and lock it up. Otherwise, I'd be happy to keep it open."

"It's perfect," she said looking around, admiring the new setting. "There's only one thing that could make this evening more perfect."

"I couldn't find any flowers," Novah sighed.

"I was thinking of something else," Rebecca replied with a seductive wink, dragging him by the hand to her new bed.

CHAPTER TWENTY

A few weeks later, Novah was becoming frustrated.

"How are we ever going to get enough supplies on board?" he exclaimed to his officers at dinner. "N'dim and V'kol are doing their best, but those scout craft are small."

Quartermaster Janice Roskov responded. "Don't worry too much about that, Captain. While we may not have a large supply of modern foodstuffs and amenities, this ship came pre-stocked with plenty of basics and food pills. I do have a concern, however."

"What is it?" inquired the Captain.

"Water. Without enough water, we're all dead halfway there. The tanks on the R'ptyr are huge, and mostly full. We run a full-fledged water and sewer system, so we have a closed loop and don't lose anything, yet if something goes wrong, if one little part of the system breaks and we have a leak or vent any water out into space, we'll have to start rationing at the very least. When you look at a four year journey with no known pit stops, we just barely have enough water with full tanks for 50,000 people with no room for error."

Rebecca peeked up at Novah from her module, but didn't say anything.

"We'll have plenty of water," stated Novah. "We're onboarding more when we land on Earth, and before we open the wormhole to

A'ala, we'll stop in the Oort cloud to refill. Almost everything out there is ice – some methane, some water, some other stuff. We'll mine a water source and refill. That'll get us the rest of the way." Novah smiled, proud that he'd actually remembered something from seventh grade science class.

Roskov looked at him skeptically. "Do you know how to mine space objects? They aren't just sitting there like a gas station, stationary, waiting for us to pull up to one."

Novah hadn't thought about that part.

"NICOLE, does the *R'ptyr* have the ability to capture and mine external space bodies for water?" asked Novah.

Affirmative. With enough advance planning, the R'ptyr can match the speed and trajectory of an external object, and then extract resources using one of twelve automatic extractors.

"Like refueling an F-22 in flight," offered Chief Tines.

Novah was satisfied. "Water will be fine, food will be fine, as crops are already starting to bear fruit on the farm deck. Medicine and arms will be fine, as we made those a higher priority for initial loading. What about bulk building materials? Steel? Computers? Transportation? Things too big to fit in a scout craft?" Novah asked.

The room fell silent.

"Captain," started Rebecca, "we should remember to be realistic about our mission. The *R'ptyr*, large as she is, is not large enough to transport every kind of equipment and technology to A'ala. The focus of the *R'ptyr*'s design was on people. People design things. People build things. We spent a lot of time formulating a method of getting the right people. With the right people, we can make steel. We can make supplies. We can make anything we need as long as the people we have know how to do it. The *R'ptyr* is not a cargo vessel. It's more like a cruise liner. The *R'ptyr* has the basics. Once we get to A'ala, we'll have to build what we need from the basics. We can't bring Earth with us. Only the minds of Earth."

Novah stared down at the table, tapping his fingers on it in thought while the room sat in silence.

"You are right, of course," he stated softly. "I hope we've picked the right people."

When the meeting adjourned for the evening, Dr. Annikov tapped Novah on the shoulder.

"Captain, please make time to come by the medbay tomorrow. I want to do some follow-up tests to make sure everything is alright. It's been over a month, and while you feel healthy, I'd feel better if you had a check-up."

"I'm fine, doctor," he replied with a sigh.

"Novah," chided Rebecca. "You'll go, and you'll go tomorrow." She nodded at the doctor. Novah's nostrils flared.

"Fine," he bit off.

The next day, just to be sure, Rebecca personally escorted Novah to Medbay One. She handed him off to Dr. Annikov.

"I'll continue on rounds while you do your thing," she told the doctor. She then looked at Novah. "Oh, don't look so sullen. Come find me on the farm deck when you're done." She waved and departed.

Dr. Annikov closed the door to the exam room. "Alright captain, up on the table. Take your shirt off."

He peeled off his uniform top over his head, and Katyrina then wrapped the blood pressure sleeve around the upper part of his right arm, the Velcro holding it fast. Novah sat there while the doctor pressed the button to inflate it. He looked up at the doctor, who was busy looking at her timer. He recalled meeting her the first time in the tactical lounge, and talking with her a few times when he recovered, but he never really *noticed* her – until now. She wasn't absurdly beautiful, wasn't particularly tall, and possessed a fit but unsculpted frame. The way she moved though, the deftness of her fingers, the sway of her hips, the periodic unconscious swoop of her hand to push away a stray lock of her red hair, all appealed to him at a base level. He decided that he found her attractive. He certainly trusted her – she'd saved his life after all. She was a brilliant and competent doctor as well. She was a decade older than him, but still in her prime.

"What?" she asked, catching him staring.

"Nothing, doctor. I was just spacing out."

"Yes, I can only imagine about what," she said snarkily. "Blood pressure is fine."

She grabbed a stethoscope and pressed the cold metal against his chest. The metal was cold, but the heel of her hand was warm.

"Your heartbeat is normal. Strong and steady." She walked around behind him, placing the stethoscope on his back. "Breathe in and hold it." He did so until she ordered him to let out his breath, and then repeated the exercise two more times.

"Ok, let me see your neck now." She went back around to his front, and pressed her warm fingertips around the area where his stitches from where D'kob had sliced him had been.

"Doctor," Novah said in a soft, courteous voice, "I don't think I ever really thanked you. Thank you for saving me."

"You're welcome, Novah," she said warmly. "It's what you pay me for." They both laughed lightly.

"Other side," she said, turning his head. Her fingers poked around the area where the incision to his neck vein had healed.

He thought the words, he suppressed them. He thought the words again, and then suppressed them again. He didn't understand how he could, or why he would, say them, and was taken aback with surprise hearing them come out of his mouth.

"You really are quite attractive, you know."

Dr. Annikov's fingers froze in place for a full second, absorbing the words. Then one set of fingers pressed up behind Novah's ears, gingerly intertwined with the hair there, slowly combing it backwards. Without looking at him, she moved her lips achingly close to his ear.

"Be careful what you say, Captain," she said in her hauntingly seductive drawl. He could feel her warm breath against him. "You don't want to take on more than you can handle."

He felt a twinge.

She turned away and bent over purposefully to pick up his shirt which had slid off of the chair he'd put it on.

"Exam's over," she said, once again in her fully-professional tone shattering the past few seconds like glass. She handed him his shirt. "Get dressed, and come back here in a month," she ordered.

"Yes, doctor," he replied, somewhat embarrassed.

"I'll see you tonight," she replied in a friendly tone.

"Yes, see you tonight." He made his way out of the exam room and towards the agriculture section of the *R'ptyr*, carrying on normally, the exchange with Dr. Annikov mostly forgotten. Mostly.

He found Rebecca talking to the head farmer, who was remarkably named farmer Brown. He was waving his hand over the fields from his observation deck when Novah walked up to them.

"Mr. Brown says the fields are growing great," said Rebecca. "We already have a full crop of tomatoes, lettuce, beans, and many other vegetables. With proper soil rotations, we'll be able to grow all year round."

Brown nodded. "Yep. This artificial lighting works just like the real thing, and I don't know what kind of dirt this is, but there are no pests and no fungi of any kind to worry about. No chemicals or pesticides needed. Everything can be all organic and still get maximum yield. The problem is harvesting it all."

"How's that?" asked Novah.

"Well, what you see laid out before you is a hundred acres, half of which is planted. We're ready for harvest, but I don't have enough people to harvest it all. Then how do we store it? Do you have a processing plant? A cannery? A monster freezer and tons of vacuum-sealing bags? It's my own damn fault...I planted too much. I was thinking about a larger crew."

"I see," replied Novah. "We'll figure something out. Make sure you show up to dinner tonight."

"Will do," farmer Brown replied. He reached behind him and picked up a large basket of tomatoes, handing it to Rebecca.

"A little something for you to snack on," he said with a smile.

She accepted the basket by the woven handle. "Thank you, Mr. Brown," she replied in kind. "See you at dinner."

Rebecca swung the basket casually with one hand, while holding Novah's hand with the other as they walked back towards the teleporter.

"He has a little crush on me," confessed Rebecca.

"Who wouldn't?" grinned Novah. "You're the best woman on this spaceship. I don't blame him a bit for being fond of you."

"You're so sweet," she said, nudging up against him. "I've seen eyes ogling you too, you know."

"Who, me?" he asked incredulously.

She rolled her eyes. "Don't play the innocent one, mister," she lightly chided, "every woman here, even the married ones, have eyed you from time to time. It's completely natural. Even your doctor has a soft spot for you."

Novah blushed.

"Oh, you've noticed as well, hmm?" continued Rebecca.

"No no.. it's..umm..no..I don't know.." he stammered.

She laughed, that echoing, delightful laugh that made Novah weak at the knees. "It's ok, Novah. It's all completely natural. I'm not the crazy-jealous wife kind. I know you love me and want me. That's all I care about. The others can flirt all they want," she said sincerely.

He stopped their walk, turned, and kissed her. Hard. He came up for breath and whispered something into her ear. Then it was her turn to blush.

They made their way leisurely back to the tactical lounge. Once there, Novah called up the current rank lists on the displays. Those names already boarded were in green, their slots frozen. The names in each section underneath changed as the *R'ptyr* did the evaluations and sorting. At the beginning, name swaps had been fast and furious. As the number of applications slowed down to thousands per day instead of tens of thousands, the lists were starting to look a bit more solid. There was, however, very little green. The vast majority would not get pre-boarded.

"We'll need to figure out a way to manage this," Novah said. "We should cut off applications at some time. Establish the concrete list and the waitlist. We'll also have to figure out loading logistics."

Rebecca nodded. "I propose ending applications at the six month mark, which is about five weeks away. We'd have to announce it soon."

"I'm glad we have NICOLE to do all of the sorting," said Novah. "It's such a huge, messy math problem. NICOLE compensates for families and keeps the right ratios and all of the stuff it would take humans forever to figure out."

"Should we publish the list and waitlist?" asked Novah.

Rebecca thought for a moment. "I don't know if that's such a good idea. We should figure out a way to let people know they're in the running, though, so that they can prepare."

"Any suggestions?" asked Novah. "You're the smart one."

She tapped her fingernails on the table for a few seconds. "How about this," she said. "After we end applications, we'll have the complete pool of folks, and they'll be ranked. We can provide each person with a notice that they are in the pool. We don't have to tell them what number they are...but we *can* tell them an estimated percentage chance that they'll be selected. NICOLE can do that math quite easily. It's not a guarantee – people still have to pass the health exam – but it'll give people a good sense of what their odds are. We only send out two notices, though, one each the last two weeks prior to pick-up. People only need enough time to get organized and reach the rendezvous point."

"I like it," replied Novah. "We should do a broadcast soon. NICOLE, send a notification to all broadcast agencies that I'll be issuing a statement tomorrow at nine p.m. GMT."

Notification sent.

The following afternoon Novah explained that applications would stop being accepted at the six month mark, and how those that made the pool would be notified. He was done in five minutes and ended the transmission.

He had intentionally sequestered himself from the planetside cacophony of opinion since his first announcement. He knew he would be hated by the majority and didn't want to hear or read any of it. There was no need to. Good people were going to get left behind. There was no avoiding that cold, hard fact. He and Rebecca had discussed it many times and had made their peace with it.

NICOLE, by accessing all of the databases of information governments had accrued on individuals, was able to cross-check responses on applications with actual data. The dossiers of those on the ranking boards were quite long and detailed. Rich people on Earth would attempt to game the application process by paying brilliant minds outrageous sums of money to fill out applications for them. Courses were created out of thin air where application "experts" received a hefty fee for their "teachings" on how to fill out their applications "correctly." A great deal of money changed hands, but none of it had any impact on NICOLE's selection algorithms. NICOLE saw through all of the shenanigans which manifested themselves as irreconcilable inconsistencies.

Predictably, there was a large increase in the number of applications the week following Novah's notice. The numbers quickly trailed off after that as the vast majority of those who wanted to apply had done so. At the six month mark, NICOLE had processed 712,345,982 applications. That total was less than ten percent of Earth's population.

The manifest of the *R'ptyr* at the six month mark listed 1381 people. Novah estimated that S'lace would be able to bring another thousand on board before the main pick-up time. He felt uneasy about that number. Five hundred would be security personnel of various flavors, but would that be enough to secure the loading area? What if people got out of hand? What if Alberto or S'heil were stupid enough to try something?

And when would he tell the rest of the crew about the sigil holders? Novah, Rebecca, and S'lace knew the plan for them, but nobody else did.

"We need to tell the chiefs sooner or later," Rebecca reminded him. "I think some will not understand. Some will openly balk. But I think what we've decided is the most just."

"Do we have to tell them everything?" asked Novah. "I think we should tell only what we have to. Ask for forgiveness later rather than set up an environment where the entire mission is jeopardized."

Novah and Rebecca discussed it further, and came up with the plan for telling the others.

During dinner the next evening, Novah addressed the table, which was by this time completely surrounded with full chairs.

"Ladies and gentlemen," he began, "the time has come to inform you about another aspect of our mission." The room grew silent.

"As you are all aware, 50,000 humans are being selected through the application process for pickup and transport to A'ala to colonize that world. People were chosen very carefully for specific roles. These 50,000 will serve as the base through which we build a civilization. However, those 50,000 will not be the only ones joining us on our journey. Sixty years ago, the Khamek made an arrangement with world leaders where certain select people would be allowed passage. Each person was given a special sigil which constitutes a boarding pass. We have no control regarding the makeup of this group. They could be thieves, sick, slackers, or decent people. It doesn't matter – if they have a sigil, they get to board."

Murmurs surrounded the table. Dr. Annikov's voice rose to the top.

"They will have to be quarantined," she stated flatly. "With no health check, who knows what they could be carrying. We can't risk jeopardizing everyone else."

Rebecca flashed a glance at Novah. Novah caught the glance but quickly turned his vision to the doctor.

"You right, doctor," he stated. "We will be boarding these 50,000 first, through the mid-ship boarding platform, into two sterile containment areas. They will be completely set apart from the rest of the ship. It will seem and feel like they are being imprisoned, but we can't take any chances. How long of a quarantine do you recommend?" He mentally crossed his fingers.

Her response was immediate. "Fourteen days," she stated. "We're going to have to be very careful with this, Captain. Nobody on board should come into contact with any of them. If it is possible to have them self-board, we should, to limit exposure."

Fourteen days…more than enough, Novah thought.

"Fourteen days it is then," Novah replied. "We'll come up with a way to limit exposure at boarding. The only thing we really have to worry about is making sure only sigil-holders board, and that the boarding is orderly." He looked at Rebecca. "I'm putting you in charge of coordinating this, Rebecca."

"Yes, Captain," she replied.

"We're scheduled to pick up the remainder of our selections three days later. That'll be more involved. It'll take longer. We need to do on-the-spot health checks and disqualify anyone who is sick, in accordance with the regular plan. We've depended on NICOLE to do the first part…it's up to human hands to finish up the process."

Nods circled the table.

"Chief Tines," Novah continued, "you will need to draw up a security plan for both boardings. I don't trust S'heil or Earth governments to leave us alone. Expect the unexpected."

"Yes, Captain," Tines replied.

Novah pressed his palms flat against the table. "This is going to be hard, everyone. We have to be clinical. Disciplined. Ordered. We have six months to come up with a solid boarding plan. We'll be having monthly review sessions to go over the plans from now until…" Novah thought for a moment.

"What shall we call this little operation? Shouldn't we think up something clever to commemorate the boarding?" He looked around the table.

"Let's just call it what it is," offered Chief Tines. "Embarkation. E1 and E2." There were murmurs of agreement.

"Ok then," continued Novah, "Embarkation it is. The sigil holders are E1, the others are E2. The first review session will be two weeks from today, lasting all day. Please plan accordingly. Is there anything else to discuss today?" There was silence until Dr. Annikov spoke up once again.

"All of the officers at this table have been working their brains out. I'd like everyone to schedule an appointment with my staff for physicals," she said. "Yourself included," she said pointedly at Novah.

"I was just there a few days ago!" he protested, but the evil eye from the doctor caused him to shut up. Rebecca smirked, which didn't escape Dr. Annikov's eye. "You too, Rebecca," the doctor continued. "You haven't even come in to donate blood like I asked. And when was the last time you had a physical?"

"Maybe when I was sixteen," confessed Rebecca. "I'll make an appointment for this week."

Dr. Annikov looked around the table and was greeted by forlorn faces. Nobody wanted to have a physical. The doctor read the body language and made her insistence known.

"Look, I know none of you want to do this," she stated, "but look at the situation we are in. We've been working hard. We're going to continue to work hard until Embarkation. And it won't end then. Once everyone gets boarded, our jobs become even harder as we try to be leaders for 100,000 people, half of whom are locked up for two weeks. We won't get a real rest for probably a year. We can't burn out too fast. We have to pace ourselves. Lots of rest, a good diet, all of that stuff. We need to stay sharp."

Reluctant nods fell like dominoes around the table, followed by various mumbled promises to comply.

"Well, now that that's settled," Novah said through a smirk, "is there anything else?"

Nobody said anything, so Novah adjourned the meeting. The bulk of those in attendance exited, with the exception of Novah, Rebecca, and Dr. Annikov, who was fiddling with her module. She finally stood up and headed for the door.

"I've scheduled Rebecca for next Tuesday, and Novah for the day after," she said without looking up.

"Thank you, Katyrina," Rebecca said.

CHAPTER TWENTY-ONE

Rebecca ended up going to see Dr. Annikov well in advance of her appointment. The morning after the big meeting, Rebecca devoured a large, fresh, ripe tomato from the basket that farmer Brown had given her the day before. Shortly after she finished, the barely-chewed tomato fled her stomach with violent intent, spreading its red, seedy mess all over the tactical lounge table, much to Novah's astonishment.

"Holy crap!" he exclaimed. "Let's get you to the medbay!"

Rebecca attempted to wave him off, to no avail. She continued to vomit forth a frothy red bile, leaning on Novah heavily as he guided her to the teleporter. In less than a minute he was dragging Rebecca to the nearest medbay table as Dr. Annikov rushed out of her office.

"What's the matter?" the doctor asked urgently.

"I'm not sure," replied Novah. "We were sitting at the table, and she just started barfing all over the place."

"I'm fine," Rebecca croaked.

"I'll be the judge of that," retorted Dr. Annikov. "I've got it from here, Captain. She's in good hands."

"Can't I stay?" he whined.

"No, best you don't. Your exposure should be limited until we find out what's going on here," replied the doctor.

"Alright," he sighed as he exited. "Call me if you need anything."

"Certainly," said the doctor. She closed the door behind him, and turned to Rebecca.

"Did you eat anything funny?" she asked.

"No," replied an ashen-faced Rebecca, "just a large tomato."

"That's funny enough these days, given we're living on pills mostly," replied the doctor with a smile.

"I'm sure it wasn't the tomato," replied Rebecca.

"What makes you so sure of that?" asked the doctor.

Rebecca simply looked up at her, tears in her eyes and fear on her face. The feeling in the doctor's gut found voice.

"Oh my goodness!" said Dr. Annikov excitedly. "Did you miss?"

"Yes. I figured it was just one of those things…but then I started feeling really sick today…"

"Let's do some tests to be sure. Do you feel okay otherwise?" The doctor reached into a drawer and pulled out a plastic-wrapped cup.

"Yes, completely fine," replied Rebecca, taking the cup from the doctor. "I assume I need to pee in this?"

"Yes. You go do that, and I'll get ready to draw some blood. We may as well give you the full regimen since you're here."

Half an hour later, Dr. Annikov came back to the exam room, a smile painted broadly across her face.

"Congratulations, Rebecca, you're going to be a mommy," she said, beginning to choke up. "This is so wonderful. Isn't it?" Tears flowed freely down the doctor's face.

Rebecca reached out and grabbed the doctor's hand. "Yes," she said through her own tears and confusion, "I'm very, very happy."

Dr. Annikov reached to the countertop and grabbed a few tissues, handing a wad to Rebecca.

"I'm sorry," said the doctor wiping away her tears, "I'm just so… happy for you. I assume Novah is the father?"

"Of course," said Rebecca with a sniffled giggle.

"When will you tell him?" the doctor asked.

"Oh, I'll tell him right away. There's no sense in delaying. He'll be fine. I'm not worried about his response. He'll take it in stride like he does most things."

A few minutes later, Novah was passed out on the tactical lounge floor, Rebecca kneeling above him, lightly tapping his cheek. He had a cut over his left eye where it had banged the table on his way down. He groggily came to, ignoring the blood stinging his eye.

"Preg…pregnant?"

Rebecca was torn between amusement and concern. "Mmhmm,

you're going to be a daddy."

Novah's eyes started to roll back in his head again. Rebecca straddled him and grabbed him by the ears.

"No more fainting, mister!" she said. "Now get up. You need a couple of stitches."

Novah remained motionless.

"Well?" she exclaimed.

"It's hard to get up when you're on top of me like this," he smirked. She sighed and pulled herself up by the edge of the table. She reached a hand down to help him up, but to her surprise, he pulled her back down beside him.

"I'm scared to death," he confided. "I know we'll be fine. I just...just..."

"Shhhh," she said, putting a finger to his lips. "You're right. We'll be fine. I'd rather not have you bleed to death though. Let's get to the medbay."

They walked into the medbay where Dr. Annikov looked up at them from her desk, a concerned look on her face as she noticed Novah holding a cloth to his eye. "Back so soon?"

"He took it in stride," said Rebecca, "it's just that he tripped on the table."

The doctor shook her head and sighed. "I'll stitch him up," she said, dragging him off to an exam room.

"Send him to the engine room once you're done," said Rebecca.

"As you wish," she replied, digging around for antiseptic. Rebecca made her way to the engine room while the doctor made her way around Novah's eyebrow with a suture needle. "This may sting a bit."

"I'm not sure how it happened," mumbled Novah.

"The cut or the pregnancy?" sassed the doctor, jabbing him with the needle.

"The cut, silly," he said through a wince.

"Hold still," she ordered.

"Be gentler," he grumbled. "You're being too rough."

She didn't want to care how much it hurt when she pierced his skin, but found she did, and softened.

"I don't like stitching you up all the time," she said softly.

"It's not so bad," he replied. "Your hands are warm."

She stifled her retort with a soft blush, replacing sass with something more professional.

"You'll want to ice this, and I advise you to stop banging your head into things."

"Yes, doctor," he replied through another wince as she tied off the knot.

She taped a square of cloth over his cut and sent him on his way. She then retreated to her office, locked her door, and wept for reasons few men would understand.

Novah met Rebecca in the engineering section of the ship, which was massive in its own right, a full fifth of the ship's length in the middle of the craft. The massive Z'korz generation cylinder was capped fore and aft by a pair of equally-massive fuel storage sections. Behind the aft section was a massive array of batteries. Each battery was three cubic meters in size. There were five thousand of them in parallel. The pair stood on the observation gangplank that bisected the battery compartment.

"How long will the batteries hold their charge?" asked Novah.

"Z'korz batteries have been notoriously poor in that regard," replied Rebecca. "The old Z'korz batteries would lose half of their charge in three days, and half again in another three. This is why Khamek ships are tethered to scores of support craft. Each craft contains batteries. Because of the Z'korz half-life, more infrastructure is needed for battery capacity than any other thing. Grandfather figured out a way to slow Z'korz battery degradation by ninety percent. The batteries in the *R'ptyr* are the prototypes. All new Khamek ships are now being outfitted with the new batteries as well. It's an amazing technological leap."

"So ours will still have enough charge to open the wormhole once we get to a safe distance?"

"No," she replied. "There's a problem. The last time I was down here to check, these batteries were over half full, plenty of capacity to get us to A'ala. They're empty now. Completely drained."

Novah stood in silence for a few seconds, withering under Rebecca's gaze.

"Do you know what happened?" he asked.

She sighed. "So this is the game we're going to play? Ok, I'll play. You see this panel over here? The one with the display that says 'batteries vented'? That shows that someone came down here and manually overrode the fire control system and emptied the batteries out into space. So I asked NICOLE who did it. *Captain Burns*, she said.

I couldn't believe it, so I went and reviewed the security records, and sure enough, your dot was down here at the time the batteries were emptied. There's no doubt it was you. Don't try to deny it."

Novah would have felt better if she'd been angry, if she'd yelled. Her compassionate yet questioning tone, like a mother asking a two year old why he got into the cookie jar, made his shame at being caught worse. His ears burned a bright crimson.

"I know why you did it," she continued. "I understand, I really do. I'm disappointed though. We should have talked about it. I'm your partner here, remember?"

Novah stared at the floor.

"Remember?" she asked again, reaching out and lifting his chin from his chest.

"I remember," he whispered.

"Good," she said. "There's nothing we can do about what's been done. I won't tell anyone."

"Thank you," Novah replied, torn between the rightness he felt in emptying the tanks and the painful wrongness in having disappointed Rebecca.

They walked silently amongst the massive banks of batteries until they reached the gangplank at the aft observation station that looked out into the aft fuel storage compartment.

"Teleporting everywhere, I sometimes forget how massive this ship is," commented Novah.

Rebecca nodded. "I spent the month before you arrived walking every hallway. That's a hundred miles across all five decks. I still don't have a good feel for if this ship is too large or too small for what we have to do. Grandfather designed it, though, so I have to believe he knew what he was doing."

"I'm sure he did," replied Novah. "I'm still in awe. Apart from the bridge and engine area, you almost can't tell you're on a spacecraft."

They turned and walked back amongst the batteries towards the teleporter.

"Have you given any thought as to where we are going to land this beast?" asked Rebecca.

"I've spent a lot of time just staring at maps," he replied. "The easy thing would be to plop the *R'ptyr* down in the middle of the U.S., since that is where I think the bulk of the colonists can easily get to. Yet when I looked at the names this morning, there are quite a large number of folks from Europe, India, China, Japan, and Australia. There are even a few in Africa and South America."

"We knew that would happen without geographical restrictions," said Rebecca. "I think it was the right call, but now we have this problem. Why can't we just make multiple stops?"

"It's possible," stated Novah, "but every second we're on Earth represents risk. What if something goes wrong with the *R'ptyr*?"

Rebecca snorted. "This ship isn't going to break down," she offered dismissively. "We can make a stop on every continent. It just needs to be arranged is all."

He reached out and grabbed her hand. "We're only making two landings. Everyone will just have to get there. Open doors are an invitation to a cruise missile or rocket grenade. I don't trust President Hernandez or any of the other sigil-holders as far as I could throw them."

They made their way to the tactical lounge, picking up Chief Tines along the way.

"Chief," Novah asked, "where do you think we should set this big bird down to pick up the second fifty thousand?"

Tines let out an exasperated sigh. "This whole operation has more security holes than a cheese grater," he said. "I don't know how we haven't been blown to the moon already. Just using S'heil's scout craft alone is crazy, even with all of the extra precautions we're taking."

"We understand," offered Rebecca. "We don't have a whole lot of options. That's why we're asking you about the landing area."

"I know," he replied. "Sometimes the magnitude of what's going on here overwhelms me a bit. Now…where to put the *R'ptyr* down…" He paused for a moment. "I'm thinking the President has already solved this problem for the sigil holders. Why don't we use the same area? It'll be secure, or at least more secure than setting down in the middle of a corn field in Kansas. There's going to be a crazy amount of people there. Media, well-wishers, protesters, lookie-loos, you name it. A gated off area will help, but to be honest Captain we simply don't have the people to guard the fence line. We're just asking to be overrun no matter where we go."

Novah pursed his lips. "We need to find a way. There's got to be a way. Something we haven't thought of yet."

"Obviously," said Rebecca with a smile.

The trio entered the tactical lounge.

"You'll want to be involved with this," Novah told Tines as they took their seats. "NICOLE, open a call to President Hernandez."

Connecting.

Alberto answered his cell phone. "Yes?"

"Mr. President, this is Captain Burns. I was hoping you would have a few minutes to talk."

"Certainly, Mr. Burns," Alberto replied. "I'm delighted to hear that you've survived your…ordeal. I'm riding to the Pentagon. I've got about five minutes."

"That's more than I need," Novah replied. "Have you determined where you want the *R'ptyr* to land to pick up the sigil-holders?"

"Yes," Alberto replied. "All sigil holders will be gathered near an abandoned coal processing facility in Virginia. It's secluded, well fenced, yet has a large enough flat area to land the *R'ptyr*. My chief of staff is handling the logistics."

"Sounds perfect," stated Novah. "I'd like my security chief, Larry Tines, to work with your chief to make sure everything goes smoothly. The day will be here before we know it."

"Certainly," Alberto said.

"There are a couple of issues regarding the sigil-holders you need to be aware of," stated Novah. "The first is that we're going to have a very cramped ship. People will only be allowed one piece of luggage. We simply don't have the room for everyone to bring a ton of stuff."

"Understood," the President replied. "What else?"

"As you know, sigil-holders are permitted on board regardless of situation, position or health. It's the health thing that's scary. We won't be doing any health screening of sigil-holders, so our chief medical officer is insisting that they be quarantined for a period of time. We have set aside substantial areas of the ship for the quarantine period. Once the quarantine is lifted, sigil-holders will be given free range of the ship just like the other colonists. It will be cramped and inconvenient, but I'm sure you understand that we cannot allow a stray germs loose amongst the rest of the crew. That could screw up the entire mission."

"How long would this quarantine be?" inquired Alberto.

"Fourteen days, maybe less," replied Novah. "It's a small price to pay to be sure of human survival."

"Alright," Alberto said reluctantly. "It makes sense. I'll make sure everyone who needs to know understands."

"Great," said Novah. "One last thing. Do you have a succession plan? If all of these world leaders and important sigil-holders suddenly disappear leaving people leaderless, people will freak out."

"We have a plan," reported Alberto. "The less you know, the better. It'll work. This isn't our first rodeo."

"You mean it's not the first time you've had to lie to and mislead the American public?" snarked Novah.

President Hernandez let his silence grind for a few seconds before speaking again.

"Is that all?" he asked.

"That's all, Mr. President. We'll be in touch if anything else comes up." Novah hung up the call.

"I can't tell if he's up to something or not," Novah confessed to Rebecca. "What do you think?"

"My gut tells me he's all about self-preservation and the preservation of his power. As long as he thinks he has those things, I don't think he'd risk jeopardizing them," Rebecca replied. "In fact, it might even be worth throwing him a bone as an insurance policy."

"What kind of bone?"

"Offer him some sort of advisory role. Even a command position. It doesn't matter what it is, as long as it strokes his ego and gives him an incentive to play nice. Give him the hope of getting what he wants in the future, and he's not likely to disrupt the present."

"I'm so glad you're on my side," he said with a smile. "You're so smart."

Novah quickly called Alberto back.

"Mr. President, I know you're in a hurry, but there was one more thing I wanted to talk to you about."

"What is it," bit off Alberto, perturbed at the interruption.

"Well," stated Novah, "as you might expect, we're going to need some sort of order on the *R'ptyr*. I can't expect everyone to become accustomed to the military-style discipline necessary to run a ship this large. We'll need some sort of interim civilian government until we get to A'ala. I'd like you to head the *R'ptyr*'s civilian government. You would also have a seat at the daily ship briefing. You can handle things however you like, so long as the ship's operations and preservation are not compromised. Those remain my under my sole authority and command. A limited number of current military command sigil-holders will be welcome to have roles in my command structure proportional to their current ranks."

Alberto was silent for a few seconds before replying. Novah waited patiently.

"This is… unexpected," Alberto replied. His countenance seemed to brighten considerably. "I accept. Thank you."

"You're welcome. Goodbye, Mr. President." Novah hung up.

Alberto sat at the head of a large table in a room in the Pentagon, a dozen high-ranking military officers surrounding it. They all stared in silence at him, waiting for him to speak.

"Gentlemen," he said with a smile, "Operation Silent Viper is hereby suspended. It seems the young captain is going to welcome us with open arms into the command structure of the *R'ptyr*. With patience, we'll be able to take it over slowly, from the inside, without firing a shot."

Novah wasn't done making calls.

"NICOLE, I want to talk to the head of the Swiss bank. I have no idea what his name is."

Connecting.

Mark Reinhard was the head of the Swiss Central Bank, the role of which had grown substantially over the few preceding years. The Swiss were the world custodians of the new world Reserve Currency after the fall of the dollar, a mixed basket of currencies backed by gold. This made gold-holding nations such as China, India and Russia very rich. It made the Swiss Central Bank rich as well. Nations couldn't agree on a suitably fancy name for the new currency, so they simply called it the New Global Dollar. Mr. Reinhard was now the most powerful banker in the world, and an argument could be made that he might be the most powerful person period. He was also, of course, a sigil-holder.

Mr. Reinhard's personal cell phone rang as he was sitting at his office desk. He looked at the unrecognized number with a cocked eyebrow, shrugged, and answered.

"Das ist Mark Reinhard spricht. Wer ist das?"

Novah plucked the name from the German, hoping the banker knew English. "Mr. Reinhard, my name is Captain Novah Burns of the *R'ptyr*. Do you have a minute to talk?"

Of course he did, though he wondered why Novah would be calling him. He settled into a comfortable banker snootiness and switched languages to English.

"Mr. Burns, it is a pleasure to speak with you. How may I assist you today?"

Fortunately, Novah had done his homework, or at least copied NICOLE's paper. Novah knew that Mr. Reinhard had attended the meeting at the Bilderberg, and knew the truth about the Earth's coming misfortune.

"I have a favor to ask, Mr. Reinhard," Novah said.

Mr. Reinhard smiled into the receiver. "Mr. Burns, I am a banker. Bankers are not in the habit of granting favors. However, since we live in extraordinary times, and because I am a curious man, I will listen to what you have to say."

Novah silently absorbed Reinhard's condescension and continued.

"There are 70,000 people on the colonist list. 50,000 who will be brought on board in addition to the sigil holders, and another 20,000 waitlisters who will step in in the event one of the first group is unable to board. Many of these people are still recovering from the recent economic hardships the globe suffered. Travel to the rendezvous point will require some capital. I am asking you to send a check for 100,000 Global Dollars to each of the 70,000 people on the list to cover travel expenses."

Mr. Reinhard did math in his head and struggled to suppress his gag reflex.

"Mr. Burns, that is seven billion dollars," he stated dryly.

"Yes, I'm aware of that," replied Novah. "But do you really think that matters?"

The question snapped Mr. Reinhard back to reality. This world was ending. What difference did a few billion dollars make? However, Reinhard was still a banker, completely unaccustomed to giving away anything without getting something back in return.

"No, I suppose not," said Mr. Reinhard. "I could arrange what you ask. Why should I, though? So much paperwork. Those that make it, make it, and those that don't, don't. I'm certain that more than enough will be able to reach the rendezvous point. Why should I care which ones do or don't?"

Novah felt his face begin to flush, but a gentle touch of Rebecca's hand on his knee refocused him.

"If you do," replied Novah, "I will put you in charge of the R'ptyr's banking system, which, by extension, would become A'ala's banking system. Furthermore, I will waive the one-piece-of-luggage requirement for you. I will allow you to bring three tons of gold coins and five tons of silver coins on board with which to begin your banking venture."

It was a great deal, one that Reinhard grew instantly excited about. Yet his pomposity leaped out of his mouth before he could control it.

"And if I do not?"

Novah sighed, and didn't try to hide it.

"Mr. Reinhard, space is a very cold, lonely and dangerous place. Accidents happen all the time. For every adventure there is a ... misadventure."

There was no mistaking the threat.

"I will see that the checks are written and delivered. Send me the list, and the time frame in which the checks are to be received," replied Reinhard evenly. "I apologize for my tone, and my...how should I say...snootiness," he continued, "These are strange times we live in."

"Yes they are," said Novah. "Thank you."

He reached and touched the disconnect button on the table.

"Boy or a girl?" asked Rebecca suddenly.

The abrupt topic transition made Novah shake his head as if trying to discard cobwebs. "What?"

"Boy or a girl? Which do you want?"

He was about to speak when Rebecca interrupted him. "And don't give me the oh-it-doesn't-matter-all-I-want-is-a-healthy-baby nonsense." Her tone was odd, different, even harsh.

Novah sat back, trying to recover. "Umm... a boy?" he offered.

"What, don't you know?" she chided. "Grow a pair and claim it."

"I haven't really given it much thought, to be honest," he said sincerely.

"Why not? Isn't it important to you?"

"Of course it is."

"Then why haven't you given it any thought?" Tears welled in her eyes.

Novah was in foreign territory. "Are you ok?" he asked.

"I'm fine!" she snapped. "Why won't you answer the question?"

"I've...we've...been *busy*, Rebecca." He reached over to take her hand, but she snatched it away. She then got up, gave Novah a deadly stare, turned, and walked out of the room. He sat there confused for several minutes unsure of what had just happened.

CHAPTER TWENTY-TWO

D r. Annikov was genuinely sympathetic to Novah's plight.
"It's completely normal, Novah," she said wearily as he sat
across from her desk looking sullen. "Pregnancy can impact
a woman's body chemistry and hormones profoundly."

"Is there something you can give her?" Novah asked.

The doctor sighed and smiled at him. "No. This is just part of
nature. She's going to have mood swings. One hour she'll be up, the
next she'll be down. You just have to let it run its course."

"How long will that take?"

She shrugged. "It depends on the woman."

"I need her to be level. I need her to be stable and consistent. If she
starts letting her emotions get the best of her, things will get more
difficult than they already are. I can't do this alone."

The doctor reached across the desk and placed her hand over his.
"You have a full room of officers that are here for you. *I'm* here for
you. You never have to be alone in *anything*."

She withdrew her hand with a smile and straightened in her chair.

"Rebecca has regularly scheduled pre-natal visits with me," she said.
"I'll keep a close eye on her. If there's anything abnormal with regards
to her body chemistry, or if she's not handling the pregnancy well
physically or emotionally, I'll let you know."

"Thank you, doctor," he replied.

"Please, Novah, we've known each other for months. We're
friends. Call me Katyrina. That's my name. If I don't have to call you

captain, you don't have to call me doctor. Now if you'll excuse me," she continued, "I'm already plumb tuckered out, and I have a full patient load today. I have a crew of thirty across three shifts, but believe it or not there's enough happening on this ship to keep everyone on their toes."

"Anything serious?" Novah asked.

"Not anything deadly. Bumps, bruises, a few stitches here and there, three other pregnancies to manage, and one of Chief Tines' men broke his arm yesterday pretty badly. Oh, and S'lace is sick."

"S'lace?"

"Yes. She came by early this morning. I don't know anything about Khamek biology, but fortunately NICOLE was able to bring up some basic reference. She's running a temperature. She said she didn't feel well, and her skin felt clammy and her eyes were a bit, for the lack of a better term, droopy. I didn't know what to tell her other than drink plenty of fluids."

"I don't like the sound of that," Novah said. "Where is she now?"

"I presume she's gone off to do her usual list pickups."

"NICOLE," said Novah, "What is S'lace's location?"

S'lace is currently returning to the ship from Earth with two passengers. ETA is three minutes, arriving in docking bay three.

"I think I'll head to docking bay three and see how she's doing myself. If she's sick, she should take some time off. I know she's been working really hard," he said.

Dr. Annikov nodded. "If I get some spare time I'll dig a little more into Khamek physiology."

Novah made his way to docking bay three. He stepped into a corner to stay out of the way of the processing team – those tasked with orienting the new colonists and showing them to their quarters and stations. S'lace's ship landed and a young couple followed S'lace out of the landing area. They were met by the processing team. Before S'lace could turn around and head back to her ship, Novah intercepted her. She looked awful.

"S'lace!" shouted Novah.

"Yes Captain?" she replied weakly.

"I order you to the medbay, now. I'll escort you personally."

"As you wish, cap..." She collapsed mid-sentence into Novah's arms. Her skin was covered with tiny blisters. He lifted her legs and carried her as quickly as he could to the teleporter. In less than a minute, he was barging into Medbay One.

"We need a doctor!" Novah shouted.

Instantly, three medical personnel were grabbing S'lace putting her on the first available bed. A loud authoritative voice boomed with urgent volume.

"EVERYONE STOP. DO NOT MOVE," yelled Dr. Annikov.

"NICOLE, lock down Medbay One. No entrance or exit without my authority."

Medbay One locked down.

The doctor pointed to those around S'lace. "Get an I.V. in her, stat. Pure saline. Hook her up. I want vitals. Captain, go to my office and have a seat. Everyone else, go back to work. Nobody leaves. This medbay is now quarantined."

The doctor suddenly went very pale.

"NICOLE, lock down the entire ship. Medical override alpha. Disable all teleporters."

Teleporters disabled.

"To work, everybody. Let's pray it doesn't get busy." She walked into her office and shut the door.

"What's going on?" Novah asked urgently.

"I don't know what S'lace has, but it isn't normal. Those blisters…that's usually a sign of something serious. I don't know if she caught something from humans, or if what she has is native to Khamek, but whatever it is, we have to contain it and keep it from spreading until we figure out what it is."

"Do you think it's contagious?" he asked.

Beads of sweat had appeared along Dr. Annikov's brow. She sat down in her chair and let her head rest on her arms. She rested a moment, then lifted her head back up.

"I'm not feeling well, Novah. I have a fever and upset stomach. There's no cause for it. I did have contact with S'lace this morning, though. So yes, I think it is could be, even across species. With a very fast reaction time. Less than six hours."

"Oh shit," said Novah.

"NICOLE, open a ship wide channel," he commanded.

Channel open.

"Attention everyone. This is the captain. The *R'ptyr* has been locked down for precautionary reasons. There is a possibility that a contagion is loose. Everyone should stay where they are. If you have had any contact today with anyone in Medbay One or with S'lace, please inform the nearest medbay and wait for instructions."

An hour later, Dr. Annikov was in a bed of her own attended to with great care by the available staff. She wasn't the only human sick – the two that S'lace had brought on board were beginning to feel unwell and had reported to Medbay Two. Dr. Stephenson had taken control of the medical staff from Medbay Two. Novah took up residence in Dr. Annikov's office, and started a conference call with all of the officers and Dr. Stephenson.

Novah began. "Chief Tines, what is the security situation? Is everyone staying put?"

"It appears that everyone has followed your instructions, Captain," stated Tines. "There's very little movement in the ship apart from what's ordinary, and it looks like people are following your order."

"Dr. Stephenson, do you have any clues yet as to what is going on?" asked Novah.

"No, I'm afraid not," offered Stephenson. "I've taken blood samples from the two that S'lace brought up from Earth. They aren't feeling too terribly bad, just tired. It's difficult to know if they are infected or simply worn out from the excitement. The lab should finish analyzing the samples in the next few minutes. How is Dr. Annikov?"

"Worsening, I'm afraid," said Novah. "High fever, and she's completely incoherent. She is being hydrated through I.V. S'lace's vitals are worsening as well. The staff here in Medbay One is holding together, but obviously concerned and frightened."

Rebecca piped up. "Are we sure S'lace is the cause? Perhaps there is something atmospheric? Something they ate?"

Dr. Stephenson shrugged and shook his head. "It's simply too early to tell. Dr. Annikov was right in demanding quarantine, though. We'll just have to stay on the lookout and see if anyone else gets sick."

Four hours later, they reconvened. The situation had worsened significantly. Doctors and nurses in Medbay One were dropping like flies.

"Status, Dr. Stephenson?" asked Novah.

Dr. Stephenson looked pale and sounded weaker, his voice more of a casual whisper than his usual self-assured. "Well, I think we can positively confirm that this is a contagion that began with S'lace. S'lace visited Dr. Annikov first thing this morning before going on her first pickup. She returned and collapsed. Dr. Annikov then fell ill. The two colonists brought by S'lace are now ill. The processing crew that greeted them are also now sick and here in Medbay Two. Many members of the staff here are sick. Those sickest the longest have small red welts all over their bodies. It looks and acts like smallpox, but it isn't. If we don't find a way to stop this, everyone that has it will be dead in twenty-four hours. The blood tests are coming back with strange results. If I didn't know better, I'd say it was leukemia. Yet leukemia isn't contagious, nor does it act this quickly."

Novah rubbed his eyes, trying to process it all. "What's your best guess, doctor?"

"I hate making guesses, Captain," he replied. "But if you force me to conjecture, I'd put my money on some sort of blood poisoning virus."

"Have you asked NICOLE?" asked Rebecca. "Surely NICOLE has enough knowledge of Khamek history to potentially help identify this virus."

The doctor smacked his forehead. "Gah! Why didn't I think of that?"

"NICOLE," Rebecca's voice rang out, "access all sick patient records and cross reference symptoms with all known human and Khamek illnesses. Deliver your findings to Dr. Stephenson as soon as..."

Processing complete.

The room fell silent. NICOLE had accomplished in ten seconds what Earth's best doctors hadn't been able to even get close to in hours.

"Report," commanded Novah.

Contagion most closely resembles Khamek disease L'kosks' Disease which takes root in the bone marrow, slowly infecting all new blood created until critical mass is reached to produce symptoms. Symptoms include high fever, body welts, delusions, loss of strength and appetite. Each Khamek is inoculated against the disease immediately upon birth or Z'korz transference. The disease appears to have mutated and infected humans, focusing on already-created blood, skipping the marrow entirely.

"What is the cure?" asked Dr. Stephenson urgently.

There is no known cure. Survival rate for afflicted Khamek is less than three percent. Survival rate for afflicted humans with this new variant is unknown.

Dr. Stephenson uttered a barely intelligible expletive before collapsing to the floor. A trio of sickly-looking nurses rushed to his side, silently looking into the camera begging for help.

"This is not good," said Novah stating the obvious.

"Captain," spoke Chief Tines, "how come you're not infected? Didn't you carry S'lace to Medbay One yourself?"

"Yes, I did. I feel totally fine though. I should be laid up like everyone else."

"The blood," spoke a suddenly pale Rebecca. "It's the blood. The disease couldn't infect your blood. It's a residual inoculation from the transfusion from when you were attacked. That's the only thing it can be."

"Rebecca," said Novah.

"Already on my way," she replied.

Everyone in both medbays was very sick. Only Novah and Rebecca in Medbay One were able to do anything, and in reality, it was only Rebecca. Novah was simply an extra set of hands.

"Ok, here's what we're going to do," she said. "We're each going to give up a pint of blood, and transfuse one quarter of a pint into the eight sickest patients. Maybe our blood will attack the virus."

Thirty minutes later, eight patients were absorbing new blood. Rebecca's went to S'lace, Dr. Annikov, and two others. Novah's went to four others in the Medbay.

An hour later, three of the four of Rebecca's patients regained consciousness. S'lace's eyes remained closed. Her skin had turned from her normal pale color to that of a brown paper sack, but she didn't appear to be worsening. Katyrina's vitals quickly returned to normal. None of Novah's blood recipients showed any signs of recovery.

"What's going on?" croaked a weak Dr. Annikov.

They quickly explained to her what had happened.

"So then, Rebecca," she said, "it appears you once again are saving the day."

"It's too early to say that," said a fatigued Rebecca. "It appears that only my blood is working. Novah's isn't. I wish I'd have listened to you about donating blood."

"How many are sick?" the doctor asked.

"Twenty-three, including Dr. Stephenson and all of Medbay Two," reported Novah.

They were silent for several seconds, all of them realizing the graveness of the situation.

"Doctor," Rebecca asked softly, "how much blood can one person safely donate?"

"With proper care, two and a half pints," said the doctor. "In your case, only one. Otherwise you put the baby in real danger."

"Can we create a vaccine?" asked Novah. "Surely NICOLE can help with that."

"Yes, we can, but that won't help any of the sick – it'll only prevent further sicknesses," said the doctor.

Novah began to panic. Twenty-three doctors, nurses, and patients were going to soon die if a solution wasn't found.

"We gave a quarter pint to each person who recovered," said Rebecca. "How much is enough? Could we get away with an eighth of a pint? Less?"

"It doesn't matter," replied a somber Dr. Annikov. "You're not giving up any more blood."

"How about just a little? Maybe we can make up a big batch using the powdered hemoglobin like before?" said Rebecca.

"I don't know if that'll work. And like I said, it doesn't matter, you're not giving up any more blood."

Rebecca reached to Dr. Annikov's bed and grabbed her hand. "Katyrina, a lot of great people are going to die if we don't try something. Please, let me give just a little more. Let's see if the hemoglobin trick works."

The doctor sighed. "For the record, your physician does not agree, but you are free to do as you wish."

Novah helped extract another pint of blood from Rebecca, which they added to the hemoglobin powder along with the requisite amount of water. They had to guess on the dosage, and decided to divide the five created pints evenly by the number of remaining sick. The pair took the concoction to Medbay Two to try it on Dr. Stephenson.

It didn't work. They doubled the dosage, then tripled it, with no impact. Seven had died in that span.

Rebecca sat down. "Novah…"

"No, absolutely not," he interjected. "You've already given up too much. Doctor Annikov says you'll hurt the baby."

"I'm aware of the risk, Novah. But if I can somehow squeeze out just one more pint, that's at least four more people we can save."

"No. Two and a half is the max for a normal, non-pregnant person."

"I'm not a normal person, Novah," she said. "We have to try. I think we can save eight with a pint."

"We'll lose the baby," whispered Novah.

"Possibly," she answered back in her own pained, low whisper, "but isn't one life worth saving…eight?"

He wasn't going to get his way, and he knew it. They quickly siphoned off another pint, which Novah clumsily administered to six people in Medbay two. He stuck the two remaining in his pocket, and wheeled a very weak and pale Rebecca back to Medbay One. Dr. Annikov was up and around, albeit still weak, but had enough energy to scream at the pair as they came through the door.

"What have you done?" she demanded.

"Saved six," said Novah handing her the remaining two samples, "and here's two more. Better get busy."

Furious, she took the two warm bags and began transfusions on two others in the medbay. Meanwhile, Novah lifted Rebecca onto a bed and plugged a liter of saline into her arm. Ten minutes later, Dr. Annikov was back with them. Rebecca was pale, weak, barely conscious and softly weeping. Dr. Annikov put her stethoscope to Rebecca's abdomen, lowered her head, and with tears in her own eyes turned to Novah.

"You better go on, Novah," she said with a quivering voice. "I'll see if I can save Rebecca."

CHAPTER TWENTY-THREE

The entire compliment of the *R'ptyr* was gathered on the observation deck. Seventeen adult-sized caskets lined a lit walkway that led from the teleporter door to the prepared seating area. At the very end of the row was a casket no larger than a loaf of bread.

The week that passed after the outbreak was filled with tears. Of the seventeen adults, twelve were medical personnel – a huge loss. The other five were the new pair from Earth and three from the processing team. Those that survived recovered almost immediately, though it took many days for them to feel completely normal again. S'lace still remained in the medbay, languishing in misery, conscious but in constant pain.

While people took the loss of the adults poorly, Dr. Annikov, who was mourning many colleagues, seemed to take the death of Rebecca's unborn child worst of all. The loss of so many of her coworkers, as well as Rebecca's baby, had broken her. The dark circles carved out under her eyes from ceaseless crying stole her stature of confidence. Her red locks were orderless, pointing randomly wherever they pleased.

Novah tried his best to stay upbeat, while struggling with his own feelings. Rebecca had made the right decision, he knew, but at great risk to herself. The fear of losing her seemed to trump all of his thoughts.

Everyone was seated, with the rows of chairs placed in circles, with one aisle left so that people could walk into the center. Novah thought a group service would be best. The crew was essentially family. It was good to grieve together. At the appointed time Novah released Rebecca's hand, stood up, and walked to the center area.

"Hi everyone. As you know, we have suffered a terrible loss. The loss has hurt us all, and will continue to do so for a long while. We will get over this tragedy though, and we must remember that tragedy is part of the price we pay for survival. Whether our ancestors travelled by boat across the Atlantic, or across the great plains by covered wagon, or journeyed somewhere else through some other dangerous means, tragedy goes hand in hand with the promise of a new world and a new life. That doesn't lessen the pain of our loss, but it is a pain we must steel ourselves against and accept." Novah paused, struggling now as he moved beyond the remarks he'd prepared and memorized so as to deliver them without crumbling.

"Though we have suffered, and though it doesn't mean much to those who have lost family or friends, we must try to take solace in the fact that it could have been worse. Eight others who would have died are still with us today thanks to the heroic sacrifice of Rebecca, who, knowing the risks to herself and our baby, gave everything she could to save as many as possible. Our daughter died so that more could live."

Sobs silently echoed throughout the cavernous deck. Even the stoic Chief Tines found himself ignoring his tears while clenching his teeth together.

"I don't have anything else to say," Novah concluded somberly. "If there is anything anyone would like to say, feel free to come into the circle, or just stand where you are. When everyone has had their say, we will adjourn to the port launch bay."

For the next two hours people spoke out in sadness, and sometimes in laughter, as memories of their friends and coworkers were shared. Through it all Novah sat silently, holding Rebecca's hand. She in turn held Dr. Annikov's. Katyrina also managed to stand and offer some words in remembrance of her destroyed medical staff. The doctor was a wet-faced, exhausted mess.

After all the words were spoken, Chief Tines' security forces, dressed in black tops, formed in groups of four. Each group, with utmost precision and care, hoisted an adult casket up onto their shoulders. Novah hoisted the final tiny casket onto his own shoulder.

Rebecca took his other hand and they waited silently for the procession to lead out before them.

The train of grief wormed three hundred yards along the seldom-used corridors to the port launch bay. Each casket was set side by side in a line along the force field. People had lined up in viewing positions in the bay overlooks, spanning three decks. Novah placed the final casket then walked out of the bay to the launch station controls. Once the light was green, indicating the launch area was clear, he released the force field. The vacuum of space sucked the caskets out in a blink, where Earth's gravity snatched them and pulled them down towards the planet. As they entered the atmosphere, they ignited. Seventeen tiny fireballs sunk over the horizon and vanished.

The crowd dispersed and returned to their routines. After a few minutes, only Novah, Rebecca, and Katyrina remained, holding hands in silence, staring out the force field to the blue and white globe below.

They eventually left the launch bay. Novah left the two women to their own devices.

"There's someone I need to talk to," he said. "I'll see you at dinner."

"Okay, Novah," replied Rebecca.

He made his way to Medbay One where the still-brown S'lace was still recuperating. It was amazing that Rebecca's blood had any impact on her whatsoever, and while it saved her from death, the side-effects S'lace suffered from – mainly a medium-grade fever and severe pain – kept her bedridden. Novah wheeled a chair up beside her bed, and held her long fingers in his hand.

"How are you feeling, S'lace?" he asked.

"S'lace would rather have suffered misadventure," she offered.

Novah smiled as best he could. "We'll have no more misadventures, please. We've had quite enough already."

S'lace nodded. "Indeed."

"I need to ask you a question, if you're up to it," said Novah.

"S'lace will attempt to answer, Captain. Ask Novah's question."

"How did you get sick?"

S'lace spoke very softly. "S'lace is sorry, Captain. S'lace has caused the misadventure of many good Humans. S'lace begs for forgiveness."

"There is nothing to forgive. You didn't know you were sick until it was too late. I just want to know if you know why you weren't given your immunizations."

S'lace did her best to think. "S'lace's Z'korz transferred to this body thirty-five Earth years ago. Usually immunizations are administered prior to regaining consciousness. S'lace didn't ask at the time."

"Can you tell me more about this Z'korz transference?" asked Novah.

S'lace nodded. "S'lace was hunting D'kob in the area on Earth known as Egypt. S'lace cornered D'kob, but D'kob had a taser weapon and stunned S'lace, allowing D'kob to escape. S'lace then went to S'heil, and S'heil was customarily displeased and shot S'lace in the face with a kinetic bolt weapon. If a Khamek has the means and foresight, a Khamek can have a Khamek's Z'korz transferred to a clone body. The transference must happen within thirty minutes else the Z'korz is nontransferable and is lost to space. S'lace, having worked for S'heil for many years, commissioned a clone and S'lace's Z'korz was transferred to the clone. S'lace awoke in the new body. S'lace's first vision was S'heil, offering S'lace a cup of foul-tasting tea, apologizing for S'heil's hasty discharge of S'heil's weapon into S'lace's face. S'heil then instructed S'lace to resume attempts at capturing D'kob.

"S'lace finally captured D'kob and deposited D'kob on S'heil's ship in the prison section. D'kob managed to escape less than a day later and crash-landed on Earth. V'kath was responsible for D'kob's containment. V'kath did not have the foresight to commission a clone."

"Do you think S'heil infected you somehow with L'kosks' Disease?"

S'lace clouded over. "Possibly. Perhaps the foul-smelling tea was the catalyst. Or perhaps S'lace was poisoned with L'kosks' Disease by some mundane method prior to leaving the *L'ghorsk*.

"Why would S'heil do that?"

"S'heil is a very clever Khamek. Perhaps S'heil sought to capture the *R'ptyr* through human attrition."

"So he thought killing everyone on board would grant him the *R'ptyr* by default. He was willing to sacrifice you and everyone else just to get the ship. Yet the *R'ptyr* is impregnable. Why bother?"

"S'heil does not believe in impossibilities," S'lace said. "Given enough time, without interruption or distraction by Humans, S'heil believes S'heil could break into the *R'ptyr*."

"Well, this is twice his plans have failed now. He should be punished for his transgressions."

S'lace looked down at her brown arms, her eyes narrowing.

"Punishing S'heil would please S'lace greatly, Captain," she said.

"I'll talk to Rebecca and see what can be done, if anything. Get better. We need you." He squeezed her fingers.

"S'lace will."

He went back to his quarters, and to his surprise, the door between him and Rebecca was closed. He put his ear to the door and heard two female voices crying in inconsolable grief. He assumed it was Rebecca and Katyrina and decided to leave them alone. He went to the small table next to his bed, and for the first time ever, cancelled dinner. *Give people the evening to get their thoughts in order*, he thought. He left his room and personally visited the officers who were available. They were grateful to have the evening off. Novah then stopped by the baths, using the extra time to have a leisurely soak, watching some miniscule percentage of the *R'ptyr*'s water supply disappear into the reclamation vents as the steam rose above him while he thought.

He'd been noodling over the security of the second embarkation for days. Nobody had any ideas that seemed reasonable. Teleportation? Not fast enough, even using all of the *R'ptyr*'s teleporters, plus there was no way to administer the health test remotely. He slapped angrily at the water.

"Is there really no way?!" he exclaimed.

No way to do what, Captain?

Novah looked up towards the ceiling, shocked. Never before had NICOLE spoken without first being invoked by name.

"Umm...NICOLE? You can now talk without being addressed directly?" Novah asked.

You asked a question. There are no other humans or Khamek within several meters of your position. I therefore concluded that it was your intent to address me.

Novah felt uncomfortable goosebumps grow on his body in spite of the hot water. *This is kind of creepy*, he thought. Since she asked, though...

"Ok Nicole, solve this problem: we must land the *R'ptyr* on Earth to pick up the selected applicants. However, there are going to be all kinds of other people there, which creates a huge security problem. I want the people we want to bring on board to be able to approach, but not the people we don't want."

The unusual delay in NICOLE's response – a full second – at first caused Novah to think that even she couldn't solve this problem. Her response, however, filled him with glee.

241

At what distance do you wish non-boarders to be kept at?

Novah thought. "Five hundred yards," he finally replied. NICOLE's response this time was immediate.

As part of the application and selection process, I was able to acquire the DNA records of all applicants, readily available from medical and government databases. This was to scan in advance for any genetic abnormalities. I can create a DNA-permissible shield at a five hundred yard radius from the R'ptyr. Those selected will be able to walk effortlessly through the shield based on their DNA profile. Those not selected will not have their profiles as part of the shield data matrix and will therefore be unable to pass through.

"That's brilliant!" Novah exclaimed. "What about their luggage? Can the shield stop things like bullets and rockets too?"

I can adjust the tolerance of the shield to accommodate items directly touching or held. Unless a foreign object enters concurrently with a selected applicant, it will be unable to pass through. I have programmed the shield. The shield engagement icon is now on your command module.

Novah was beaming as he hopped out of the bath, hurriedly dried off, and dressed.

"Thank you, NICOLE! You've saved us!"

That problem solved, Novah's brain turned to another issue as he made his way to the bridge: what, if anything, should be done about S'heil?

"NICOLE, what is the R'ptyr's offensive military capacity?"

The R'ptyr is primarily a transport vessel. It is equipped with adequate defensive weaponry, but primarily relies on its trichristalline alloy hull. Offensive capability is minimal, limited to five pairs of Khamek variable-sensor torpedoes, each capable of crippling if not destroying the average Khamek ship.

So, thought Novah, *pretty much as expected. Designed to get to A'ala and nothing else.*

Still, if he wanted to drop the hammer on S'heil, he could. He assumed S'heil knew that as well. He swiveled out of the chair and made his way back to his quarters. The door to Rebecca's was still closed, but when he guiltily listened this time, the women were having a giggle-fest. He knocked politely on the door.

Rebecca unlocked it, and it swooshed open into its pocket.

"Novah!" she giggled, hugging him tightly. "Come join us."

She led him by the hand into her room. Katyrina stood silently by, greeting him with a smile.

"I think we've passed beyond the emotional worst of it, right doctor?" Rebecca asked.

"Yes, I think so," the doctor replied with a giggle. "I should be going, however. I've been away from the medbay far too long. Come see me tomorrow, Rebecca. I need to keep an eye on you for a few days."

"Yes, doctor," Rebecca replied. "I'll come by after lunch."

Dr. Annikov turned to Novah. "You need to make some time to come by as well. Someone needs to teach you the *right* way to administer an I.V."

"Dismissed, doctor," he said with a smile. Katyrina exited.

"She's in love with you, you know," Rebecca offered matter-of-factly.

Red lights flashed in Novah's head. *What to say…what to say.*

"What makes you think that?" he asked.

"She told me."

Novah still stood in silence, figuring silence was the best possible response.

"We talked about it a good long while," continued Rebecca lightly. "She's head over heels in love and I'm fine with it. Be nice to her. She's a professional but lonely woman who has made lots of painful sacrifices for her career. For some reason she's latched on to us as her social circle. She won't even consider other men, oddly enough. She'd rather love you in silence than go through the trouble."

Rebecca talked about it as if it was the most natural thing in the world, without a hint of jealousy or concern. Novah wasn't sure what to do with the information. His gut told him it was a trap. He'd be nice to the doctor, but not go too far.

Rebecca wrapped her arms around Novah's neck. "Don't worry, I still love you too. More than she or anyone else possibly could." She planted a long, hard kiss on his lips. He tried to go further, but she brushed him aside.

"No, Novah. It's too soon. I'm not up for that yet."

Before he could sober up completely she gave him another kiss. "You should stay with me, though." So he did.

CHAPTER TWENTY-FOUR

K atyrina approached S'lace's bedside swirling a test-tube filled with S'lace's blood.

"Do you see this?" she asked, holding the test tube out in front of S'lace's face. "Down at the very bottom. Very dark. Those are what I'm calling nanomites. You were poisoned on purpose, long before boarding the *R'ptyr.*"

"Probably S'heil's foul tea!" S'lace exclaimed. "Nanomites?"

"Yes. Microscopically small machines. Somehow you ingested some, and they used trace metals in your bloodstream to replicate inside of you. Then they attached to your bones. At some point they were activated remotely and began altering your blood cells as they were created, effectively giving you L'kosks' Disease. It took many weeks to produce symptoms. Your body is plumb full of nanomites. Somehow – I don't know how – Rebecca's blood is helping your body fight them."

"Can S'lace be purged of nanomites?" S'lace asked.

"I've been giving this some thought," replied the doctor, "and I think I can adjust the magnetism on one of our MRI machines to dislodge them from your bones. From there, we can use the magnetic field to push them out of your bloodstream and body through normal means. It will be very painful, however, so I'll want to anesthetize you. Knock you out."

"Proceed immediately," S'lace demanded.

"I thought you'd say that," replied Katyrina with a smile as she slipped a needle into a vein in S'lace's right arm.

The following day Katyrina brought a small clear bag to the recovering and normal-colored S'lace, placing it on her lap.

"A souvenir," the doctor said with a grin. S'lace picked up the clear bag by the top and peered at the shiny contents quizzically.

"S'lace does not recognize these contents," S'lace said, looking closer with a tilted head. "What material is this? Where did this material originate?"

"Those, sugar, are your nanomites, and they came out of your ass while you were knocked out. A nice little loaf of metal. Isn't it pretty?" The doctor giggled.

S'lace handed the bag back to Katyrina. "While S'lace appreciates Katyrina's gesture, S'lace must decline Katyrina's gift. These nanomites belong to S'heil. S'lace wishes to return them. Please store these nanomites until such a time can be arranged."

The doctor let out an airy chuckle. "Okay S'lace. I'm glad you're feeling better."

Now that S'lace was well enough to resume her pickups she was determined to make up for lost time, starting with the new, reprioritized list NICOLE had created to bring aboard replacement medical personnel.

Life aboard the R'ptyr had returned to normal, and everyone was busy making preparations for the boardings which were only three months away. The two Khamek supply runners, under S'lace's urging, worked just as hard as she did, adding in an extra run or two each day.

After consultation with the officers it was decided to ignore S'heil for the time being. It would serve no purpose to antagonize him further by damaging his ship or causing chaos in the Khamek ranks should he be killed. An extra layer of security was added to supply runs, with each box and crate going through an expanded battery of scans to check for bombs or other devices S'heil might try to sneak on board.

Rebecca recovered fully in short order, though Dr. Annikov monitored her constantly, almost to a point of annoyance.

After two weeks of avoiding social calls to the doctor, Novah finally stopped by Medbay One for his I.V. lesson.

"Good afternoon, doctor," he said with a smile upon entering. "I'm here for my lesson."

"Well it's about time, Novah," she replied. "I was beginning to think you were ignoring me."

"Me? Never," he replied. "I've just been busy. So who am I going to poke today?"

"Me," she said, lightly blushing after she recognized the double-entendre. "You're going to set me up with a basic saline I.V."

Novah rolled his eyes. "That's easy," he said.

Katyrina sat back on the bed after setting it to an upright position. Novah grabbed an I.V. needle and came for the doctor's arm.

"Stop, you hairless ape! Are you trying to kill me?"

Novah stopped, confused. "What?"

"You have to clean the area first. Alcohol wipes, to your left, top drawer." Novah reached for a packet.

"Infections," she continued, "are going to be our biggest problem. We have a limited number of antibiotics, and even if the supply was limitless, nearly everything becomes antibiotic resistant over time. We are going to have to be totally militant about cleanliness and sterilization. Without antibiotics a simple scratch could end up killing someone if it isn't dealt with properly. You must never, ever perform any medical procedure without washing your hands and cleaning any insertion or incision points."

After making sure everything was clean, she guided him through the rest of the steps. He did know what he was doing, but the doctor was able to give him some key advice to make things easier and more efficient.

Novah noticed the slight tremble in her voice, however, though she tried to mask it with medical professionalism. She couldn't hide her blush, though, as he touched her arm. It was purely benign, necessary touching for the task, but Novah felt awkward knowing that she was reacting so. It was also flattering. Katyrina was attractive in her own way, and the way she looked at him with big doe eyes made him feel special. He pulled the I.V. out at her instruction, and wrapped a small cotton square on the tiny spot of blood that bubbled up from her arm.

"Any other ailments, doctor?" he asked playfully.

"Have you ever heard a real heartbeat before?" she asked.

"Well, not as a doctor with that ear thingy," he said warily.

"Come closer," she commanded. He obeyed, and she removed her stethoscope from her neck and placed the ends in Novah's ears. She placed her hand on top of his, and guided the cool metal 'ear' up under her shirt to a warm place between her breasts. Novah lightly resisted, but the doctor's hand was firm.

"Listen," she said.

The thoughts he was having were soon drowned out as he concentrated on the fast *boom-bhum, boom-bhum* echoing in his eardrums. Her heart sounded loud and strong. Her skin was warm and smooth.

"You're alive," Novah offered.

"Very much so," she purred in a sultry, seductive tone.

"Katyrina," he said extricating his hand.

"Yes doctor?" she giggled.

"I'm out of time today," he continued. "Perhaps next time I can examine your liver."

He meant it as a joke, but she thought he was mocking her. Hurt and crestfallen, she stood up from the bed, snatching her stethoscope back.

"You're right, Captain. Time's up. See you at dinner." She bolted the room.

Shaking his head in confusion, he left the medbay and continued on his rounds. Everything was normal at the evening meeting with nothing out of the ordinary to report. Katyrina had greeted him warmly and professionally, as always.

Later that evening, Rebecca chided him harshly.

"I asked you to be nice to her!" she exclaimed. He knew who she was talking about.

"I was!" he retorted. He wasn't about to spill the details, though he figured she already knew them.

Rebecca rolled her eyes. "Do I have to spell it out for you?"

Novah plopped down on a chair, frustrated. "I wish you would," he said. "I'm confused. I don't know what the hell is going on."

Her tone changed instantly, realizing that Novah's naivety and inexperience put him at a disadvantage. She didn't quite reach the level of condescension, but Novah still felt as if he was being talked down to.

"Do you think Katyrina is attractive?" she asked.

He wasn't in the mood for games, so he answered her directly. "Yes, in her own way. She's not as classically beautiful as you, but it would be a stretch to say she was in any way unattractive."

"Good. Thank you for being honest. And thanks for the compliment," she offered sincerely. "Now let me ask you another question. What is our primary mission?"

He raised his eyebrow at the sudden topic change. "To transport all of these humans to A'ala."

"Why?" she prodded.

"To save the human race."

"Yes, to save the human race!" she said. "And how do we do that? Do you think it stops with getting all these people to A'ala safely?"

"Well that's the most of it," he said.

"No," she said softly. "That's just the beginning. In order for humanity to survive, there needs to be more of us. We have to procreate as fast as possible. Every available womb needs to be filled, then filled again to replace those that are inevitably going to die from any countless number of things. That is the goal – to build a large, healthy, growing population. That's the only way humanity survives."

"What does that have to do with Dr. Annikov?" he asked densely.

She took both of his hands in hers. "Novah, my womb is out of commission for a little bit. Katyrina loves you. She wants nothing more than to bear your child. She knows you and I are together, so adores you in silence. She and I have talked about it, and about priorities. She and I are as close as friends can be. I'm asking you to sleep with Katyrina. Give her a child. Love her. You have my blessing. But remember, you belong to me, and as soon as possible, I want another baby of yours growing inside me."

Novah sat silent for a moment. "So let me get this straight," he finally said, "you want me to knock up Dr. Annikov, treat her, essentially, as a …second wife, all with your blessing?"

"I insist," Rebecca said.

"This is a bit unorthodox," Novah said. "What would your grandfather say?"

"Things are different now, Novah," she said. "For humanity to survive, we have to adjust our mindsets. I'm sure grandfather would feel the same way. Human culture is filled with examples of men having multiple wives – even in the Bible. Times changed, though, and it no longer became necessary. Times have changed again."

She looked at him in the eyes with utmost sincerity, squeezing his hands. "No empty wombs."

"Should we make that the ship motto?" he joked.

"Yes, we should," she said in all seriousness.

"Why me though? She's attractive and smart and she can probably have any man on the ship she chooses."

"Katyrina, like most women, knows what she wants. Sure, she could arrange to get pregnant by some other guy, but she would always be wondering 'what if.' She would love the child, but probably not as much as the one she wanted."

"Like buying the car you liked second-best," he offered.

Rebecca laughed. "Yes, I suppose exactly like that."

He looked at Rebecca, and she read his mind.

"No, this isn't a trick or a trap," she said. "No empty wombs."

Novah sighed. "Very well then. I'll go see Katyrina."

"Not tonight you won't," said Rebecca. "I want to cuddle."

The following morning, Novah poked his head into Medbay One. "Dr. Annikov?"

She greeted him warmly. "Yes Captain?"

"Coffee at lunch? I'll stop by and get you."

She approached him cautiously, and with a whisper. "Novah, are you asking me out on a coffee date?"

"Yes," he replied promptly.

"I'll be ready at noon," she said, suddenly giddy. Novah walked out of the medbay shaking his head.

No empty wombs, he kept telling himself.

As promised, he collected her at noon. They chatted casually as they made their way to her quarters. They did not have coffee.

CHAPTER TWENTY-FIVE

The three months leading up to Embarkation Day One passed quickly. Everyone seemed happy and excited, particularly now that the E2 security problem had been solved. Dr. Annikov had a rosy glow and a noticeable swelling in her abdomen. Novah sometimes couldn't tell who was happier - she or Rebecca. With a day to go, Novah placed a call to President Hernandez.

"Is everything ready on your end?" inquired Novah.

"Yes," replied Alberto. "We'll be expecting you at the landing spot at midnight. The field will be lit up. You won't be able to miss it."

"Good. We'll be coming in dark. Sigil holders should congregate at the edges of the landing area so that they don't get squished. Embarkation will happen both starboard and port near midship. We'll load people first, then supplies. Loading will be fully automated so as to minimize risk of contagion to those already on board. Remember, all sigil-holders will have to be quarantined."

"Everyone is aware," relied Alberto. "We'll do what we can on our end to make boarding as smooth and quick as possible. Oh, and there's one more thing."

"What's that?" asked Novah.

"Ignore the news. Just be at the landing area at the appointed time."

Novah shrugged. He didn't pay attention to the news anyway. "Very well, Mr. President. See you in thirty-three hours."

The news Novah was supposed to ignore couldn't really be ignored. It was being broadcast world-wide. All of the world's leaders, along with high-ranking economists, bankers, judges and media, had gathered at a castle outside of Versailles for the World Economic Conference. Never before had so many high-ranking members of government and finance gathered in one place. The agenda was to discuss the acceptable global level of fractional reserve lending. Unfortunately, just as the proceedings were beginning, a massive explosion rocked the castle. In fact, the historic castle was turned to utter rubble. Everything within a square kilometer was flattened. The explosion wasn't nuclear but it was clearly effective. The fifteen hundred delegates in attendance were presumed dead. Few human remains were found. Within an hour an organization that called themselves The Black Hand had claimed responsibility. It was the first time anyone had heard of The Black Hand.

Shortly after the explosion, at a secure and private airstrip ten kilometers away, a door to a massive tunnel opened. A long caravan of vans began to spew forth from the hole, lining up along the runway. Three hundred vans and four armored trucks parked alongside the tarmac. On the airstrip, their engines buzzing in eagerness to leave, were six American C-130 transport planes. The vehicle passengers walked on to the extended rear ramps of the aircraft, each carrying one large carry-on. The last plane was reserved for a particularly special cargo – the Swiss banking head and his cargo of precious metals. Each in turn, the armored trucks drove up the ramp in reverse and deposited their heavily-guarded cargo. The trucks were then abandoned on the side of the runway. As the sun was setting on the French countryside, the airplane doors closed. Twelve minutes later, the sextet was flying in a loose formation westward towards the Atlantic, escorted by a half-dozen F-22 fighter jets. Eight hours later, with an in-flight refueling along the way, all of the planes landed at the large hidden airfield in the mountains of Virginia.

Immediately after dinner, S'lace intercepted Novah.

"The time has come, Captain," she said. "And S'lace has a special gift for Novah."

"A gift?" said Novah.

"Yes. Come with S'lace. Novah shall see."

Novah followed S'lace to the bridge, which, for the first time, was literally buzzing with activity. There were people at various stations around the bridge, all taking their business very seriously.

"Captain on the bridge!" S'lace bellowed.

Instantly, everyone snapped to attention. There were twelve

humans, who quickly formed a line.

"Captain," said S'lace, "May S'lace present Novah's bridge crew. NICOLE helped S'lace identify the closest Human equivalent to a starship crew. Before Novah is the command crew of the United States submarine named *Kentucky*. This crew brings tactical and logistical knowledge the Captain may find useful."

Novah felt instantly intimidated. Every one of the dozen before him had way more military background than he had – which was none. He couldn't be weak, though. He was the captain. He did his best to project an air of command.

He walked towards them pretending he knew what he was doing. He could see the skepticism – but also the excitement – in their eyes.

Novah chose the third one from the left.

"What's your name, sailor?"

"Lieutenant Samantha Perkins, Sir!"

"What is your specialty, Lieutenant Perkins?"

"Navigation, Sir."

"What do you think of the *R'ptyr*? Do you think you can steer her?"

"She's an amazing craft, sir. Easy to learn. She appears easy to drive."

"Thank you, Lieutenant Perkins."

Novah chose the seventh in line, a man in his forties, grey around the temple.

"And your name, sailor?"

"Executive Officer Victor Jimenez, Sir. My job is to keep these deck-swabbers in order."

"Thank you, Mr. Jimenez," Novah said with a light laugh. "How do you prefer to be addressed?"

"XO is fine, sir."

Novah nodded. He then chose the man at the end of the line, a grey-haired man who had to be approaching sixty. Novah assumed he was the captain, but let him speak for himself.

"Captain Henry Riggs of the *U.S.S. Kentucky*, Captain, at your service."

"It's a pleasure to meet you, Captain Riggs," Novah said, shaking the captain's hand. Novah turned to S'lace.

"Thank you, S'lace, this is just what we needed. Please wait for me in the tactical lounge."

For the first time in a long while, S'lace smiled. Novah then turned back to the dozen.

"Gentlemen…and lady," he began, "welcome aboard the *R'ptyr*. I'm sure you know the purpose of this vessel, so I won't go into that. I'm also sure that each of you is here by your own choice, knowing that this is a very different mission that what you may be used to. If you are not here by your own choice, or don't want to take orders under my command, please say so now."

He was met with silence.

"Great! I know you are the best, because we only take the best on this ship. I expect you to live up to your reputation. Stations, gentlemen, and errr…lady. Captain, with me please."

Everyone returned to their posts, except Captain Riggs, who fell in beside Novah. Novah walked to the very front of the bridge, which looked out over the front part of the ship and out into the universe.

"Captain Riggs," said Novah, "Where does your allegiance lie?"

Riggs answered immediately. "With the *R'ptyr*, sir."

"Not with the United States?"

"No, sir."

"Why not?" Novah could tell the captain wasn't accustomed to being interrogated by someone well less than half his age. Riggs held it well, however.

"Permission to speak freely, sir."

"Granted."

"I have been the captain of the *Kentucky* for five years. I paid my dues, working my way up the ranks. When I was made captain of the *Kentucky*, I was promised that she would be my ship for as long as I wanted her. A year later, I was given orders to fire cruise missiles on 'insurgents' in Los Angeles. Cruise missiles! On civilians! Hundreds were killed. We returned to port and I and my entire crew tendered our resignations. The resignations were rejected. We were sent back out to sea. One month later, the *Kentucky* was ordered to serve as escort for an arms shipment from Iran to North Korea, and then later to deliver three tons of gold from New York to China. Then last week, in spite of years of service, the *Kentucky* was ordered to return to Bangor for decommissioning, and her entire crew discharged. Forced into early retirement due to alleged budget cuts. The United States is corrupt and rotten to the core, Captain. Nothing has changed since the Fall. The same policies that were in place before are still in place now. All opposition is silenced or "disappeared." Anyone who stands up for common sense, accountability, or the Constitution is punished. All of the best military officers have been forced out. The only ones left are either the boot-lickers trying to earn a fat pension or those like us who grit our teeth and follow orders because we still believe in serving our offices with honor in spite of the paper pushers in Washington. When your alien friend approached us just before we walked off of the *Kentucky* for the last time and gave us the offer, debate lasted all of three minutes, and the officers were unanimous. We're grateful to be a part of something great again. To have a noble and honest purpose. My officers and I will do everything we know how to do to protect this ship and her passengers, and to be honest, Captain, you're going to need our help. You and I both know you aren't really ready for something this big."

Novah bit the inside of his lower lip, crossed his arms behind his back and stood silently for a few seconds.

"Captain," Novah said, "I think you're going to fit in here just fine. Novah turned around and pointed back at the command chair. "Your place is there. You are in charge of all bridge operations. All tactical and ship movement authority belongs to you, unless overridden by me. We have a pair of takeoffs and landings in the next few days, starting at midnight tonight. My Chief of Security Mr. Tines is my right hand man with regards to on-ship security. I expect you two will get along fine. Dinner is at seven p.m. each evening in the tactical lounge. I expect you to attend."

"Thank you, Captain," the captain said with a smile. "We won't let you down."

Novah turned to leave the bridge, but stopped for a moment and turned.

"It appears we have one captain too many," noticed Novah. "I don't know the rules for this type of situation. Any ideas?"

Captain Riggs grinned. "As a general rule, there shouldn't be two captains on the same ship. I don't know the particular protocols here on the *R'ptyr*, but I assume you can't promote yourself to admiral. To avoid confusion with the crew, let's just define my title as Commander or skipper."

"That sounds reasonable to me," replied Novah. "Thank you, Commander Riggs. Now that the formalities are over, I need to tell you the rest of the story."

"Oh?" replied Riggs with a raised eyebrow.

"It's a very long story," said Novah, "but I'll give you the short version. You won't like it. I know I don't – yet these are the cards we've been dealt. Earth is doomed. It's basically about to turn itself inside-out with volcanoes and earthquakes. In exchange for passage to a new world for a select few, the President and other world leaders sold humanity out. This first group we're about to pick up are sigil-holders, those that Earth's leaders decided to save. Politicians, lawyers, bankers, and the like. The second group we're going to pick up are the ones that count – doctors, farmers, soldiers, etcetera. It's been a bit of a Mexican standoff to get this far. Once we get both groups, the Khamek are going to, for the lack of a better word, harvest those left on Earth to fuel their journey to a planet called V'laha, which, as I understand it, their god compels them to travel to or face destruction. The logic is that since everyone on Earth is going to die anyway, they might as well die for a cause. I realize that's a rather plain and heartless explanation, but we don't have time now to get all weepy about it."

Riggs turned white as a sheet and turned to face Novah, his brow furrowed with the conflict between duty and the impact of what he'd just heard. "You're right. I don't like it. It sounds though like the horse is already out of the barn. It's going to be a bloody mess down there."

"I'm afraid so," replied Novah. "Are you still with us?"

Riggs let out a heavy sigh, his emotions held in check by his military training. "Yes, Captain. There's little choice in it now. I wish your alien friend would have explained the whole story before we signed on."

"Would it have mattered?"

"Maybe," replied the commander. "I don't know. Are there any other surprises?"

"I'm sorry you found out like this," offered Novah. "As far as other surprises, I have a feeling we'll all be talking to Jesus before this is all over." Novah clapped Riggs on the shoulder lightly, turned, and left the bridge while Riggs stood there silently, his wheels spinning.

Novah made his way to the tactical lounge and found S'lace waiting there for him. He approached her and gave her a hug.

"Thank you for the bridge crew," he said. "I trust they were completely vetted?"

"Completely, captain," said S'lace. "S'lace used NICOLE for selection."

Novah was uneasy not knowing the criteria S'lace had entered for NICOLE to interpret, but decided to check on that later.

"What about their families?"

"Already on board, Captain," she said.

"You've been busy."

She nodded, but spoke no further. Novah could tell she wanted something.

"Ok, spit it out S'lace. What's on your mind?"

"S'lace wants to rescue S'lace's clone," she stated simply.

"Where is your clone?"

"Aboard the *L'ghorsk*."

Novah looked at her as if she were crazy. "You want to just fly up to S'heil's ship and take your clone? S'heil won't let you. The *R'ptyr* can't help, either. We have to focus on getting people off the planet and getting out of here."

"S'lace understands. S'lace asks to take a scout ship and accomplish this mission without support."

"S'lace," Novah said sympathetically, "we can't wait for you. Besides, it is a suicide mission. S'heil will capture and kill you."

"Possibly," stated S'lace, "yet S'lace asks for permission anyway. Please, Captain."

Novah rubbed his forehead with his fingers.

"Alright. It's the least I can do. You can have a scouts ship after the pick-ups. But we can't wait for you. You'll be on your own. You'll have to rescue your clone, and if you are successful, catch up to the *R'ptyr* before we're too far gone."

"Agreed," S'lace said with a smile.

Novah smiled back. "Please come back, S'lace. We need you."

"S'lace will. S'lace promises."

S'lace hurried out of the room, and Novah paged Chief Tines.

"Chief, how are we doing? Only three hours until E1."

"Everything is in order, Captain. Automation protocols are tested and functioning. Each door is fortified and guarded. All access from the entry points has been blocked off except for the path to the quarantine areas. If everything goes according to plan we should have everyone on board in thirty-six hours."

"Nobody gets out of the quarantine areas. Nobody. Got it?"

"Yes Captain. There's no reason for anyone to want to leave. It's fully provisioned. A bit sterile and cramped, and Cohagen set it up with modified versions of some of those awful Roman toilet benches he borrowed from the rest of the ship, but it will be tolerable for a couple weeks."

"Excellent, thank you Chief." Novah smirked at the thought of President Hernandez taking a dump in full view of everyone.

Novah found Rebecca in Medbay One chatting with Dr. Annikov. He walked up to the pair and rubbed Katyrina's belly.

"Everything in order here?" he asked.

"There's not much to worry about medical-wise," said Dr. Annikov. "With everyone in quarantine we'll pretty much be sitting on our thumbs. Even if something does happen in quarantine there's little we can do about it. I have some bio-suits and quick-response kits just in case, though."

Novah gave a quick glance towards Rebecca. In the most subtle of ways known only between lovers, she shook her head at him. She hadn't yet told Katyrina the plan.

"Well, stay on alert nevertheless. You never know what old Alberto – or S'heil for that matter – might be planning for tonight. Both the ladies nodded.

"I'll be watching everything from the bridge," Novah said. "It seems we have a new bridge crew and I want to get a feel for them."

"May I join you there?" asked Rebecca.

"Of course. I wouldn't want you any other place."

At eleven thirty p.m., Novah was seated in the command chair with Rebecca at his side. All of the proper introductions had been made and now it was showtime.

"Commander Riggs," Novah said punching in some coordinates into his command module, which instantly transmitted them to all view screens, "Bring the R'ptyr to ground to these coordinates. Stay cloaked."

"Aye Captain!" Riggs bellowed, back to his normal self. "Perkins! Make your descent thirty degrees. Engage thrusters."

"Decent thirty degrees, engaging thrusters, aye!" replied Perkins.

"Lock in designated coordinates," continued Riggs.

"Coordinates locked, aye!"

Novah and Rebecca grinned at each other, knowing full well that the R'ptyr could make the landing autonomously. Either of them, in fact, could land the craft with a few gestures on their command modules. The play before them was exciting, though, so they sat back and enjoyed the show.

"Atmospheric penetration in twenty seconds," stated Perkins.

"Contact!! Multiple contacts!" shouted the man at the tactical console named Knudsen.

"On screen," commanded Riggs.

On the screen, appearing out of nowhere, were three hundred Khamek ships. S'heil's fleet had received its reinforcements.

Novah raised an eyebrow. Surely S'heil wouldn't be so stupid.

"Position?" asked Commander Riggs.

"Stationary," replied Knudsen. "They are maintaining position with the main Khamek fleet. I detect no weapons armed."

The captain turned to Novah. "Thoughts, Captain?"

"Ignore them," Novah replied. "Stay on task."

"Aye Captain," replied Riggs.

"Atmospheric penetration now," stated Perkins. "ETA to landing zone is ten minutes."

"Keep her steady, Perkins," ordered the captain. "Prepare the antigravity landing array."

"Aye, captain," replied Perkins, who's only real duty was to watch the map. The *R'ptyr* was doing the hard work.

Those on the ground at the Virginia landing area could hear the *R'ptyr* long before they could see it. Even when the ship landed, with the cloaking turned off, it was hard to see. Steaming jets surrounded the massive craft in mist, and only after it cleared did the jaw-dropping enormity of the *R'ptyr* truly sink in.

Novah watched the crowds outside from dual monitors. There was a nervous energy amongst the sigil holders, and nearly all of them had white knuckles from holding them so tightly. The rules were made clear and ironclad a long time ago – no sigil, no boarding.

Two massive doors opened into giant ramps, one on each side of the *R'ptyr*. Once they touched the ground, a voice boomed out. It was the *R'ptyr*'s friendly, pure, female voice.

Please proceed single file to the entrance ramps. Maintain order. Processing will stop if order is not maintained. Present your sigil for scanning at the terminal at the top of the ramp, then proceed down the walkway.

Novah watched as the lines filed in, looking for one face in particular – that of his father. He watched, he waited. He snoozed, and started watching once again. Thirty three hours later, 49,743 sigil-holders were on board. The last up the ramp, strutting as if he was a conquering hero or Santa Claus in the Macy's parade, was Alberto and his wife. Novah's father was not with him.

Novah pressed a red icon on his command module and the automated sigil recognition system stopped. He pressed another icon, which was the intercom to the boarding ramp.

"Alberto, where is my father?"

"Novah, I'm sorry to say that your father rejected a sigil," replied the president.

"Rejected? Or did you conveniently misplace his?"

"Rejected. He was rather surly. I believe the quote was "I'd rather rot in the seventh circle of Hell for all eternity than be trapped for two weeks with the likes of you.""

Novah grinned to himself. That sounded exactly like something his father would say.

"My father never did like you very much. Do you know where he is?"

Alberto shook his head. "No, but he gave me a letter to give to you." He reached into his lapel and pulled out a legal-sized envelope.

Novah had a sinking feeling in the pit of his stomach. Rebecca sensed it too, and reached for Novah's hand. Novah's dad wouldn't be coming along.

"I believe you, Alberto," Novah said. "Leave the letter right where you are standing. Come aboard."

Alberto left the envelope on the walkway and he and his wife entered the R'ptyr. With all the people on board, the door ramps began retracting into the hull. At the same time a different set of doors opened. Chief Tines' security dispatch quickly exited the R'ptyr to begin the boarding of the supplies. Tines snatched the envelope out of the retracting door, folded it in half and shoved it into his pocket.

Five hours later the supplies had been security scanned and loaded. It was mostly food, water, and weapons, along with the Swiss banker's bullion.

With everything was secured the R'ptyr returned to orbit. The countdown to E2 was started – thirty-six hours to go.

Fatigued, Novah called down to the equally-fatigued Chief Tines. "Is everyone secure in the quarantine chambers?" Novah asked.

"Yes sir. It's all sealed up, and nobody has been in contact with them or even breathed the same air. The chambers have their own air supply. The centripetal artificial gravity spinning started flawlessly, so they've been able to spread out and be less cramped. They are in their own isolated little world. No windows even. For all they know, they were loaded into a giant freight car."

"Thank you, Chief Tines. These people will likely find something to complain about. I don't want to hear one word of it. I won't take calls from the President or anyone else. We have too much to accomplish in the next week to be distracted by nonsense. Oh, and when you get a minute, I'd really like to have that envelope."

"As soon as I can, sir. And trust me, you won't be hearing a word from these people. They can bitch amongst themselves for the time being. That seems to be what they're good at anyway."

Novah turned off the intercom and addressed Commander Riggs.

"You have the con, commander. I'm off to get some rest before E2."

"Sleep well, Captain," replied Riggs.

Novah and Rebecca retired to their quarters, falling asleep as soon as their heads hit the pillows.

The applicant colonists had each received a pass with a percentage printed on it. Everyone with a pass was instructed to journey to the pick-up site. The percentage indicated the odds of being selected to board. Those with numbers between eighty and ninety-nine felt pretty good. Those under fifty percent were rightfully pessimistic. There was a chance that a person could fail the health check, which would increase everyone's odds behind that person just a little bit.

When the R'ptyr descended towards the seemingly infinite cornfields twenty-five miles outside of Independence, Missouri on E2 day, Novah was once again sitting at the command chair. He marveled at what he saw.

"How many do you think are down there?" Novah asked out loud to nobody in particular.

"I'd say at least half a million people," replied an impressed Commander Riggs. "I'm glad we have a lot of room to maneuver. Perkins, set her down where you can outside the mob. Try not to crush anyone."

"Aye skipper," replied Perkins.

Perkins set the R'ptyr down a full quarter-mile from the huge sea of humanity, and Novah simultaneously engaged the DNA-filtering shield. From the north an endless sea of people ran towards them, some cheering, and some screaming as they were trampled by the throng. Novah, seeing the chaos outside, engaged the exterior loudspeakers.

"STOP!" he yelled. His voice echoed halfway to St. Louis. Amazingly, the massive herd of humans froze in place.

"Behave yourselves," chided Novah. "No running. People are getting hurt. Walk at a normal pace. Those that run, or even walk fast, will be disqualified from boarding. Walk towards the blue shield surrounding the ship. Those selected for boarding will be able to pass through it. Those not selected must remain outside of the shield."

The *R'ptyr*'s crew watched as the sea of people below walked very slowly towards the shield. It wasn't long until the shield was completely surrounded, with people slowly pressing through it. Just as NICOLE had advertised, those without the proper DNA signature found themselves helplessly pounding an impenetrable shield, even as their neighbor with an approved signature slipped through effortlessly. Before those that made it through could get too close to the *R'ptyr*, a score of outer doors opened, each with a large, unmistakable letter of the alphabet painted on the ramp. Novah once again let his voice be heard.

"Greetings. Boarding will begin shortly. Please be patient, because as you can see, there are a lot of you. You will be doing a lot of waiting, both outside and once you enter the *R'ptyr*. Each person will be called by name. You should be standing in the appropriate line, marked by the first letter of your last name. You will be brought up the ramp and a pair of doctors wearing bio-hazard suits will administer your health test. The test takes ten seconds. If you pass you will be forwarded to the Orientation Center. The orientation session won't begin until everyone is boarded, so please be patient. Read over the individualized packet you'll be given upon boarding. Food, drink, and restrooms will be available as well. Please, no crowding or pushing. We want this to be a fun and exciting experience, but if anyone gets out of hand, they will forfeit their pass and be sedated. Welcome aboard."

Those inside the shield cheered jubilantly. The boarding proceeded quickly, apart from the protests of the few that failed the health test, only of few of which had to be sedated. Novah fidgeted from the command chair wishing the boarding would go more quickly. He kept waiting for the other shoe to drop – for S'heil to try to take the ship.

Commander Riggs walked over to him nonchalantly and stood watching the same screens.

"Captain," Riggs stated softly, "More and more Khamek ships are arriving in the vicinity of Earth. Hundreds of them. They are small craft. They're parking in a super-high orbit."

Novah nodded. "I expect that S'heil will waste little time once we've picked up our passengers before he starts – "

Novah paused. Riggs just nodded solemnly.

"There's no turning back, Commander," reminded Novah. "Keep an eye on the Khamek fleet. Let me know if anything changes. Keep your feelings to yourself – there will be plenty of time for them after we get everyone loaded and get away from the Khamek."

"Understood, Captain," said Riggs. "We'll stay focused."

Novah nodded, and the Commander returned to his station. Novah had worked hard to compartmentalize everything – to not acknowledge what was really going to happen down on Earth. He struggled to put the mental genie back into the bottle. He called Tines.

"How are we looking, Chief?" he asked.

"All passengers are loaded, but we can't get to the supplies. They are just outside of the shield. Some of them are already being ransacked by the mob. I'm not sure what to do," Chief Tines replied.

"Hang on, Chief," replied Novah. "NICOLE, can you slowly expand the DNA shield outwards until the supplies are inside it?"

Affirmative. Expanding shield.

Novah watched as the shield very slowly expanded, pushing everyone backwards, much to their dismay. Within five minutes the supplies were safely inside the shield.

"There you go, Chief," Novah told Tines. "Scan that stuff thoroughly. We don't want any surprise packages."

"You got it, Captain! We should be ready to go shortly." Tines waved his arms and a swarm of crew came out with scanners and movers to check and load the supplies. In under an hour, Tines reported back.

"We're ready to go, Captain! Closing the doors!"

Novah paused. His eyes continued to scan the massive crowd still gathered outside the shield.

"Chief, how many alternates do you think are still out there?" he asked.

"There's no telling," replied Tines. "Could be five thousand, could be a close to the full twenty."

Novah drummed his fingers for a few seconds on the arm of his chair. Rebecca reached up with her hand to stop his tapping.

"Just do it," she whispered with a smile. "We'll figure it out."

Novah grinned and nodded. "Ok then. Chief Tines, board the alternates. All of them. Do it as quickly as you can."

"Yes sir!" replied a relieved Tines, who was feeling just as uncomfortable as anyone at the prospect of leaving all of the alternate people behind.

"It looks like we're going to have company soon, so we're clearing out just as soon as those doors close."

"Roger that," Tines replied.

Novah made the announcement to the crowd outside, asking those with printed alternate papers to enter the shield. A fresh batch of cheering passengers made their way to the ramps from all directions.

Four hours later, the doors began to fold up in unison. Sprinting towards the ramp labeled "M", wearing a black utili-kilt and dragging a hard piece of oddly-shaped luggage was one final straggler.

"Wait! Wait!" the voice cried.

The man was helped up into the ship by the pair of medical personnel, who administered the health test. His luggage was scanned, and with a nod, they ushered the final colonist – one Mr. Frank MacDoughall from Whitefish, Montana – towards the orientation area. The doors sealed shut, once again securing the *R'ptyr* from any outside influence. Novah let out a sigh of relief as the crew cheered wildly.

"Contact! Multiple contacts on rapid approach!" yelled Knudsen over the cheers. "They are approaching all major cities."

"Commander, get us off the ground," ordered Novah.

"Aye Captain!"

Dust enveloped the *R'ptyr* as the antigravity array engaged, lifting the craft slowly off of the surface of the Earth for the final time. As the *R'ptyr* was leaving, Khamek scout ships by the score were descending and landing all over the planet. The *R'ptyr* made its way up into the atmosphere, and all eyes on the bridge were glued to the monitors. Fully-armed Khamek exited the scout crafts and started shooting every human in sight with some sort of orange beam weapon. It was pandemonium on the surface.

"What the hell!" exclaimed XO Jimenez. "Skipper, what's going on?"

Riggs turned to Jimenez, but he addressed all of the former *Kentucky* crew. "Do your jobs, people. Focus. We need to get this ship out of here."

"Monitors off," commanded Novah. "There's nothing we can do

about what's going on down there. Our mission is to get this ship to A'ala."

The *R'ptyr* left the final vapors of Earth's atmosphere. Novah fought back the sentimentality building within him, gritting his teeth and gripping the arms of the command chair.

"NICOLE, plot the course to the nearest heliosphere exit point."
Course plotted.
"Commander, all ahead full."
"All ahead full, sir," said Riggs, nodding to the helmsman.
"All ahead full!" came the reply.
"S'lace!" Novah spoke into the intercom.
"S'lace is here," she replied.
"You can launch just as soon as we clear the atmosphere. Good luck."
"Gratitude, Captain. S'lace will see Novah again in a few hours."
"More contacts!" shouted Knudsen. "A massive Khamek fleet! Different markings! They are out a ways though."
"On screen," said Novah calmly.
Nothing appeared visually. The fleet was way out of visual range.
"Tactical view," ordered Novah.
A top-down view of the solar system appeared on the screen. Small triangles represented the Khamek fleet near Earth, while the new fleet was represented by another group of small triangles. The new triangles had just passed the asteroid belt, hastily proceeding towards Earth.
"They are headed right for us, sirs," said Johnson. "They appear to have come from right where we want to go."
"Hold course," replied Novah. "They can't harm us. Reduce to half speed."
"Reduce to half speed," ordered Riggs.
"Aye skipper. Half speed."
"We're being hailed," said Rebecca, who until then had been sitting quietly in her normal spot beside Novah.
"Bring it up," said Novah. Appearing on the screen was the Lord Commander.
"Hello, Captain," said Jesus.
"Jesus!" replied Novah.
"On your way out?" asked Jesus with a warm casualness that contrasted with the stress of the moment.
"Yes. We lifted off about fifteen minutes ago on our way to A'ala,"

said Novah. "It seems the Khamek are wasting little time harvesting every human left on the planet."

Jesus frowned. "Yes. S'heil knows I'm coming and is trying to indiscriminately take as much Z'korz as he can."

"You're here to stop him?"

"Yes. I have told him that no being can get to V'laha except through me, but he refuses to acknowledge this reality. No matter how much Z'korz he takes, he won't be able to accomplish his mission. Khamek can be as stubborn as humans," stated the Lord Commander.

"I imagine there's a lot more to that," said Novah.

"Yes. I promise, one day I'll sit down and explain it all to you," said Jesus, "but right now I have to prepare for battle. I cannot let S'heil do what he is doing. He is a blind fool. The Thirteen Houses of the Khamek Grand Council are split on the issue. Many are secretly applauding S'heil's initiative to get to V'laha no matter what. Others openly condemn S'heil's genocide now, even though they were in favor of the deal in the first place. I was able to gather enough ships in the vicinity that aren't loyal to S'heil and put them under my command to move to stop him. This is developing into a full-fledged Khamek civil war."

"I thought you were all about peace and love and whatnot," asked Novah.

Jesus furrowed his brow. "In this case, I did not come to bring peace – but a sword. All of this was set in motion a very long time ago. But let me worry about that – you have your mission, I have mine. You need to get to A'ala."

"Understood, Lord Commander," replied Novah.

"Oh, and Novah," continued Jesus, "I know what you're going to do. It isn't easy to be a judge. It comes with a price. It happens that in this case vengeance and logic coincide. It's a gray area that I am also uncomfortable with, but I understand."

Novah hung his head. "I could see no other way, and since there are no coincidences, I figured this is the way it is supposed to be."

"Don't lie to me," replied Jesus sternly. "There were other ways, even if you were too blind to see them." Jesus turned his head and fixed his gaze on Rebecca.

"Rebecca, *sangreal*, my beloved granddaughter," he continued, "I also know what *you* have done. Believe me when I say that you are most blessed among all human women. Your suffering has not been in vain.

You have saved humanity, and for that, I and my father are eternally grateful." Jesus and Rebecca both had tears in their eyes.

"Thank you, grandfather," she replied. "When shall I see you again?"

"I shall visit soon after your sons arrive," he said.

"Sons?" said Novah and Rebecca in unison.

Jesus smiled. "I have a war to win. Complete your mission. Survive. Prosper. I shall be with you again in time. Jesus out."

The screen went blank.

The bridge crew stood frozen, mouths agape.

Novah found himself amused. "Gentlemen, that was Lord Commander Jesus. Yes, *the* Jesus. Your minds do not want to believe it, but that extra hard thumping you feel in your chest – that we all do – tells you it's true."

Commander Riggs spoke softly. "There's a lot you haven't told us," he said.

Novah stared at the commander with steely seriousness. "You've been on the *R'ptyr* for less than a week. I can't tell you everything in that time. We've had to focus on the mission. Trust me, you'll get the full story soon. We're on a two year journey to interstellar space, through a wormhole, and then another two year leg to A'ala. We'll have plenty of time to talk."

"I suppose you're right," replied the commander. "It's hard to believe that not long ago none of this could have even been imagined."

"We live in a new time now, Commander," said Rebecca with restrained solemnity. "This is our new reality. A reality in which we're free to make our own rules. A reality in which we can wipe the slate clean and start new. We're now living a life of excitement and horrible dangers, a couple of which we've already experienced. A life that feels more real and more harsh because every decision really counts. Everything counts because we are the last vestige of humanity, all crammed onto this special ship. Everything has changed."

CHAPTER TWENTY-SIX

While the 50,000 sigil holders remained in quarantine, the remainder went through a full day of formal orientation. They were shown to their quarters and shown where they would be working during the day. Each adult was given a "civilian-appropriate" command module and shown how to use it. At the end of the day everyone was shepherded to the theater deck. Thirty thousand were able to sit inside the theater proper, and the remainder sat or stood outside in the surrounding courtyard and concourse, tightly packed, viewing the proceedings on giant view screens or on their modules.

Novah was nervous. Everyone with the exception of those in quarantine would be listening to his speech, the most important words likely to ever pour out of his mouth. He didn't know how people would react to what he was going to say. When he finally told his officers what had to be done, they were understandably horrified. Logic, and the imperative for survival, eventually grounded them, and they understood there was no other way. The debate then centered around whether everyone should be told or not in Novah's speech. Some were for, some against.

"Everyone must understand the price that is being paid for humanity's survival," said Rebecca. "We all must realize how precious life is, and how precarious our situation is. Hard choices will need to be made every step of the way."

In the end, nobody envied Novah as he concurred with Rebecca. It was his burden, and his alone. The group spent three hours crafting the speech Novah would give.

Soon after, Novah stood backstage, reminded of the first time he was there. He could hear the same energy in the theater as people talked amongst each other excitedly. Novah insisted on the lights being on – this wasn't a show, wasn't a performance. He wanted to see the eyes of his audience. He didn't want to hide behind the cloak of darkness or a blinding spotlight. He thumbed through the pages on his module a final time. He'd read this speech a hundred times yet still didn't feel comfortable with it.

Rebecca came up beside him and took his hand. "You'll do fine," she said encouragingly.

"I hope so," he replied uncertainly.

"Do you want me to do it?" she asked. The question was like being poked in his eye.

"No," he said firmly. Having his ego tweaked gave him a sharper edge. A commander's edge. He turned and kissed her. "Thank you, gorgeous."

She smiled up at him. "Go get 'em, tiger."

He walked up the four stairs separating the dark backstage area from the brightly lit theater. The crowd went wild, probably because they didn't know what else to do. Novah smiled and walked to the center of the stage. Out before him was a massive sea of people crammed into three deep levels of seating. He stood for a few seconds gaining his bearing and fortifying his nerves before trying to calm the crowd with a downward motion of his hands.

"Good evening," he said. "Welcome aboard the R'ptyr."

The crowd cheered again and wouldn't seem to calm down. Novah looked sideways along the stage at Rebecca, who was standing with her arms folded leaning against the doorway. She shrugged at him and smiled.

Novah assumed a more commanding voice. "Ok, ok, that's enough. Everyone settle down. We don't want to be here all night."

The crowd took their seats, and the room fell utterly silent. Novah took a deep breath and began.

"You are not who you were a month ago," he said. "You are not employees of a company. You are not taxpayers to a government. You are not Americans, or Indians, or Chinese, or any nationality. You are not even citizens of Earth anymore. All of that stuff is now in the past. It has become your heritage, not your identity. You are the select few, the chosen colonists to build a new life on a new planet. You are the best at what you do. You have the character and the fortitude to be pioneers. You have the courage of your ancestors, who began similar journeys decades and centuries ago. I am going to count on that courage tonight. I am going to ask you to be brave.

"As we speak, the *R'ptyr* is headed towards the outer solar system. It will take us two years to reach a point safe enough to open a wormhole to the Gamma Serpentis system, thirty-six light years away. We'll then have another two years of travel before we reach the planet A'ala itself, our new home. The journey from here to there is the easy part. The *R'ptyr* has enough provisions and self-sustainability to allow us to make the journey in relative comfort and not go hungry. We have no idea what we'll find when we reach A'ala. It is a new world filled with new adventures and new dangers. We have some data given to us by the Khamek, and an empty, pre-built city to call our home, but otherwise we need to rely on each other and our inventiveness and ingenuity. That part will be difficult but I believe in all of you. We'll do well.

"We ended up taking on board 77,432 people in Independence. That may seem like a lot of people, but in reality it isn't. Space is a dangerous place. Accidents happen. While we know of nothing that can damage the *R'ptyr* from the outside, we must be vigilant in keeping an eye out for potential risks from the inside. If you are feeling sick, even if it is just a sniffle, stay in your quarters and call a doctor. We must all stay healthy as much as possible. Along with that we must put a focus on procreation. By the time we reach A'ala this ship should be filled with toddlers and newborns. The only way humanity survives is if we create more of us. It is our top priority here on the *R'ptyr*, and apart from security, shelter, food, and water, will continue to be our priority on A'ala. Be fruitful and multiply! Those of you that are married and of child-bearing age, get busy! For those of you that are single, there are roughly as many men as there are women. Match up! Socialize! Find a partner you want to raise children with, and then get to it!" Novah performed a trio of hip-thrusts, and the crowd laughed.

"Those of you who are older, we're counting on you to help out. Pass on your knowledge and wisdom. Your experience is vitally important. Do not feel bad if you cannot have a child. You are here for a reason. You were specifically chosen to be here. Do what you do best, and use your skills to forward the cause of growth and survival.

"So, to summarize, and to make it abundantly clear, our goal on this ship is to make as many babies as is possible. Life is what we treasure most." His words quaked and his heart pounded ruthlessly in his chest.

"All of our rules on this ship center on the protection of life – the protection of humanity. They are all important. Why have any rules at all? Because, as good as we are or think we are, we are humans and have human emotions and weaknesses. Leaving Earth doesn't mean we're leaving our humanity and all of its warts behind. We are individuals, but we are also a community. As has been said before in our history, if we do not stand together, we shall fall separately. With that said here are the basic rules. You may have already noticed them on your command modules – they are and will always be the first page you see, to remind you.

"The first rule is no murdering. We can't be going around killing each other. You are free to defend yourself, however. Saving your own life, or the life of your friends and family, is paramount.

"The second rule is don't fool around with someone who is already in a committed relationship. Doing so will only inflame human jealousy and passions, which lead to anger and violence. If you are in a committed relationship, please signify this by adjusting the lighted band color of your personal command module to orange. This will be the universal signal on the R'ptyr that you are in a relationship or otherwise not interested in being bothered by flirtatious or sexual gestures or talk. Be the master of your passions. Don't flirt with, lead on, or sleep with someone who's band is lit up orange.

"The third rule is the 'golden rule.' Treat each other as you want to be treated. Be kind and respectful. Love each other. Remember that each of you is special, and critical to the success of our mission.

"The fourth rule is no stealing. Do not take something that doesn't belong to you without permission of the owner. Again, we are preserving life by guarding against human passions. If you steal something, you're going to piss someone off, which could lead to injury or death.

"The fifth rule is no raping. As much as we want a baby in every womb, we won't tolerate putting them there by force. All sex must be consensual.

"The sixth rule is don't expect to get something for nothing. There is no concept of entitlement on this ship. Everyone works for what they get. Everyone has a job to do. If you don't work, you don't eat.

Common sense exceptions will be made of course for those who are sick or injured.

We value life and the preservation of life. However, if eliminating one life prevents the potential loss of others, we will regretfully sacrifice one for many. Therefore, if you are caught murdering, breaking the rule of orange, stealing, or raping, the penalty is death. You will be thrown out an airlock and your name will be etched on the Wall of Shame. That wall currently has no names on it. Don't be the first!"

A wave of murmurs rose from the crowd. Novah let it naturally subside and continued.

"Yes, I realize that the death penalty is harsh, but if humanity is to survive, we need to be serious about surviving. That means the elimination of threats that present themselves. If you break these rules, you are a threat to do it again. Putting you in jail is a burden on others who instead of doing their productive work must now be taken off task to monitor and care for you – you, who not only broke the rules, but are currently producing nothing of value because you are in jail.

"These are the rules for our journey to A'ala, and like all rules, there may be rare exceptions based on individual, particular circumstances. Common sense must prevail. I and my circle of officers will be the arbiters of such cases, and our ruling will be final. I'm hopeful, however, that everyone will simply abide by the rules and not force me and the other officers to be buried in petty court cases for the whole trip – we have plenty of other things to do. Once settled on our new planet my mission is complete. At that time we as a community can feel free to change the rules as we see fit.

"Changing subjects now. As you have learned or will soon discover, the R'ptyr is a very large craft. It is essentially a small city. It contains a city's infrastructure. It is that of ancient cities, yet easily recognizable. It has storefronts and farms and small factories. It has schools and buildings for every sort of business. As much as possible, we should strive to live normal lives as we see fit. Each of you has been assigned a role on the ship based on your aptitude and specialty. We hope you enjoy this role and stick with it. However, this role is only temporary. One month from today you will be free to change roles. The ship-run cafeterias will stop giving out food for free. Medical services will no longer be free. Your quarters, however, will be yours. Your property until we leave the R'ptyr. You are *free* people. You'll be free to do whatever you like. Remember that resources are limited, though, and that the laws of supply and demand are universal.

"To help facilitate this freedom of mobility, and to help grow an actual shipboard economy, every person aged sixteen and over will be given a fixed amount of gold and silver. Real metals. Everyone will get the same amount. It is up to you to use it wisely. You can use this currency to buy one of the vacant available areas and maybe rent it out. You can start a business of your own. Whatever you want to do. You can market your services to the highest bidder. Or you could be foolish and do nothing, living off of your gold until none is left. Do this and you will go hungry. There are no food stamps, Social Security, nor any welfare of any kind on the *R'ptyr*. You are responsible for providing for your own well-being.

"There will be no income taxes. No estate taxes. No property taxes. These taxes are immoral, as they punishments for success. There will be only one tax levied to support the operation of the *R'ptyr*. This will be a three percent transaction tax on all transactions except the purchase of food.

"As hauling around pounds of gold and silver is hard, there will be a bank which will have one purpose and one purpose only – to hold your metals and transfer monies from account to account. Each account holder can access their account through their command module, and transactions can happen via the module. There will be no need to carry around a credit or debit card. Your balance will at all times show you your available balance in the bank. You can, of course, always use the metals themselves.

"The bank will never lend your money to other people without your permission in the form of a contract which clearly defines the terms of your agreement with the bank, and the bank will make no money on lending. The bank will only act as a facilitator. Unlike on Earth, your money is not simply a faith-based construct. The sum total of all of the money on the *R'ptyr* will always be the same. Once each month the bank will be audited. You are encouraged to go to the bank whenever you wish and actually view your holdings there. Together, we can build a real economy based on real efforts and real rewards. You will not be punished for your success. However, just as with the ship rules, once we reach A'ala you will be free as a community to change things. We'll discuss and develop the mechanism for change, and the form of A'ala's government, during our journey there."

The crowd offered approval via polite applause. The small handful of real economists were less enthusiastic.

Novah's tone then turned softer and noticeably somber.

"Reaching A'ala, however, requires a sacrifice. A human sacrifice, and I am not speaking metaphorically. I am now going to share with you the truth of how you are here, and how we must get to A'ala. I have hidden this from you. I no longer want to be the latest in a long string of leaders who has built on lie after lie after lie. This will be difficult for you to hear. It was for me. It still is."

That was a lie, of course, and the irony didn't escape him. In his heart he didn't regret for one moment what had to be done. He wasn't going to make the same mistake he made with Penny. He was in fact looking forward to atoning for that lapse in judgment.

So many people had never been so silent as they sat rapt, waiting for Novah to continue.

"I'm going to make a very long story much shorter," continued Novah. "There isn't the time to talk about everything tonight. As you may have expected, the Khamek have been visiting and studying Earth for a very long time. They are able to predict significant disruptions within the earth that are causing earthquakes and volcanos to erupt. Within the next year, these geological events will climax and wipe out humanity on Earth."

Novah waited for the din of gasps and cries to die down before continuing.

"Sixty years ago, the Khamek made a deal with the leaders of Earth. The Khamek found a suitable planet for us to migrate to. The Khamek built this ship for humanity in preparation for this migration. The ship is designed to hold 50,000, and the Khamek gave our governments 50,000 sigils like this one," he said holding up a sigil. "Over the years, these were used as bargaining chips by the powerful and elite to buy favors and influence. Government officials, lawyers, media moguls, billionaires, but mostly bankers, accumulated the sigils for themselves and their business associates. Now imagine, if you will, 50,000 politicians, bankers and lawyers trying to build a new society from scratch."

A few giggles rippled through the audience.

"Exactly," nodded Novah. "Humanity would be doomed. However, due to a series of fortunate events – and what some might call divine intervention – I came into possession of the R'ptyr and decided that 50,000 *different* people had to be chosen. The best and the brightest across humanity, so that humanity could have a real chance. That's how all of you came to be here today. You are the very best and brightest that we could find."

Spontaneous applause broke out, and Novah waited patiently for it to die down.

"But on to the sacrifice I mentioned. There is some serious physics involved in generating a wormhole. Without the wormhole, we can't get to A'ala. We'll starve to death. There is a quantum force known as Z'korz that provides the energy needed to create a wormhole. Only Z'korz contains enough energy. Z'korz is created through conscious thought, therefore only sentient life forms carry with them the Z'korz energy needed to open a wormhole. To capture this Z'korz energy, sentient life forms must be killed, and their Z'korz fields syphoned off into giant batteries. These batteries can then – when the time comes – provide the energy needed to open a wormhole. To open up a wormhole sufficiently large enough to get us to A'ala, around 50,000 people need to give up their Z'korz energy."

The room gasped and rumbled with fear, many assuming that they were going to be killed.

"Hold on, hold on," beckoned Novah. "Nobody here is in any danger. Everyone listening to me is safe. There's no need to panic. Remember when I talked a minute ago about those 50,000 sigil holders?" Novah switched on the view screens using his command module. The screens immediately switched to a view of the quarantine holding areas, slowly rotating near the Z'korz batteries and engine.

Novah pointed at the screens. "They are our fuel. They, who for decades stole our wealth and freedom are now the source of our power. They, who condoned the rape and murder of many thousands of innocent people during the Fall. They, whose sole purpose is to keep us under control so that they can feel powerful. They are now the fuel for humanity's survival. Are there some good people in these chambers? I'm sure there are… just like there are millions upon millions of good people we had to leave behind on Earth." *Just like I was sure there was some good in Penny*, he thought. "It isn't fair. None of this is fair. It is, however, necessary if humanity is to survive. We will all die if the people in these chambers do not."

Novah waited a few moments for the reactions – some of horror, some of shock, some of ambivalence – to die down. While this was happening, a man sitting in the very last seat at the end of the first row slid out a hard, oddly-shaped plastic case and opened it. He slowly withdrew the pieces of the device and began to assemble it. Nobody seemed to notice.

"There really is no other way," continued Novah. "So for us to survive, they must burn." He turned his chin upward, speaking to the ceiling.

"NICOLE, engage the Z'korz extraction chambers."

Chambers engaging.

The chambers, already rotating to provide an artificial gravity to the storage compartments, began to accelerate their rotation. The soundless bodies on the view screen fell to the floor of the chambers unable to stand against the increased centripetal force. Silent screams poured forth from almost 50,000 mouths as the rotation grew faster and faster. As the speed reached the point where distinction was a blur, NICOLE ignited the chambers. Bright orange flames filled the view screen. Novah stood, painfully listening to the horrified screams coming from the theater. In less than ten seconds the orange flames retreated and the spinning chambers slowed quickly to a stop. Nothing organic was left. No bone, no bodies, no carbon. The chambers were clean and reflective. Coins, belt buckles, metal buttons, jewelry, and nearly 50,000 sigils rolled into a pile at the lowermost part of the chamber.

Z'korz extraction successful.

It took a couple of minutes for the shocked and horrified audience to sit back down. Then a lone pair of hands, somewhere deep in the crowd, slowly and persistently slapped together. They were soon followed by another set, then another, and then another. Soon the theater was erupting in applause. Then people stood.

I just fried 50,000 people, and I'm getting a standing ovation, thought Novah. Anger and frustration welled up in him as he stood, head bowed and fists clenched on the stage, the roar of the audience washing down over him. The sense of wrongness tasted like vomit in the back of his throat.

The crowd cheered harder until the man in the front row snapped the final, long cylinder in place, stood, took a deep breath, and aimed his stare and intentions at Novah. He squeezed, and the theater was filled with an entirely different sound – a chilling yet familiar hum that held fast, long and droning. Novah felt the vibrations before he heard them, and turned to face their source. He didn't recognize the man, but as the audience quickly hushed, Novah understood and felt a warm sense of calm fill his soul. *An ending far better than I deserve*, he thought to himself. Novah nodded a single time at the man, giving him permission to proceed, and closed his eyes.

The pipes sang forth the mournful notes of *Amazing Grace* in slow, deliberate fashion, each phrase quivering with solemnity as a collective gasp was drawn in by the audience, their approval turned instantly to shame, a shame soon drenched in rueful tears. Novah motioned the kilt-wearing pipes-player up onto the stage to a place beside him. Without missing a note, the man made his way up the five steps at stage left and stood beside Novah, pipes singing their gentle scolding for all to hear and weep to.

Long after the final note faded, weeping still filled the theater. Novah opened his eyes and turned to shake the hand of the pipes-player, but he was gone. Novah sighed and turned back to address the audience, summoning the last of his leaderly reserves.

"That's all for tonight. Remember this night. Remember the price that was paid, and remember your duty to honor that price by being the very best you can be."

Rebecca and Katyrina met him as he stepped into the shadows off of the stage, their faces streaked with tears. With each step down, Novah felt his knees – and his certainty – grow ever weaker. At the bottom, he collapsed into their arms.

"What have I done?!" he wailed.

"What you chose to do," answered Rebecca.

CHAPTER TWENTY-SEVEN

Novah awoke tangled in arms. Rebecca's were wrapped around him from the front, while Katyrina's were wrapped from behind. His brain was just as tangled. He only vaguely remembered last night's speech. He remembered feeling sick. He heard the ghostly echoes of bagpipes in his head. He didn't remember being escorted – more like carried – back to his quarters. He could only in pale fragments recall Rebecca and Katyrina peeling his clothes off of him, crawling into bed with him, holding him, comforting him, wrapping him in the cocoon of their arms and love.

He remained still, wedged between two lightly snoring bodies, a bit too warm. Their arms were in a way like a prison, trapping him there, forcing him to deal with thoughts he normally obscured with busyness. He found himself wondering about his dad, wondering if he was killed by S'heil's forces yet, or if he was surviving and fighting back. He had his father's letter but hadn't found the time, or the courage, to read it.

He thought about the sheer absurdity of his life. Here he was, wedged between two naked, beautiful women, one of whom was the umpteenth-great granddaughter of Jesus Christ. He was the commander of an interstellar spaceship, full of wondrous technology that he couldn't have imagined a couple of years ago, hurtling off into the outer fringe of his home star's influence. His doomed planet was under siege by opposing Khamek factions – one led by an egomaniacal Khamek, the other by a legendary super-human that many of his kind called God.

He couldn't take the confinement any longer and tried to wiggle out of the quartet of surrounding limbs without waking their owners. They rustled, grunting in the inconvenience of being jostled, but remained asleep as he slipped away. He looked back at the two slumbering women as he slid into his pants, their bodies barely visible, softly heaving with each breath. He walked over to his desk and sat down, waving his hand under the small desk light which ignited in a warm white glow. He slid the drawer open and pulled out the folded envelope, ironing it flat again as best he could on the desktop. Finally, after staring at the envelope for a full minute, Novah lifted it off of the desk, tore it open, pulled out the hand-written letter, and read it.

Novah,

First and foremost, let me say how proud I am of you. When I saw you on TV, I stood in awe of the man you've become and the role you've been thrust into. I don't know how you became connected with the aliens, or how you were given command of that big ship, but I suppose that doesn't really matter now.

As you know by now, I won't be joining you on your journey. The President did offer me a sigil, which I declined. That man, and all of his kind, repulse me. Government goons raped and killed your mother, then sent me to some godforsaken Alaskan gulag to rot. Hate is a harsh word, as I've always told you, but I really hate Hernandez. He's rotten, and the fish rots from the head down. I hope, for your sake and all of humanity's, that you can find a way to keep him contained. Don't back down, don't let him assume control. He'll ruin everything.

I don't know all the details about what's going to happen here on Earth. I've gathered that it won't be pleasant. This is my home, though. I'm too old and too stubborn to leave it. I'm content to die here in whatever fashion fate has decided for me. I am greatly comforted knowing that you are on that ship away from the mess down here. I suspect few things ease the transition to the afterlife quite like the feeling of pride in one's children. When my time comes, I'll go with a smile.

I do wish I'd have had another hour with you, to try to cram what knowledge and wisdom I have into you, now that you're old enough to really listen. I don't have an hour, though, so I'll try to distill everything into its essence.

You're in a unique position, Novah. Don't let it go to your head. It has almost always been the case — with very few exceptions - that the more power a man has, the more power he wants. Power corrupts. That's what happened to Hernandez and our government as a whole. Don't let that happen to you. Be principled, not political.

You can't outrun your humanity no matter how far you go, so don't try. Just try to be the best person you can be and encourage others to do the same.

Hernandez is getting ready to leave, so I need to wrap this up. Know that I love you, and as I said, I'm very, very proud of you. I'll leave you with one last thing, which is probably the most important piece of advice I can give you: don't take anything for granted.

Good luck!

Love,

Dad

Teary eyed, Novah refolded the letter and stuck it back in the envelope. He then turned and looked one more time at the sleeping tangle of limbs and hair he'd climbed out of. He smiled.

Don't take anything for granted.

Following his dad's advice, he turned off the light, stripped off his pants and slowly wiggled back into his previous position between the two women. His mind finally at peace, Novah lost himself between the heartbeats of the present and the future, and fell back to sleep.

ABOUT THE AUTHOR

Robert Reynolds was born, raised, and still lives in Washington State. Married with two children, he spends his time writing, thinking, playing games and acquiescing to his dog's every whim.

Follow me on Twitter: @NovahBurns
Visit my website! http://robert-reynolds.net

~~~

Thank you for reading my book. If you enjoyed it, would you please take a moment to leave a review at your favorite retailer?